Daniel Appleton White

New England Congregationalism in its Origin and Purity

illustrated by the foundation and early records of the First Church in Salem, and

various discussions pertaining to the subject

Daniel Appleton White

New England Congregationalism in its Origin and Purity
illustrated by the foundation and early records of the First Church in Salem, and various discussions pertaining to the subject

ISBN/EAN: 9783337262280

Printed in Europe, USA, Canada, Australia, Japan

Cover: Foto ©Andreas Hilbeck / pixelio.de

More available books at **www.hansebooks.com**

NEW ENGLAND CONGREGATIONALISM

IN ITS ORIGIN AND PURITY;

ILLUSTRATED BY THE

FOUNDATION

AND

EARLY RECORDS

OF THE

FIRST CHURCH IN SALEM,

AND

Various Discussions Pertaining to the Subject.

BY DANIEL APPLETON WHITE,

———————

SALEM:
1861.

PREFACE.

The following work, (with the exception of the Index and Table of Contents, which a young friend has prepared without his supervision,) is altogether the work of the Compiler. But after being enabled, through the favor of Providence, to bring these pages to a conclusion, he now finds himself, as he approaches the completion of his eighty-fifth year, so far prostrated by illness as to be compelled to entrust the preparation of this preface to friends who can truly state his views.

As he has regarded the subject, Congregationalism, such as it was when planted here, in its form of government and its essential principles, recognizing the largest liberty compatible with the necessary restraints of moral and religious obligation, contained within itself the elements of our greatness and our glory. He has therefore looked, with constantly increasing interest, into the ecclesiastical records of our New England settlements, anxious that controversies and opinions belonging to a later period, should not be permitted to color statements of facts purporting to be drawn from these sources of historical authority; and especially that the records themselves should be guarded against the admission of foreign ingredients, and preserved alike in their purity and their integrity.

He has felt that the example which the First Church presented, of a foundation built upon the New Testament, rather than upon creeds of man's device, is invaluable.

It will be perceived (see note, p. 184) that the Compiler was drawn into the first discussion by peculiar circumstances, which seemed to demand, at the time, a vindication of those principles upon which he deemed the First Church to have been founded.

The Second Discussion (see Extract from Salem Gazette, on p. 193,) owes its origin to a lecture delivered in his presence before the Essex Institute, which sought to invalidate what he has regarded as well-established historical truth. To this lecture he saw fit to make a rejoinder ; and, in this " second discussion," the newspaper articles which subsequently appeared on both sides, are, in substance, inserted.

The *Third Discussion,* (see p. 235) was occasioned by what seemed to him a persistent attempt to embody error in the solemn form of Ecclesiastical History.

The obvious advantage of *printing* the original Records of the First Church, commenced by Rev. John Higginson, will be readily perceived, as rescuing them from the accidents of time and chance. The curious and interesting original records of Rev. John Fiske, under date of 1637, are also important, from their close relation to the early history of the Church.

The Notices (see p. 283) of the several pastors and teachers of the First Church, seem appropriately to follow the publication of its early records.

It will thus be seen, that, throughout, the Compiler has acted upon the defensive ; first, in defence of the truly Protestant foundation of the First Church ; secondly, in defence of historical truth ; thirdly, in a renewed effort in the same direction, when, without any recognition of the Compiler's views as published in the second discussion, an attempt was made to incorporate what he regards as gross error, into the sober truth of history.

The whole work, though it contains more than the discussions and records, of which a manuscript copy was requested by the Essex Institute, is presented to that Society, that they may distribute and dispose of the published copies in such manner as they may see fit.

Salem, March 12, 1861.

TABLE OF CONTENTS.

FOUNDATION.. 1-10
    Gott's Letter.. 1
    Morton's Memorial... 3
    Mather's Magnalia... 5
    Hubbard's History of New England.............................. 8
    Bentley's Description of Salem................................ 9

EARLY RECORDS.. 11-119
    Transcript Records... 13-17
    Rev. John Fiske's Salem Record, 1637......................... 25-40
    Certificate to the same of Mr. David Pulsifer................ 307
    Extract from Rev. John Fiske's Chelmsford Church Record....... 38-40
    Original Records of Rev. John Higginson...................... 45-96
    Specimens of Records of Messrs Noyes, Curwin, and Sam'l Fisk,.... 96-111
    Re-organization of the First Church, and Ordination of Rev. John
        Sparhawk... 112-116
    Remarks on the Ancient Church-Book........................... 117-119

FIRST DISCUSSION... 121-184
    Statement of the occasion of it.............................. 121-122
    " Correspondence, etc.".................................... 122-183
    Note (from First Church Records of Feb. 18, 1832)............ 184

SECOND DISCUSSION... 185-234

THIRD DISCUSSION.. 235-260

NOTE A. On " Felt's Ecclesiastical History," etc............. 261-268

NOTE B. On Appendix to New Edition of Morton 269-274

NOTE C. On Principles of Congregationalism................... 275-282

SUPPLEMENT. Notices of Pastors and Teachers.................. 283-306

ADDITIONAL NOTE, including a Reference to the Old Newbury Church..... 307-308

TABLE OF CONTENTS.

FIRST CHURCH.

FOUNDATION.

No church or town records appear to have been kept in Salem till about the year 1637. But fortunately we are enabled to supply the deficiency in respect to the foundation of the First Church, by the testimony of original witnesses whose relations are more explicit and satisfactory than could have been expected from church records. These witnesses were CHARLES GOTT, one of the two first deacons of the Church, and a representative from Salem in the General Court, in 1635, and JOHN HIGGINSON, son of Francis Higginson, and the Pastor of the Church for nearly half a century, and conversant with its history for more than seventy years. His father, Francis Higginson, and Samuel Skelton, were the first ministers.

Mr. Gott, in a letter to Governor Bradford, dated Salem, July 30, 1629, informs him as follows:—"The 20th of July, it pleased God to move the heart of our Governor to set it apart for a solemn day of humiliation for the choice of a pastor and teacher; the former part of the day being spent in praise and teaching, the latter part was spent about the election, which was after this manner: the per-

1

sons thought on (who had been ministers in England) were demanded concerning their callings; they acknowledged there was a two-fold calling; the one and inward calling, when the Lord moved the heart of a man to take that calling upon him, and fitted him with gifts for the same; the second (the outward calling) was from the people, when a company of believers are joined together in covenant, to walk together in all the ways of God, every member (being men) are to have a free voice in the choice of their officers, &c. Now we being persuaded that these two were so qualified as the apostle speaks of to Timothy, where he saith a bishop must be blameless, sober, apt to teach, &c., so these two servants of God, clearing all things by their answers, and being thus fitted, we saw no reason but that we might freely give our voices for their election after this trial. Their choice was after this manner: every fit member wrote, in a note, his name whom the Lord moved him to think was fit for a pastor, and so likewise, whom they would have for teacher; so the most voice was for Mr. Skelton to be Pastor, and Mr. Higginson to be Teacher; and they accepting the choice, Mr. Higginson, with three or four more of the gravest members of the Church, laid their hands on Mr. Skelton, using prayers therewith. This being done, then there was imposition of hands on Mr. Higginson. Then there was proceeding in election of elders and deacons, but they were only named, and laying on of hands deferred, to see if it pleased God to send us more able men over; but since Thursday, (being as I take it, the 5th of August) is appointed for another solemn day of humiliation, for the full choice of elders and deacons, and ordaining them. Now, good sir, I hope that you and the rest of God's people (who are acquainted with the ways of God) with you, will say that here was a right foundation laid, and that these two blessed servants of the Lord came in at the door, and not at the window."*

Morton's "New England's Memorial" was first published in 1669, when John Higginson was Pastor of the First Church, who together with Thomas Thacher, the first minister of the Old South Church, in Boston, prefixed to it a cordial recommendation of the work, as being "compiled with modesty of spirit, simplicity of style and truth of matter." Mr. Higginson must have read with particular attention what related to his own Church, which, doubtless, he had himself chiefly furnished, as well as thus entirely sanctioned. The following extract from Morton's Memorial shows the true foundation and constitution of the Church:

"Mr. Higginson and Mr. Skelton, in pursuance of the ends of their coming over into this wilderness, acquainted the Governor, Mr. Endicott, and the rest of the godly people whom they found inhabitants of the place, and the chief of the passengers who came over with them, with their professed intentions, and consulted with them about settling a reformed congregation ; from whom they found a general and hearty concurrence, so that, after some conference together about this matter, they pitched upon the 6th of August for their entering into a solemn covenant with God and one another, and also for the ordaining of their ministers ; of which they gave notice to the Church of Plymouth, that being the only Church that was in the country before them. The people made choice of Mr. Skelton for their Pastor, and Mr. Higginson for their Teacher. And accordingly it was desired of Mr. Higginson to draw up a confession of faith and covenant in scripture language ; which being done was agreed upon. And because they foresaw that this wilderness might be looked upon as a place of liberty, and therefore might in time be troubled with erroneous spirits, therefore they did put in one article into the confession of faith, on purpose, about the duty and power of the magistrate in

* 1 Hist. Coll. III. 67.

matters of religion: Thirty copies of the aforesaid confession of faith and covenant being written out for the use of thirty persons who were to begin the work. When the 6th of August came, it was kept as a day of fasting and prayer, in which, after the sermons and prayers of the two ministers, in the end of the day, the aforesaid confession of faith and covenant being solemnly read, the fore-named persons did solemnly profess their consent thereunto; and then proceeded to the ordaining of Mr. Skelton Pastor, and Mr. Higginson Teacher, of the Church there. Mr. Bradford, the Governor of Plymouth, and some others with him, coming by sea, were hindered by cross winds, that they could not be there at the beginning of the day, but they came into the assembly afterward, and gave them the right hand of fellowship, wishing all prosperity, and a blessed success unto such good beginnings. After which, at several times, many others joined to the Church in the same way. The confession of faith and covenant forementioned was acknowledged only as a direc-tion, pointing unto that faith and covenant contained in the holy Scripture, and therefore no man was confined unto that form of words, but only to the substance, end and scope of the matter contained therein. And for the circumstantial manner of joining to the church, it was ordered according to the wisdom and faithfulness of the Elders, together with the liberty and ability of any person. Hence it was that some were admitted by expressing their consent to that written confession of faith and covenant; others did answer to questions about the principles of religion that were publicly propounded to them; some did present their confession in writing, which was read for them; and some, that were able and willing, did make their confes-sion in their own words and way; a due respect was also had unto the conversations of men, viz: that they were without scandal."†

About twenty-eight years after the publication of Mor-ton's Memorial, Cotton Mather completed his "Magnalia, or Church History of New England," in which he acknowl-edged assistance received in his work from John Higgin-son, and from Nicolas Noyes, then ministers of the First Church, both of whom prefixed to his history their testi-mony to its truthfulness. The former, in his "Attesta-

----

† New England's Memorial, Davis's Ed. 145.

tion," dated "Salem, 25th of the first month, 1697," says : "As for myself, having been, by the mercy of God, now above sixty-eight years in New England, and served the Lord and his people in my weak measure, sixty years in the ministry of the Gospel, I may now say in my old age, I have seen all that the Lord hath done for his people in New England, and have known the beginning and progress of these Churches unto this day, and having read over much of this history, I cannot but in the love and fear of God bear witness to the truth of it."

"JOHN HIGGINSON."

The following account, therefore, contained in the first Book of the Magnalia, is entitled to the same degree of credit as if it had been recorded by Mr. Higginson himself.

BOOK I. CHAP. IV. § 6 & § 7.

§ 6. "Mr. Higginson and Mr. Skelton, and other good people that arrived at Salem, in the year 1629, resolved, like their father Abraham, to begin their plantation with calling on the name of the Lord. The great Mr. Hildersham had advised our first planters to agree fully upon their form of Church Government, before their coming into New England ; but they had indeed agreed little further than in this general principle, That the Reformation of the Church was to be endeavored according to the written word of God. Accordingly ours, now arrived at Salem, consulted with their brethren at Plymouth, what steps to take for the more exact acquainting of themselves with, and conforming themselves to that written word : And the Plymotheans, to their great satisfaction laid before them what warrant, they judged that they had in the laws of our Lord Jesus Christ, for every particular in their Church Order.

Whereupon having the concurrence and countenance of their Deputy Governor, the worshipful John Endicot, Esq., and the approving presence of messengers from the Church of Plymouth, they set apart the sixth day of August, after their arrival, for Fasting and Prayer, for the settling of a Church-State among them, and for their making a confession of their faith, and entering into an holy Covenant, whereby that Church-State was formed.

Mr. Higginson then became the Teacher, and Mr. Skelton the Pastor of the Church thus constituted at Salem; and they lived very peaceably in Salem together, till the death of Mr. Higginson, which was about a twelvemonth after, and then of Mr. Skelton, who did not long survive him. Now the Covenant whereto these Christians engaged themselves, which was about seven years after solemnly renewed among them, I shall here lay before all the Churches of God as it was then expressed and inforced :

"We covenant with our Lord, and one with another; and we do bind ourselves in the presence of God, to walk together in all his ways, according as he is pleased to reveal himself unto us in his blessed word of truth; and do explicitly, in the name and fear of God, profess and protest to walk as followeth, through the power and grace of our Lord Jesus Christ.

"We avouch the Lord to be our God, and ourselves to be his people in the truth and simplicity of our spirits.

"We give ourselves to the Lord Jesus Christ, and the word of his grace, for the teaching, ruling and sanctifying of us, in matters of worship and conversation, resolving to cleave unto him alone for life and glory, and to reject all contrary ways, canons, and constitutions of men in his worship.

"We promise to walk with our brethren, with all watchfulness and tenderness, avoiding jealousies and suspicions, backbitings, censurings, provokings, secret risings of spirit against them ; but in all offences, to follow the rule of our Lord Jesus, and to bear and forbear, give and forgive, as he hath taught us.

"In public or private, we will willingly do nothing to the offence of the Church ; but will be willing to take advice for ourselves and ours, as occasion shall be presented.

"We will not in the congregation be forward, either to show our own gifts and parts in speaking, or scrupling; or there discover the weakness or failings of our brethren; but attend an orderly call thereunto, knowing how much the Lord may be dishonored, and his Gospel, and the profession of it, slighted by our distempers and weaknesses in public.

"We bind ourselves to study the advancement of the Gospel, in all truth and peace, both in regard of those that are within or without; no way slighting our sister Churches, but using their counsel as need shall be; not laying a stumbling-block before any, no, not the Indians, whose good we desire to promote; and so to converse, as we may avoid the very appearance of evil.

"We do hereby promise to carry ourselves in all lawful obedience to those that are over us in, Church or Commonwealth, knowing how well pleasing it will be to the Lord, that they should have encouragement in their places, by our not grieving their spirits through our irregularities.

"We resolve to approve ourselves to the Lord, in our particular callings; shunning idleness as the bane of any state; nor will we deal hardly or oppressingly with any, wherein we are the Lord's stewards.

"Promising also unto our best ability to teach our children and servants the knowledge of God and of his will, that they may serve him also; and all this not by any strength of our own, but by the Lord Christ; whose blood we desire may sprinkle this our Covenant made in his name."

By this Instrument was the covenant of grace explained, received, and recognized, by the First Church in this Colony, and applied unto the evangelical designs of a church-estate before the Lord. This Instrument they afterwards often read over, and renewed the consent of their souls unto every article in it; especially when their days of humiliation invited them to lay hold on particular opportunities for doing so.

So you have seen the nativity of the First Church in the Massachusetts Colony.

§ 7. As for the circumstances of admission into this Church, they left it very much unto the discretion and faithfulness of their Elders, together with the condition of the persons to be admitted. Some were admitted by expresssing their consent unto their confession and covenant; some were admitted after their first answering to questions about religion, propounded unto them ; some were admitted, when they had presented in writing such things, as might give satisfaction unto the people of God concerning them ; and some that were admitted, orally addressed the people of God in such terms, as they thought proper to ask their communion with; which diversity was perhaps more beautiful, than would have been a more punctilious uniformity ; but none were admitted without regard unto a blameless and holy conversation. They did all agree with their brethren of Plymouth in this point,—That the children of the faithful were church members with their parents ; and that their baptism was a seal of their being so; only before their admission to fellowship in a particular church it was judged necessary, that being free from scandal, they should be examined by the Elders of the Church, upon whose approbation of their fitness, they should publicly and personally own the covenant ; so they were to be received unto to the table of the Lord; and, accordingly, the eldest son of Mr. Higginson, being about fifteen years of age and laudably answering all the characters expected in a communicant, was then so received.''

We take a single passage from Hubbard's History of New England. The author, who was the minister of Ipswich Church, was intimately acquainted with Rev. John Higginson and with Roger Conant and other founders of the First Church, from whom he doubtless obtained information which entitles him to be regarded as one of the original authorities on the subject. He says of these founders, p. 118 :

" They had not as yet waded so far into the controversy of church discipline, as to be very positive in any of those points wherein the main hinge of the controversy lay between them and others ; yet aiming, as near as well they could, to come up to the rules of the Gospel, in the first settling of a church state, and apprehending it necessary for those, who intended to be of the Church, solemnly to enter into a covenant engagement one with another in the presence of God, to walk together before him according to the word of God, and then to ordain their ministers unto their several offices, to which they were by the election of the people designed, scil., Mr. Skelton

to be their Pastor, and Mr. Higginson to be their Teacher. In order to the carrying on of that work, or preparation thereunto, the
said Mr. Higginson, according as he was desired, drew up a confession of faith and form of a church covenant according to the Scriptures; several copies whereof being written out, they publicly owned the same, on the day set apart for that work, a copy of which is
retained at this day, by some that succeed in the same Church. Further also, notice was given of their intended proceedings to the
Church at New Plymouth, that so they might have their approbation
and concurrence, if not their direction and assistance in a matter of
that nature, wherein themselves had been but little before exercised.
There were at that time thirty persons joined together in that church
covenant; for which end so many copies being prepared aforehand,
it was publicly read in the assembly, and the persons concerned solemnly expressing their assent and consent thereunto, they immediately
proceeded to ordain their ministers. Mr. Bradford and others, as
messengers of Plymouth Church, were hindered by cross winds from
being present in the former part of the day, but came time enough to
give them the right hand of fellowship, wishing all prosperity and
success to those hopeful beginnings, as they then accounted them,
although in some points of church discipline Mr. Higginson's principles were a little discrepant from theirs of Plymouth. Those that
were afterward admitted unto church fellowship, were, with the confession of their faith, required to enter into a like covenant engagement with the Church, to walk according to the rules of the Gospel,
as to the substance, the same as at the first; but for the manner and
circumstances, it was left to the wisdom and faithfulness of the Elders,
to be so ordered as was judged most conducing to the end, respect
being by them always had to the liberty and ability of the person."

We add to the ancient historical authorities that of Dr.
Bentley, who, in writing his "Description of Salem," had
the freeest access to the Town records, as well as to those
of the Church, from which he copied the original Covenant, together with the preamble to its renewal in 1636,
and the clause against the Quakers, added upon its renewal in 1660.

"Mr. Higginson," says Dr. B., "found Mr. Endicott at Salem,
who had explained his intentions to the Church already formed in

2

Plymouth. Two articles were fixed by consent, that the Church at Salem should not acknowledge any ecclesiastical jurisdiction in the Church at Plymouth, if any assistance should be given at Salem; and that the authority of ordination should not exist in the clergy, as in the Protestant Churches, but, as in the unqualified sense of the Reformed Churches, should depend entirely upon the free election of the members of the Church, and that there should be a representative of this power continually in the Church..........A covenant or religious obligation was formed, and publicly signed, at the institution of the Church, and it is recorded in every history of New England. It may be esteemed, if not for its theology, for its simplicity. If it speak not the language of a sect, it breathes the spirit of Christian union. It never could be intended so much to display opinions, as by written obligation to fasten men together. It is the inartificial range of thought, forgetting the eyes of posterity, and without polemic or scholastic refinement. It was more an act of piety than of study. And it was recollected afterwards more from devotion and patriotism than religious prejudice. It did all the good which was intended, and from its peculiar character it could not live for the purposes of superstition. It was revived and signed again in 1660, when Mr. John Higginson was established in Salem, rather as a grateful memorial than as an innovation upon any practices which had obtained. Had its spirit been regarded, an attempt would not have been made to change the language of reproof, in general, into an unmanly invective against a particular denomination of Christians. But the abuse of this instrument consigned it to the sole care of the historian, who has preserved it for us as a precious relic of antiquity."*

---

* 1 Hist. Coll., vi. 242.

As already observed, no public records are known to have been kept in Salem, till about the year 1637. The present Old Church Book is a large folio volume, strongly bound, and lettered, " RECORDS OF THE FIRST CHURCH OF SALEM, FROM 1629 TO 1736." It contains transcript records from a former book, and original records commencing with the settlement of Rev. John Higginson, in 1660. The former include the original Covenant with the preamble to its renewal in 1636, followed by a catalogue of the names of church members, males and females, in separate columns, without note of the time of admission, till near the end of the year 1636, and after that time promiscuously in the order of admission, (the time of which is noted,) to the year 1659; and then a catalogue of the names of children baptized, from 1636 to 1659. These transcript records are evidently in the same hand-writing, and appear to have been transcribed with great care. There is a note in the margin of the covenant indicating the time of its adoption, which is in a different hand, doubtless that of Rev. Samuel Fisk; and a clause at the end against the "Quakers' doctrine," added upon the renewal of the Covenant in 1660, and in the hand of Rev. John Higginson, apparently with the same pen and ink with which he recorded the vote of the Church respecting it. We present here a copy of the original Covenant, with the preamble, Quaker clause, and marginal note, and the entire separate lists of male and female members of the Church, admitted before 11th mo., 1636; followed by the record of admissions during the two last months of that year, and also the record of baptisms from 25 of 10th mo., 1636, to the end of the year; which are added as specimens of the respective records continued to 1659. The note subjoined to the transcript records, by Rev. Samuel Fisk, upon his ordination in 1718, is copied for the information it affords respecting the original records contained in the then new book. The reason why more was not transcribed from the old book may sufficiently appear from Mr. Higginson's record of the proceedings of the Church in relation to that book, at their first meeting after his settlement in August, 1660. It is our purpose to add, as a supplement to these transcript records, a curious original record, under the date of 1637, existing in the well known hand-writing of Rev. John Fiske, some time assistant preacher with Hugh Peters, the Pastor of the First Church, lately brought to light, and of which we had no knowledge till very recently. This, undoubtedly, is more ancient as well as more valuable, than any thing left in the lost book, and will, we think, afford decisive evidence respecting the original constitution of the First Church.

In these Transcript Records we retain the same orthography that we find in the Church book, and give, in italics, the renewing preamble, Quaker postscript, and marginal note.

Gather my Saints together unto me that have made a Covenant with me by sacrifyce. Psa. 50 : 5 :

6 *of 6th Month.* 1629, *This Covenant was publickly Signed and Declared, as may appear from page* 85, *in this Book.*

Wee whose names are here under written, members of the present Church of Christ in Salem, having found by sad experience how dangerous it is to sitt loose to the Covenant wee make with our God: and how apt wee are to wander into by pathes, even to the looseing of our first aimes in entring into Church fellowship: Doe therefore solemnly in the presence of the Eternall God, both for our own comforts, and those which shall or maye be joyned unto us, renewe that Church Covenant we find this Church bound unto at theire first beginning, viz: That We Covenant with the Lord and one with an other ; and doe bynd our selves in the presence of God, to walke together in all his waies, according as he is pleased to reveale himself unto us in his Blessed word of truth. And doe more explicitely in the name and feare of God, profess and protest to walke as followeth through the power and grace of our Lord Jesus.

1 first wee avowe the Lord to be our God, and our selves his people in the truth and simplicitie of our spirits.

2 Wee give our selves to the Lord Jesus Christ, and the word of his grace, fore the teaching, ruleing and sanctifyeing of us in matters of worship, and Conversation, resolveing to cleave to him alone for life and glorie ; and oppose all contrarie wayes, cannons and constitutions of men in his worship.

3 Wee promise to walke with our brethren and sisters in this Congregation with all watchfullnes and tendernes, avoyding all jelousies, suspitions, backbyteings, censurings, provoakings, secrete risings of spirite against them ; but in all offences to follow the rule of the Lord Jesus, and to beare and forbeare, give and forgive as he hath taught us.

4 In publick or in private, we will willingly doe nothing to the ofence of the Church but will be willing to take advise for our selves and ours as ocasion shalbe presented.

5 Wee will not in the Congregation be forward eyther to shew oure owne gifts or parts in speaking or scrupling, or there discover the fayling of oure brethren or sisters butt atend an orderly cale there unto ; knowing how much the Lord may be dishonoured, and his Gos-

pell in the profession of it, sleighted, by our distempers, and weaknesses in publyck.

6 Wee bynd our selves to studdy the advancement of the Gospell in all truth and peace, both in regard of those that are within, or without, noe way sleighting our sister Churches, but useing theire Counsell as need shalbe : nor laying a stumbling block before any, noe not the Indians, whose good we desire to promote, and soe to converse, as we may avoyd the verrye appearance of evill.

7 Wee hearbye promise to carrye our selves in all lawfull obedience, to those that are over us, in Church or Commonweale, knowing how well pleasing it will be to the Lord, that they should have incouragement in theire places, by our not greiveing theyre spirites through our Irregularities.

8 Wee resolve to approve our selves to the Lord in our perticular calings, shunning ydleness as the bane of any state, nor will wee deale hardly, or oppressingly with any, wherein we are the Lord's stewards:

9 alsoe promyseing to our best abilitie to teach our children and servants, the knowledg of God and his will, that they may serve him also ; and all this, not by any strength of our owne, but by the Lord Christ, whose bloud we desire may sprinckle this our Covenant made in his name.

This Covenant was renewed by the Church on a sollemne day of Humiliation 6 of 1 moneth 1660. When also considering the power of Temptation amongst us by reason of ye Quakers doctrine to the leavening of some in the place where we are and endangering of others, doe see cause to remember the Admonition of our Saviour Christ to his disciples Math. 16.   Take heed and beware of ye leaven of the doctrine of the Pharisees and doe judge so farre as we understand it yt ye Quakers doctrine is as bad or worse than that of ye Pharisees ; Therefore we doe Covenant by the help of Jesus Christ to take heed and beware of the leaven of the doctrine of the Quakers.

CATALOGUE OF THE NAMES OF THOSE PERSONS THAT ARE JOINED
IN FULL COMMUNION.

Samuell Sharp.
John Endecott.
Phillip Veren.
Hugh Laskin.
Roger Connant.
Laurance Leach.
William Auger.
Francis Johnson.
Thomas Eborne.
George Williams.
George Norton.
Henry Herricke.
Peeter Palfrye.
Roger Maurye.
Thomas Gardener.
John Sibly.
John Baulch.
Samuell Moore.
John Holgrove.
Ralph Fogge.
John Horne.
John Woodberye.
William Traske.
Townsend Bishop.
Thomas Read.
Richard Rayment.
Jeffry Massy.
Edmond Batter.
Elias Stileman.
Edmond Giles,
Richard Davenport.
John Blackleech.
Thomas Scrugges.
William Allen.
William Kinge.
Richard Rootes.

John Moore.
William Dixy.
John Sanders.
Jacob Barney.
Richard Brackenbury.
John Blacke.
Joseph Pope.
Peeter Woolfe.
William Bownd.
Samuell Archer.
Thomas Lothrop.

Elizabeth Endecott.
Alice Hutchison.
Elizabeth Leech.
Alice Sharpe.
Johane Johnson.
Elizabeth Holgrove.
Margarett Bright.
Elizabeth Davenport.
Mary Alford.
Sarah Connant.
Jane Alderman.
Agnes Woodbery.
Judith Raymond.
Johane Cotta.
Dorcas Veren.
Sarah Batter.
Eedith Palfery.
Eedith Herrick.
Hanna Moore.
Susana Fogge.
Johane Watson.
Alice Ager.
Anne Ingersoll.
Ellen Felton.

Elizabeth Allen.
Martha Woolfe.
Ellyn Backenbury.
Anne·Dixy.
Anne Bound.

Ann Horne.
Margery Balch.
Presca Kendall.
Anne Skarlett.
Gartrude Ellerd.

———

1636.
8. 11 mo. Hugh Peters.
Edmond Marshall.
Anne Moore, widdow.
16. 11 mo. John Humphy.
Lyddea Bankes.

5. 12 mo. Mary Jeggells.
12. "   Frances Skerry.
Abigail Lord.
17. "   Ann Garford.
John Alderman.
27. "   Henry Bartholomew.

[So continued to 1659.]

———

A CATALOGUE OF THE NAMES OF THE CHILDREN OF THE CHURCH
THAT ARE BAPTIZED.

1636.
25. 10mo. Recompence, son of John Horne.
Jonathan, son,   } of Peeter Palfreye.
Jehodan, daughter, }
Zachariah, son of Henry Herrick.
Hanna: da: of Jon. Woodbery.
Jon: so: of George Williams.
James, so: of Will: Bownd.
Abigaile: da: of Will: Dixy.
Lydea: da: of Jon: Black.
Jerusha: da: of John Moore.
Sam'll: so: of Sam'll: Moore.
John: son of Will: Dodge.
Difficulty: da: of Jon: Talby.
Mehitabell: da: of Will: Kinge.
Seeth: da: of Tho: Gardener.
Abigaile: da: of Richd: Hucheson.
1. 11 mo. Elias: son of Sam'll: Sharp.
Mary: da: of Will: Trask.

24. 11 mo. Theophilus: son of Jon: Humphry.
      Exersise: da: of Jon: Blacklecch.
      Naomy: da: of Edmo: Marshall.
      Joseph: son of Joseph Grafton.
12. 12   Deborah: da: of Charles Gott.
      Benjamin: son of Will: Ager.
17. 12 mo. Benjamin: son of Tho: Smith.
         [So continued to 1659.]

The following is the explanatory note of Rev. S. Fisk, before alluded to, which is subjoined to the catalogue of church members terminating in 1659 :

"The Rev. Mr. John Higginson did, on his settlement in this Church, begin a record of the admission of members at page 75, in this book, where and in the following pages the reader must look till the re-settlement of this Church in *Samuel Fisk, pastor,* on Oct. 8, 1718, who continued the record of baptisms, beginning page 17, and the record of church settlements, and meetings, acts, &c., beginning distinctly page 140, and the record of such as entered into or re-newed their covenant, page 240, and the record of such as came to the holy communion of the Lord's Supper, beginning page 280,—
         "SAMUEL FISK, Pastor."
Salem First Parish, Oct. 9, 1718.

It seems proper here to add a few remarks to Mr. Fisk's note. The names of church members, doubtless, were pre-served from the beginning in connection with the Cove-nant, though without date of the time of admission till the keeping of church records commenced. This, we think, must have been soon after the settlement of Hugh Peters and the first renewal of the Covenant. The record of bap-tisms appears to have been always kept by itself; but it is probable that the admission of church members was recorded together with "church meetings, acts, &c.," as con-
3

tinued by Rev. John Higginson, and that the transcript catalogue of members from 1636 to 1659, was formed from such miscellaneous records contained in the first church book. Throughout this catalogue various members are noted as dead, removed, &c., apparently in the transcriber's hand-writing. The plan of keeping a distinct record of admissions to the Church, appears to have originated with Mr. Fisk.

The record of baptisms from 1660 to 1695, is in the handwriting of Rev. John Higginson; from which time to 1714, it is in the hand of his colleague, Rev. Nicholas Noyes, and from 1714 to November 1717, in that of Mr. Noyes's colleague, Rev. George Curwin. On the 23d day of the same November, Mr. Curwin died, and in about three weeks after Mr. Noyes followed him, dying on the 13th day of December. During the ten or eleven months from their decease baptisms are recorded as administered by Mr. Blowers, Rev. Benj. Prescott, Rev. Aaron Porter, and Rev. Joseph Gerrish. Then commences a record in a more systematic and complete form according to the following statement at the head of it:

" Here followeth a catalogue of the names of such persons, either adult or infants, who have received baptism from the 12th of October, anno. 1718, by Sam'l Fisk, Pastor. The males baptized are distinguished by the letter *m*, and the females by *f*, preceding their Christian name ; and when this following line ———— is drawn under either of the Christian names of the parents who bring their children to baptism, it signifies that the child is baptized upon that parent's account which is so marked. The mark of a star signifies the person deceased."

The record is kept in this manner, by Mr. Fisk, to the year 1744, eight years after his dismission from the first society, and while he continued minister of the new society formed by his adherents, he still retaining the Church book. The two last baptisms recorded by him in this book are those of his own sons, John and Joseph; the former of whom, born April 16th, and baptized May 6th, 1744, by his uncle, Rev. Nathan Bucknam, of Medway, became the distinguished General Fiske, upon whose death the late Dr. Bentley delivered an appropriate discourse, in which, alluding to the father and his pastoral relations with the First Church, he represents him as "a man of eminent talents in the pulpit, of a firm and persevering mind, and of great ambition;" adding that he married into one of the most flourishing families of the town, and was very highly esteemed till dissensions in the society, from the ill defined discipline of our churches, interrupted the harmony and prevented his usefulness."[*]

He was the son of Rev. Moses Fiske, and a grandson of Rev. John Fiske, to whom we have before alluded. In the 10th volume, third series, of the Massachusetts Historical Collections, may be seen some interesting notices of the Fiske family; "a Suffolk family which produced many emigrants, and which struck deep root in the New England soil."

Rev. John Fiske was a graduate of King's College, Cambridge, and arrived here in 1637. Besides being assistant preacher with Rev. Hugh Peters, he became at once distinguished as a classical instructor, and had among his pupils the famous George Downing, who was a graduate in the first class of Harvard College. Afterwards Mr. Fiske was successively the minister of Wenham and of Chelmsford, and the book of church records, a quarto manuscript

---

* He married Anne Gerrish. His grandfather, John Fiske, married Ann Gipps, his great grandfather, John Fiske, (who died 1633) married Anne Lantersee, and his great grandfather's father, William Fiske, married Anne Ansty.—3 Hist. Coll. X. 157.

volume, which he kept throughout his ministry, is now in the custody of that intelligent and faithful antiquarian, Mr. David Pulsifer, of Boston.* In this book we find recorded, in the handwriting of Mr. Fiske, the first covenant of the Salem Church, with the preamble to its renewal, and the names of church members appended to the year 1639; and also under the date of 1637, an original record of certain proceedings before the church when he was assistant preacher, which appears to us worthy of preservation among the records of the First Church, both as being illustrative of the early times of the Church, and as affording together with his record of the covenant, sufficient evidence to settle the two main questions that have been agitated, respecting the original constitution of the Church. Mr. Fiske's record of the covenant being essentially the same as that which we have taken from the Salem Church book, need not be repeated here in full; we copy from it only the passage which contains the latter part of the renewing preamble and the first sentence of the covenant renewed, including the whole of what has been lately imagined to constitute the original covenant and which we inclose within brackets that it may be distinctly perceived, as follows:

"We, &c., Do therefore solemnly, &c., renew that church covenant we find this church bound unto at their first beginning, viz:—That [we covenant with the Lord, and one with another, and do bind

---

* This curious old book was bought at the sale of the effects of the late Dr. Charles Coffin, of Newburyport, by a gentleman who presented it to Mr. Pulsifer. Dr. Coffin, was a graduate of Harvard College in the class of 1759, and died in 1821. He was the father of Rev. Dr. Charles Coffin, a graduate of the same College in 1793. How the book got into Dr. Coffin's hands is a mystery. But Mr. Pulsifer is able, doubtless, to furnish copies to Wenham and Chelmsford of their respective records, which would be more useful to them than even the originals. Several leaves are torn so as to mutilate a number of the names of Salem Church members, but not so as to prevent their being ascertained excepting in a single instance.

ourselves in the presence of God to walk together in all his ways, according as he is pleased to reveal himself unto us in his blessed word of truth,] and do more explicitly in the name and fear of the Lord, profess and protest to walk as followeth, through the help and power of the Lord Jesus."

From the structure and punctuation of this sentence, it may be seen at once how far from Mr. Fiske's imagination must have been the thought that the half of it within brackets was the whole covenant so solemnly renewed. He, as well as Mr. Higginson, must have perfectly understood what it was; and not a doubt appears to have existed, or been suggested for more than two hundred years, that it was the very "confession of faith and covenant" described by Morton as drawn up at the first gathering of the Church, and recorded by Mather under the sanction of Mr. Higginson himself, as "the Instrument" showing "the nativity of the First Church;" the "venerable instrument," as represented by the accomplished editor of Morton's Memorial, used by "the people of Salem in the settlement of their church order," and "to be considered as expressing the character and views of those memorable worthies;" the "covenant or religious obligation," as stated by Dr. Bentley, "which was formed at the institution of the church."

Mr. Fiske's record of the covenant agrees not only with that found in the Salem Church book but with the copy printed in London in 1643, as quoted by Hanbury, in his Historical Memorials of the Independents,* in retaining the "preamble" to its renewal, and in connecting the word "sisters" with "brethren" where the latter term occurs. The copy in Mather's Magnalia, being designed to present clearly the original covenant, and that only, omits, of course, this preamble as well as the postscript, added in 1660. It also omits the word "sisters" in the cases just mentioned,— which is the most material variation that we have observed among the numerous editions of this covenant. The copy printed in Dr. Bentley's "Description of Salem," abounds in typographical errors, owing, probably, to his not having had opportunity to correct the proof-sheets himself. Neal, in his History of New England, and in the History of the Puritans, presents the genuine original covenant, and so does Judge Davis in his edition of Morton's Memorial. The learned Neander and Uhden give it a conspicuous place in their luminous and interesting History of the Congregationalists of New England; and their representation of it deserves particular notice for the illustration it affords of the various manner of designating this instrument. They introduce it as follows:—"Higginson thereupon drew up the following covenant as an expression of the sentiment of these colonists;" and at the close they add the following statement:—"In presence of the delegates of the church of New Plymouth, the persons assembled thereupon declared solemnly and each one for himself their agreement with this confession of faith." Thus the same which is first called *covenant* is here called *confession of faith.* Morton, it will be remembered, in his New England's Memorial, denominates the instrument which Francis Higginson was commissioned to "draw up in scripture language a confession of faith and covenant;" yet in the very next sentence, in alluding to a certain article (the 7th) as put into it "on purpose," he calls it more briefly "the confession of faith." Sometimes, too, as by Mather, it is called "confession and covenant," but its general designation is simply the Covenant.

Mr. Fiske's record of the Covenant is undoubtedly the most ancient now in existence. It precedes, in his church book, the particular original record, under the year 1637, before mentioned, and with this record, and the names of church members subjoined to the covenant, is all that the book contains relating to the Salem Church. His list of church members accords entirely with that in the Salem Church book, being the same and placed in the same order to the end of the year 1636, excepting that in Mr. Fiske's record the name of Hugh Peters, is taken from among those recorded as admitted in 1636, and placed next after that of John Endicott, the Governor, and there written, Peter.[*] After the particular time of admission begins to be noted, as will be observed, the names of male and female members appear promiscuously in the order of the time of admission, whereas before they were placed in separate columns; and so Mr. Fiske continued to place them to the end of his list, that is, till 1639.

Mr. Fiske's Salem records, as we have intimated, afford sufficient evidence, not only *positively* as to what was the original covenant of the First Church, but *negatively* that there could not have been a distinct confession of faith to which candidates for church membership were required to give their assent. For it is not conceivable that Mr. Fiske with his strong religious faith and while so careful to preserve a record of the covenant, should have taken no notice whatever of a separate confession of faith, had any such appertained to the Church. Besides, the original record now to be introduced, though but a fragment, happens to

---

[*] Thus written also by Mr. Peters himself; but we write the name as we find it in the Salem Church book. So we do that of Samuel Fisk, though both his father and his grandfather added the final *e*. In the index to Harvard College Catalogue, consequently, Samuel and his father, Moses Fiske, appear under different surnames.

contain particular, and as we think, decisive evidence to the same effect in regard to each question. We refer to the case of " Rob. Cotty," who claimed church member-ship on the ground of having been admitted to subscribe to the covenant,—to which it was answered, "The covenant then not first made but renewed.' And also to the record of the manner in which " Deborah Holme " and others were "received into church communion,"—where no allusion whatever is made to subscription or assent to any con-fession of faith.

This original record abounds in abbreviated words, and marks standing for words, the meaning of which we have endeavored, with Mr. Pulsifer's aid, to give in language intelligible to common readers. Our interpretation may be tested by reference to the copy of the same original, recently printed (as well as might be with common types) in " Historical Collections of the Essex Institute." Some abbreviations and single letters we leave as we find them. The small letter "a," at the beginning of certain lines or sentences, may be as well understood, perhaps, without as with any explanation from us ; so also the capital letters in the margin, indicating, as we suppose, the speakers or source of what is expressed in the text.

Dr. Bentley, in speaking of the settlement of Mr. Pe-ters, in the Salem Church, says :—"He disclaimed all the errors of Mr. Williams, and in his zeal, as he tells Dor-chester Church, he excommunicated his adherents upon the reports about them."* Probably most of the proceed-ings here sketched by Mr. Fiske, related to such adherents.

---

* 1 Hist. Coll. vi. 251.

MR. FISKE's ORIGINAL RECORD.

"Salem, 1637.

At a Church Meeting.

A question propounded to the Church by the desire of the Maj istrates of this Country. <small>Maintenance of Church Officer s</small>

What way or course is best to be taken of the Churches, for ministers' maintenance, and the continuance and upholding of Church ordinances?

R. The Church hath taken it into their consideration.

———

Our Bro. Walker's Case brought to the Church.

He had been distempered in head and distracted, and <small>William Walker.</small> since that time, suspended from the sacrament of the Lord's Supper. Now that he is judged to be recovered thereof, he is considered.

Eld.   1. that he hath not manifested himself to be humbled for his miscarriages in that time.

2. that he refuseth to come to assembly and to partake in the seals.

3. that he hath not brought his child lately born to him unto baptism.

4. that commonly he neglects to beg a blessing, and to give thanks at his eating.

W.   he answers—

1. To the keeping back his child—
that he judged himself as insufficient to one ordinance as to the other.

now the church had judged him as insufficient for one.

E.   during the time of his distraction and since the Elder had told him now of the necessity of it.

W.   yet he could not conceive but in the opinion of the church, he was yet accounted insufficient because of his distraction.

E.   Then this should have humbled him before the Church.

But whither does he now desire communion with the Church?

For he had manifested his desire of return to Engl.

4

w.   he would demur on it, and by reason because of his unfitness, through God's visiting of him.

E.   Thus he charges God, not himself.
      a, he charges the devil, because his fall came from his tempting of him.

r.   Charged him of a lazy desposition—idleness,—as the cause.

w.   he justifies himself against that—

R.   he hath sometimes desired freedom for the Church communion.
      a. for coming into the assemblies, that he hath said that he is not bound to sit within the watch of the congregation, but may be abroad in time of God's worship without the meeting house.

w.   This he justifies also.

E.R.&c. There eyes (it is said) were fastened upon him.
      a. Many objects are tendered abroad to draw away the mind.

To Giving of Thanks at Meat

w.   That he is not bound to give appearance of it.

E.   1. in regard of offence.
      2. in regard of reverence some gesture is to be used there.

w.   that soul reverence suffice: and the hat may be on, &c.

E.   to that 1 Cor. 6, 20.
      when he had nothing to say in his defense further—they said he was convicted. They urged why he did not confess his sin.

w.   that he desired not communion with the Church, unless the Church were contented with the hand of God on him.
      Twas objected against him,
      1. that he would not stay from eating till others with him had begged a blessing.
      2. that he would answer the Church why he saw cause only.
      3. that he was not bound in giving thanks to express words before God.
      4. that was supposed he was very ignorant.

r.   What the 5th commandment was? he could not tell, and asked what difference between vocation and justification; he would, but could not tell.
      a. he confessed that he read not a chapter by the whole week together.

a. that he neglected the duty of prayer commonly in family.

a. that he had said that points of evidencing of salvation are not to be meddled with by evil men.

a. that the Pastor should catechise his boy and not him.

☞ And the day after he was taken with a distracted distemper in his head.

P.   The Church gave him an admonition out of Ps. 15, **Issue.** 19 and 21. And upon it presently turning his back he went forth the assembly.

Rob. Cotty.

His case decided by the Church, which was that he conceived himself a member of this Church.

[he came before the Church with a portugal cap on: against this objected—

1. from the danger of it—intimating that soul reverence only is very contrary to 1 Cor. 11, 7.

2. contrary to good report. Warranted things are of good report, provide all things honest in the sight of all men.]

c.   he a member of this Church.

1. Because he recommended to the Church.

2. because he was admitted to subscription to the covenant.

R.   1. that he was not dismissed, but only recommended to the Church—which implied a purpose of stay for a time only here.

to 2. if he were, it was thro' mistake of the Church.

c.   the Church now dissolved from whence he recommended. Es. 44, 5. Numb. 13.

R.   1. it is denied.

2. grant it that recommendations be so; a man may be of many churches together.

P.   to the 2. Scriptures, Numb. 13, was a rash vow.

a. that the Church enquired further upon him why he would subscribe, and that the same day.

a. for recommendations there are texts, tho' not so manifest for dismission, and that in Col. 4, 8, 9, shews there is a distinction of members, and a propriety to every church,—one of you, and one of us.

a. the covenant then not first made, but renewed.*

R.   that dismission is but a term of distinction from recommendation ; since letters dismissive are nothing but letters recommendatory.

a. as our Lord hath divers households, now the Lord sends a servant of one by the bye upon a message or the like to the other. Those servants shall give him entertainment. But he shall have no power of transacting anything in that house, like as there from whence he came. So here.

———

Contribution.   A question was moved to the Church, viz :
whither contribution was—
1. to be every Sabbath.
2. to be done so as every one might take notice what each doth contribute.

R,   It is referred to the further thoughts of the Church.

———

Upon another Day.

S. Weston.   The case of our sister Weston brought before the Church. When a matter of difference between her and another was at the Court put unto the Jury : she excepted against two of the Jury men, who were therefore offended and with them others also.

E.   demanded her reason.

S.   that she did think it her liberty.

E.   True, that there is a liberty ; but exception implies a just cause or 't is not equal : viz. that he will not do justice ;
or, that he regards not an oath ;
or, that he bear some spleen.

M.   The law grants it,
in case of consanguinity,
or some nigh relation :
But then the ground or reason must be shown to the Judge of the Court.

S.   She denied to render a reason, lest that impeachment of his

———

* Explicit and decisive as to the first covenant—certainly not made when renewed—not a "covenant of 1636."

good name whom she excepted against : and said that _{Mr. Batter.} the other was all one with the party against her, and more frequent with him than any one member.

R.   Mr Batter at Mr. Pesters with Mr. Noyes, Pter Ward—the others have had frequent dealings there.

And that S. hath broken a rule, Matt. 18, and Lev. 19. that suspecting evil in them she dealt not with them. For the things were some long time before the Court.

s.   She knew not they should be of the Jury, she intended not a scandal.

a. that she conceived them in a temptation, and gifts blind the eyes of the wise.

R.   In aggravation of her fault, it brought in against her, her carriage to our bro. Johnson,—her disorderly carriage then before the Church,—her there taxing our Pastor of hypocrisy,—her opening the grievance there against a bro: in her own case,—her not dealing with such suspected brethren before after so long a time,—her confessing she saw no sin in them which aggravates her exception,—her taking the occasion from suspicious reports against them.

So she referred to the next Church meeting.

————

Eld'r,   He asks our Bro. Walker how the case stands now with him. _{Br. Walker the 2d time.}

w.   1. that he justifies not his practice in the time of his distraction.

2. that 't is not in his power to reform himself.

3. that he stands at the dispose of the Church.

E.   The Church expects his repentance.

w.   he knows not what to say to it.

E.   What he answer to the Church as touching the withholding his child from baptism.

w.   he silent.

E.   the Church desires satisfaction.

w.   that he looks not upon himself as meet for communion.

But that he shall be meet when God shall turn his heart, (yet that he well understands the Church's expectation) and that because—

    1. distempered

    2. faithless.

Pastor. that it appears he is under a temptation and 't were fit his case were commended to God by fasting and prayer.

E. whither he desires this?

w. that he knows not what to say to it.

———

Mr.
Humfry. Mr. Humfres Case brought to the Church.

Eld'r he complains against the Church of Lin: that twice he was there hindered the seals:

the 1 because of some difference between him and Leiften. How, who excepted against him.

the 2d time, because one Thomkins was received into Church communion that day, notwithstanding he excepted against him.

Pastr. it seems as if the Church there denied him not that communion.

It was agreed upon that if the Church and he so consent, this Church may have the whole matter discovered by writing from both sides, &c.

This day, Deborah Holme,

       Bro: Gidnies wife,

       Bro: Marshal's wife,

         Ja: Moulton—made their professions, and testimoies were given of their godly life; and the next Sabbath they were received into Church communion.*

Some others propounded should have come in but were excepted against. Whereupon warning was given by the Elder that the reasons for their exceptions might be brought in to him before the next Church meeting.

Deacons. Propounds to the Church to consider of the dispose of Mr. Skelton's children.

———

* No allusion whatever to any confession of faith to be subscribed or assented to.

10th of 11th month.

Mr. Humfres case the 2d time. In the interim our Pas- Mr.Hum-
tor was sent for to meet the Elders of the Church at Lin to
confer with them ; who from both parties brings this relation
to the Church :—

1. That he withdrew himself, because he was loth to offend the
Church.

2. that the second time he withdrew himself because he was
offended by the Church who took in an unworthy member.

To this 't was determined,

1. that the Church is to deal with Mr. Humfrey for withdrawing himself, and not rather for dealing with the first Bro: privately according to rule first.

r.   here in the interim fell in this discourse, viz. qu. whither an
irritation unfits for the sacrament—

it should appear because anger is a short madness.

A. 1. Cor. xi. an examined man 't is his duty to eat.

qu. whither a bro: may abstain when he is like else to give
offence to another.

A. no.

2. that this Church is to write to those Elders and Church.

1 because they take on members against opposition

and 2 privately.

2. because they suffer the unseasonable opposition of members.
For members are not to reason between themselves before the
Church by way of opposition, but members must speak their
case to the Church.

This writing to be sent by virtue of the community that is between these Churches.

————

The Case of the brethren that withdrew themselves from this Church
brought forth.

Pastor. that they do it 1. out of contempt.   Separa-
tists.
                  2. because they would the peace of the Church
seeing they cannot peacefully hold communion with the Church.

                  3. they are not resolved, as they pretend,
whither to go.

a. that they object not against the Church only, that those that received on did not renounce publicly the government of Engl. and that one, about hearing in Engl. and that one, that they no liberty of objecting in the Church against what is taught.

It was put to the Church's consideration—whither if six or eight of the Church, and which we hope to be godly, yet not agreeing with us in their judgment, may not have a peaceable departure from us to gather a Church?

R.   1. These persons must first give the Church satisfaction for their schism.

2. 't is probable that these would not keep communion with this Church.

3. These have not asked leave of the Church, but do take leave of the Church.

It was determined these should be sent for.

Eld'r.   ^{Bro.}/_{Weston.} desires of our Bro: Weston the grounds of his withdrawing from the Church.

W.   that he had already told the Elders his grounds.

E.   he desired him to declare them to the Church.

W.   that the Church he counts to walk according to her light or apprehension.
and he walks according to his.

1. ground, because he not suffered to ask questions in public, but 't is imputed to him for pride.

E.   'T is desired that he should refrain in regard of the season : viz. Lord's day.
but qu. is this a ground of his withdrawing?

W.   yes because he count himself bound presently to object and so seek clearing of truths.

E.   he never dealt in private with the Elders for it.

W.   2. reas. because when he questioned about our Pastor touching his coming off at Rotterdam: and what kind of Church that was : 'T was answered by some, that he was neither fit for church nor commonwealth.

3. reas. because some are admitted into this Church from Rotterdam, touching whom they write that they came disorderly away: then if that be a true Church, why are these received without satisfaction first given.

Pastor. 1. that he in town two years and a half, and not objected against.

2. that the 2d meant of his wife, who had no letters of dismission from thence.

qu. How far, or whither a wife ought to seek letters of dismission, if the man be dismissed.

R. by M. 1. that not needful.

Obj. she must come in, in a way of God here.

M. 'Tis satisfaction enough that she be a member of another church.

Obj. That church hath manifested itself offended for her disorderly coming away.

Pastor. she thought not herself bound to require their letters her husband being here.

Obj. It should appear as if there might be something disorderly observed in her carriage since her husband's coming away.

Past. the fault was of negligence by the Elders in not propounding her to the Church.

It was concluded that letters should be written to Rotterdam about the persons that did disorderly come off thence.

W. 4 reas. because our Pastor often hath said in public to this effect: We had better part than live contentiously.

Pa. meant in a way of Christ.

Ma. to the 2d reas that t was he that said he was neither fit for church nor commonwealth, because by his oft questioning grieves magistrates and ministers, and so that he thinks still : so long as he holds that way.

Here Bro. Talby obj. that it was an uncharitable speech.

R. that he breaks a rule, seeing he should have dealt with our Ma. privately, and this kind of speaking is disorderly.

W. 5 reas. because this Church holds communion with such as do hold communion with the Church of Engl. viz. the members of Mr. Lathrop's congregation, which hath both communion with this Church and the Church of Engl.

E. that he should have dealt with those members privately.

W. 6. because he is counselled to follow peace : and this is the end of his practice.

E. But the beginning must be peaceable too.

5

Ma.   The case may be resolved in this one question : qu. whither one under sin in his opinion, not in the opinion of the Church, is a just ground of his leaving the Church ?

W.   a private scruple against any is not to be made public, lest others should be brought to scruple too.

Ma.   whither a private scruple a ground of separation. This course tends but to schism, and so to heresy, which is damnable.

W.   This which is now called damnable, was once called lawful.

M.   He which holds and teaches: that one may break off from a Church, upon any discontent, or at taking offence against a brother &c., is in a damnable heresy for it rases the foundation of grace.

E.   that Bro: Weston shew a text of Scripture for his separation.

W.   he is silent.

E.   he is desired to be at the next Church meeting.

Bro. Ony.   He is desired of the Church the grounds of his separation.

Ony.   that he had told them to our Pastor, and he desired him to discover them to the Church, and his withdrawing was but for the present, because the sacrament came suddenly before he could inform the Church of his scruple. Whereupon it presently went abroad that he was quite broken off. Whereas he conceived himself under a temptation and having touched a dead body ought to refrain.

qu. by one. whither a man may break off communion with a church, if he see or suppose some practice in the church that he allow not of ?

M.or P.Neg.   Gal. 5. Circumcision a fundamental error yet not a ground or rule there through the Epist. of separation from that Church. So in the Church of Corinth—Fornication—so holding of Paul, so of Apollos. So in Thyatira, Jezebell's doctrine, and yet no rule given for separating from either.

o.   Were such members admitted ?

M.   There is the same reason of admission and keeping in of members.

o.   Such as have been defiled with idolatry have been here admitted without washing their hands by repentance.

м. Their practice gives satisfaction, in that they join with the true Church of Christ.

o. They may yet retain Babylon in their hearts.

м. we are to be more charitably affected to such.

o. Esech. 43, 9, 10, 11.

м. are not our brethren ashamed of their doings when they will not abide by it?

Bro. Oldney. he gave the right hand of fellowship to me.

r. Why then, so lately, and not now?

o. that his judgment so altered, so as not know how to give the right hand of fellowship to the Church.

Pa. that you are so newly altered in your judgment:

Consider,

1. the frame of your heart at that time, were you in a humble, praying frame, and in the way of an ordin:

2. does it carry you nigher to Christ now and to more humbleness.

3. you should have told it to the Elders. Prov. 9, 7, rebuke a wise man, &c.

4. that place in Ezech. 43, you misapply, for from thence we ᴱᶻᵉᶜʰ. ⁴³· note.

1. Those are most capable of the things of God, that are ashamed of their iniquities.

2. God will never show the true forms of his house, but to them that are washed from their iniquities; and these forms are the inwards, which are the seals.

3. The story is this. This Church had revolted and relapsed, and the prophet exhorts her to her first love again: and told her what she should see upon her return. For in their falling off they lost the patterns of the house.

s. 5. Can you challenge any of spiritual whoredom amongst us.

o. 1. that if those that relapsed, being in a church state, ought to be ashamed ere they capable, &c., much more those that never, in a church state.

2. he could not challenge any without prejudice or offence, but these professors, of all men, were most bitter against separation at first, who now join without being ashamed of that.

r. such breaches as these in Churches gave occasion to them of their bitterness.

o.   there ought to be yet a public detestation against these courses.
His texts for separation.   2 Cor. 6, be not unequally yoked.

M.   that yields no reason of his withdrawing, unless we were proved idolaters ; and we have a text opposing this practice of his.
Rev. 2, 18, 20.—

Where the Lord :   1. acknowledges the good in that Church,
then he speaks of her sins and judgments, and in verse 24, he
says to those not so sinned—I'll lay no other burden upon you
but, &c.

The sin of idolatry, or of circumcision, may be held in a
Church, and yet the Church a true Church.

P.   that place, 2 Cor. 6, meant of idolatry out of the Church, and
the Apostle wrote to the whole Church.

o.   meant that they should come out from the idolators amongst
themselves.

B.   meant of their being among idolators and their joining to
their idol feasts.
a. Christ separated not from the Jewish synagogues.

o.   there divers reasons of that, for the prophecies were not fulfilled ;—and Christ communicated not in their corruptions.

P.   In Zach. 11. there is set down the worship Christ did communicate in.

Thus closes Mr. Fiske's record of proceedings in the
Salem Church, or rather of a sketch of certain proceedings, especially interesting, at the time. Reversing his
old book, we find at the other end, the beginning of Wenham Church records. The first thing, however, that meets
our eye here, is the following family record, in his own
hand writing, which appears to us of sufficient interest to
be copied in this connection.

" The children of John and Anna Fiske, born in N. E.

1638.   John, borne ye 29th of 6t.   ⎫
             bapt. ye 2d, of 7.   ⎬ Salem Mr. Peter.
                                   ⎭

Escaped a greate danger at Wenham, in passing with the stream under the mill-wheele, when the mill was agoing. An. 1617, 6t of 3d, at what time he rec'd (as twere) a new life. Not a bone broken, &c.

1640. Sarah, borne 24 of 5t. } Salem, Mr. Peter.
   bapt. 26 of 5. }

1642. Moses, borne 12 of 2d. at Wenham.
   bapt. 0 of 4t, at Salem, by Mr. Norice.

1644. Anna, borne 15t of 11th. } at Wenham
1645. ——— bapt. 2 of 1st. (ye 1st child bapt.) }

1646. Eli-ezer, borne 8t of 12th, } Wenham.
   bapt. 15 of 12. }
   he deceased 16 of 10, 49.

1671. The sd Anne Fiske, wife to the sd Jno. ffiske, having lived with him about 37 years, deceased 14 of 12th mo. at Chelmsford.

1672. Elizabeth Hinksman, marryed to the sd Jno. ffiske 1 of 6mo. at Chelmsford.

"1644, 18th of 8th," is the date of the first Church meeting at Wenham. Mr. Fiske must have preached at Enon, or Wenham, a number of years before that time, and probably also resided there with his family, his son Moses being recorded as born in 1642, at Wenham.

In 1654, Mr. Fiske and his Church were invited to join those "engaged in the N. plantation at Chelmsford." Much inquiry and deliberation followed on the subject, and certain questions arose, "touching the building of the house, terms of accommodation and of yearly maintenance,"—which were referred for counsel to "Mr. Endicot, Governor, Mr. Mather, Mr. Allen, of Dedham, Mr. Cobbet, Mr. Sherman, Capt. Johnson, of Wooburn;" and upon their decision, "on either side preparation was made for the removal of the Church." And "accordingly about the 13th of 9 mo. 55, there were met at Chelmsford, the Pastor with the engaged Brethren........to whom such of the Brethren of Woburn and Concord Ch: who had before propounded themselves to join with the Ch : late at Wenham, now in removing to Chelmsford, presenting themselves with their letters of dismission and testimony given, were by a unanimous vote received into fellowship."

There is one transaction recorded by Mr. Fiske, after his removal to Chelmsford, which strikes us as particularly interesting, and worthy of a place in connection with the records of the First Church. We refer to the proceedings before the Chelmsford Church, when his son, Moses Fiske, (father of Rev. Samuel Fiske,) was about leaving home, at the age of sixteen years, to enter Harvard College. These proceedings were in perfect accordance with the evangelical spirit of the First Church Covenant,—the spirit of Christ's Sermon on the Mount,—while they present, a beautiful instance of the sisterly relation which was cherished by the early New England Churches. The following is Mr. Fiske's record of the case:

12 of 7
'58.

Moses Fiske. This day, Moses Fiske, being suddenly to depart for the College, was called forth before the Church, and owned there his parents' covenant, in presence of the Church, personally engaging himself to the Church, and the Church to him, as in the form as follows :

1st. it being moved to the Church whether any had aught against him for matter of offence, as touching his life and conversation, alledging that in Psal. 50, 16, 17,—and there being no objection :

It was then proposed to him :

You (M) do here before the Lord, his angels, and us his people, promise and engage yourself personally to own and stand to your parents' covenant with this Church.

And in particular,

1. To own no other God, but only the true and living God, even the maker, preserver and governor of all things, to be your covenant God, and do give up yourself unto him.

2. To own the Lord Christ in all his offices, as to be your media-

torial Prophet to teach you the will of his Father, your Priest to reconcile you to his Father, and your mediatorial King to rule and govern you.

3. To walk according to the holy Order and Rule of the Gospel, according to your best light, without giving just offence unto any.

4. And you do here by your own personal act give up yourself to the watch and care of this Church;—and all this by the help of God's spirit and grace.

To which he answered personally in the affirmative.

The Church then by the help of the same spirit doth promise to perform unto you her duty of Church Inspection and care ;—and also to be ready to own you afterwards, to further Privileges in the Church as the Lord shall qualify you thereunto.

Letters also of Recommendation were voted in his behalf to the Church at Cambridge, which were to this effect.

To the Rev'd, &c.

Rev'd and Beloved,

We being (for our parts,) convinced according to the light appearing to us, that it is our duty to own such the children of members in personal covenant with us, as who were in their minority at what time these their parents entered in covenant with this Church, to be also members thereof from that time forward, and consequently to have right unto Baptism, and to [constant] inspection and care as parts of the same body :   And considering that the ordering hand of divine providence hath disposed of one in such wise related to us, (Moses Fiske by name,) to be for a certain space of time amongst you, a member of the College, for his better advantage in good learning ;—notwithstanding we are in some good measure competently satisfied touching the pious care of the Reverend, the President and Fellows of the said College, as in reference to all the members, so even to this in particular :   Yet out of conscience of discharging the uttermost of our trust over him: He being now more removed from under our eye and observation : we beg and entreat of you (Brethren) that you would please to take cognizance of him ; and to do both us and him this office of brotherly love, as to extend your inspection and watch over him, as may concern both the preventing of scandal by him, and the furtherance of his spiritual good according to God, and to the rule of his holy Gospel : in which respects we do commend him over unto you for the time being, coveting of you your prayers for him as for ourselves. So leaving you to the gracious guidance of the spirit of Christ in, and his blessing upon all your pious administrations and endeavors : we rest

Yours in the &c.

Jno. Fiske,

Tho: Adams,

Chelmsford,

Ja: Parker,

12 of 7,

In the name and with the

58.

consent of the Church.

We now come to the original records of Rev. John Higginson. But before entering upon them let us recur for a moment to Mr. Fiske's Salem records, especially that of the renewed covenant and church members, and see what light it affords in relation to the first old church book which Mr. Higginson found upon his settlement here, and which, as will be seen. became immediately the subject of examination and revision. This record of Mr. Fiske, being essentially the same with the corresponding transcript record, as copied in the preceding pages, proves that the transcript is true to an original like itself, and that itself is a duplicate of that original, or derived from the same source. Did the original record, contained in this old book, present a true copy of the genuine "confession of faith and covenant in scripture language," drawn up by Francis Higginson in 1629, and "about seven years after solemnly renewed," upon the settlement of Hugh Peters ? A few historical reminiscences will answer the question. Mr. Peters became the Pastor of the First Church on 21st of December, 1636, and the baptism of sixteen children on the 25th of the same month, forms the first record in the list of baptisms. On the 8th of the next month, that is, January, 1637, he joined the church, and his name stands first in the record of admissions to full communion, the date against his name being 8, 11 mo. 1636, the year, as then reckoned, ending with February, 1637. Thus commenced the records of Mr. Peters and the use of the first church book. The renewal of the Covenant, the preamble to which he evidently wrote, must have taken place about the same time. The first seven words and some striking expressions in this preamble are the same as used by him in renewing the Covenant of his Church at Rotterdam which he had left on coming to America.* Mr. Fiske, who speedily became associated with Mr. Peters, would naturally form his own record of the renewed Covenant from the Salem Church book, then just introduced. But, however this might be, we may be sure that both Mr. Peters and Mr. Fiske would avail themselves of the best means of information in their power, to ascertain the true original Covenant with everything material to a right understanding of the constitution of the Church. Now what were those means? At the beginning, we may remember, "Thirty·copies" of the Covenant were "written out for the use of the thirty persons who were to begin the work." Consequently there must have been just so many records of it to start with; and we cannot doubt that the officers and other principal members of the Church would have carefully preserved their copies and been ready to furnish all desirable information, whether for renewing the Covenant, or setting up a church book of records. It is well known, as stated by Mr. Felt, that Deacon John Orne (writing his name as he did in his will and as Dr. Bentley writes it) "was a friend and confident of Hugh Peters. He and Deacon Charles Gott," Mr. F. adds, "were Mr. P's agents till his death."† None could be better qualified than these confidential friends to enlighten Mr. Peters on the subject of the orig-

* 2 Hanbury's Hist. Memorials, 309.　　　† Annals of Salem, 275.

inal " confession of faith and covenant " of the First Church. We may be certain, therefore, that the old church book, started under his direction, contained a true and complete record of the genuine Covenant to which "the Church was bound at their first beginning," together with his "preamble," so expressed and applied as would leave no room to doubt which was the one and which the other. But further still, this old record bore the sanction of all the members of the Church whose names were subscribed to the renewed Covenant—actually subscribed—as indicated in the preamble. In the case of " Rob. Cotty," (as presented by Mr. Fiske,) it is seen that one of his reasons for claiming church membership was his being admitted to subscription to the Covenant; the answer to which, that "the Covenant then not first made but renewed,"—shows the renewing of the Covenant to have been the occasion of his subscription, and shows, also, the probability that the members of the Church generally subscribed their names on the same occasion. The signatures in Mr. Fiske's record appear closely subjoined to the Covenant, as was probably the case in the first Church book, though the transcript from it, being designed to include subsequent as well as preceding members, has a general heading to the list accordingly. It has been understood that this list included no names of members who had "deceased or taken up their connection."[*] It does not, indeed, contain the names of all who were then living and connected with the Church. Charles Gott is not on the list, yet he was a Deacon of the Church, and not long after the renewal of the Covenant, he, with Deacon Orne, received from the town a grant of the five acres of land, ever since known as the " Deacons' Marsh." [†] But it would seem that nearly all who had ever been con-

---

* Annals of Salem, 2d, edi., 171.   † Ibid. 183.

nected with the Church were represented on this list; the Salem annalist, in undertaking to designate those among the first settlers who were members of the First Church, but not thus represented, finds only the first two ministers and Henry Haughton, the first ruling elder, all deceased, and Rev. John Higginson and Charles Gott, who were probably absent from Salem at the time. It consequently appears that the renewed covenant, as recorded in the first church book, bore with it the testimony to its genuineness of nearly all the living members of the Church, most of whom were original members,—the very persons, who, at the beginning, "did solemnly profess their consent thereunto." Now all this we certainly have, and as certainly know that we have it, as if the old church book itself had been brought to light instead of Mr. Fiske's duplicate record which identifies the original of the transcript contained in it.

Of Mr. Fiske's duplicate record we have said that it is *essentially* the same as the corresponding transcript from the old church book. It may be well to indicate the immaterial differences which would seem to be implied. In the renewing preamble, Mr. Fiske's record has "yea" before "even," which is not in the transcript; and the latter has "into" after "entering," not in the former. Otherwise the words are the same in both, excepting that Mr. Fiske uses "who" instead of "which" between "those" and "shall." In the Covenant itself the most considerable variance appears at the close of the introductory clause, where Mr. Fiske's record has "help and power" instead of "power and grace," before "our Lord Jesus." The names of the forty-seven male and thirty-four female Church members, subjoined to the renewed covenant, are the same in both, and arranged in the same order, excepting only Mr.

Fiske's respectful transfer of the name of Hugh Peters to a higher place in the list.

But it has heretofore been imagined that something very precious may have been lost with the first church book. But what can this have been? Every thing contained in it relating to the original constitution and members of the Church, was, as we have seen, faithfully transcribed into the present volume, as were also its records of baptisms and of admissions to church communion during the ministry of Hugh Peters, and that of his colleague and successor, Rev. Edward Norris, extending together through twenty-two years. What other important matters could the old book contain? Mr. Norris, indeed, like his immediate predecessor, was troubled by divers sectaries, but Mr. Fiske's graphic sketches relating to a portion of these will doubtless suffice for the whole. The moral discipline of the Church, so strictly carried out as it then was, would of course lead to proceedings, the record of which, however interesting to the families concerned, and their descendants, could be of little general importance. Undoubtedly the venerable and judicious committee of the Church, who were appointed to examine the old church book, took care that every thing in it of any permanent value should be transferred to the new book. We may therefore confidently rest satisfied that the records of the First Church, so far as they were ever made, are still, to all valuable intents and purposes, complete.

We now enter upon Rev. John Higginson's church records, and shall endeavor to select from them all admissions to the Church during the first ten years of his ministry, with other proceedings of general interest, and illustrative of the spirit and character of the First Church.

"1660.

John Higginson, formerly a member of this Church, being removed from Gilford, and come to the Bay in order to his going for England, was by importunity prevailed with to stay here for one year, and desired by two general votes of the Church and town to continue with them in the work of the ministry.

After his continuance here almost a year he gave his answer to the call of the Church and people here in these words:

"It hath been matter of serious inquiry to me what should be the "will of God and my duty in this great turn of my life, especially in "ordering my abode here amongst you for a time, which hath been "overruled by the Providence of God wholly beyond my own inten-"tion in my removal from the place where I was before. And yet "truly when I have considered all, I incline to look at the call of the "people here as the call of God for my continuance amongst you. "I desire to be thankful to God and thankful to you all for your love "to me and mine, and am willing to settle amongst you. As in Acts "2, 42, so when I join in Church fellowship with you,

1. "So long as the Church and people of God here continue in "the stedfastness of faith in Christ and order of the gospel as now "you do.

2. "So long as I find that I can (with a good conscience) carry "on that part of the work of Christ which may belong to me and "discharge my duty to my family: I do express myself willing to "settle amongst you with a true intention, and a true affection, hav-"ing no other thoughts or desires but to live and die amongst you as "my Father did before.

"There is but one thing, I would commend unto the congregated "that you would seriously think of a Ruling Elder, for though I "should not be unwilling to do what the Lord shall enable me, yet I "am not free to undertake church work without the assistance of a "Ruling Elder, the place being great, the people many, and the work "like to be much, especially in such times as these.

"And for myself I know my own weakness many ways and that "I *shall have need of the freedom of my spirit and command of my* "*time,* that I may in some measure fulfill the work of the ministry "into which I am called of God by yourselves."

A motion being made for choosing a Ruling Elder, Mr. John Brown being nominated, after some consideration he was (in his absence) chosen by the Church with general consent: On the 8th of the 5th month, the call of the Church was signified unto himself being then present; he expressed his acceptance of the Church's call the Lord's day after to this effect. "That though he judged himself un-"fit, and many others more able for the work, yet considering the "call of God and the people in it, and that he might be any means "of the Church's settlement, he did give up himself to the Lord and "to the Church in the work so far as the Lord should enable him "thereunto, only his occasions at Virginia did require his presence "there the following winter, and when the Lord should please to re-"turn him safely from thence he should then continue at home and "apply himself to the work as the Lord should enable him."

On — of — month, "Letters of Recommendation and dismission from the Church of Gilford concerning J. Higginson and his wife, were read unto the Church, and they were both received members of this Church after the usual manner. After which the Church did signify by a vote (with general consent) their election of him to the office of Pastor in this Church, and he did manifest his acceptance of their call thereunto promising to attend the work of that office amongst us as the Lord should help him.

It was thought meet in regard that many of the brethren would be shortly absent upon the necessary occasions of their callings at sea, to hasten the ordination of the Pastor and Elder, which was accordingly agreed upon to be on the   of the 6th month ; and letters were sent unto four of the neighbor Churches of Ipswich, Linne, Reading and Boston, to give them notice of the Church's intention about the ordination at that time, desiring the presence of their Elders and Messengers then.

The day above said, J. Higginson was ordained Pastor with prayer and fasting and imposition of hands, preaching out of 1 Cor. 3, 7. He that plants is nothing, and he that watereth is nothing, but God that gives the increase.

The Church having no Elders then, our honored brother Major Hawthorn and the two Deacons imposed hands on the Pastor and then the Pastor and the two Deacons imposed hands on the Ruling Elder. The Elders of the foresaid Churches being present (with many others) Mr. Norton, Teacher of the Church of Boston, did in the name of the rest give the right hand of fellowship to both our Elders, showing from Gal : 2, 9, that the right hand of fellowship was the sign of the communion and helpfulness which both Churches and Elders were engaged in one towards another as the case might require.

___

At a meeting of the Church Sept. 10.

A church meeting Sept. 10. It was agreed upon and voted by the Church. 1. concerning catechising : That Mr. Cotton's Catechism be used in their families in teaching their children in order to public catechising in the congregation.

2. Concerning the Lord's Supper:

1. For the time of the administration of it, to be in ordinary course once a month.

2. For the charge of it ; the Lord's Supper being proper to the Church, it was thought meet not to take in the help of non-members' contribution for it ; therefore it was agreed upon : That every member of the church (except the poor) do bring in to the Deacons half a crown in merchantable pay, it being left unto their discretion to provide the bread and wine, and when the sum raised by the half crowns is spent, then the Deacons to propound unto the Church for another contribution in the same way for the same end.

3. That on days of Humiliation and Thanksgiving, the Deacons propound for a contribution for the poor of the Church.

4. That Major Hawthorn, Mr. Batter, Mr. Price, the two Deacons, together with the Pastor, be desired to review the Church book and to report such things to the Church as they conceive worthy of consideration.

___

Review of the former Church book. After a sufficient time spent by the forenamed brethren in reviewing the Church book, they gave this account unto the Church : That they conceived the book itself and paper of it being old, not well bound, and in some places having been wet and torn, and not legible, is not like to last long to be of use for posterity, therefore they thought it best if it were kept in safety by the Elders,—*by that means it will be of use so long as it will last.* Only some few passages in it which do reflect upon particular persons, or upon the whole Church, without any Church vote, and without due proof, they did mark in the book as thinking they should be struck out.

48

1. Also that in the new book : that in all matters tending to censure nothing to be brought to the Church, nor left upon record, without sufficient proof.

2. That all Church acts (or votes) be so recorded as to be read unto the Church, if it may be, at the time when the vote is passed; if not, to be read the first thing done the next Church meeting.

5. That any brother have liberty to see the Church book for his satisfaction. These things were consented unto by the Church, only some of the brethren propounded, which was readily consented to, that there might be liberty to such as desired it to see those passages mentioned in the former book for a month's time.

It was also then agreed to have a public day of Humiliation.

1. To humble ourselves under the afflicting hand of God in the general sickly time this winter, and in letting loose seducers to prevail so far with so many in this place.

2. To seek the Lord for his presence with us in carrying on Church work, and for his mercy in reducing those that go astray.

3. To renew our covenant, and to add that clause of taking heed of the leven of the doctrine of the Quakers.

4. To seek the Lord for the peace and welfare of ourselves, and of our native land.

Accordingly on the first week of the first month, the Church and people here assembled in a day of Fasting and prayer, and the Pastor spoke something from Rev. 3, 10, concerning the power of temptation, and also concerning our duty of covenant from Psal. 50, 5. In the close of the day the Church covenant was renewed, and that clause added, that

By the help of Christ we would endeavor to take heed and beware of the leven of the doctrine of the Quakers according to the command of our Saviour Christ in Math. 16.

1661. It pleased God to return home our Elder, Mr. Brown, in safety from Virginia in the 3d month, notwithstanding the casting away of his vessel and goods to his great loss, and a great danger he was in afterwards by the Indians, which preservation and deliverance was related by himself and for which solemn thanks was rendered to the Lord in the congregation.

Elders attending every 2d day. Soon after, the Elders gave public notice that they should be present at the Pastor's house every 2d day of the week at one o'clock, and so spend the afternoon (and more if there should be need) with any that should come to them in a preparative way in order to the Church's knowledge and consent.

At a meeting of the Church, Sept: 9.

State of the chil- **1.** These following propositions concerning the state of the dren of memb rs. children of members were agreed upon and voted by the Church according to Scripture. That the chil.lren of members born in the Church, or received with their parents in their minority, are true and real members by virtue of divine institution, according to that in Gen. 17, 7. I will establish my covenant with thee and thy seed after thee to be a God unto thee and thy seed. The name of the children are put into the covenant by the Lord as well as the parents' name. Acts 3, 25: such children are expressly called the children of the covenant which God made with Abraham.

2. The membership of such children doth not cease but by virtue of some other divine institution, viz: that of excommunication.

Math. 18, 1 Cor. 5. they are brethren, therefore not to be accounted as heathens, publicans, or wicked persons, but by a just and orderly excommunication. Hence it follows.

1. Such children have a right of claim to all the ordinances as they are capable of enjoying them in an orderly way, because they are chil lren of the covenant, Acts 3, 25: and brethren, Math. 18.

2. They have a right unto baptism in their infancy, that being now the first seal of the covenant, and these being chil lren of the covenant, Acts 3, 25, and our Saviour witnessing for them that such children belong to the Kingdom of Heaven, Math. 19, 14.

3. They are under the watch and care of the Elders who are to take heed unto all the flock over which the Holy Ghost hath ma le them overseers, but such chil.lren belong to the flock,—they must take care of the Church of Go.l, 1 Tim. 3, 5.

4. They are under the watch and care of the whole Church, and in case of just offences they m ly and ought to be proceede l with either privately or p iblicly in an or lerly way, accor ling to Math. 18. and Luke 17, 3. If thy brother offen.l thee,—these are brethren.

5. That it is the parents' duty by diligent instruction of their children to prepare them for and bring them to the trial of their fitness for full communion. Deutr. 6, 7. Thou shalt teach the se words dil-

7

igently unto thy children. Gen. 18, 19, Abraham will command his children to keep the way of the Lord. Jos. 24: 15, I and my house will serve the Lord.

6. When they are at years of discretion and desire to join in full communion, it belongs to the Church to judge of their fitness for full communion in an orderly way; 1 Cor. 5, 12, do not you judge those within.

[In the margin, against this, Mr. H. writes as follow :—"This last was added another time. But afterwards this last was otherwise agreed upon and consented unto,—first in the case of Barth. Gidny and after that in all others of the children of the covenant, vide 65, page 84."]

1. It belongs to the Elders duly to examine them of their knowledge with application to themselves : that it may be known they are able to examine themselves, judge themselves and discern the Lord's body; according to 1 Cor. 11. The Elders making known to the Church their desires for full communion, the parties are in a Church meeting to express their own desire, their owning their parents' covenant, and their knowledge with application to themselves, if they can : or, the Elders to read for them what they have received from them.

And if there be no exception against them in a month's time, they are to be received unto full communion to enjoy and use their right in the Lord's Supper, and in votes as other members do. Acts 10, 47. Can any man forbid, &c.

———

At a meeting of the Church about Octob. last.

Richard Harvey. Mary Lay. Richard Harvey, and Mary Lay, having stood propounded for a month's time, and no exception against them, they were received unto membership by consent of the brethren; they making their confession, and testimony given of their conversation.

Letters to ye members a-broad. The Elders propounding the case of divers members removed from us divers years ; it was consented unto that the Elders should write unto them to desire them that as the Lord gives them opportunity they would either return to us, or else join unto some other church : which was accordingly done.

———

And whereas divers members of the Church, as Joseph Boys, John

Kichin, Joseph Pope and his wife, Mrs. Gardiner and John Maston, were generally known to absent themselves from the ordinances of Christ amongst us ; some of them appearing and giving no just reason for their withdrawing, to avoid tediousness our brethren, Major Hawthorne, Mr. Bartholmew, and bro: Prince, were desired to bestow as much time in private discourse with them as they should think meet, that if it be possible they might gain them, and to report what success they find the next Church meeting.

A motion being made by some Elders in the Bay unto this Church to join with them in a day of Humiliation to seek the Lord for his mercy and favor in removing the judgment of sickness, and for preventing our fears, and continuing the blessings of Church and Commonwealth: which was consented to and kept on Dec. 22.

Mr Black-leach dis-missed. Mr. Blackleach and his wife being removed to live at Hartford, desired dismission unto that Church ; which was consented unto by the Church here and sent unto them by the Elders.

A Fast. The General Court of this Colony being exercised this winter time with many difficulties, taking into consideration the many sins that might provoke the Lord against his people ; in particular, unprofitableness under the means, decay of first love, neglect of the order of the gospel, inclinations in the young generation to profaneness, &c., and the many dangers we are liable to in these times from complaints against us, intrusion of heretics, the combination of antichrist against all the servants of God. The Court did commend unto all the Churches and inhabitants of this jurisdiction, and appoint the 2d day of the 11th month, to be kept as a day of Humiliation and supplication to the Lord for a thorough returning from our provoking evils, and for the diverting of such calamities as may be coming upon us and the people of God elsewhere : which day was accordingly kept at the time appointed.

At a Church meeting 22 of the 11th month.

Charles Gott. Ex. Conant, These being children of the Church, having been propound-

Jeh Harvey.
H Sull's.
Ab. Hill. —ed a month's time and no exception against them, they made their confession and renewing their covenant, were admitted unto full communion.

The answer returned concerning the forementioned withdrawing members was, that they were some of them in a more pliable way than formerly, and therefore any further proceeding was respited till the next meeting, that the Elders and some brethren might have opportunity of conference with them in the meantime.

The Elders and our bro. Bartholmew and Price were desired to consider of the cases of any of the children of the Church which have given offence before their membership was acknowledged by the Church's vote, to speak with them, and to make report at the next Church meeting.

J.
Rising. James Rising admitted to the Lord's Supper as recommended by Mr. White's letter, if no just exception be against him before the next sacrament ; he to procure his dismission as soon as he can.

The Church consented to the baptizing of Mrs: Eliz: Conant's child upon the letter from the Church at Corke testifying of her membership there.

At a Church meeting 19th of the 12th month.

Josuah Ray.
Eliz. Croad
Ab. Kipping.
Mary Woodbery. These being members of the Church, having been propounded a month's time, and no exception against them, they made their confession and renewing their covenant were admitted to full communion.

Eliz:
Hill. Eliz: Hill, the wife of Zebulon Hill, also made her confession and had good testimony for her conversation ; and so to be admitted unto membership the Lord's day following.

Excom of
J. Boys,
J Maston
J.Kichin. The case of the six members who had forsaken the Church assemblies was again considered, and they not being gained

by all the forementioned dealings of the Church with them, nor so much as coming to the Elders for conference as was desired, nor making their appearance before the Church as they were warned to do; they having so long a time forsaken the fellowship of the Church, and in so doing cast out themselves and cast off the Church; in the issue of the consideration by a vote of the Church it was consented to that these three, J. Maston, John Kichin and Joseph Boys, should have the sentence of excom. pronounced against them; and by another vote of the Church that the other three, J. Pope and his wife, and Mrs. Gardner, should be admonished, and further time given to them. Accordingly on the Sabbath following the Pastor preaching on Heb. 10, 25 :—Not forsaking the assembling ourselves together as the manner of some is ; showed from thence the greatness of the evil of those brethren and sisters in a constant way and course of breaking the 2d and 4th commandments, and that their way was a casting off the Church, and casting out themselves, &c. In the close of the afternoon's exercise, according to the forementioned votes of the Church, he pronounced the sentence of excommunication upon John Maston,

Admon. of J. Pope & wife, and Mrs. Gardiner. John Kichen, J. Boys, and the sentence of admonition upon J. Pope and his wife, and Mrs. Gardiner ; which latter was sent unto them, in writing, by two of the brethren.

Hill Eliz: Hill was then received unto membership.

1662.

A Synod at Boston March 10. On the 26th of 12th month, being the Sabbath day, was read an order from the Gen. Court, for calling of a Synod, this Church (as the rest of the Churches in the Colony) being desired to send their messengers of Elders and brethren to Boston on the 10th of the 1st month, there to discuss and declare what they shall judge to be the mind of God revealed in his word concerning these two questions :

1. Who are the subjects of Baptism?

2. Whether according to the word of God there ought to be a consociation of churches, and what should be the manner of it ?

It was left unto consideration till the Lord's day following, when Major Hawthorne, Mr. Bartholmew, and the Pastor were chosen to go to the Synod at the time appointed ; which accordingly they did ; the Synod continuing together almost a fortnight, finding the questions to be weighty, and that divers of them could not then stay longer

Adjourned till June 10. together, they adjourned the Synod to the 10th of the 4th month next,—this the messengers of this Church gave notice of on the next Sabbath after their return home.

About two months after sentence of admonition was sent unto Mrs. Gardiner, Joseph Pope and his wife, they sent in their answer in **Excom. of Mrs. Gardiner, J. Pope and wife.** writing, denying to continue their fellowship with the Church in the ordinances of God, charging the Church with bloody cruelty, &c., which writing of theirs being read unto the Church, they did vote the sentence of excom: which accordingly was pronounced by the Pastor.

The Synod meeting again on the 10th of 4th mo. was adjourned again till the 10th of September, of which notice was given to the Church.

Our bro. Rayment and his wife, removing their dwelling to Seabrook, desired letters of recommendation to the Churches in those parts, which was granted by the Church.

Octob: 19. The Church was acquainted with two orders from the **A day of Thanks.** General Court, the one recommending to the Churches a day of Thanksgiving on Nov. 5, with reference to the safe return of the messengers, giving such a portion of the fruits of the earth after threatening to deprive us of all, and the continuance of the mercy of the Gospel to us hitherto. The other recommending also a day of Humiliation on Dec. 5th, in consideration of the afflicted and low **A Fast.** estate of the cause and people of God universally in these times, together with some public rebukes of God amongst ourselves; which two days were accordingly kept at the times agreed upon.

Mr Croad, Sara Ray. Mr. Croad and S. Ray, making their confession, were received unto membership on the Lord's Day.

Lot Conant, Mark Bachelor. Lot Conant and Mark Bachelor making their confession and owning the covenant in a Church meeting were admitted unto full communion.

Mr Brock's Ordin. The Pastor and Mr. Bartholmew being desired by the Church, were present at the ordination of Mr. Brock, Pastor of the Church at Reading, Nov. 12.

At a Church meeting 12th of 11th month.

Synod Book. The Pastor gave notice to the Church that now the result of the forementioned Synod was printed, and to be had at Boston, and the consideration of the matters therein contained was commended to the Churches by the General Court.

Ab. Bach. Eliz. Bach. Ab. Bachiler, daughter of John Bachiler, and Eliz: Bachiler, daughter of Joseph Bachiler, having been propounded a month's time, and no exception against them, they making their confession and renewing their covenant, were admitted to full communion.

J Dodge, J. Hill, M. Westgate. John Dodge, John Hill, Mary Westgate, having been propounded a month's time, no exception against them, making their confession, and having good testimony for their conversation, they were to be admitted unto membership on the Sabbath following.

J. Rising, S. Ruck. James Rising having a letter of dismission from the Church at Bermudas, and Mrs. Sarah Ruck having a letter of dismission from the Church at Concord; these letters of dismission were read and accepted by the Church, and they also to be admitted unto membership in this Church on the Sabbath following.

Rob. Allen Recom. Robert Allen's recommendation granted to the Church at Norwich according to his desire.

On the Lord's day following, John Dodge, John Hill, M. Westgate, James Rising, Sara Ruck, were admitted unto membership, after the usual manner.

———

1663. At a Church meeting March 30,

Mary Balch, Eliz: Williams, and Damaris Mansfield, being propounded a month and no exception against them; (the daughter of our bro. Conant, of H. Skerry, of Mr. Stileman) making their confession and renewing their covenant, were admitted unto full communion.

Ambrose Gale. Ambrose Gale having been propounded a month, no exception against him, he making his confession was admitted unto membership on the Lord's day following, by consenting to the covenant.

Eliz. Woodbery was also received unto membership the Lord's day following, in the same manner.

Also a day of public Humiliation was then propounded and consented unto ; which was observed on the 22 of the 2d month.

———

At a Church meeting last of 6 month.

Mrs. Helwis, the daughter of Major Hawthorn, Rachel Raiment, the daughter of T. Scrugs, Eliz. Haskal, d. of J. Hardy, H. Baker, d. of J. Woodbery, having been propounded a month and no just exception against them, making their confession and renewing their covenant, were admitted unto full communion.

Edmond Pach having been propounded a month and no just exception agst. him, he made his confession, and had good testimony for his conversation, was on the Lord's day following admitted unto membership by the vote of the Church.

Eunice Smith, the wife of bro. Potter, now living at Fairfield, her dismission having been formerly granted was now sent unto that Church.

———

Beginning of Octob: Letters were sent from the Church at Gloster, giving notice of their intention to ordain Mr. Emerson as their Pastor, and desiring this Church to send their messengers to be present at the ordination. The Pastor and Captain Lothrop and W. Allen were desired by this Church to go thither at the time appointed ; which they did, and at their return an account was given to the Church by the Pastor that the ordination was approved of by the messengers of the Churches then present.

———

9 Novemb: Letters were sent unto the Church from Topsfiel l signifying their intention of joining in church fellowship and in or laining Mr. Gilbert their Pastor, and desiring this Church to send their messengers to be present with them on the day appointed. Accordingly the Pastor and brother Porter were desired by the Church here to go thither then ; which they did, and after their return an account was given to the Church by the Pastor, that for the *substance* their pro-

ceedings at Topsfield in the Church gathering and ordination there was approved of by the messengers of the Churches then present.

Also our brother Browning living at Topsfield ·and desiring his dismission that he might join in church fellowship there, it was granted by the Church here.

———

Nov. 20. A day of Thanksgiving was propounded and consented to by the Church with relation to the mercies of the year, and the Lord's continuance of our peace and liberty thus long in such times as we live in : which was accordingly kept, at the time appointed.

———

Dec, 12 4 Fasts in one winter. It was propounded to the consideration of the Church whether God did not call us unto more frequency in Public days of Humiliation and seeking to the Lord for mercy with respect unto that great affliction and reproach which is come upon so many thousands of Ministers and Christians in these times by means of Episcopal usurpation, and human impositions in the worship of God. Also with respect unto dangers threatening ourselves. It was cheerfully consented unto that once a month for the four following months to set apart a day for seeking the face of God in solemn Humiliation and prayer, which was accordingly done. On the last of which four days viz. the 16th of the first month, the Church covenant was read and solemnly renewed by this Church.

———

Dec. 10. Wenham. There was a Church gathering and ordination of Mr. Newman Pastor there, at their request unto this Church, the Pastor, Mr. Conant, and Capt. Lothrop were desired to be present there, who gave account afterward that the proceedings there were approved by the messengers of the Churches. Also Mr. Gott and his wife, and his son Charles, and Math. Bachilor, at their desire, were dismissed then from hence to join with the Church there.

———

1664.   At a meeting of the Church March 17.

Freeborne Sallo's, daughter of bro. Wolfe, having made her cofession and renewing her covenant, there being no exception against her, she was admitted to partake of the Lord's Supper.

8

58

Christopher Babbidge, Mrs. Woodcocke, Margery Williams, the wife of Isaac Williams, and Jone Pitman, the wife of Tho. Pitman, of Marblehead, having been propounded the usual time, there being no exception against them, and sufficient testimony for their conversation, they were on the Lord's day following admitted unto membership by the vote of the Church.

---

4 m. 5 day.
Elder Brown's dismission from his office. Elder Brown upon his return from Virginia this Spring, finding by experience his occasions such as he could not attend the office of an Elder with that constancy and expence of time that the work of it did require, and professing a need of attending his calling as a seaman, wherein he was to be much absent from the Church, he desired of the Church that they would dismiss him from his office, that he might with more freedom of spirit, attend the necessary duties of his calling. The Church, after some time of consideration, consented to his desire, and accordingly on the 5th day of the 4th month, he was dismissed from his office.

W. Dounton's Recommendation. A letter of recommendation was read unto the Church from a Church in Weymouth, wherein William Dounton and his wife, and Edward Humber were recommended unto the communion of this Church, which was accepted and they admitted to communion with us by virtue of the communion of Churches.

A Fast. An order from the General Court was read, wherein in regard of the many distractions and troubles of the Colony, and the afflicted state of the people of God in other places, was recommended to all the Churches of this Colony the 15th day of the 4th month as a day of Humiliation and prayer; which was accordingly on the day appointed.

4th mo 19. A letter of dismission was desired by Johanna Town and Margaret Reddington to the Church at Topsfield, which was accordingly granted by the Church here and sent unto them.

[Thus far we have given Mr. Higginson's records entire. Here occurs a case of disciplinary proceedings against a member of the Church "for drunkenness," who, having been duly dealt with, and failing to reform, was finally excommunicated. This is omitted, as other cases of the kind will be hereafter.]

———

There was another Fast recommended from the General Court in regard of the Lord's frown in taking away much of the fruits of the
Fast. earth, and in sundry other signs of God's displeasure against us; which was accordingly observed on the day propounded, viz: 1 of 7 month.

Fast. Another Fast was also kept on the 16th of Nov. upon the same grounds, for the same ends with the former.

———

On the 6th of 9th month the Church was acquainted with the de-
Mrs. sire of Mrs. Lydia Banks, who had been absent from the
Banks. Church 22 years, that she might be dismissed to a Church in London, of which Mr. Nye is pastor; which was consented to by the Church.

The Gover-
nor's dis- Also the desire of our honored Governor and his wife was
mission. made known to the Church for their dismission to the Church at Boston, which was accordingly consented to by the Church and sent unto them.

———

Synod's prop- About the same time was a meeting of the Church for the
ositions read. reading of the Propositions of the Synod touching Baptism and consociation of churches; at the end of which the Pastor promised that in time convenient he would communicate unto the brethren a short writing as a help for the practice of the Synod's propositions.

———

1665. The General Court, sitting at Boston, finding many difficulties in the transaction of affairs with his Majesty's commissioners, did send abroad a writing wherein they desired all the Churches and people of God to be sensible of the many provoking sins that are amongst us, as also the many signs of God's displeasure against us, and that all would apply themselves to Humiliation and Reformation, and to cry mightily unto God that he would be reconciled to us and that in particular he would graciously incline his Majesty's heart to favor us. Accordingly they recommended the 22d day of the 4th month to be kept as a general day of Humiliation and prayer— which was observed amongst us at the time appointed, as in other places.

Children of the Covenant. On the 18th day of the 5th month, being the sacrament day, the Pastor preached on Acts 3: 25—You are the children of the covenant which God made with your fathers;—whence he delivered this doctrine, that " children born of parents in cove-"nant, they are children of the covenant, and continue so to be until " they be discovenanted in a way of God."

4 of them claiming their right. At the end of the sermon he acquainted the Church with the desire of four of the children of the covenant born and baptized in this Church, having now children born unto them, desired that their children might be baptized. The parties themselves, viz. John Massy, John Gidney, Bartholmew Gidney and Sam. Williams, did stand forth and profess their willingness to own the covenant of the God of their fathers, and did modestly claim the right of their children unto baptism, and desired they might be baptized.

The Pastor's Speech. The Pastor professed his willingness and readiness to baptize these or any other children of the covenant amongst us according to his office, if he might do it with the consent of the Church, it being clear to him to be his duty, and that he apprehended it as one of the great sins of the country that so many of the children of the covenant were unbaptized, and that he would not that the sin should be any longer at his door, being ready to do his duty in that respect. He also did bring to remembrance that this mattter had been in debate at times in this Church this thirteen years. That in the year '52 it was propounded by the former Teacher, Mr. Norris, as a question to be agitated, concerning the baptizing of members' children and their children upon that right, which was in several Church meetings debated in his time, when it was agreed that the children of confederates were real members. And if he had not had ground to believe that it was the Church's judgment that they were real members, he had not ventured upon taking office in this Church.

And after he was in office it was brought into consideration again in several Church meetings, when these two things were agreed upon and voted by the Church :

1. That the children of members born in the Church, or received in minority, are true and real members by divine institution.

2. That their membership doth not cease but by some other divine institution, viz. excommunication.

After which there was a Synod, the result whereof was published and had been read in the Church, the scope of which was to show the Scripture grounds of the doctrine that had now been delivered, and that the children of such are to be baptized.

The Pastor also acquainted the Church with the straight he was in, many of the children of the covenant claiming baptism for their children, which he knew not how to deny, and yet with respect unto some brethren that were otherwise minded he had forborn as long as he could, but truly he did not see how he should be able to hold it long except he might have liberty to act in a peaceable way in this matter of baptizing the children of the covenant according to his own judgment, and according to the Scriptures, (Luke 12, 42,) and though it was to be desired that we might all be of one judgment in this matter, yet it was not to be expected, but must be left unto God and time, we forbearing one another in love, as Eph. 4: 2.

After some agitation the issue was: It was put to vote—whether Vote of the Church. the brethren of the Church did consent that the Pastor should act in the baptizing of the children of the covenant in this Church in a peaceable way ; which was consented unto by the vote of the Church at that time.

———

The children of the children of the Covenant baptized. Accordingly the Sabbath following, viz : the 30th day of the 5th month, the aforesaid John Massy, John Gidney, Bartholmew Gidney and Sam. Williams, having been privately examined by the Pastor, did publicly profess their taking hold of the covenant, after which their children were baptized, and the names of which are recorded in the catalogue of the children baptized in this Church.

On the 20th day of the 6th month Eliz. Stone, the daughter of bro. Dixy, after private examination by the Pastor, did publicly profess her taking hold of the covenant, whereupon her four children were baptized, the names of which are also recorded in the catalogue of children baptized in this Church.

Curwithy recommended. Mr. Curwithy and his daughter Curtis, and our bro. and sister Harvy, removing to Southhold, desired letters of recommendation to the Church there; which was granted by the Church and accordingly sent with them.

At a meeting of the Church, Octob. 5.

The Pastor did then also acquaint the Church with the writing he had formerly mentioned and read unto them as a help to reduce the doctrine of the Synod into practice; it being a Direction for a public Profession after private Examination by the Elders, which Direction is taken out of the Scripture, and points to the Faith and Covenant contained in the Scripture, it being the same for substance propounded to and agreed upon by the Church of Salem in their first beginning, 1629, 6t of the 6t month: it being now printed any that desired it should have one of them for their use.

A direction for a public profession after private Examination.

[We have now come to an important passage in these records which deserves particular attention. It is on the 85th page—the page referred to in the "marginal note" to the covenant, as affording evidence that, on the "6th of the 6th month, 1629, this covenant was publicly signed and declared;" which evidence we accordingly find in Mr. Higginson's commendation of the "Direction, &c."—prepared by him "as a help to reduce the doctrine of the Synod into practice," in relation to Baptism," it being the same for substance as propounded to and agreed upon by the Church of Salem in their first beginning, 1629, 6th of 6th month."

It is also the passage in which it has recently been imagined that Mr. Higginson referred to something very different from "this covenant"—nothing less, in short, than a test creed or articles of faith, to which subscription or assent was required, in order to church communion. And the editors of the new edition of Morton's New England's Memorial, published by the Congregational Board of Publication, in 1855, have been so carried away by this novel theory, as to set forth, in an appendix,* the covenant and articles contained in this "Direction, &c." thus prepared in 1665, as—"The Articles of Faith, and Covenant of 1629 ;" while the genuine old Covenant to which Mr. Higginson had always been understood to refer, is (all but a single sentence) transferred for its origin, from 1629 to 1636. Dr. Felt, too, in his Ecclesiastical History of New England†, published in the same year, appears to have been carried away in like manner, and this very "Direction, &c."—printed at first without date—is doubtless the "Pamphlet printed about 1660," (as then stated by him,) to which he alludes as proof, "that the first independent church of Salem at their outset, had articles of faith."

It therefore becomes proper to apply to Mr. Higginson himself for explanation of his meaning in this important passage. Having been with his father at the formation of the Church, and a member of it in the beginning, he must have known exactly what was then "propounded to and agreed upon by the Church ;" and he was too constantly appealed to for many years as the living oracle on the subject, ever to have forgotten what he first knew. Any one of his transactions or statements respecting it is sufficient to clear the passage from all possible doubt as to its meaning on this point.

Let us first look at the renewal of the Covenant which

---

*p. 459.   †p. 116.

he and the Church had then just accomplished, and consider for a moment the material circumstances attending it. Upon the settlement of Hugh Peters, the Church Covenant had been renewed, as we have seen, with a preamble identifying it as "that Church Covenant" to which the Church was bound "at their first beginning." It was this identical Covenant, with this preamble at its head, which Mr. Higginson and the Church now renewed; and he added with his own hand the clause against the Quakers' doctrine, which the Church had voted, evidently with the same pen and ink with which he recorded the vote—as may still be seen by inspection of both in the present old Church Book. Thus we have his solemn recognition of the Covenant and the fact stated in the preamble, that it was the Covenant to which this Church was bound "at their first beginning." It is worthy of remark, that Mr. Higginson adopts the peculiar expression used in the preamble—"first beginning"—as if to fix the certainty of his reference to the same.

Next let us look at the account of the foundation of the First Church, contained in Morton's New England's Memorial, furnished, doubtless, by Mr. Higginson, soon after this time, (1665,) as the Memorial was first published in 1669. A single sentence from that account, which is marked by some striking expressions, here used by Mr. Higginson, sufficiently illustrates his meaning in the passage of his records before us, and at the same time represents the exalted Scriptural character of the document first " propounded to and agreed upon by the Church,"—the very "confession of faith and covenant" drawn up by his father, " in Scripture language." The sentence is as follows:—"The confession of faith and covenant, forementioned, was acknowledged only as a direction, pointing unto that faith and covenant contained in the holy Scripture, and therefore no man was confined unto that form of words, but only to the substance, end and scope of the matter contained therein."[*]

Mr. Higginson's statements on this subject, in the Magnalia—statements expressly approved as true, if not expressly made by him—afford evidence alike clear and satisfactory, in regard to the point in question. In the account of his father's life, contained in the Magnalia, after stating the arrival at Salem of Mr. Francis Higginson with Mr. Skelton, in June, 1629, "their laying before the chief of the people their desires and their designs of settling a reformed congregation," &c., and the consequent appointment of "a day in the following August for it;" the writer adds: "In order hereunto Mr. Higginson drew up a confession of faith, with a Scriptural representation of the covenant of grace applied unto their present purpose, whereof thirty copies were taken for the thirty persons which were to begin the work of gathering the Church. The day was kept as a Fast; wherein, after the prayers and sermons of the two ministers, these thirty persons did solemnly and severally profess their consent unto the Confession and Covenant then read unto them."[†]

Now the "Confession and Covenant" here described, is certainly the same that was "propounded to and agreed upon by the Church of Salem in their first beginning;" the very "Covenant whereto these Christians engaged themselves," as already shown,[‡] which was about seven years after solemnly renewed among them;" viz., upon the settlement of Hugh Peters, in 1636, who prefixed the Preamble; which was again renewed in 1660, when Mr. Higginson added the Postscript, and which, under his

---

*See ante, p. 3.   †Magnal. III. 74, fol. ed.   ‡Ante, p. 5.

9

sanction, was recorded at length in the Magnalia, without preamble or postscript,—the venerated "Instrument" it-self, adopted at "The Nativity of the First Church in the Massachusetts Colony."

Thus over and over again did the Rev. John Higginson identify the venerable old Covenant of the First Church as what was "propounded to and agreed upon by the Church of Salem, in their fist beginning, 1629, 6th of the 6th month."

Mr. Higginson, as will be remembered, upon his first reading to the Church the Propositions of the Synod touching Baptism, &c., "promised that in time convenient he would communicate to the brethren a short writing, as a help, &c." The records show how earnestly he sought to carry out to the fullest extent the "doctrine of the Synod" on this subject, and what opposition to his views he had to encounter from some of the brethren. It was necessary for his purpose that he should present the "short writing," he had promised, in a form and phraseology different from the first Covenant, and it was natural that he should commend it as "the same for substance,"—esteeming both, undoubtedly, as partaking alike the substance of vital Christianity. But he did not submit it to the brethren for their adoption, or even approval. They, in fact, took no vote or order respecting it. This "new Direction," was not "issued by the First Church;" nor does it appear ever to have been used by them in the admission of members to the Church. It seems to have been designed for the Pastor's own accommodation in matters pertaining to his office, as well as for the "help" of those who might wish to avail themselves of it, in order to Baptism and the "Half-way Covenant;" and "children of the Covenant," perhaps, after examination by the Pastor.]

B. Gidney admitted to the Lord's Supper. Bartholmew Gidney propounded his desire of partaking of the Lord's Supper, saying he had submitted unto exam. of the Pastor, and publicly professed his faith and owning of the covenant, he saw not that anything more was required of him from Scripture. This being considered of and spoken to by the Pastor and several brethren, it was in the issue consented unto with respect to himself, though with respect unto others it was left unto further consideration.

Mrs. Sherman. Also Mrs. Sherman, the daughter of Mr. Johnson, (our brother) living at Boston, but belonging to this Church, being here she submitted to the examination of the Pastor and publicly professed her assent to the doctrine of faith, and her consent to the covenant, and her subjection to discipline, and so had her child baptized; and staying here to Lord's day after, she having been with the Pastor the day before, who examining of her declared unto the Church that he did apprehend her as able to examine herself and discern the Lord's body; and so she was permitted to partake of the Lord's Supper.*

Day of Thanksgiving. The General Court, considering the mercies of the last summer in giving seasonable rain when there were fears of a drought, and diverting a squadron of Dutch ships that threatened to invade our coasts, together with our peace and liberties yet continued, they appointed the 8th day of November to be kept as a solemn day of Thanksgiving.

Fast. Also considering divers causes of Humiliation among ourselves, and the sad condition of the people of God in other parts, especially the severe hand of God in the pestilence raging in London, &c., did appoint Nov. 22, to be kept as a solemn day of Humiliation; both of which days were observed at the time appointed.

At a Church meeting 4th of 11th month.

Edm. Gale, H. West, El. West, Tho. West, admitted to membership. Edmond Gale, Henry West, and Elizabeth West his wife, and Thomas West, being non-members, having stood propounded a month, and no exception against them, they made their confession, and were on the Lord's day following re-

* Here we find the following marginal note in the hand-writing of Rev. S. Fisk:— Such as had renewed their baptismal engagements, claimed their right to the Lord's Table, and by the Pastor were admitted without requiring anything farther of them.

ceived unto membership with this Church by the vote of the Church, and by their own entering into covenant.

II. Brown, Love Stevens, J. Massy, J. Ingersoll, as children of the covenant admitted to the Lord's Supper.
Also at the same time Mrs. Hanna Brown, Love Stevens, John Massy, and John Ingersoll were presented to the Church, as children of the covenant, such as had been either born in the Church or received with their parents in their minority : and such having been formerly at several times owned as members of the Church. The Pastor expressed that after his examinntion of them he did approve of them as able to examine themselves and discern the Lord's body, and that they being not under any Church censure, he knew not of any Church, bar, according to the Scripture, that might hinder them from partaking of the Lord's Supper. Several of the bre·hren did speak for it ; only two of the brethren who were absent the former Church meeting when the same thing had been considered consented to, and practised in the case of Bartholmew Gidney ; they peaceably expressed their dissent, and that they woul l not oppose. The weather being cold, and having been long togeth·r, the Pastor propounded to them the substance of the doctrine of faith an·l covenant which God had ma·le with their fathers, and the covenant duties they were engaged in in the Church; which they all professed their consent unto, and so they had their liberty to partake of the Lord's Supper.

The Council of this jurisdiction, held at Boston on the 15th of the 1st month, appointed the 5th day of the 2d month to be kept as a day of Fast. solemn Humiliation and prayer, in consideration of the provoking sins amongst us and the tokens of God's displeasure against us : also considering the sins, calamities and sufferings of the people of God in other parts, and expecting that many of God's great works and gracious promises are not far off from accomplishment, as the conversion of God's ancient people, and the destruction of antichrist, &c. This day was accordingly observed at the time appointed.

1666. On the 27th of the 3d m. being the Lord's day, a writing was read, subscribed by six hands, wherein some brethren, living at The Farmers' proposition. the Farms, did acquaint the rest of the Church and people living at the town, that by reason of their distance from the meeting-house, they found many inconveniences, that they and their families could not so comfortably attend the Church assembly for the worship of God on the Lord's day as they desired ; and therefore made a motion to the rest, that either they would help them to a minister, or leave them to their liberty to procure one themselves. This proposition was left unto consideration.

At a Church meeting, 23d of 5th month.

J. Maskall, Mrs. Endecot, and Sara Henly, received to membership.
John Maskall, Mrs. Endecot and Sara Henly, of Marblehead, being non-members, having stood propounded a month's time, did now make their profession, and had good testimony for their conversation, they were on the Lord's day following received unto membership with this Church, by the vote of the Church, and by their own entering into the covenant of the Church.

10 of the children of ye covenant admitted to the Lord's Supper.
Also at the same time Thomas Giggles, Mrs. Anne Gardiner, Mrs. Elizabeth Grafton, Mary Swasy, Lydia Pitman, Mary Herick, Lydia Herick, Hanna Woodbery, Elizabeth Patch, and Mary Looms, who had been either born or baptized in the Church, or received with their parents in minority, were presented before the Church : The Pastor expressing that after examination of them he did approve of them as able to examine themselves and discern the Lord's body, and that they being not under any church censure he knew not of any Church bar to hinder them from partaking of the Lord's Supper. After some speeches of some of the brethren, they expressing their assent and consent to the confession of faith and Covenant read unto them, they had their liberty to partake of the Lord's Supper as other children of the Covenant formerly.

Farmers' proposition considered.
There was some consideration of the Farmers' motion for another minister, but another writing being at this time propounded by five of the near neighbors and brethren thereabouts desiring that they might not be engaged in that design, it did not appear they had a competent number, also (by such of the brethren as spake) it was thought not to be at present seasonable to prosecute such a matter. Also that the agitation of some things that did concern it was more proper to a town meeting.

At a Church meeting, 6th of November.

6 children of the Covenant admitted to the Lord's Supper.
Mr. Zerub. Endecot, Mr. James Brown, Mr. Jonathan Corwin, Hanna Gidney, the wife of Barth. Gidney, Rebecca Putman, the wife of John Putman and Eliz. Hol-

linwood, the wife of Richard Hollinwood, were presented before the Church, the Pastor expressed himself that after examination he approved of them as able to examine themselves and discern the Lord's body, they professing their consent to the Confession of Faith and Covenant read unto them, they had their liberty to partake of the Lord's Supper, as other children of the Covenant formerly.

Concerning the baptizing of elder children such as Pasca Foote's, in another Church book, Nov. 28, 1652. At the same time the Pastor gave notice of the desire of divers of the members of the Church to have their elder as well as their younger children baptized: he did also bring to remembrance what was recorded concerning this case in the other church-book, namely, in the case of the eight children of Pasca Foote, Nov. 28, 1652, that it was agreed upon then that the elder children should resort to the Elders and give some account of their faith, and that no more should be done in that matter. After which, on the 6th of the 12th month, the aforesaid *eight children were all baptized by Mr. Norris, the Teacher* of this Church. The present Pastor expressed himself to concur with the judgment of the Church and their former Teacher in this matter. And further said that he looked upon those two grounds to be taken together with respect to the children of members grown up. 1. That they were the seed of confederates, acc. to Gen., 17, 7. 2. That they were sons and daughters that had knowledge, and und: acc. to Neh. 10. Accordingly he desired that such as had children unbaptized that were grown or growing up to years of discretion, that they would first bring them to him to be examined; if upon due inquiry he found them neither ignorant nor scandalous, but such as according to their capacity did understandingly desire baptism, he was ready then to baptize their elder as well as their younger children. Divers of the brethren did also speak for the encouragement of the Pastor in baptizing of such children in such a way.

On 9th Nov., there was observed a public day of Thanksgiving Day of Thanksgiving. according to the Court's order, with respect unto the mercies of the year and continuance of our peace, in such a troublesome time.

On the 22d of Nov., there was also observed a day of Humiliation Fast. and prayer (according to the Court's order) to humble ourselves under the many signs of God's displeasure against us. and to make supplication for his mercy and the continuance of our blessings as hitherto.

———

Motion of brethren on Bass River. This winter was a motion made by the brethren on Bass River to the rest of the Church here at the town, that they might have their consent to be a Church by themselves, and to have Mr. Hale for their Pastor, which was left unto consideration. And the last of the 12th month, by the consent of the brethren both on that side the River and here at the town was publicly observed as a day of solemn Fasting and prayer to seek unto God for his direction and presence in such a weighty matter.

Fast. Also in the 2d month another public day of Humiliation and prayer was observed by order from the Court of Magistrates, as a means of our farther humiliation under the signs of God's displeasure against the English nation, and in particular the burning of London, together with some lesser judgments of God amongst ourselves. as the small pox in the Bay, and the many dangers we were exposed unto ; and to seek the Lord's mercy for the English nation, and unto ourselves here in this wilderness.

———

1667. At a Church meeting. 4th of 5th month.

5 children of the Covenant admitted to the Lord's Supper. John Gidney, Sam. Archer, jun., Jo. Peas, Martha Barten, Martha Foster, were presented before the Church, the Pastor expressed himself that after examination he approved of them as able to examine themselves, and discern the Lord's body, they professing their consent to the Confession of Faith and Covenant read unto them, they had their liberty to partake of the Lord's Supper, as other children of the Covenant formerly.

3 admitted to membership. Goodie Guppa, Eliz. Clifford, Mary Merit, being non-members, having been propounded a month, and no exception against them, they made their confession and were on the Lord's day following received unto membership by the vote of the Church, and by their own entering into Covenant.

Susanna Walker at her desire was dismissed to the Church of Boston.

About baptiz-
ing the children
of S. Starr.

The Pastor acquainted the Church with two cases. The one wherein it was desired by sister Hollinwood that her daughter Starr's children might be baptized, their mother though dead, yet being in minority when she was received into the Church, and there being good testimony of her hopeful godliness, the Q. was, why might not her children be baptized according to the 6 prop. of the Synod, which was read and left unto consideration.

About baptiz-
ing adopted
children.

The other about baptizing adopted children. Mary Hodges, concerning whom there were many that would testify her eminent godliness, and was in the way to join to the Church herself, yet dying before her joining to the Church, she did on her death bed give her little child to sister Root, who with her husband's consent took it for her own child, and did solemnly own it before the Church, desiring if it might be according to rule, that the child might be baptized. The Pastor propounded and read several passages out of Mr. Cotton's Way of the Churches, Mr. Shepard's Church membership of Children, and the Answer to the 21st Qu. tending to favor the baptism of Adopted Children. Both which being new cases and not within the compass of that consent which the Pastor had by the Church's vote for baptizing the children of the Covenant in this Church in the year '65, he did therefore propound and leave these cases to consideration against some other time.

Liberty to use
the Bay psalm
book, together
with Ainsworth.

The Pastor having formerly propounded and given reasons for the use of the Bay psalm books in regard of the difficulty of the tunes, and that we could not sing them so well as formerly, and that there was a singularity in our using Ainsworth's tunes, but especially because we had not the liberty of singing all the Scripture psalms according to 3 Col., 16—he did now again propound the same; and after several brethren had spoken, there was at last a unanimous consent with respect to the last reason mentioned, that the Bay psalm book should be made use of together with Ainsworth's to supply the * * * [several words illegible.]

July 4.
The Church's

1667. The motion and desire of the brethren and sisters on Bass River side to be a Church of themselves, hav-

consent to the
brethren on
Bass River side,
to be a Church
of themselves.
ing been left unto consideration for a good space of time,
was now again renewed, and a writing read which is as
followeth:

We whose names are under written, the brethren and sisters on
Bass River side, do present our desires to the rest of the Church of
Salem, that with their consent we and our children may be a Church
of ourselves; which we also present unto Mr. Hale, desiring him to
join with us and to be our Pastor, with the approbation of the rest of
the Church. Subscribed :

Roger Conant.

Tho. Lothrop
and his wife.

W. Dodge
and his wife.

R. Dodge, sen., and
his wife.

H. Woodbery and
his wife.

W. Dixey and
his wife.

Jo. Stone, sen.

Robt. Morgan.

Hugh Woodbery
and his wife.

Sam. Corning and
his wife.

Jo. Hill and
his wife.

Exercise Conant.

Edw. Bishop.

Rich. Brackenbury
and his wife.

Jo. Black, sen.

W. Woodbery, sen.

Nicholas Patch.

Josiah Roots.

John Dodge.

Hanna Woodbery.

Mary Dodge.

Lydia Herick.

H. Herick and
his wife.

Lot Conant.

Mary Herick.

Eliz. Woodbery.

Eliz. Haskol.

Ralph Ellan.

Peter Wolfe and
his wife.

Freeborn Black.

An. Woodbery, the
wife of N. Woodb.

Mary Lovet.

Eliz. Patch.

H. Sallos.

Goodie Biose.

Lydia Herick.

Wido Woodbery.

An. Baker.

Sara Leech.

*Such as are members
yet not in full com-
munion desire to be
dismissed with their
parents:*

Peter Woodbery.

Jo. Dodge.

Jo. Black.

Sam. Corning.

Nath. Howard.

Humph. Woodbery.

Sus. Woodbery.

Jo. Woodbery.

H. Woodbery.

W. Dodge.

H. Rayment.

Sara Conant.

H. Herick.

Ephr. Herick.

Jo. Herick.

Eliz. Herick.

Ab. Stone.

Eliz. Howard.

Jos. Roots.

Tho.* Woodbery.

Jos. Lovet.

Bethia Lovet.

Rem. Stone.

Eliz. Howard.

74 in all.

This writing being read together with the names subscribed, there was a unanimous consent of the brethren present unto their desire, only it was left to the Sacrament day after, when, in the fullest Church assembly, the consent of the rest of the Church was signified by their vote in lifting up their hands. And so they have their liberty to be a Church by themselves, only they continue members here until their being a Church. The Lord grant his gracious presence with them.

Their Church Covenant and ordination of Mr. Hale as their Pastor. On the 9th of Sept. these brethren of the Church gave us notice that they intended (if the Lord please) to join in Church fellowship together on the 20th day of the same month, desiring the presence of the Church here either by ourselves or messengers. In regard of our nearness and that they are a Church issuing out of ourselves, it was thought meet for as many to be present as could. So when the day came, divers of the brethren were present, as also the messengers of the Churches of Ipswich and Wenham. Mr. Hale propounded and read a Confession of Faith and Covenant, which they had often considered of among themselves, and did then (all that had been in full communion in the Church of Salem) express their consent unto that Confession and Covenant, and so were owned as a distinct Church of themselves, by the messengers of the Churches present; and the brethren of that Church desiring of it the Pastor of this Church was helpful to them in the transaction of the business of the ordination of Mr. Hale as Pastor of the Church.

———

1668. On the 25th day of the 1st month at the time of the Sacrament of the Lord's Supper were read letters of dismission from the Church of Boston in the behalf of Joseph Phipeny and Dorcas his wife, they having lived some considerable time here; they were accepted by the vote of the Church unto membership in this Church, and so they entered into covenant with this Church.

There was an order read from the Governor and Council for the **Fast** observation of a public solemn day of Humiliation and prayer on the 26th day of March with relation to the great concernments of the Churches and people of God here, and also in our native land and other parts of the world; which was accordingly observed.

On the 29th day Mr. Hale's motion concerning the dismission of some other of the children of the Church that had not been formerly mentioned, was considered; and the answer returned was, viz:— That it was intended to dismiss all the children at once and together with their parents that had been members here, so that there needed not a particular dismission of any of them.

Jo. Hathorne, examined by the Pastor, at his earnest desire was admitted to the Lord's Supper on a Sacrament day, upon his solemn owning the covenant of God before the Church.

The General Court in the 8th month having not appointed any Fast. public days of Thanksgiving or Fasting and prayer as formerly, it was propounded by the Pastor for us to keep a public day of Humiliation and prayer, particularly with respect unto the reasons in common with others, as with respect unto the afflicted state of the Church of God abroad, the many difficulties in carrying on the work of God in Church and Court, and the death of so many ministers amongst us of late ; particularly with respect unto some reasons more proper to ourselves, as the late breaking out of sin and profaneness amongst us, and the sad appearance of divisions amongst us ; that we might seek to God that he would heal our spirits and give us peace. This motion was in the issue agreed unto by the brethren of the Church ; and the day was kept by us on the 23d of Dec.

Also with respect unto the mercies of the year past, and the con-
Day of
Thanksgiving. stancy of God's goodness to us here, with continuance of our peace, and the news of peace in England ; and that liberty is granted to the people of God in England in such a measure, it was considered and agreed on to keep a day of Thanksgiving afterward ; which was accordingly done on the 14th day of the 11th month.

1669. In the beginning of the first month on the Sabbath an order from the Governor and Council was read, wherein they recommended to all the Churches in this Colony to keep the
Fast
March 25. 25th day of the month in public Fasting and prayer, in

the sense of the many provoking evils amongst us, and the many tokens of God's displeasure against us, and the uncomfortable breaches
in sundry places, the present low estate of the Churches abroad:
Stirring us up to seek to the Lord for mercy in these regards; which
day was accordingly observed here at the time appointed.

———

On the 3d of the 2d month was read a letter from the dissenting
brethren at Boston, sent unto this Church, wherein they expressed
Dissenting brethren's case at Boston. that the result and advice of the Council called by the
Elder and brethren the last summer, was to grant them
an amicable dismission, in order to the propagation of another church;
this advice they had attended, having several times moved for a dismission, but in vain. Therefore they made this address to sundry
other Churches, as their only next refuge left them by Christ in his
word; professing their firmness to the government, according to the
Their letter. patent, and that they are not for any other way of church order,
than that solemnly declared from the Scriptures, in the Platform of Discipline, and the last Synod about the subject of Baptism
and consociation of Churches, desiring ever to maintain brotherly
love and communion with the Church they desired to be dismissed
from as also with the rest of the Churches. They did humbly again
and again desire us, in the bowels of Jesus Christ request and desire
us, not to receive sinister reports against them, but to send the Elder
and messengers of our Church to meet with others in council at Boston upon the 13th of April, to consider, consult, and give their helpful advice in their labouring case.

———

After the reading of this letter it was desired to defer the issue
till the Lord's day after, till it might be known from the Elders of
Boston Church whether the Church there consented to such a coun-
The Pastor and Capt. Price sent to the Council, and how. cil, or would give them a meeting: which by the Pastor
(and others) was enquired of the week following, who
brought a negative answer from the Elders. Yet the
brethren of the Church generally did agree in this, that there was
and ought to be relief against miscarriages in particular churches in
the Congregational way. And in the issue by a vote they desired
the Pastor and Capt. Price, to go not as members of the Council to
vote therein, but to be present at the Council, and so to do what

good they could, as they heard Mr. Whiting and Mr. Laiten of Lin Church were desired so to go.

At a Church meeting, April 30, 1669.

Council at Boston.

The Pastor made some report of what was done at the Council, wherein there was a meeting of messengers from thirteen other Churches besides Salem and Linne, and that they applied themselves first unto the Elders twice, and then to the Elders and brethren of the Church of Boston; the 3d time in way of mediation for a pacification, but were three times denied to admit of any conference with them. So the Council considered of the advice of the first Council, and the Scripture grounds of it, and saw cause to approve of it, viz., that the dissenting brethren might have their dismission, and in case the Church persisted in denying their dismission, they might take their liberty seasonably to be a Church of themselves, as if they had had a formal dismission.

Mrs. Putman, (Lieft. Putman's wife,) Mrs. Abigail Ward and Sarah Pickworth, were presented before the Church, the Pastor expressed himself that after examination he approved them

3 children of the Covenant admitted to the Lord's Supper.

as able to examine themselves and discern the Lord's body; they solemnly owning and renewing their Covenant, it was declared they had their liberty to partake of the Lord's Supper.

William Bartoll, Mary Bartoll and Martha Beal of Marblehead,

4 non members admitted.

also Abigail Clark, having stood propounded a month made their confession, and, in the issue, there being n o just exception against them, and some testimony for them, they were, on the Lord's day following, admitted to membership in this Church by expressing their consent unto the Covenant, and by the Church's vote. G. Beal and H. Gilbert were not admitted.

On the 16 day, being the Sabbath, was read in the public assembly, a letter sent from the three Elders of the first Church at Boston, to

Letter from the Elders of the Church at Boston.

the Church of Salem, expressing their desires of a charitable construction of their actions, and their willingness to declare the reasons of their actions, when it should be desired. The Pastor declared that the week past the dissenting brethren had made use of their liberty at Charlestown in gathering into a Church body of themselves, according to the advice of two Councils in their case, with the approbation of Magistrates and Elders according to the law, and had the right hand of fellowship given them by the messengers from five Churches,—so he saw not any need of any further discourse about the contents of the former letter at present. So it rested at the present.

On the 27 day of Nov. was observed a day of Thanksgiving for the mercies of the year, by order from Gen. Court, dated October 28.

A letter was received and read on the Lord's day, from the Pastor and some brethren of the Church at Newbury, signifying the divided and broken state of the Church there, and earnestly entreating the Church here to send them Elders and messengers to help, with others, in the case on the 3d of Nov. next. Our honored brethren, Major Hawthorn and Capt. Price were sent as messengers from this Church, and were present at the time appointed. When they returned, they shortly gave account that the Council was adjourned unto the 19th day of April. At which time only the Pastor went from hence with the consent of the Church, (the other two brethren being hindered by weighty reasons.) At his return from thence, he made report unto the Church, that, though at first there was a sad appearance of an irreconcilable breach, yet afterwards the Lord was pleased so to bless the motion made for accommodation as to bow their hearts unto a reconciliation on all sides. The Pastor being the leader, acknowledging his own failings, desiring forgiveness from God and them, and expressing his forgiveness of those that had appeared in opposition against him. Many others did the like on both sides, and so there was a comfortable issue; they mutually binding themselves to observe the directions of the Platform of Discipline for the time to come.

Letter from the Pastor and Br. at Newbury.

Council at Newbury.

Thanksgiving. In the beginning of the 9th month, an order was read from the General Court, for a day of Thanksgiving on the 17th day, with respect unto the mercies of the year past, and in special with respect unto the merciful moderation of the rains that had threatened a famine, which was observed at the time appointed. Also James Rising's dismission was propounded, and granted to Windsor Church.

1670.

On the   day of the 4th month, the Pastor propounded whether it might not be expedient to admit members on the Sabbath, after the evening sermon, except when they were so many that it would take up too much time,—which was assented to. Accordingly old Mrs. Stileman, having stood propounded a month, and no exception ag'st her, was admitted by consent of the Church: the Pastor reading her relation, and she consenting to the covenant which was propounded to her—on the Sabbath day, July 10.

*The first taking in of members on the Sunday evening.

Mrs. Stileman.

[Here end the first ten years of Mr. Higginson's records, from which we proposed to select all admissions to the Church, with other matters illustrative of the spirit and character of the First Church. This we have now done, and for the first four years have given the records entire. It will be observed that "non-members" were admitted by a vote of the Church upon their making confession of their faith and repentance and consenting to the Covenant. "Children of the covenant," being already members, were admitted to partake of the Lord's Supper without any vote of the Church, after private examination and approval by the Pastor and publicly making their confession and renewing their covenant. After Mr. Higginson had prepared his "short writing," before mentioned, containing a brief confession and covenant "as a help," &c., it would seem that assent to this was sometimes given by those who were thus admitted to the Lord's Supper; but nothing of the kind appears to have been done in admissions to church membership. Our further selections

----

*Note by Rev. S. Fisk.

from the records will be comparatively few. For a number of years they abound with matters relating to the assistant preacher, Mr. Nicholet, who became a great favorite with a portion of the people, but proved a thorn in the side of their minister. We introduce a very condensed statement respecting them, from Dr. Bentley's " Description and History of Salem," in connection with what we shall take from Mr. Higginson's records on the subject:

"In 1672," says Dr. Bentley, "Mr. Charles Nicholet, from Virginia, came to Salem, and he was invited to tarry, for a year, as an assistant minister. After two years he was chosen to continue for life, and was to be supported by a voluntary contribution. The vote was taken in the congregation, and not in the church. The Church remonstrated, and in 1675, the General Court, by Governor Leverett and others, declare their disapprobation of a vote taken contrary to a law of the jurisdiction, and the established usages of the church. The objections of the Pastor were asked, and he gave them; that in his judgment, the doctrine was inconsistent in terms, the measures unfriendly to peace, and the duty without any mutual assistance. Mr. Nicholet explained himself, corrected his expressions, and promised caution, and a council was called. But the animosity could not be removed. A new meeting-house was raised on the northern part of the Common. Mr Nicholet saw no prospect of peace. And, after many farewell sermons, in 1676, he departed from America forever."*

The council here mentioned by Dr. B. was never actually called, though recommended by the Governor and Council and considered of by the Church.]

1675. This spring the greatest number of the town, and many of the Church joining with them, attempted the building of another

Attempt for another meeting house.

meeting-house, which they carried to such a forwardness as to raise the roof of it upon the Green; they were so confident as to join in a petition to the General Court for their approbation of Mr. Nicholet to be minister therein; the General Court appointed a committee to consider the case, who came to Salem on

June 8, '75. After three days hearing of the case, they gave in a Result, subscribing all their names to it, which, for the memorableness of it, is here recorded.

June 10, '75.

Committee of the Court's Result. We, the Committee of the General Court, met at Salem, having given free and public liberty for each party to express themselves in the matters of their present differences unto a full hearing of the case committed to us, cannot but first manifest our deep and sorrowful sense of the sinful causes, sad concomitants and fruits of the unbrotherly distance of affection and spirit of contention which hath been so long prevailing in the Church and amongst the inhabitants there. More especially we have observed, to our great grief, how much advantage Satan is getting by those strange and sinful animosities, and highly reflecting and provoking carriages and expressions that have passed between those that are chief in this place, whose disunion in no wise consists with the flourishing and much to be desired efficacy and beauty of civil and sacred order amongst this people; all which we do solemnly bear our testimony against. And that we may further attend the errand about which we are sent, and in some measure (as God shall be pleased to give success,) attain the great end aimed at by the Honoured Court, we declare and advise as followeth.

1. We declare the course and way that hath been attended in the calling and settling of Mr. Nicholet as a preacher, by a promiscuous vote of the Town, is very irregular and expressly contrary to the known wholesome laws of this jurisdiction, and of dangerous tendency and influence as to the state and order of the churches here established. And alike irregular and of evil consequence, we declare the general voting of such inhabitants in Town affairs who are not expressly qualified so to vote by law.

2. As an expedient for the recovery and settlement of peace and order of this place, we advise and direct that they do seriously endeavor a mutual agreement to walk together in love; and for that end,—

1. That the whole Church and Town meet together in a public day of Humiliation, to be set apart to that end, and that the work of the day be carried on by the Rev. Pastors, Mr. Higginson and Mr. Nicholet, that the whole assembly may humble themselves before God for past irregularities, and seek reconciliation with him and one with

2. another And so the work of public preaching for the future be carried on jointly by Mr. Higginson and Mr. Nicholet as before; that so the whole people may be in a way of mutual accord. And 3. when there shall be need of issuing forth into another congregation, so weighty a work may be done with mutual love and satisfaction, and according to the rules of God's word, and the laws here established.

John Leveret, Gov.,	Hugh Mason,
Sam. Simons, dep. Gov.,	Joseph Dudly,
Edward Ting,	Peter Buckly,
Will. Stoughton,	Daniel Fisher,
John Richards,	John Wait.

————

War with the Indians, Exod. 17, 13. Then came Amalek and fought with Israel. At the same time when the Committee was here at Salem, there came news that Philip and the Indians began to make war with the English in Plymouth Colony. There were soldiers sent from this colony to join with those of Plymouth. Afterwards the war proved more dangerous than was expected, both to the Eastward and on Connecticut River, the Indians burning, spoiling and killing many of the English in many towns. The war continued all the summer and also the winter following, in which time, by the order of the Court and Council, there were sundry days of Fasting and prayer appointed and observed here in Salem, and in other churches and places in this colony: as on June 29, and on October 7th, and on December 25, and on Jan. 12; many companies of horse and foot being also sent forth; many of our men were killed, and the anger of God manifested against the country.

————

1677. July 25. The Lord having given a commission to the In-*A Fast upon occasion of the Indians taking the ketches at Cape Sables.* dians to take no less than thirteen of the Fishing Ketches of Salem, and captivate the men, (though divers of them cleared themselves and came home,) it struck a great consternation into all the people here. The Pastor moved on the Lord's Day, and the whole people readily consented, to keep the Lecture day following as a Fast day; which was accordingly done, and the work carried on by the Pastor,—Mr. Hale, Mr. Cheevers, and Mr. Gerrish, the neighbor ministers, helping in prayer. The

Lord was pleased to send us some of the Ketches on the Fast day, which was looked on as a gracious smile of Providence.

Also there had been nineteen wounded men sent in to Salem a little before. Also a Ketch with forty men sent out from Salem as a man of war, to recover the rest of the Ketches. The Lord give them good success.

———

1678. At a Church Meeting, March 9.

Admission of eight members. Sam. Eburn, Fra. Girdler, Rich. Reith, Roger Hill, Mary Hill, Rebecca Booth, Miriam Pethrick, Agnes Stacy, these eight having been propounded a month, no exception coming against them, they making their profession of faith and repentance in their own way, some by speech, others by writing, which was read for them, they were admitted to membership in this Church, by consent of the brethren, they engaging themselves in the Covenant.

———

1679.

Synod. Aug. 3, being the sacram't day, was read unto the Church an order from the General Court, informing us of a Synod appointed on Sept. 10, at Boston, to revise the Platform of Discipline agreed upon by the Churches in 1647, and what else might appear necessary for the preventing of schisms, heresies and profaneness, and establishment of the Churches in the faith and order of the Gospel, &c.

Aug. 31. The brethren of the Church staying in the afternoon chose Mr. William Brown sen. and Mr. Jo. Brown sen. as messengers to go with the Pastor to the Synod.

Account of the Synod. Sept. 7 being sacram't day, the Pastor being returned from Boston, gave an account to the Church what was done at the Synod, viz:

That after the reading over and considering the Platform of Discipline published by the Synod in the year 1648, it was agreed on by a vote of the Synod, nemine contradicente, that we do all own, approve and profess the same for the substance of it as the profession of these Churches.

Also, that in answer to the two questions propounded by the

Court, there was an agreement in several things propounded in writing, as provoking evils in this time of God's judgments, and the remedies thereof, as to the substance, end and scope of them, by the unanimous vote of the Synod. Also, a confession of faith to be drawn up by a committee agreed upon and presented to the Synod, which adjourned till the week before the next Court of Election.

At a Church Meeting, Jan. 12.

Synod book. The Synod book in answer to these two questions:—1. What are the provoking evils procuring the late and dreadful judgments of God against New England? 2.—What are remedies and means for reformation?—was read over and considered.

Two Deacons chosen Also our bro. Horne* having been Deacon of this Church above this fifty years, being now very antient, the Church proceeded and agreed to choose two Deacons to be added unto him; and so Mr. Hilyard Verin and Mr. John Hawthorne were chosen Deacons. Also the Church voted the continuance of the contribution for the poor.

A day of Thanksgiving was ordered by the Council to be observed
Thanksgiving. throughout the Colony, in relation to the return of our two agents from England, who had been resident there three years on the country's service, and other mercies; which was accordingly observed here in Salem Jan. 22.

At a Church Meeting, Febr.
The Pastor propounded and read a direction for the renewing of our Church Covenant, which was also left to consideration.

1680. At a Church Meeting, March 10.
The direction for renewing our Church Covenant, after several agi-

---

*John Horne, one of the first thirty members of the Church. In his will, proved in 1684, he signed his name Orne. From him have descended all the Salem Ornes. He left four sons, John, Symon, Joseph, Benjamin. Joseph was great grandfather to the late Dr. Joseph Orne, of H. C. class of 1765.

tations about it, was agreed on by the Church to be solemnly read as consented to by the Church the next Fast day.

Fast. April 15 was a Fast observed according to the order of the Council, when the first Church Covenant was read, and the new Direction propounded by the Pastor, and more accommodated unto our **Covenant renewed.** times, was also read, and both of them consented to as helps in renewing our covenant with God and one with another. **2 deacons ordained.** Also, at the same time, Mr. Hilyard Verin and Mr. Eli Gidney were ordained unto the Deacon's office in this Church.

[Here we come to a passage which deserves particular attention, like the one before noticed respecting the "Direction," &c., proposed by Mr. Higginson "as a help" to carry into practice the doctrine of the Synod of 1662, on the subject of Baptism. As the discovery of an old pamphlet containing that "Direction," &c. in print, (consisting, as it did, of a brief confession of faith, and a covenant with questions and answers suitable for baptism) furnished occasion for imputing to the founders of the First Church the adoption of test articles of faith along with their covenant; so the present existence of an ancient "transcript" of a pamphlet containing a copy of "the first Church Covenant," with the penitential preamble to its renewal in 1636, and the postscript against the Quakers' doctrine, added in 1660,—and also a copy of the "New Direction," &c., prepared pursuant to the Reforming Synod of 1679,—seems to have suggested the notion that what had been always and universally understood as the *first* Covenant of the First Church, agreed upon "6th of 6th month, 1629," was really (all but a single sentence) "adopted as a special covenant in 1636."

The original of this old "transcript pamphlet" appears to have been entitled,

"A copy of the Church covenants which have been used in the Church of Salem; both formerly and in the late renewing of their covenant on the day of the public Fast, April 15, 1680. A direction pointing to that covenant of God's grace in Christ, made with his Church and people in the Holy Scriptures. . . . . Boston, printed at the desire and for the use of many in Salem, for themselves and children. By J. F. 1680."

"There was a Church covenant agreed upon and consented to by the Church of Salem, at their first beginning, in the year 1629, Aug. 6th."

"This following covenant was propounded by the Pastor, agreed upon and consented to by the brethren of the Church in the year 1636."

These declaratory sentences introduce "the first Church Covenant," with the preamble of 1636, in which it is specified as "the Church Covenant" which "this Church was bound unto at their first beginning." At the end of it, and before the postscript, it is stated as follows:

"The forementioned covenant was often read and renewed by the Church at the end of days of humiliation, especially in the year 1660, on the 6th of the first month."

Then comes the postscript, added at the time of this renewal in 1660. The "New Direction" is next thus introduced:

"Also the following covenant was in several Church meetings in the beginning of the year 1680, considered and agreed upon, and consented to by the generality of the Church, to be used as a direction for the renewing of our Church covenant, as being more accommodated to the present times and state of things amongst us. Accordingly it was made use of in that way at the conclusion of the public Fast, April 15, 1680, viz:

"We who—through the mercy of God—are members of this Church of Salem," &c.,

to the end of the New Direction, constituting about one-half of the pamphlet.

Rev. Samuel Fisk, as before observed, when forcibly dismissed from the First Church, took away with him the Church book, and used it in the new society, formed by his adherents, till he was in like manner dismissed from that society. Upon Mr. Leavitt's settlement in 1745, he and his church adopted the first part of this New Direction as their covenant; the old First Church having re-organized itself upon the original Covenant alone without the preamble or the postscript, or any part of the New Direction. The old "transcript pamphlet," containing all these, it is understood, has been attached to the Church book of Mr Leavitt's society ever since his settlement. But never till very recently has it been known to suggest a thought that anything more than the "penitential preamble" was originated in 1636. The new notion appears to have been taken entirely from the above declaratory sentences, without perceiving that the "Church Covenant" mentioned in the first of those sentences is distinctly set forth in that which the second states to have been "propounded," &c. It matters not, therefore, whether these sentences came from the transcriber or the editor of the pamphlet. But a reference to the vote of the Church on which the pamphlet was founded, clears the subject from all possible doubt. Mr. Higginson's record of this vote states most explicitly that "the first Church Covenant was read," and also "the New Direction," &c., unquestionably the *same* first Covenant which he and the Church renewed upon his settlement in 1660, to which he affixed the postscript against the doctrine of the Quakers; the same original Covenant which, without preamble or postscript, he afterwards certified to Cotton Mather for insertion in the Magnalia, or Church History of New England.

In respect to the imputation of test articles of faith, the

favorite phraseology of Mr. Higginson in describing the first Church Covenant, and other "writings," designed "as helps" in Christian ordinances, deserves special notice as manifesting how studiously he sought to exclude all thought of human requisition and to keep in view the supremacy of the Scriptures.*]

On the Sabbath day, Dec. 5, the Pastor gave an account that the
Synod's
confession.
Confession of Faith and Platform of Discipline by agreement of the Synod and General Court, were now printed together.

1681.
Jo. Leech,
Mary English.
On the Sacrament day, John Leech and Mary English were admitted to full communion as children of the Covenant in this Church, in the usual way.

At a Church Meeting, May 5.

Ez. Cheevers,
Benj. Gerrish,
Mary Hodge,
Alice Booth.
Ezekiel Cheevers, Benjamin Gerrish, Mary Hodge, and Alice Booth, after they had stood propounded a month, and no exception came in against them, they made their profession of faith and repentance, and were accepted by the vote of the Church ; and were admitted to the Church Covenant on the Sabbath day following.

1682.   At a Church meeting, June 5.
Also the Pastor did speak to the Church about their duty of observing and encouraging such as they know to be godly to join to the Church. And that they should watch over such as were reported to be given to drinking and company keeping, to deal with them in a regular way.

Also he did recommend the Scripture, Math 9, 1, to the serious
Motion for
another minister.
consideration of the Church, that in regard of his age and weakness they would look out for another minister to be joined with him, one that is well known and approved to be

*See Ante pp. 4, C2, C4, 86.

89

godly and an able preacher of the gospel; and so left it as an object of their serious consideration.

Fast. June 22 was observed as a general Fast by the Court's Order, principally to beg mercy from God in relation to our two agents sent for England. The Pastor did then also renew his motion for another minister as matter of prayer to the whole congregation.

1683. The Church and people having considered the Pastor's motion for another minister to be joined with him, they observing the **Mr. Noys his call.** infirmities of age growing upon him, and not knowing how soon they might be deprived of him and left destitute of a minister; having heard a good report of Mr. N. Noys, and that he was free ; having also the creditable testimony of divers magistrates and ministers concerning him, for his ability, piety and suitableness for Salem, they did unanimously agree to call him to the work of the ministry amongst us here, and it pleased God to facilitate some difficulties that were in the way, that in the issue he came to us, and entered on the work of the ministry the 1st week of May.

At a Church meeting, 1st week of November.

Also the Church having agreed, did, by their vote, choose and call Mr. Noys to the office of a Teacher in this Church ; agreeing also, on **Mr. Noys, his ordination, Nov. 14.** Nov. 14, for the day of ordination. Accordingly letters were sent to the Churches of Newberry, Rowly, Ipswich, Wenham and Beverly, to give notice of it, and to desire the presence and assistance on the day appointed, which being come, the Elders and messengers of the forenamed Churches were present. Mr. Noys preached on Mark 1, 7, 8. He was ordained by imposition of hands of the Pastor, and Mr. Hubbard of Ipswich, and Mr. Phillips of Rowly. Also Mr. Hubbard gave the right hand of fellowship in the name of the neighbor Elders. He observed that as Enoch was the seventh from Adam, so Mr. Noys was the seventh ordained church officer in Salem, &c. The calling, ordaining and settling of Mr. Noys in Salem was with general acceptation of all, both in town and

12

country. The good Lord grant his presence and blessing with his ministry for the conversion, edification, and salvation of souls.

It should have been remembered before, that in the beginning of Nov., Mr. Noys, by a dismission from the Church of Newberry, was received unto membership in this Church. Also Mr. Daniel Epes and his wife were both received unto membership here by a dismission from the Church of Ipswich, all three after the usual manner.

1684. At a Church meeting, May 19.

11 members of Marblehead. These persons following being all of Marblehead, were admitted unto Church fellowship after the usual manner, viz., Benj. Gale, Miriam Hanniford, Johanna Hawly, Dorcas Pedrick, Mary Rowles, Mary Clattery, Charles Pitman, Deliverance Gale, Mary Ferguson, Abigail Hinds, Mary Doliver.

Baston. June 6 being Sacrament day, Thomas Baston, of the village, was received to membership in this Church, after the usual manner.

After this the church members living at Marblehead presented their names, together with their desire that the Church here would grant unto them with their children a dismission, that by consent they might become a Church by themselves, viz:

Samuel Cheevers,	G. Dixy,	G. Henly,
Moses Maverick,	G. Bartoll,	Mrs. Conant,
Ambrose Gale,	G. Watts,	G. Darby,
Richard Reith,	G. Ellis,	Reb. Carder,
Benj. Parmiter,	Sarah Dod,	Eliz. Glasse,
Edward Read,	Mary Fortune,	Anna Sims,
William Bartoll,	Eliz. Russell,	G. Sandin,
Francis Girdler,	G. Pedrick,	Grace Coes,
Sam. Sandin,	Agnes Stacy,	Miriam Hanniford,
Georg Bonfield,	G. Meritt,	G. Hanly,
John Merit,	G. Meritt,	Deliverance Gale,
John Stacy,	Abig. Merit,	Mary Rowles,
Benjamin Gale,	Tab. Pedrick,	Mary Clattery,

John Sayward,	Abig. Hinds,	Mary Ferguson,
Eunice Mavrick,	Charles Pitman,	Mary Dallabar,
Elizab. Leg,	Jane Blackler,	Elizab. Gatchel,
Jone Pitman,	G. Clarke,	50 in all.

The church at Marblehead gathered, and Mr. Cheevers ordained Pastor. There was a unanimous vote of the Church, granting the desire of the brethren and sisters of Marblehead, that they (and their children) might become a Church of themselves. Afterwards, they did signify to the Church that they had agreed upon Aug. 13, when they intended, if the Lord please, to join in church fellowship together, and also to choose and ordain Mr. Cheevers Pastor of their Church. They desired also the presence of messengers from this Church, as also from the Churches of Lin, Beverly, Wenham, and Ipswich. On the foresaid Aug. 13, after Mr. Cheevers had prayed and preached, he presented and read a confession of faith and covenant which they had all considered of and agreed upon among themselves, and which then they did express their consent unto. And so they were owned and approved by the Elders and messengers of the Churches present, as a particular and distinct Church of Christ amongst themselves. Then the brethren of the Church, by their vote expressing their calling and election of Mr. Cheevers to be their Pastor, who was ordained by the laying on of the hands of the Pastor of Salem, together with three other Elders; Mr. Hubbard of Ipswich was desired to give the right hand of fellowship, and the Pastor of Salem to manage the whole action.

Chebacko Church, Bradford Church. The year before Chebacko Church was gathered, and Mr. Wise the Pastor ordained in the same way, messengers from Salem being present. As also the year before that, the Church of Bradford was, and Mr. Sims ordained there the same way.

1684. At a Church meeting, Nov. 6.

Whereas in the former Church meeting, the Elders acquainted the *Consent of the Church to the Elders in baptizing of children in these and such like cases.* Church with variety of cases they met withal in baptizing beyond what was hitherto practised. After some discourse about it, and because many of the brethren were absent, it was agreed then to appoint this Church meeting on purpose that the matter might be maturely considered, and that there might be full notice of it, and that the whole Church might come together.

Accordingly being met together, the Pastor informed them that they might remember that the Synod book, containing the Scripture grounds for 7 propos. touching the subject of baptism, had been (almost 20 years since,) read and considered in the Church, and that then they consented to the baptizing of the children of such parents as were born in the Church, or received with their parents in minority—though they be not yet admitted to the Lord's Supper, according to the scope of the Synod's 5th proposition ; and accordingly we have practised ever since. But as time and experience hath showed, there are many other cases wherein we are as yet defective in baptizing.

As in the case of:

1. The children (of such brethren as have scrupled the baptizing any infants at all) that are grown up and yet are unbaptized, and they have children also.

2. The children of other churches, who live amongst us, and they have children also.

3. The children of church members whose parents are dead.

4. The children of such Christians as live amongst us, though not members of this or any other particular church.

The P. and T. both did express their own judgments : that in these and such like cases the children ought to be baptized as well as those we do already, viz : The parents submitting to the examination of the Elders, and we find them qualified as those whose children we have hitherto baptized, though they dare not as yet offer themselves to the Lord's Supper.

They also professed they intended not the baptizing of the children of all promiscuously, viz., not of any ignorant, scandalous persons, who contradict the profession of Christianity.

The P. also expressed that the reason why he had forborne to baptize in sundry of these cases hitherto, was for want of the brethren's consent. But now they met with so many such cases of those that did frequently and importunately desire bapt. for their children, that they could no longer forbear, but desired to have the consent of the brethren that they might act freely in baptizing according to their own judgments ; and that for such reasons as these :

1. Because baptizing belongs to their office, Math. 28, 19, Luke

Reasons. 12, 42, Heb. 13, 17.

2. These and such like cases are included in the Scripture grounds of the Synod in 1662.

3. Though brethren differ in their apprehensions about baptizing, yet they may, on the principle of forbearing one another in love, consent to their Elders to act in things belonging to their own office, according to their own light. 1 Thes., 2, 4. 1 Tim., 1, 11. Eph., 4, 2. Also Mr. Noys, the Teacher, did fully and freely express himself to concur with the Pastor in this matter, not merely in way of compliance, but as his own judgment wherein he was fully persuaded.

In the agitation, discourse and conference about this matter, many of the chief of the brethren did express themselves as concurring in judgment with the Pastor and Teacher, and that they thought they should not only have liberty, but countenance and encouragement in their way and work; and though some others of the brethren that were otherwise minded, did express their scruples, fears and doubts, yet they would not oppose, but suffer the Elders to act peaceably in this matter: so that in the issue, the liberty of the P. and T. to act in

Voted. baptizing in these and such like cases as they hold themselves bound to do by virtue of their office, was voted, nemine contradicente."

——

1686. July 14 was kept as a public Fast, by order of the President and Council; for seeking the mercy of rain in a time of great drought, and for the Lord's gracious presence and assistance with the new Government, and for the afflicted state of the Church of God in the world.

——

Contribution for the French Protestants. By an order from the President and Council, there was a general contribution through the Colony, for the distressed French Protestants that were come to New England, &c. Accordingly there was a contribution at Salem on the Lord's Day, Sept. 5, which amounted to six and twenty pounds odd money, which was sent to Boston by Mr. Benjamin Gerrish, who returned with a receipt of the money from the persons appointed to receive it. As there had been a contribution some years ago for thirteen men, that suffered shipwreck coming from Ireland, to whom was given seventeen pounds in money.

John Maston, Benj. Gerrish, chosen and ordained Deacons, Octob 14. Whereas on March 11, '84, our brother John Maston and our brother Benj. Gerrish, were desired by the Church to assist in the Deacon's work; finding by experience there were neglects and murmurings growing amongst us, as in Acts 6, 1, the Church, after consideration of the matter at several times, did on the Sabbath, Octob. 1, proceed unto a free election and choosing (by a general vote) of the two foresaid brethren to the office of Deacon—viz. on the Sacram't day; and after their acceptance, notice being publicly given to the congregation that if there was no just exception brought in we should the next Lord's Day after proceed to their ordination; which accordingly was done—viz. on the Lord's day, Nov. 14, the two forenamed brethren were by the two Elders ordained to the office of Deacon in this Church, with prayer and imposition of hands, according to the pattern, Acts 6.

1687.

On Nov., 7, was a day of Thanksgiving kept (as by agreement in other Churches, so here.) For 1, the mercy of the harvest: 2, the Thanksgiving. mercy of the King's declaration for liberty of Religion, and confirmation of our properties: and 3, for the general health and peace amongst us here.

On Nov. 27, Joanna Cooms was admitted to Church membership. Thanksgiving, Dec. 4. Then was read also an order from the Governor and Council for a general day of Thanksgiving throughout all New England, expressing in a general way the three forementioned grounds and causes of thanksgiving; which day was accordingly kept and observed in Salem on Decemb. 1.

On Nov. 10, 1689, was presented the desire of the Church members at the village to have their dismission that they might be a Church of themselves, for themselves and their children, viz:

The Church at Salem Village.

Mr. Paris, ordained Pastor.

Bray Wilkin and his wife,	John Putman, jr., and his wife,
Nathan Putman,	Henry Wilkes,
John Putman and his wife,	Benjamin Wilkes, and his wife,

Joshua Ray	Benjamin Putman
and his wife,	and his wife,
Nathan Ingersoll,	Jonathan Putman
Thomas Putman,	and his wife,
Ezek Cheevers,	Sara, the wife of James
Edward Putman,	Putman,
Peter Prescot,	Deliverance Walcott,
Peter Cloys,	25 [24] in all.

The Church here consented to their dismission for that end; desiring the honored Major Gidney, Mr. Hawthorn, and Mr. Corwin to be as their messengers present and assistant to them in that work, which was carried on and completed on a day of Fasting and prayer on Nov. after the usual manner and custom of such churches, as where one Church becomes two by consent, with the approbation of the magistrates and neighbor churches, whose messengers were present. At the same time, Mr. Paris was chosen and ordained their Pastor. The whole business was transacted by Mr. Noys, Teacher of the Church of Salem.

———

1691.

By reason of many captives taken of late by the Indians, especially from York, there was a general contribution propounded by the

Contrib. for the redemption of Captives. Governor and Council throughout the Colony for the redemption of them, Febr. 21. The contribution at Salem, amounting to thirty-two pounds in money, was sent unto Captain Sewall and Mr. Jer. Dumer, who were appointed to receive it: a receipt of which was sent to us under Captain Samuel Sewall's hand, dated at Boston, Febr. 26, 1691-2.

———

In December there was a council at Lyn, in relation to some differences between some brethren and Mr. Shepard, their Pastor.

Council at Lyn. Mr. Noys and three other brethren were, by a vote of the Church, desired to go thither and join with other Elders and messengers of the Churches of Boston and Malden, to help to make peace: which, through the blessing of God on their endeavors, was attained to the general satisfaction of all.

1692.

July 14, by order of the General Court, was kept a public
Thanksgiving. general Thanksgiving throughout the Province of Massachusetts, for the return of the Governor and Mr. Mather bringing
over with them a settlement of government, &c.

———

Aug. 28, by an order from the Governor and Council was observed
Fast. as a day of Fasting and prayer, to seek mercy from God in relation to the present afflicted state of things in both Englands: to
which was added, by the said order, an exhortation to all the churches
to keep the wheel of prayer in continual motion, by successive and repeated agreements for days of prayer with fasting, in their several
vicinities, till our God hath spoke peace to us, and we find his salvation nigh unto us, with glory dwelling in our land.

———

1694.

Nov. 29 was observed as a day of Thanksgiving.

Dec. 13 was observed as a day of Humiliation.

Jan. 27, Martha, wife of Sam. Robinson, was received to membership in the usual way.

———

[We have now come to the end of Mr. Higginson's records. Those which follow in the present old Church
book, are in the hand-writing of Mr. Noyes and his colleague, Mr. Curwin, till near the time of their death, in
1717; and from 1718 to the end of the book, in the hand
of Rev. Samuel Fisk.

We take from Mr. Noyes's what comes immediately after
Mr. Higginson's last record for three or four months entire,
as a specimen of his manner; and shall add a few selections from his and subsequent records chiefly for the historical facts contained in them.]

———

Admitted. Feb., last Sabbath, Tamizen Woodwell, wife of Samuel
Woodwell, was admitted to full communion.

1695.

Mrs. Glover admitted. March. Elizabeth Glover was admitted to full communion with the Church on the Sabbath day before Sacrament.

Mrs. Margaret Sewall was a child of the Church at Cambridge, and desiring communion with this Church, was propound-
Mrs. Sewall admitted. ed the last Sabbath in March, was received to full communion the first Sabbath in April, before the Sacrament of the Lord's Supper.

Fast. April 25 was observed a public Fast, being appointed by the government.

Abigail Punchard admitted. On the 2d of June Abigail Punchard was admitted to full communion with the Church, just before the Lord's Supper; she was propounded the Sabbath before.

June 23. Mehitabel Fountain owned the covenant and had her five children baptized.

June 30. Mary, wife of Samuel Gale, owned the covenant and had her two children baptized.

July 7. Sarah Leach was admitted to full communion with the Church, before the Sacrament, being propounded the Sabbath before.

1696.

Feb. 7. After the Sacrament the Teacher earnestly desired the communicants, such of them as had adult children, to put them in mind of their baptismal covenant, and told them that although God accepted the parents' covenanting for their children in their minority, yet God expected their personal owning the covenant at age, and that such as the parents should think qualified they should stir them up to seek full communion with the Church.

1703.

Mar. 8. With the consent of the brethren of the Church, was given unto our brother, John Massey, an old great Church Bible, it having been often lent to aged people, and misused, and not like to be any way more serviceable than by giving it to some aged person, and he being considered as the first Town born child, it was given to him and delivered to him before the brethren.

13

1704.

Dec. 3.   Mr. George Curwin, having been approved by the Elders and propounded, and nothing objected against him, renewed his covenant with God and the Church and was received to full communion with consent of the Church.

———

1707.

Octob. 5.   Samuel Phillips, junior,* and the wife of Mr. Nathaniel Higginson, having been examined and propounded, renewed their covenant with God and the Church and were received to full communion with consent of the brethren.

———

1711

Octob'r 7. The Rev'd Mr. Samuel Phillips was dismissed from this Church, to join in church fellowship with the church in the South part of Andover.

The communicants in the South part of Andover desired the Elder and messengers of this Church to be present with them on Octob. 17, and join with the Elders and messengers of other churches, to counsel and help them in their embodying and becoming a church themselves, and the ordaining the Rev'd Mr. Samuel Phillips to be their pastor.   The Elder not being able to go, the Church chose and desired Major Sewal, Esq., and the Rev'd Mr. George Curwin, and Capt. Peter Osgood to go as messengers from this Church; and they did go, and the affairs of the day were orderly carried on, the Church embodied, and Mr. Phillips ordained their Pastor.

———

1712.

Sept. 28. Colonel Higginson was propounded in order to full communion with the Church.

Octob. 5th.   Col. Higginson was received to full communion upon his renewing the covenant with God and the Church, the brethren consenting.

* The first minister of Andover, South Parish.

SALEM, April 24th, 1713.

To the Rev'd Mr. Nicholas Noyes, Teacher of the Church in Salem, and to the Church of Christ there:

Hon'd, Rev'd, and Beloved:

Whereas it hath pleased our gracious God to smile upon our endeavors for the erecting of an house for the carrying on the public worship of God, and settling a minister amongst us, and we being called by divine providence (as we apprehend) to settle a particular church according to the Gospel, under the ministry of the Rev'd Mr. Benj. Prescot:

Our humble request to yourselves is that you will please to dismiss us and our children with your approbation and blessing, to be a church of ourselves, and until we are so, with the consent and approbation of the Elders and messengers of the churches that shall assist at the ordination of the Rev'd Mr. Prescot, to continue members of Salem Church, and as there shall be occasion assist and help us, especially by your prayers unto the God of all grace, that in so great an affair we may be directed and assisted to proceed in all things according to the will of God, unto whom be glory in the church by Jesus Christ, throughout all ages, world without end.

Your unworthy brethren and sisters living within the bounds of the Middle District in Salem.

Hanna King,	Martha Adams,	Sam'l Goldthwait, sen.,
Judah Mackintire,	Elizabeth Cook,	Ebenezer Gyles,
Elizabeth Nurse,	Sarah Gardiner,	Abraham Pierce,
Sarah Robinson,	Elizabeth Gardiner,	John Foster,
Ales Shafflin,	Isabel Pease,	John Felton,
Hanna Small,	Hanna Felton,	David Foster,
Hanna Southwick,	Hanna Foster,	Abel Gardiner,
Mary Tompkins,	Abigail French,	John Gardiner,
Elizabeth Tompkins,	Elizabeth Gyles,	Samuel Goldthwait,
Elizabeth Verry,	Elizabeth Goldthwait,	William King,
Jemima Verry,	Hanna Goldthwait,	Richard Waters,
Sarah Waters,	Debora Gool,	Robert Pease.
Elizabeth Waters,	Elizabeth King,	
Susanna Daniel,	Samuel Gardiner,	

At a Church meeting at the Teacher's house, June 25th.
The Church having received a petition from our brethren and sis-

ters living in the District, wherein they desire a dismission from us for themselves and their children, in order to be a church of themselves. The Church giveth in answer as followeth : That although we cannot praise or justify our brethren's proceeding so far as they have done in order to be a church of themselves without advising with or using means to obtain the consent of the Church they belonged to ; yet at the request of our brethren and sisters, and for peace sake, we permit them and their children to become a church of themselves ; provided they have the approbation and consent of the Elders and messengers of some other churches in communion with us, that shall assist at their church gathering and ordaining them a pastor. And until they have so done, they continue members of this Church. And so we commit them to the grace of God in Christ Jesus, praying that they may have divine direction and assistance in the great work they are upon, and that they may become an holy and orderly and peaceable church, and that the Lord would add to them of such as are within their own limits, many such as shall be saved. The above answer was twice distinctly read to the brethren of the Church before it was voted, and then consented to by the vote of the Church, nemine contradicente.

[Rev. Benjamin Prescott was accordingly ordained, Sept 23, 1713.]

1714.

The Reverend Mr. George Curwin was ordained a Pastor of this May 19. Church. The Teacher gave him the charge, D. Cotton Mather gave him the right hand of fellowship. The Elders and messengers of the North Church in Boston, and of the Church in Brattle Street, in Boston, and of the first Church in Ipswich, and of the Church in Beverly, and of the Church of Marblehead, and of the Church at Wenham, and of the Church at Salem Village, most, if not all of the Elders, laid on hands. D. Mather began with prayer, Mr. Curwin preacht on 2 Cor., 2, 16, the last clause of the text ; Mr. Gerrish made the concluding prayer, Mr. Curwin pronounced the blessing.

[The following entries are in Mr. Curwin's hand writing.]

1715.

Nov. 27. The Rev'd Mr. Joseph Green, Pastor of the Church at the Village, died the 26th instant, to the great loss of the Church of God, and was exceedingly lamented.

———

Dec. 4. John Holyman and Mrs. Elizabeth Hunt, having been examined, propounded, and nothing objected against them, entered into covenant with God and the Church, and were both admitted to full communion.

———

Dec. 23. The Rev. Mr. Chipman was ordained Pastor of the North Church at Royall side; which was also gathered the same day by the assistance of one of the Elders, with the messengers from this Church in conjunction with others.

———

1716.

April 26. The Rev. Mr. Edward Holyoke was ordained pastor of the New Church in Marblehead, which was the same day gathered by the assistance of the Elders and messengers from this Church in conjunction with others.

———

23 May. The Rev. Mr. William Cooper was ordained assistant to the Rev. Mr. Colman, with the assistance of one of the Elders and messengers from the Church.

———

Nov'r 4. A letter from our neighbors in Manchester was read to the Church, wherein they signified their desire to the Elders and Church that they would assist them on the 7th instant, in gathering into a church state, and in ordaining the Rev. Mr. Ames Cheever to the office of a pastor among them; and there were chosen as messengers from the Church, Daniel Epes, Esq., Steven Sewall, Esq., Mr. Sam'l Ruck, and Capt. Thos. Barton. Accordingly on the day appointed, the work was christianly and peaceably carried on, to the satisfaction of the Elders and messengers.

1717.

June 2. Was read a letter from the Church in the Village, desiring the presence and assistance of the Elders and messengers from the Church at the ordination of the Rev'd Mr. Peter Clark ; and there were chosen to attend the Pastors our worthy brothers, Daniel Epes and Steven Sewall, Esqs., and Deacon Simon Willard.

June 5. The Rev'd Mr. Peter Clark was ordained Pastor of the Church in Salem Village, where things were comfortably carried on.

On Nov'r 23, 1717.

The Rev'd Mr. George Curwin's death and character. Died the Reverend Mr. GEORGE CURWIN, in the 35th year of his age, and the 4th year of his ordained ministry in this Church. He was highly esteemed in his life, and very deservedly lamented at his death ; having been very eminent for his early improvements in learning and piety, his singular abilities and great labors, his remarkable zeal and faithfulness in the service of his master. A great Benefactor to our poor. The Reverend Mr. Noyes his life was much bound up in him.

On Dec'r 13, 1717.

The Rev'd Mr. Nicholas Noyes, his death and character. Died the very Reverend and famous Mr. NICHOLAS NOYES, near 70 years of age, and in the 35th year of his ordained ministry in this Church.

He was extraordinarily accomplished for the work of the ministry, whereunto he was called, and wherein he found mercy to be faithful ; and was made a rich, extensive, and long continued blessing. Considering his superior genius ; his pregnant wit ; strong memory ; solid judgment ; his great acquisition in human learning and knowledge ; his conversation among men, especially with his friends, so very pleasant, entertaining and profitable ; his uncommon attainments in the study of divinity ; his eminent sanctity, gravity and virtue ; his serious, learned, and pious performances in the pulpit ; his more than ordinary skill in the prophetical parts of Scripture ; his wisdom and usefulness in human affairs ; and his constant solicitude for the public good: it is no wonder that Salem and the adjacent part of the country, as also the Churches, University and people of New England, justly esteem him as a principal part of their glory. He was born at Newbury, 22d Dec., 1647; and died a bachelor.

These characters were drawn by persons well acquainted with the Rev'd persons deceased, and published in the Public News Letter, in Boston.

At a meeting of the First Church, in Salem, Sept. 8th, 1718,— John Higginson, Esq., chosen Moderator.

Voted. That the eighth day of Octob'r next is appointed for the ordination of the Rev'd Mr. Sam'l Fisk.

Voted. That the Church will call in the help and assistance of the Elders and messengers of the following Churches, viz : The First Church in Ipswich, the Church in Wenham, the First Church in Beverly, the Fourth Church in Boston, the First Church in Marblehead, the Church in Salem Village, the Church in the Precinct in Salem : to assist at the ordination of the Rev'd Mr. Sam'l Fisk.

Voted. That John Higginson, Esq., Daniel Epes, Esq., and Deacon John Marston, are chosen a committee to write unto and notify the several churches above-named ; and to desire the Rev'd Mr. Joseph Gerrish, or the Rev'd Mr. John Rogers, or the Rev'd Mr. Benjamin Colman, or the Rev'd Mr. Thomas Blowers, or either of them which they shall see meet, and can prevail with, to give the Rev'd Mr. Fisk his charge at his ordination.

Voted. That Mr. Epes and Deacon Marston do enquire and take a list of the names of all the children that have been baptized since the death of the Rev'd Mr. George Curwin.

A copy of the Letter sent by this first Church in Salem, to invite the Churches aforenamed, to assist at the ordination of Mr. Fisk in this parish.

The First Church of Christ in Salem, to the First Church of Christ in Ipswich, sendeth greeting.

Rev'd and Beloved in our Lord Jesus Christ:

It having pleased the Sovereign God, after he had, in the close of the last year, called to himself our Rev'd and dear Pastors, Mr. Nicholas Noyes and Mr. George Curwin, to bring to our help the Rev'd Mr. Samuel Fisk ; whose ministerial qualifications and labors we have been so satisfied in as unanimously to call him to the office of a Pastor over us, having the unanimous concurrence of our neighbors, the inhabitants of this Parish herein : and it having pleased God to incline the heart of the Rev'd Mr. Fisk to accept of the call we have given him, we have thought fit to appoint Wednesday, the eighth day of October next ensuing, as a suitable time for his ordination to that office.

These, therefore, are to request the presence and assistance of your Rev'd Pastors and messengers on that day, in that affair ; having likewise sent letters of this import to other churches on this occasion ; hoping this office of communion may tend to our mutual edification and the strengthening our holy fellowship.

Thus commending you to the grace of God in our Lord Jesus Christ, and asking your continual prayers to God for us,

We rest,   Your Brethr'n and Serv'ts,

JOHN HIGGINSON,   ⎫ In the
DANIEL EPES,   ⎬ name of
Salem, Sept. 8th, 1718.   JOHN MARSTON.   ⎭ the Ch'h.

————

On the eighth of Oct'r, 1718.

Oct. 8, 1718.
Mr. Fisk now
ordained Pastor.
The Rev'd Elders and messengers of the Churches which were invited, assembled in Council at Salem, in pursuance of their invitation, and the Rev'd Mr. Thomas Blowers opened the public service by prayer; the Rev'd Mr. Benjamin Colman preached on 2 Corinthians, 4, 5,—an excellent sermon to the vast assembly. After sermon, Mr. Fisk prayed; then the Rev'd Mr. Gerrish prayed and gave the charge ; the Rev'd Mr. John Rogers and Mr. Benj. Colman, and Mr. Thomas Blowers, imposing hands with him. Next, the Rev. Mr. John Rogers gave the right hand of fellowship to the ordained Pastor, in the name of the Rev'd Elders present : after which, the fourth part of the hundred and eighteenth Psalm was sung, and the Pastor pronounced the blessing: 2 Corin'ns, 2d chap., 16th v., and 12th chap., 9th v.

On this ordination day, the assembly met at the New Church, which was now almost perfectly finished: a vast and beautiful, yet grave house it is. It was begun to be raised on May 21st, 1718, and it was completely raised May 24th, 1718. The congregation first met to worship God in it, on July 13th, 1718. No hurt was sustained either in pulling down the old house, or raising the new one. Laus Deo Salvatori.

A new church or house built for the public worship of God.

This is the third house erected for the public worship of God, on the same spot of land, on which the first church was built in this Town, and which was the first in the Province.

———

Salem, Nov. 14, 1718.

To the Rev. Mr. Sam'l Fisk, Pastor of the First Church in Salem, and to the Church.

Hon'd, Rev'd and Beloved :

Whereas all of us, the subscribers, have been for some time under covenant obligations to this Church, and whereas now Divine Providence opens a way for our embodying into a church state ourselves, under the pastoral care of the Rev'd Mr. Robert Stanton, whom we design to have ordained for that purpose as soon as conveniently may be.

And altho' some few of us have failed in our duty, in our former proceedings, we pray it may be overlooked and passed by.

And we humbly and heartily request of you, that you would be pleased so to release us from our covenant obligations, as that we with our children may have your free consent, to embody into a church by ourselves, and may be by you recommended to the pastoral care of our intended Pastor, Mr. Stanton. And we entreat we may have the benefit of the Sacrament with you, until our Church is settled; and as there shall be occasion, that you will assist and help us, especially by your prayers unto the God of all grace, that in so great an affair we maybe directed and assisted, to proceed in all things according to the will of God; unto whom be glory in the Churches by Jesus Christ thro'out all ages, Amen.

Martha Willard,	Eliz. Gerrish,	Christopher Babbidge,
Hannah Willard,	Hannah Pickering,	Simon Willard,
Mary Prince,	Mercy Swinnerton,	Jonathan Webb,
Abigail Andrew,	Eliz. Barton,	Richard Prince,

14

Jane Willard,	Dorothy Neal,	Benj. Ives,
Sarah Hardy,	Priscilla Hilliard.	Joseph Hardy,
Silence Rogers,	Abigail Punchard,	Daniel Rogers,
Eliz. Bush,	Sarah Ward,	Malachi Foot,
Eliz. Dean,	Martha Pope,	Josiah Willard,
Margaret Beadle,	Abigail Foot,	John Browne,
Mary Murrey,	Abigail Foot, Jun'r,	
Deborah Masters,	Mary Foot,	
Mary Collins, Jun'r,	Mary Collins,	

And whereas I, Simon Willard, have served this Church in the office of a Deacon, I pray now to be excused.   S. W.

At a meeting of the First Church in Salem on Dec'r 25th, 1718, being Thursday P. M.

Voted. An answer to the request of the brethren and sisters, who dwell in the eastern part of this Town.

A dismission and recommendation granted to the brethren and sisters, with their children, who dwell in the Eastern Precinct.   Whereas our neighbors who dwell in the eastern part of this town have erected a house for the public worship of God; and the first parish hath granted them a separate district for the support of the ministry among them:—

And whereas they have hereupon called a learned, orthodox and pious minister to dispense the gospel to them, and in order to settlement and ordination among them:—

Altho' we cannot but bear due testimony against the irregular proceedings of some of the said brethren in their management of that affair, of building a house for a separate assembly, contrary to the usage and proceedings of other brethren formerly belonging to this Church, in the gathering of a church, and contrary to good order: Yet for peace sake, considering that those of our said brethren who request dismission, and who have been faulty, have confessed their fault, and desired that it might be everlooked;—and we being ready to encourage the work of the Gospel among us in this Town:—

Do dismiss our said brethren and sisters with their children, who dwell to the eastward of the said line, from this Church, (so as that they attend communion and church order with us till their Pastor is ordained,) and recommend them to the care of the Rev'd Mr. Robert Stanton, whom they intend to have ordained their Pastor.

Voted. That Deacon Simon Willard be dismissed from the service of this Church as a Deacon, according to his desire, with thanks for his good service.

1719.

April 5. Then was communicated to the Church a letter from the brethren in the Eastern Parish in this Town, (who some time since embodied into a particular Church by fasting and prayer and signing a covenant, present thereat the Rev'd Mr. Thomas Blowers, of Beverly, and the Pastor of this Church, who assisted those brethren,) requesting the presence and assistance of the Pastor and messengers of this Church in the ordination of the Rev'd Mr. Robert Stanton, on Wednesday, the 8th instant; and the Church delegated Deacon Marston, and Col. John Higginson, and Col. Sam'l Brown, for that service.

———

April 8th. The Rev'd Mr. Rob't Stanton was ordained; the Pastor and delegates being present.

———

1727.

Oct. 15. After evening service the Pastor stayed the brethren of the Church, and read to them a letter from the First Church of Christ in Ipswich, inviting the Pastor and messengers of this Church to assist in the ordination of Mr. Nathaneel Rogers, a colleague Pastor to his Father, the Rev'd Mr. John Rogers, in that Church. Then two votes were called, viz:

1. That this Church will send their messengers as desired on the specified occasion.

2. That our brethren, Deacon Peter Osgood, Samuel Brown, Benjamin Lynde, sen'r, James Lindall and Thomas Barton, do represent this Church on the aboves'd occasion. Both voted in the affirmative.

———

Oct. 18th. The Pastor and two of the messengers above named (the other three being providentially hindered) went to Ipswich and there met the Elders and messengers of several other Churches which convened upon the same account, and ordained Mr. Nathaneel Rogers colleague Pastor with his Father, the Rev'd Mr. John Rogers. The Lord make them both very great blessings.

———

Nov. 4th. A public meeting was held in the afternoon of this day (being Saturday,) in the House of God, partly on account of the sudden and we fear unnatural death of our sister

Public Meeting on acc't of the Earthquake.

Hannah Moses, a member of this Church for many years past; also partly on account of a terrible earthquake, which was on Lord's day night last, at half an hour after ten ; both Parishes met on this occasion; and there was a vast assembly. The Pastor preached, from 1 Peter, 4, 17, 18. The Lord hear us!

Dec. 21. A public Fast was appointed by the civil government on account of the late surprising and dreadful earthquake, which happened on the night between the 29th and 30th days of October last past, about half an hour after ten-clock, and which lasted, that is, the first shock, about 6 minutes, at least in this Town, and which was followed by many others during that night, and afterwards; especially in the Northern parts of this Province till this time. This extended, as we have been informed, as far as Pennsylvania Southwards, and how far Northwards we cannot tell, only we are informed, as far as any of our Northeast settlements reach. This day was observed by us and the Eastern Parish in this Town, who joined with us. Now there was collected by a contribution for the poor,—Twenty-one pounds, seven shillings and nine pence.

1728.

May 22. The Pastor and some of the messengers chosen [Samuel Brown, Deacon Osgood, Thomas Barton, James Lindall, John Nutting and Samuel Ruck,] went down to the place appointed for meeting in the Eastern Parish in this town, where they met the Elders and messengers of several other Churches which convened upon the same account, and ordained Mr. Wm. Jenison Pastor of the Eastern Church and Parish in this Town. The Lord make him and his people mutually very great blessings. Mr. Clark preached, Mr. Blowers gave the charge, Mr. Barnard gave the right hand of fellowship, and the Pastor of this Church prayed.

[Mr. Fisk notices also the following ordinations, viz : of Rev. Nathaniel Henchman at Lynn, Nov. 2, 1720; of Rev. James Osgood at Stoneham, Sept. 10, 1729; of

Rev. Joseph Champney at Beverly, Dec'r 10, 1729; of Rev. John Warren at Wenham, Jan'y 10, 1732.

It may here be added that Mr. Fisk was particular in recording annual Fasts and Thanksgivings, with the exact amount of contributions received for the poor. In some years during his ministry no other records appear.]

After the public worship was ended, the Pastor stayed the brethren of the Church, and propounded to them, that they would meet publicly in this house on the *6th of August next*, to give thanks to God for his great goodness in bringing our fathers hither and planting them as a Church, and continuing it till this time; on which sixth day of August next one hundred years will be accomplished, and the second commence. The Church were desired to speak their mind for or against it as they inclined; but one spake who was for it, the rest were silent, whom therefore I told, I should, because it was our custom, take as consenting. I suppose they were all for it, by what I had heard, for I had propounded this matter (not only to the neighboring pastors, who much approved it, which I told this Church, but) to the people in private conversation; so that they had sure expectation of this public proposal.

November 27.

August 3. I propounded publicly to the congregation, what the Church had agreed as above, and prayed their presence and assistance on the said day. At this time the Eastern Church and Parish in this town were present.

1729, August 6th.

In pursuance of the above vote of the Church, the Church and parish in considerable number (with all the neighboring pastors of this association, and some number of the neighboring congregations) met at the First Church in this Town, at eleven o'clock, A. M.

This Church's first century Jubilee.

The public worship began with singing the 122d Psalm; then the Rev'd Mr. John Barnard (pastor of the First Church in Marblehead,) made a very excellent and adapted prayer: upon which the 107th Psalm, the three first stanzas in it, was sung; next, the Pastor of this Church preached on the 78th Psalm, the first seven verses; after which was sung the 44th Psalm, the 1, 2, 6 and 7th verses; after which the Rev'd Mr. Benjamin Prescott, pastor of the third Church in this Town, prayed, short but full; next we sang, as a proper close, the 100th Psalm, the long metre. In the close the Pastor pronounced the blessing. The Lord accept the offering of thanks we have made. Amen.

[Rev. S. Fisk, as indicated by his "explanatory note," at the end of the transcript record of church members,* adopted a new method of recording the names of "such as entered into or renewed their covenant," and also "such as came to the communion of the Lord's Supper," entering them under distinct heads, as in recording baptisms.† His manner of proceeding in these cases, may be seen from the respective statements placed by him at the head, which are the following.

Here followeth a catalogue of the names of such persons who have entered into covenant with God in this Church, or renewed their baptismal covenant; but generally have not had light sufficient at present to come to the Lord's Supper, but through their scruples are as yet hindered; beginning Nov'r 2, 1718.

These persons were first propounded to the Church and examined.

Here followeth a catalogue of the names of such persons who have been received to communion at the Lord's Table in this Church, from the 28th Dec., 1718—whose desires to communicate with us were first propounded to the Church, and were examined by the Pastor, according to the usage of this *first gathered* Church in this Province.

---

*See ante, 17.　　　　　† 18

In other and more important respects Mr. Fisk departed from the practice of his predecessors, and in such manner as to produce great uneasiness and disaffection among his people. He appears to have dispensed entirely with Church meetings, excepting when he stayed the Church after religious exercises for some particular purpose. Even when importuned to call the Church together to consider impending difficulties, occasioned by his official conduct, he persisted in refusing compliance. The disastrous results which followed are well known from publications of the time, but no trace of them appears in Mr. Fisk's records, excepting an incidental allusion made by him after his expulsion from the pulpit of the First Church. As already mentioned, Mr. Fisk kept possession of the Church book, and continued to use it throughout his ministry in the new Church formed by his adherents. We extract from his record of "such as entered into or renewed their covenant," a brief passage containing the allusion referred to, and stating the time and manner of his expulsion.

1738, July 30.

Joseph Orne, jun'r, being sick with a consumption, nigh to death, entered into covenant with God in this Church, and was baptized in the dwelling-house of his uncle, Joseph Orne, who educated him publicly from his youth up. This is the dwelling house where the First Church met and worshipped God for several Lord's days, after it was (with its Pastor) driven together from the public meeting-house, on Lord's day, April 27, 1735.

We shall now introduce from the succeeding Church book an account of the re-organization of the old Church, which contains a renewal and final sanction of the genu-inc original confession of faith and covenant of the First Church ; here, as generally, called simply the Covenant.]

At a meeting of the Brethren adhering to the ancient principles of the first Church in Salem, at the house of Benjamin Lynde, Esq., on the 5th Aug., 1736, for the renewal of their Covenant, and in order to the having a compleat organick Church :

After humble prayer to Almighty God by the Rev. Mr. Prescott, at the desire of the Brethren then met—

The first Covenant of the Church, with a more explicit declaration as it was before drawn up, was again read over, and after mature deliberation renewed and subscribed.

The same is as follows :

SALEM, Aug. 5, 1736.

Whereas it hath pleased the Holy God in his sovereignty to permit long and grievous afflictions and distresses to be on the first Church of Christ in the first parish in Salem, by their woful divisions, occasioned, as to us appears, by the malcconduct of their late pastor, Mr. Sam'l Fisk ; who, after the calling and advices of a Council on the matters alleged against him, and an ecclesiastical process thereupon, tho' without any proper regard had to them by the said pastor, he finally was dismissed by a major part of the Brethren of the Church of the first parish, qualified by law to act in that matter :

And whereas a number of the Brethren of the said Church, notwithstanding the repeated advices and admonitions to them by the aforesaid councils, through the prevailing influence of Mr. Fisk upon them (as we apprehend) still persist in refusing the reasonable advice of the said council, and by their continuing to adhere to the said Mr. Fisk, make themselves in some sort partakers of his guilt :

Wherefore we, the subscribers, members of the said first Church, and adhering to their first principles, both as to doctrine and discipline, esteeming it our duty to bear testimony against such of our Brethren as walk disorderly, depart from their first principles and order of discipline, and being concerned to keep ourselves free from offence, as well as to enjoy the institutions and sacraments of our Lord Jesus Christ, regularly administered to us.

We do, humbly sensible of the frowns of God upon us in the breach and rent now made in the Church, hereby separate ourselves from our Brethren walking disorderly as before mentioned, declaring at the same time our readiness to receive them to our communion and fellowship, upon their regular walk, and return to the first principles of the Church. And furthermore, we, the subscribers, the major part of the brethren regularly admitted into the Church, now in the Church, who by law are empowered to vote in calling, settling, supporting and continuing a minister, in order to the calling an orthodox minister to be settled among us, and to perform the ministerial office in the ancient place of public worship in the first parish ; and in order to proceed to a full and organic state of the Church, according to its primitive and original constitution :

Do, in the first place, solemnly renew the dedication of ourselves and our offspring to the Lord Jehova, the one true and living God, Father, Son and Holy Ghost.

2. We do confirm, recognize, and renew the first Covenant, made and entered into by our forefathers at their first settlement into a Church state in this place, which runs in the following words :

We covenant with our Lord and one with another, and we do bind ourselves in the presence of God to walk together in all his ways according as he is pleased to reveal himself to us in his blessed word of truth, and do explicitly, in the name and fear of God, profess and protest to walk as followeth through the power and grace of our Lord Jesus Christ. We avouch the Lord to be our God, and ourselves to be his people, in the truth and simplicity of our spirits. We give ourselves to the Lord Jesus Christ, and the word of his grace for the teaching, ruling, and sanctifying of us in matters of worship and conversation, resolving to cleave to him alone for life and glory, and to reject all contrary ways, canons and constitutions of men in his worship.

We promise to walk with our brethren with all watchfulness and tenderness, avoiding jealousies and suspicions, backbitings, censurings, provokings, secret risings of spirit against them, but, in all offences, to follow the rule of our Lord Jesus, and to bear and forbear, give and forgive, as he hath taught us.

In public or private, we will do nothing to the offence of the

Church, but will be willing to take advice for ourselves and ours as occasion shall be presented.

We will not in the congregation be forward either to show our own gifts and parts in speaking or scrupling, or there discover the weakness or failings of our brethren, but attend an orderly call thereunto, knowing how much the Lord may be dishonored, and his gospel and the profession of it slighted by our distempers and weaknesses in public.

We bind ourselves to study the advancement of the gospel in all truth and peace, both in regard of those that are within or without, no ways slighting our sister Churches, but using their counsel as need shall be, not laying a stumbling-block before any, no, not the Indians, whose good we desire to promote; and so to converse as we may avoid the very appearance of evil.

We do hereby promise to carry ourselves in all lawful obedience to those that are over us in Church or Commonwealth, knowing how well-pleasing it will be to the Lord that they should have encouragement in their places by our not grieving their spirits by our irregularities.

We resolve to approve ourselves to the Lord in our particular callings; shunning idleness as the bane of any state; nor will we deal hardly or oppressingly with any wherein we are the Lord's stewards.

Promising also to our best ability to teach our children and servants the knowledge of God and of his will, that they may serve him also, and all this not by any strength of our own, but by the Lord Christ, whose blood we desire may sprinkle this our covenant made in his name.

3dly. We do further covenant and engage in the presence of God and by his grace, that we will walk together as a Congregational Church of Christ in the faith and order of the gospel; more particularly as to our faith, we are persuaded of the Christian religion contained in the Scriptures of the books of the old and new Testament, as explained in the Catechism compiled by the Rev'd assembly of divines at Westminster, as to the substance of it. And as to the order of the gospel among us, we profess and take the Platform of Church Discipline in New England, composed by the Synod at Cambridge, 1648, to be our rule and method of Church discipline.

And all this we promise, not through any strength of our own, but through the aids and assistances of the Holy Spirit, flying to the blood of the everlasting covenant for the pardon of our manifold sins and praying that the glorious Jesus, the great head of the Church, would keep us from falling, establish, strengthen and settle us, and at last present us, faultless, before the presence of his glory with exceeding joy.

Geo. Daland,	Benj'a Lynde,
James Grant,	James Lindall,
John Bickford, Jr.,	Ben'a Lynde, Jun'r,
Miles Ward, Jun'r,	Jno. Nutting,
John Archer,	Henry West,
Ben'a Lambert,	Sam'l Ropes,
James Odell, as to Discipline } I take the Platform as to the } substance for my rule. }	Nath. Phippen,
	Jos. Hathorne,
	Samuel West,
Ben'a Marston,	Sam'l Gyles,
Samuel Osgood,	Nath'l Ropes,
	Jona. Gardner.

It was agreed that our brother, Judge Lynde, should be moderator of the present meeting.

The question was put to the brethren severally, whether they would now proceed to the choice of some meet person to discharge the office of a gospel minister among them.

Voted in the affirmative unanimously.

It was then resolved that the brethren would severally give their voices for the choice of a minister; which being done, it appeared that Mr. John Sparhawk was chosen by a great majority.

———

Letters missive from the "Brethren of the Church of Christ, meeting in the ancient place for public worship in the first parish in Salem," were addressed " to the churches of Christ under the pastoral care of Mr. Holyoke of Marblehead, Rev'd Mr. Benj. Prescott, Mr. John Chipman,

Mr. Peter Clarke, Mr. Champney, Mr. William Hobby, and Mr. John Warren," for the ordination of Rev. John Sparhawk, which took place on the 8th day of December, 1736. Mr. Chipman began with prayer; Mr. Appleton preached from 11 Prov., 30 ; Mr. Holyoke gave the charge, and Mr. Prescott the right hand of fellowship.*

We close our selections with some brief extracts from Mr. Sparhawk's earlier records, illustrative of the spirit and manner in which the Church proceeded in its re-organization.

At a meeting of the Church, Dec'r 27, 1736, after humble prayer to God for his blessing upon their affairs : Upon reading a letter from Deacon Peter Osgood, bearing date Dec'r 25, 1736, signifying his uneasiness and concern that he has so long continued with Mr. Fisk and his adherents, and likewise his desire to join with this Church ; the brethren unanimously voted their satisfaction, and heartily received him to their former communion and fellowship.

Voted that our brother, Peter Osgood, be continued in the office of a Deacon.

Voted, that the Scriptures be read as part of public worship.

———

May 17, 1737.
Mr. John Nutting then accepted of the office of Ruling Elder.

———

At a meeting of the Church, April 18, 1738.
Voted, that a Lecture be set up among us, and be had every fourth week, on Wednesday, at eleven o'clock, forenoon.

---

* From a note in the hand of the late Rev. Dr. Prince, it appears that the "Boston News Letter, of Dec'r 16, 1736," in its account of the ordination, gives the places of residence as follows: "Chipman of Beverly; Appleton, Cambridge; Holyoke, Marblehead; Prescott and Clarke, Salem, (afterwards Danvers;) Hobby of Reading; Champney of Beverly, lower parish."

At a meeting Sept. 18, 1738.

Whereas Mr. Samuel Barton has declared himself not fully satisfied of the particular form and method of discipline in the Congregational Churches, and so is content to have no hand in the rule and discipline of this Church, but still is desirous to partake with the brethren in the ordinance of the Lord's Supper:—wherefore, Voted, that upon his open profession of repentance toward God, and faith toward our Lord Jesus Christ, and his sincere endeavors to walk agreeable to the rules of the gospel, he be admitted to the holy communion among us.

In taking leave of the ancient "Records of the First Church—1629 to 1736,"—from which we have made such copious extracts, we would observe that while careful to copy exactly the words of the original, we have generally written them according to modern orthography, excepting proper names, which we have endeavored to give as we found them, though variously spelt.

As in making these extracts for a special purpose, it was not thought necessary to note particularly their connection with other matters, or to indicate what was omitted, we now wish, in addition to the general view already given of the old records* to state more particularly the contents of the ancient Church book.

These contents, as we have seen, consist of *transcript* records and *original* records. The former take up a little more than eighteen pages, viz: the Covenant of 1629, with the preamble of 1636, and the Quaker postscript of 1660, covering the first two pages; the list of Church members to 1659, with Mr. Fisk's explanatory note, six and a half pages, and the catalogue of baptisms, from 1636 to 1659, ten pages. The original records occupy

---

* pp. 11 and 13.

nearly one hundred and forty pages, viz: the catalogue of baptisms, extended from 1659 to 1735, about forty-three pages, and the record of Church proceedings and general matters, from 1660 to 1735, about ninety-seven pages. Of these, Mr. Higginson's, from 1660 to 1695, cover nearly thirty-seven pages: Mr. Noyes's, from 1695 to 1712, fifteen closely written pages; Messrs. Noyes and Curwin's, from 1712 to 1717, twelve pages; and Mr. Fisk's, including his call and ordination, twenty pages, besides the thirteen given to his catalogues of those "entered into covenant," and those "received to communion"; but his pages average much less in amount than the rest.

It is due to the venerable old Church Book that some notice should be taken of its perilous captivity, of more than seventy years, and its final auspicious return to its native home.

We learn from the succeeding Church records, that, at a meeting of the First Church, May 21, 1811, the Pastor called the attention of the brethren to "the book containing the ancient Records of the Church, from its first establishment—in 1629 to 1736"—stating "that this book, which had been withheld from the Church by Mr. Fisk, the former pastor, when he was dismissed from that office, had remained in the care and keeping of his son, Gen. John Fisk, until his death, his father having made him promise not to give it up during his (the son's) life. ....At the time of Gen'l Fisk's death, the book was in the hands of the Rev. Mr. Bentley, who, when called upon for it, refused to give it up to the Pastor of the Church, though requested to do it by the remaining family of Gen'l Fisk. The Church therefore voted "that a Committee be appointed," consisting of "Brother Elder Beckford, Deacon Hartshorne and bro'r John Pickering, to wait on Mr.

Bentley and request him to deliver up the book to the Church." The Committee, at a subsequent meeting of the Church, reported "that Mr. Bentley, after their calling on him, had sent the book to Mr. Eben'r Putnam, one of the heirs of Gen'l Fisk, and Mr. Putnam had delivered it to the Pastor of this Church. The book being much out of binding, and in an unsafe state, the Church voted that the Pastor be requested to have it bound in a strong manner, in order to preserve it; and THAT A COPY OF THIS ANCIENT RECORD BE MADE FOR THE CHURCH, and that the Pastor take such measures as he may think proper for the preservation of the Church books."

FIRST DISCUSSION.

From the foregoing pages, it will appear how clearly the foundation, constitution, and discipline of the First Church illustrate the genuine spirit of New England Congregationalism, which is the spirit of Christian freedom; and it is important that this great fact should be kept in mind through the review which we now proceed to take of various public discussions that have arisen from time to time, within the last thirty years, in relation to this Church.

In 1832 was published a pamphlet, entitled, "Correspondence between the First Church and the Tabernacle Church, in Salem, in which the Duties of Churches are discussed, and the Rights of Conscience vindicated," with the following motto :

"How vain, then, are those, that, assuming a liberty to themselves, would yet tie all men to their tenets; conjuring all men to the trace of their steps, when it may be what is truth to them, is error to another as wise." FELLTHAM'S RESOLVES.

The occasion of this "Correspondence" may be seen from the following proceedings of the respective churches :

At a meeting of the First Church, August 27, 1831, Mrs. Martha Baker, having applied for admission to this Church, stating that she had for some time "been a member of the Tabernacle Church," but "that she had been unable to procure the usual recommendation" from that Church to this ;—a committee, consisting of brothers D. A. White and H. Devereux, was appointed, respectfully to inquire of the Tabernacle Church the reasons for "declining to recommend Mrs. Baker to our communion." An answer to the inquiry, made accord-

16

ingly by the committee, was duly received from the Tabernacle Church, containing a copy of the proceedings of that Church, Sep'r 26, 1831, on Mrs. Baker's request to "be recommended to the First Church in this town," when "it was *unanimously* voted : That this Church cannot grant Mrs. Martha Baker's request, for the reasons following, viz :

First, Because this Church cannot consistently recognize any church as a "sister church," which, in our judgment, rejects those doctrines which we feel bound to receive as the fundamental doctrines of Christianity ; and

Secondly, Because this Church cannot consent to hold fellowship with any Church which manifests an entire disregard to the *discipline* of this Church, and which by readily admitting to its communion those who have been excommunicated by us, virtually declares the disciplinary acts of this Church to be 'null and void.' "

This second charge was first discussed as printed in an appendix to the "Correspondence," and a final reply on the subject, was received from the Tabernacle Church ; when the Committee, in behalf of the First Church, addressed to the Tabernacle Church the following communication, here somewhat abridged, dated February 18, 1832, to which no reply was made :

CHRISTIAN BRETHREN,

We have duly received your reply dated the 17th of January, to our communication addressed to you on the 8th of November last, vindicating this church from your charge against it of having manifested "an entire disregard to the discipline of your church, by readily admitting to its communion those who had been excommunicated by you." Our refutation of that charge appeared to us so complete and satisfactory, that we cannot conceal our surprise at the manner in which it has been received by you. But it is not our intention here to go into any examination of your reply, having no disposition to extend this discussion unnecessarily, and finding nothing in the principles or facts stated by you, which materially affects the merits of our defence against that charge.

But the manner in which you allude to and reiterate your other charge, which you now represent as a "charge of a dereliction from the great doctrines of Christianity," has led us to think it more important than we had supposed, to give to that also a full consideration. We are the more encouraged to undertake this from your having expressed "the pleasure which you should experience on ascertaining that this, your *far weightier* charge, is equally unfounded." We may, therefore, expect your candid attention, and if you will but favor us with that, we have no doubt of being able to afford you such pleasure in the fullest degree, and also to convince you, upon serious reflection, that your charge is not less presumptuous than unwarrantable, not less inconsistent with your own character as Protestant professors, than it is injurious to ours as Christian believers.

You justly regard the charge first alleged, especially as now represented by you, to be "far weightier" than the other, for so it certainly is as to those who make the charge; but to those who think it "a very small thing to be judged of you, or by man's judgment," it is light. We differ from you no further than you do from us; and if we are to be judged as rejecting fundamental doctrines, because we adhere to the Bible alone, exclusive of human systems of divinity, you, for coupling such systems with the Bible, may be judged as "receiving for doctrines the commandments of men," and "making the word of God of none effect," through your unscriptural creeds and confessions. "Let us not, therefore, judge one another any more." If we are conscientious in our opinions, no error in our respective views of Christian doctrine can be so great as that of uncharitably judging and condemning each other. The following passage from a discourse of the amiable and learned Seed, deserves the serious attention of all who are liable to fall into this great error. "Whether a good man," says he, "who is a misbeliever in some points, without any faultiness or irregularity of will, will be damned for his *erroneous* way of thinking, may be a question with some people; but I think it admits of none, that a man will be damned for an *uncharitable* way of thinking and acting."[*] And this, you will perceive, is but a comment upon the Apostle's declaration, that although he understood all mysteries, and had all faith, and yet had not charity, he was nothing.

We beg leave, in the first place, to make a few remarks upon certain statements in your Rev. Pastor's letter communicating the vote of your church respecting Mrs. Baker. This vote appears to us to

[*] "Discourses"—Vol. 2, p. 81.

present a rule of proceeding as novel as it is extraordinary; but your Rev. Pastor states that it "is not regarded as presenting any new view of the principle on which, in relation to other churches, you have long felt it your duty to act." This representation, we think, must have proceeded from a misrecollection, or inexperience, as to the past history and affairs of your church; for so recently as since the settlement of our junior pastor, an instance has occurred of a recommendation from this church to yours, which we have always understood was received with the usual courtesy. And it is deserving of remark, that, in considering Mr. Brown's application to be recommended by you to this church, you do not appear to intimate that there was any question about recommending him, on account of the church to which he wished to become united. On the contrary, the question, at that time, seems never to have been raised. This church, certainly, during its existence of more than two hundred years, has known of no such principle, as you now set up, in its intercourse with other churches, either in receiving or granting recommendations of members who wished to transfer their connexion to or from this church. Within our own knowledge, repeated instances of this kind of Christian courtesy, both in recommending and receiving members, have taken place between this and other churches, of as high reputed orthodoxy as your church, and whose pastors are in full fellowship with your pastor. It is but a few years since, that a member of the Third Church in this town, who for some time had worshipped with us, and who requested of that church a "dismission and recommendation to the First Church," was, agreeably to his request, "unanimously recommended to the Christian watch and fellowship of the said First Church." This recommendation was signed by the present worthy pastor of the Third Church, who in so doing did but act in conformity to immemorial Christian usage, and in that spirit of "orthodoxy and charity united," which led the excellent Dr. Watts to exclaim, "I see, I feel, and am assured, that several men may be very sincere, and yet entertain notions of divinity all widely different."

Here was an example worthy of your imitation. Why should it not have been followed in the case of Mrs. Baker? We regret that your Rev. Pastor should see occasion so emphatically to state to us, that in taking a directly opposite course, there was "not the slightest hesitation or difference of opinion, on the part of the church, as to the course proper to be pursued." This would seem to indicate that you had already yielded to the influence of that exclusive spirit, which is at war with the charity of the gospel, and which we had hoped would not reach our peaceful community. How otherwise can we account for such unanimity, upon such a question, and under such circumstances? Could it have resulted from a dispassionate exercise of your reason and judgment upon the merits of the question? Could you have been thus unanimous, had you impartially examined the subject in all its important relations? Could you have wholly set at nought the claims of the First Church to your Christian courtesy? Could you have regarded as nothing its ancient foundation in Christ, its devotion to the Bible alone as the rule of faith and worship, and its uniform support of the great principles of Christian truth, freedom and charity? Could you have established a precedent so adverse to the Christian liberty of your own members, had you well considered that it is their individual right and duty, whenever conscience, enlightened by divine truth, shall require it of them, to leave your communion for such as may be more conducive to their edification? And could you have been wholly indifferent to the influence of your example upon the peace and harmony of the Christian community? We feel persuaded that had you thus dispassionately considered the subject, you would have doubted the soundness of the principle upon which you proceeded; and had you considered also that the great responsibility which rests upon us all, respects not the faith of others so much as it does our own practice, you would have chosen to err, if err you must, on the side of Christian charity and peace.

If our apprehensions of the influence of such an exclusive spirit among you be well founded, suffer us to entreat you to resist and suppress it, as the deadliest foe to the true Christian spirit. Freed from this influence, you might enjoy that divine charity, which would restrain you from charging us with a " dereliction from the great doctrines of Christianity," and might possibly be led into that free and impartial inquiry after truth, which would enable you to see those doctrines in the same light with us. For, as the venerated Baxter says, " be you never so peremptory in your opinions, you cannot resolve to hold them to the end; for light is powerful, and may change you whether you will or no; you cannot tell what that light will do which you never saw. But prejudice will make you resist the light, and make it harder for you to understand."*

"The only means by which religious knowledge can be advanced," says Bishop Lowth, "is freedom of inquiry. An opinion is not therefore false, because it contradicts received notions ; but, whether true or false, let it be submitted to a fair examination. Truth must in the end be a gainer by it, and appear with greater advantage."†

"Truth and error," says a late eloquent Baptist divine, "as they are essentially opposite in their nature, so the causes to which they are indebted for their perpetuity and triumph are not less so. Whatever retards a spirit of inquiry, is favorable to error ; whatever promotes it, to truth. But nothing, it will be acknowledged, has a greater tendency to obstruct the exercise of free inquiry, than the spirit and feeling of a party."‡

The vote of your church, containing your "weightier charge," and exhibiting the main principle upon which you refuse to recommend Mrs. Baker to the First Church, is important in a general view, and deserves from you, certainly, a fuller consideration than you appear to have given it. This principle in its operation concerns not merely the First Church and the Tabernacle Church, but other Churches also, and affects the rights of the individual members of your church, and of all churches which may be influenced by the example of yours. The subject thus becomes identified with the great cause of Christian truth and freedom, as well as with that of Christian peace and charity, and acquires an importance which could not attach to the particular question which has led to this discussion. But it did not appear to affect the character of this church so directly, or make it so incumbent upon us to reply to it, as your more specific charge of a wanton disregard to your rules of discipline.

It could not appear to us of any great consequence, as respects our Christian standing, that you should judge us to have rejected what you deem fundamental doctrines, while we were conscious of retaining all which we deem fundamental. We know that wise and good men, in all ages of the world, have differed in opinion, especially on the subject of religion, which, from the very constitution of the human mind, must always be the case, and that, while some Christians embrace certain doctrines as fundamental, others will re-

* 1 Baxter's Works, 42.   †Visitation Sermon, 1758.
‡ Robert Hall—"Terms of Communion."

ject them as erroneous, who are equally conscientious and faithful in the study of the holy Scriptures. Such differences of opinion do not necessarily bring reproach upon any party, nor need they occasion a breach of the great law of love and charity which all admit to be the fundamental law of Christianity.

Our sole object is to convince you of the truth of these great principles. We have no disposition to enter into a controversy with you upon any of the doctrines which you may be supposed to hold. On the contrary, we would strenuously maintain your right to hold and avow them, coupled only with the obligation to allow us the exercise of the same right. Why may it not be so?

Professing, as we do, to hold to the Bible as the standard of Christian faith, and to be under the same obligation to examine it for ourselves, without attaching authority to any human interpretation, it necessarily follows that we ought to admit each other's integrity in this high trust, as readily as in lower ones, and recognize each other's Christian claims accordingly. Shall we, instead of this, judge the integrity of others by comparing the result of their inquiries with that to which we have attained, and thus make our interpretation of scripture a test for trying their soundness in faith, or their claim to our charity? Is not such conduct presumptuous and essentially unchristian, and has it not ever led to animosities and dissensions, and thus prevented the genuine influence of our holy religion among men?

It must then be a common object with the enlightened friends of Christianity to remove this scandal from the church, and to promote an opposite spirit, the spirit of love and peace, which is the true badge of the disciples of Christ.

DUTY OF CHURCHES.

From the time of the primitive ages of Christianity, churches, formed professedly upon its principles, have been prone to forget the design of their institution, and the laws to which they were subject, and to manifest a spirit directly opposite to that of Christ. We therefore propose, before proceeding to consider the subject of your vote in particular reference to this church, to take a view of the duties of Christian churches in relation to each other, and in respect to the admission and recommendation of church members.

The general duty of churches has been well stated by the late Robert Hall, who applied to this subject the force of his clear and powerful mind. "The duty of churches," says he, "originates in that of the individuals of which they consist, so that when we have ascertained the sentiments and principles which ought to actuate the Christian in his private capacity, we possess the standard to which the practice of churches should be uniformly adjusted."* Here we see the obligation which rests upon all churches, not only to adhere strictly to the laws of Christ in conducting their government and discipline, but to manifest, in all their conduct and proceedings, those sentiments of justice, candor, charity, humility and good will, which the gospel so constantly enjoins upon individuals. Considering, indeed, that these virtues constitute so principal a part of the religion of Christ, and that churches are formed to promote this religion in the world, as well as for their own edification, it is peculiarly incumbent on them to exhibit a bright example of all the Christian virtues.

From the writings of the New Testament we learn the nature, duties, and mutual connexion of churches. There we find that the word church, which is of the same import as assembly or congregation, is used to signify either the whole body of believers, the universal church, or those particular societies of Christians, formed in different places, which together constituted the universal church, and sustained the same relation to Christ their common head and lawgiver. These of course were sister churches, a relation resulting from their very nature and condition. "However familiar," says the eloquent writer just referred to, "the spectacle of Christian societies, who have no fellowship or intercourse with each other, has become, he who consults the New Testament [will instantly perceive that nothing more repugnant to the dictates of inspiration, or the practice of the first and purest age, can be conceived. When we turn our eyes to the primitive times, we behold one church of Christ, and one only, in which, when new assemblies of Christians arose, they were considered, not as multiplying, but diffusing it ; not as destroying its unity, or impairing its harmony, but being fitly compacted together on the same foundation, as a mere accession to the beauty and grandeur of the whole."

The same relation still subsists among all Christian societies, or particular churches, certainly all that are formed after the primitive model, and built upon the true principles of gospel liberty. Such churches are sister churches, whether they acknowledge the connection or not. Even should they so far forget it, as to indulge in bitter

* Reasons for Christian in opposition to Party Communion.

recriminations towards each other, and even make it a point of conscience to deny that they have any Christian connection whatever ; yet it remains a fact, independent of their will, that they are sister churches, having one common Master, and subject to the same divine rules of faith and duty, and that they owe to each other the courtesy and kindness which such a relation implies.

But "if," adds the same admired writer, "amidst the infinite diversity of opinions, each society deems it necessary to render its own peculiarities the basis of union, as though the design of Christians in forming themselves into a church, were not to exhibit the great principles of the gospel, but to give publicity and effect to party distinctions ; all hope of restoring Christian harmony and unanimity must be abandoned. When churches are thus constituted, instead of enlarging the sphere of Christian charity, they become so many hostile confederacies."* What a dereliction is this of every principle of protestantism, as well as gospel liberty and peace ! Nothing can be clearer, than that receiving the Scriptures as the common standard of faith, with the acknowledged right of private judgment, involves the obligation of mutual candor and charity, in our endeavors to understand them and ascertain the truths which they reveal. "Can any man," says Dr. Doddridge, "with the least color of reason, pretend that I have a right to judge for myself, and yet punish me for using it ? That is, for doing that which he acknowledges I have a right to do. To plead for it would be a direct contradiction in terms."†

You will find in the works of this learned author, who was not less catholic than orthodox, much that is calculated to subserve the cause of Christian peace and charity. "Union of affection, amidst diversity of opinions," appears to have been his motto. In explaining the apostolic direction, "be like minded, having the same love, being of one accord, of one mind," he says, "be unanimous in affection, if you cannot be so in opinion, agree on cultivating the same love, however your judgments, yea, and in some instances your practices, may be divided." "The best of men differ, their understandings differ, various associations have been accidentally formed, and different principles have been innocently, and perhaps devoutly admitted, which, even in a course of just and sensible reasoning, must necessarily lead to different conclusions. Accordingly we find that the wis-

* Terms of Communion.   † Works, 4v. 473.

est and the best of men have pleaded the cause on either side of various questions, which to both have seemed important, without being able to produce conviction.—Let us be greatly upon our guard that we do not condemn our brethren, as having forfeited all title to the name of Christians, because their creeds or confessions of faith do not come up to the standard of our own."*

A learned contemporary author, and of the like catholic spirit with Doddridge, has also well described that kind of union, which it is the duty of churches to cultivate. "Herein it is," says he, "that true *Christian unity* does consist; not so much in uniformity of opinion as in unanimity of affection, in love and peace, in mutual charity and good will, and in all kind and friendly offices, as it becometh brethren in Jesus Christ. We are therefore exhorted as Christians, to keep, not an unity of opinion in the bond of *ignorance*, nor an unity of profession in the bond of *hypocrisy*, but an *unity of spirit in the bond of peace*."†

Another contemporary and kindred genius, the distinguished Dr. Foster, observes: "If we are contented with the Scripture rule, we may unite in affection and brotherly communion, though we cannot in opinion." "To agree in opinion is entirely out of our power; to profess alike, while we believe differently, is base and dishonest, and destructive of the most sacred obligations, and upon that account, ought never to be the matter of our choice; so that neither of these can be any part of that unity which we are bound to cultivate as a religious and moral duty; but the whole sum of it must be resolved into this, that condescension, mutual forbearance, and an harmony of mild, benevolent affections, supply the place of that uniformity of faith and profession, which is, morally speaking, impossible."‡

The learned and excellent Howe, author of "The Living Temple," speaks as follows of the wisdom of the apostolic practice upon this subject: "The case was at that time urging and important. A great and numerous party was formed of such as did nauseate the simplicity of the Christian religion, and the true design of it. All the care was, what course was most proper and suitable to preserve the rest. Counsel was not taken to this effect; let us bind them by certain devised preter-evangelical canons to things never thought to be enjoined by Christ himself, severely urge the strict and uniform

---

* Idem, 282.   †True Doctrine of the N. T. 16.
+ Discourses on Natural Religion and Social Virtue—v. 2, p. 331.

observance of them, make the terms of Christian communion straiter than he ever made them, add new rituals of our own to his institution, and cut off from us all that never so conscientiously scruple them. No; this was the practice of their enemies, and it was to narrow and weaken the too much already diminished Christian interest."

"Yea, the attempt of imposing anything upon the disciples, but what was necessary, is judged a tempting of God; a bringing the matter to a trial of skill with him, whether he could keep the church quiet, when they took so direct a course to distemper and trouble it. The prudence and piety of those unerring guides of the church, themselves under the guidance of the spirit of truth, directed them to bring the things wherein they would have Christians unite within as narrow a compass as possible, neither multiplying articles of faith, nor rites of worship. These two principles, as they were thought to answer the apostles', would fully answer our design."

"How soon did the Christian church cease to be itself: and the early vigor of primitive Christianity degenerate into insipid spiritless formality, when once it became contentious! It broke into parties, sects multiplied, animosities grew high, and the grieved spirit of love retired from it!"*

We here invite your attention to some remarks of those eminent and learned divines, Stillingfleet and Taylor, upon the duty of churches as to Christian communion, which will lead us directly to the next topic under consideration, the principles which ought to govern them in the admission of members.

"What charter," says bishop Stillingfleet, "hath Christ given the church to bind men up to, more than himself hath done? Or to exclude those from her society who may be admitted into heaven? Will Christ ever thank men at the great day for keeping such out from communion with his church? The grand commission the apostles were sent out with, was only *to teach what Christ had commanded them.* Not the least intimation of any 'power given them to impose or require anything beyond what himself had spoken, or they were directed to by the immediate guidance of the spirit of God."†

"As for particular churches," says bishop Taylor, "they are bound to allow communion to all those that profess the same faith upon

---

* Discourse on Union among Protestants.   † Irenicum.

132

which the apostles did give communion. To make the way to heaven straighter than God made it, or to deny to communicate with those whom God will vouchsafe to be united, and to refuse our charity to those who have the same faith, because they have not all our opinions, and believe not every thing necessary which we overvalue, is impious and schismatical, it infers tyranny on one part, and persuades and tempts to uncharitableness and animosities on both."

Few churches that have framed bodies of confession and articles, will endure any person that is not of the same confession; which is a plain demonstration that such bodies of confession and articles do much hurt, by becoming instruments of separating and dividing communions, and making unnecessary or uncertain propositions a certain means of schism and disunion."*

TERMS OF CHRISTIAN COMMUNION.

Thus we are guided to the principles which determine the duty of churches in the admission of members. All Christians belonging to the same place where a particular church is formed, or to the same congregation of worshippers, have a right to participate in the ordinances and all the privileges of the gospel, "upon professing the same faith on which the apostles did give communion." Nothing more in the way of doctrines to be believed, or experiences to be related, than Christ and his apostles made necessary, can now be lawfully required as a condition of Christian communion. These principles result from the very nature and design of a Christian church; which is not a mere voluntary society, empowered to establish whatever laws it may choose, but a community which is subject to the authority and laws of Christ only, and has no right to make rules which vary his terms of communion, or in any respect abridge the privileges granted by him to his disciples and followers.

How widely, then, must those churches depart from the line of their duty, which require assent to human creeds, containing abstruse, perhaps incomprehensible, articles of faith as a necessary condition of communion; more especially, if they hold their members to continued adherence to such articles, when by further light from God's word they feel bound to reject them! Is not this making their own articles paramount to the Scriptures, and themselves masters, claiming that very allegiance from the consciences of their brethren which

*Liberty of Prophesying.

is due to Christ alone, who "is the head of the body, the church," and in all things to "have the pre eminence?"

The principles here stated, you will find to be fully sustained by the old standard orthodox writers on church government, who yet could not be expected to view the subject in all its primitive simplicity.

Dr. Owen, who was called by one of the old American divines, "The Atlas of Congregationalism," says, "No warrant from the light of nature, or from the laws of men, or their own voluntary confederation, can enable any to constitute a church society, unless they do all things expressly in obedience unto the authority of Christ; for his church is his kingdom, his house, which none can constitute or build but himself. Wherefore it is necessary that the power of admission into, and exclusion from the church, doth arise from his grant and institution."

"The power of rule in the church, then, is nothing but a *right to yield obedience* unto the commands of Christ."*

John Cotton, who stood at the head of the early divines of Massachusetts, in his "Doctrine of a Church and its Government," says "It is not in the hand of the church to make laws or ordinances, to choose officers or members, to administer sacraments or ordinances, or any part of worship or government, of their own heads, but to receive all as from the hand of Christ, and to dispense all according to the will of Christ, revealed in his word."†

Thomas Hooker, another of the learned fathers of New England, in his "Survey of Church Discipline," says, "Christ, the king of his church, and master of his house, he only in reason can make laws that are authentic for the government thereof.—It is not left in the power of persons, officers, churches, nor all states in the world, to add or diminish or alter anything in the least measure."‡

"Christ himself, the institutor and maker of his church," says Richard Baxter, "hath made the terms of essential catholic union : and we have nothing to do herein but to find out what are the terms that he hath made, and not to inquire what any men since have made or added, as being not authorized thereto."‖

"The church of Christ," says the learned Dr. Gale, "is that which

---

* True Nature of a Gospel Church, &c. p. 199.
† p. 9. ‡ p. 5. ‖ Works, v. 4, 650.

is founded according to the direction and model by him laid down; that, therefore, which is not so founded, but upon principles and regulations laid down by men, is not a church of Christ, but of men. To pretend to constitute a church by mutual agreement, as some have done, upon any principles which are not in Scripture made and declared to be of the foundation of a Christian church, and to receive and exclude members according as they conform to the foundation the church is built upon, is no other than setting up an illegal judicature, and judging the members of Christ's body without any just authority."*

We might refer to many others who maintain the same principles, but shall content ourselves with a single quotation from the works of bishop Warburton, who, having stated that "the terms of salvation, as they are delivered in the gospel, are faith in Christ and repentance towards God," proceeds to observe, that "to change the fundamental laws of Christ's spiritual kingdom, where he is the only lawgiver, is an offence of the highest nature, as not only implying simple disobedience, but usurpation likewise. A church acting with this spirit, not only throws off subjection, but assumes the sovereignty."†

Let us now inquire what were the terms, or professions of faith, upon which Christ and his apostles received those who would become his followers and members of his church. This can be ascertained only from the New Testament. And what are the creeds and confessions of faith which we find there? What was that which drew from our Lord the solemn declaration to Peter, as to the foundation of his church? This only, "Thou art the Christ, the son of the living God." What said Martha, in answer to our Lord's question, "Believest thou this?" "Yea, Lord, I believe that thou art the Christ, the son of God, which should come into the world." What was the faith declared by John in his gospel, as the end for which the miracles of our blessed saviour were wrought? "These are written that ye might believe that Jesus is the son of God, and that believing ye might have life through his name." What was the sum of Peter's first preaching, upon which were added to the church about three thousand souls? "Therefore, let all the house of Israel know assuredly that God hath made that same Jesus, whom ye have crucified, both Lord and Christ." What was the profession upon

---

* Gale's Sermons, 3, 153.   † Works, 4to ed. 5 v. 173.

which Philip baptized the Eunuch? "I believe that Jesus Christ is the son of God." And what was the faith upon which Paul promised salvation? "If thou shalt confess with thy mouth the Lord Jesus, and believe in thy heart that God raised him from the dead, thou shalt be saved." What says the beloved disciple of our Lord? "Whosoever believeth that Jesus is the Christ, is born of God." And again, "Whosoever shall confess that Jesus is the son of God, God dwelleth in him and he in God." "To us, says the great apostle of the Gentiles, there is but one God, the Father, of whom are all things, and we in him; and one Lord, Jesus Christ, by whom are all things, and we by him."

Such are the true Scripture creeds. Such were the terms upon which the apostles received men to communion, as members of Christ's church, subjects of his kingdom, and entitled to all the privileges of the gospel dispensation for attaining eternal life through faith and repentance. Such, too, for some time after the apostles' days, continued to be the terms of admission into Christ's church. " Whoever through the powerful operation of divine truth, had been brought to profess a faith in Christ as the Saviour of the human race, although they might in other respects be uninformed, and various errors might still remain to be rooted out of their minds, were yet baptized, and admitted into the fellowship of Christ's kingdom."*

"If," says bishop Taylor, " we have found out what foundation Christ and his apostles did lay, that is, what body and system of articles simply necessary they taught and required of us to believe, we need not, we cannot enlarge that system or collection.......The articles of necessary belief to all, (which are the only foundation,) they cannot be several in several ages and to several persons."†

It was by departing from this foundation principle, and imposing upon Christians other and abstruser articles of belief than those required in the gospel, that the system of ecclesiastical tyranny commenced, which became intolerable under the Roman pontiffs, and roused the spirit of Luther and others, who assailed it with the Bible and their own reason as their mighty weapons. Appealing to the pure word of God, as their guide in matters of faith, and asserting the right to a free exercise of their judgment in ascertaining its meaning, their arguments were irresistible. Had all these reform-

* Mosheim's Commentaries by Vidal, 1, 242.   † Liberty of Prophesying.

ers and their followers continued constant to their first principles, we might have seen the church restored to the purity of its primitive days. But some of those who were most resolute in breaking from the papal tyranny, brought away their chains to fasten them upon brother reformers, who would not stop in the career of improvement precisely where they judged proper. Hence succeeded, among the half reformed churches themselves, fresh impositions, persecutions, and struggles.

Should not these lamentable delusions teach all such half-reformed churches the value of Christian freedom, and the importance of returning to the gospel terms of communion? Much may be found in the conduct and sentiments of our Puritan ancestors to animate those churches of the present day which most need reformation, thus to retrace their steps. The Puritan fathers contended against the impositions of the English hierarchy with the same weapons which had been successfully wielded against the tyranny of the Romish church. They urged the duty of advancing the reformation, of conforming the church to Scripture, and bringing it back to apostolic purity.

Such was the spirit so nobly manifested by Robinson, when, on parting with those of his congregation in Holland who were about transplanting themselves to America, he solemnly charged them to be always ready to receive whatever further truth should be made known to them; for he was verily persuaded the Lord had more truth to break forth out of his holy word. "For my part," he adds, "I cannot sufficiently bewail the condition of the reformed churches, who are come to a period in religion, and will go at present no further than the instruments of their reformation. I beseech you to remember, it is an article of your church covenant, that you be ready to receive whatever truth shall be made known to you from the written word of God. But I must here withal exhort you to take heed what you receive as truth; examine it, consider it, and compare it with other scriptures of truth, before you receive it; for it is not possible the Christian world should come so lately out of such antichristian darkness, and that perfection of knowledge should break forth at once."[*]

The same spirit of Christian freedom and progress actuated our forefathers, and breathes through the covenants adopted by the churches first gathered in Massachusetts as well as that of Mr.

* Neale's Hist. of the Puritans, 2, 146.   † p. 60.

137

Robinson's church, settled in Plymouth. The famous Mr. Cotton, in his work before referred to, bears witness to this as well as the covenants themselves. "Nor do we," says he, "pinch upon any godly man's conscience in point of covenant, in case he be willing to profess his subjection to Christ in his church, according to the order of the gospel. Nor do we limit him to our own way of the order of the gospel, but as it shall be cleared and approved to his own conscience."* The covenant adopted by the first church in Boston, simply engaged them to walk in all their ways, "according to the rule of the gospel, and in all sincere conformity to his holy ordinances, and in mutual love and respect to each other, as God shall give us grace." The church in Charlestown, and various others, had the same simple covenant. That of the First Church in Salem was alike practical and free from all disputed dogmas in theology; besides containing some distinguishing principles which deserve particular notice. It engaged them to walk together in all the ways of God, "according as he is pleased to reveal himself to us in his blessed word of truth;" "to reject all contrary ways, canons, and constitutions of men;" and "to study the advancement of the gospel in all truth and peace." These principles were worthy of the founders of the First Church. Morton, in his New England's Memorial, says furthermore of this covenant, what accords with the general statement of Mr. Cotton, that "it was acknowledged only as a direction pointing unto that faith and covenant contained in the holy Scripture, and therefore no man was confined unto that form of words, but only to the substance, end, and scope of the matter contained therein." Thus liberal and consistently protestant has the First Church remained from its foundation to the present day.

May not some of our churches be justly charged with a dereliction of protestant principles? Is it not desirable that they should return to them and recover the foundation upon which the first churches of New England were built? Would not this redound to the honor of Christianity and advance its influence in the world? Together with the consideration of these questions, we would commend to your special attention the sentiments of two eminent advocates of Christian liberty, the one in behalf of protestants against the Romish church, the other of dissenters from the Church of England.

---

* p. 60.

18

"If," says the incomparable Chillingworth, as archbishop Tillotson styles him, "all men would believe the Scripture, and, freeing themselves from prejudice and passion, would endeavor to find the true sense of it, and live according to it, and require no more of others but to do so; nor denying their communion to any that do so; who doth not see, that as all necessary truths are plainly and evidently set down in Scripture, there would of necessity be among all men, in all things necessary, unity of communion, and charity, and mutual toleration.......This presumptuous imposing of the senses of men upon the words of God, the special senses of men upon the general words of God, and laying them upon men's consciences together. This vain conceit that we can speak of the things of God, better than in the words of God; this deifying our own interpretations and enforcing them upon others; this restraining of the word of God from that latitude and generality, and the understandings of men from that liberty, wherein Christ and the apostles left them, is, and hath been, the only fountain of all the schisms of the church, and that which makes them immortal."*

Dr. Chandler, the able defender of Christianity, as well as of religious liberty, speaks; as follows: "In matters of religion, I own no human authority. In these I submit only to the most high God. Him only I call and reverence as the father of my faith. I have but one Lord, even Christ. I acknowledge no divinely authorized and inspired teachers, but the apostles; nor will yield my conscience or judgment to be determined by the dictates of any mortal men. The Scriptures I receive as a divine revelation. By these I humbly endeavor to form my own sentiments of Christianity. All who receive these as the rule of their faith, and live by them as the rule of their morals, I own so far as the sound members of Christ's body; I embrace them as my brethren, I will gladly communicate with them, and I will never debar them from my communion. And this I declare, without exception of any denomination or party of Christians whatsoever, or whatever be the external disadvantages they are under, or opprobrious names that are given them. Hard names and party reproaches terrify me not. Without this latitude of principle, I can see no possible end to the divisions of the church; and if I should mark or avoid any Christians who thus adhere to the only rule of

---

* Works, fol. ed. 131.

Christianity, I transgress this apostolical canon, and am myself chargeable with a schismatical and unchristian spirit."*

An impartial attention to the views here presented could hardly fail to lead you to a correct judgment on the subject of Christian communion, and also to the proper course to be pursued by a church in relation to members who may ask a recommendation to some other church. Various causes, besides removal from the neighborhood of the church, may exist to prevent their edification in that church. It then becomes their duty to seek it elsewhere, for edification is the principal end of church communion; and it is for them to judge where they may hope to find it. The church, of which they take leave, can have no responsibility in the decision of this question, but only as to the truth of the recommendation required to be given; and it is not called upon to recommend the church to which they desire to go. Whatever difference of opinion, therefore, may exist between them and their brethren, as to the doctrines of the church whose communion they prefer, they are alike entitled to the recommendation which their Christian character deserves. This difference of opinion may be the very reason which justifies their removing from the Church; of course it cannot justify the Church in attempting to prevent it by withholding what would otherwise be their acknowledged right.

"If my own conscience," says the learned Matthew Henry, "be not satisfied in the lawfulness of any terms of communion imposed, as far as I fall under that imposition, I may justify a separation from them and a joining with other churches, where I may be freed from that imposition."†

"Whereas," says Dr. Owen, "the principal end of all particular churches is edification, there may be many just and sufficient reasons why a person may remove himself from the constant communion of one church unto that of another. And of these reasons he himself is judge, on whom it is incumbent to take care of his own edification above all other things. Nor ought the church to deny unto any such persons their liberty desired peaceably and according unto order."‡

In thus considering the duty of particular churches, we have en-

---

* Case of Subscription, p. 39. † Henry's Works, p 663.
‡ True Nature of a Gospel Church, &c., p. 225.

deavored to confine ourselves to such views as appeared best calculated to lead you to reconsider your vote respecting Mrs. Baker's application, and return to the ancient practice in such cases, and to the true principles of Christian freedom.

Here arises a natural inquiry, why these great principles, sustained and illustrated, as we have seen, by the most learned and venerated protestant writers, as well as enforced by the Bible itself, should not have become more completely established in this land of boasted light and liberty. Various reasons might be assigned, which we cannot now consider ; but there is one source of error and delusion on this subject, to which we would call your particular attention.

Mistaken ideas attached to certain terms used in Scripture, of which Heresy and Schism are perhaps the most remarkable, appear to have been among the principal obstacles to the enjoyment and progress of Christian freedom and charity. The distortion of these terms from their scriptural meaning, has led many pious Christians to visit with all the persecution in their power, the sincere opinions of other Christians equally pious as themselves, believing, doubtless, that they were doing God service while they were committing the very offence which they wished to punish. It cannot then be unseasonable here to inquire particularly into the true import of the words Heresy and Schism, as used in Scripture, which, in the judgment of the most learned, of all denominations, are now considered as having no reference to the belief and profession of conscientious opinions, or a peaceable separation from any church communion, but to pravities of the will, and actions tending to strife and divisions in the church.

The excellent Dr. Campbell, a Scotch divine, and Principal of Aberdeen College, in the Dissertations prefixed to his Translation of the Four Gospels, has critically and fully examined the scriptural meaning of Schism and Heresy. As to the first, he observes, that though in the original Greek the word frequently occurs in the New Testament, it has but once been rendered 'schism' by our translators, yet its frequent "use among theologians has made it a kind of technical term in relation to ecclesiastical matters, and the way it has been bandied, as a term of ignominy, from sect to sect reciprocally, makes it a matter of some consequence to ascertain the genuine meaning it bears in holy writ."

Speaking of Saint Paul's use of this term, in his first epistle to the Corinthians, Dr. Campbell says, "In order to obtain a proper i̇ ci̇ of what is meant by a breach or schism in this application, we must form a just notion of that which constituted the union whereof the schism was a violation. Now the great and powerful cement, which united the souls of Christians, was their mutual love. This had been declared by their master to be the distinguishing badge of their profession. As this, therefore, is the great criterion of the Christian character, and the foundation of the Christian unity, whatever alienates the affections of Christians from one another, is manifestly subversive of both, and may consequently, with the greatest truth and energy, be denominated schism."

Dr. Campbell concludes his observations on the words schism and heresy, as follows : " How much soever of a schismatical or heretical spirit, in the apostolic sense of the terms, may have contributed to the formation of the different sects into which the Christian world is at present divided ; no person who, in the spirit of candor and charity, adheres to that, which, to the best of his judgment, is right, though, in this opinion, he should be mistaken, is, in the scriptural sense, either schismatical or heretic ; and that he, on the contrary, whatever sect he belongs to, is more entitled to these odious appellations, who is most apt to throw the imputation upon others. Both terms, for they denote only different degrees of the same bad quality, always indicate a disposition and practice unfriendly to peace, harmony, and love."

"That is schism," says the learned commentator, Matthew Henry, "which breaks or slackens the bond by which the members are knit together. Now, that bond is not an act of uniformity in point of communion in the same modes and ceremonies, but true love and charity in point of affection. It is charity which is the 'bond of perfectness ;' it is 'the unity of the spirit,' which is the 'bond of peace ;' and schism is that which breaks this bond."*

John Wesley, founder of the Methodists, says that schism in Scripture means "not a separation from the church, but uncharitable divisions in it. The indulging any unkind temper towards our fellow Christians, is the true scriptural schism.—So wonderfully," adds he, " have later ages distorted the words 'heresy' and 'schism'

* Works, p. 663.

142

from their scriptural meaning. Heresy is not in all the Bible taken for an error in fundamentals, or in any thing else. Therefore, both heresy and schism, in the modern sense of the words, are sins that the Scripture knows nothing of."*

"The spirit of Truth," says John Newton, "produces unity. The spirit of division is heresy. And the man who fiercely stickles for opinions of his own, who acts contrary to the peaceable, forbearing, humble spirit of the gospel, who affects to form a party, and to be thought considerable in it, is so far a heretic."†

Chillingworth, in the preface to his works, declares that "he who believes the Scripture sincerely, and endeavors to believe it in the true sense, cannot possibly be a heretic."

Milton, in his 'Treatise on Civil Power in Ecclesiastical Causes,' says, "Seeing that no man, no synod, no session of men, though called the church, can judge definitely the sense of Scripture to another man's conscience, which is well known to be a general maxim of the protestant religion, it follows plainly, that he who holds in religion that belief, or those opinions, which to his conscience and utmost understanding appear with most evidence or probability in the Scripture, though to others he seem erroneous, can no more be justly censured for a heretic than his censurers, who do but the same thing themselves, while they censure him for so doing. For ask them, or any protestant, which hath most authority, the Church or the Scripture? They will answer, doubtless, the Scripture; and what hath most authority, that no doubt but they will confess is to be followed. He, then, who to his best apprehension follows the Scripture, though against any point of doctrine by the whole church received, is not the heretic, but he who follows the church against his conscience and persuasion, grounded on Scripture."

Bishop Taylor has many excellent remarks on this subject, in his work before referred to. "Heresy," says he, "is not an error of the understanding, but an error of the will.—If a man mingles not a vice with his opinion, if he be innocent in his life, though deceived in his doctrine, his error is his misery, not his crime. A good man that believes what according to his light, and upon the use of his moral industry he thinks true, whether he hits upon the right or not, because he hath a mind desirous of truth, and prepared to believe

* Works, vol. 10, p. 238.   † Works, vol. 3, p. 175.

every truth, is therefore acceptable to God.—The name 'heretic' is made a bugbear to affright people from their belief, or to discountenance the persons of men, and disrepute them, that their schools may be empty and their disciples few."

Very similar to this last remark is the observation, with which the "ever memorable Hales," so called for his singular piety and learning, introduces his Tract on Schism. "Heresy and schism," says he, "as they are in common use, are two theological scarecrows, which they, who uphold a party in religion, use to fright away such, as making inquiry into it, are ready to relinquish and oppose it, if it appear either erroneous or suspicious."*

"Deluded people!" exclaims Archbishop Tillotson, "who do not consider that the greatest heresy in the world is a wicked life, because it is so directly and fundamentally opposite to the whole design of the Christian faith and religion ; and who do not consider that God will sooner forgive a man a hundred defects of his understanding, than one fault of his will."†

So also Archbishop Sharp declares that "none but a wicked person" can be a heretic. "He is not a heretic," says this eminent prelate in his discourse on Heresy, "however he may be mistaken in matters of religion, who holds to the foundation of the Christian faith, and means honestly, and endeavors to inform himself as well as he can.—It is the want of honesty and virtue, it is vice and sin, it is pride or ambition, or envy or discontent ; it is the love of the world, and the desire of serving some secular interest ; these are the things that make an heretic."

We shall close these brief extracts with the venerated names of Owen and Baxter, the one upon Heresy, including also an admirable sentiment from Salvian, and the other upon Schism, such schism as one church may be guilty of towards another.

" No judge of heresy," says Dr. Owen, "since the apostles' days, but hath been obnoxious to error in that judgment ; and those who have been forwardest to assume a judicature, and power of discerning between truth and error, so far as to have others regulated thereby, have erred most foully.—Ignorance of men's invincible prejudices, of their convictions, strong persuasions, desires, aims, hopes, fears, inducements ; sensibleness of our own infirmities, failings,

---

* Works, vol. 1, p. 125.   † Works, vol. 1, p. 316.

misapprehensions, darkness, knowing but in part, should work in us
a charitable opinion of poor erring creatures, who do it, perhaps,
with as upright sincere hearts and affections as some enjoy truth."

"How tender is Salvian in his judgment of the Arians! They are,
says he, heretics, but know it not; heretics to us, but not to themselves. Nay, they think themselves so catholic, that they judge us
to be heretics. What they are to us, that we are to them. They
err, but with a good mind; and for this cause God shows mercy towards them."*

"It is a greater schism," says Baxter, "when churches do not
only separate from each other causelessly, but also *unchurch* each
other, and endeavor to cut off each other from the church universal,
by denying each other to be true churches of Christ."†

Thus we see that the guilt of heresy and schism, in the scriptural
sense of the terms, consists in a violation of Christian unity, peace,
and charity, and never in mere errors of opinion.

"THE FUNDAMENTAL DOCTRINES OF CHRISTIANITY."

In considering more particularly your "far weightier charge" against
this church, two leading inquiries are suggested by it; first, as to
the fact which you suppose; secondly, as to the principle you assume upon the supposition of it.

In the first place, how do you ascertain the fact, and form your
judgment that this church rejects those doctrines, which you receive
as fundamental? What are those doctrines? Have you ever ascertained and designated them? Where can a complete list of them be
found? You give us no intimations as to what they are, or whether
you have ever settled this question for yourselves. Yet if you are so
confident that there are certain particular doctrines, which are fundamental, essential to be believed by all Christians, as to feel authorized to charge us with rejecting them, is it not of the highest importance, on your own account, that you should be able to state precisely what they are? Unless you have it in your power to do this, how
can you be satisfied that your own faith is sufficient to make you
Christians? For, should you fail of a belief in any one of these fundamental, essential doctrines, your faith would be as clearly insufficient, as if you failed in regard to the whole; otherwise they could
not all be fundamental. Where, then, we ask, are to be found desig-

* Sermons and Tracts, p. 227.　　　† Works, vol. 1, p. 292.

nated, all the particular doctrines, which, and which alone, are essentially necessary to be believed by every man, in order to his being a Christian?

Without a complete list of your fundamental doctrines, in what manner do you form your judgment whether, and how far, this church rejects them; and how are we to comprehend the nature and extent of your judgment; what it includes, and whether it extends to all the doctrines which you receive as fundamental, or to a part only, and if to a part only, to what part? We look for satisfaction into the printed Articles and Covenant of your church; but we look in vain. Here we find no enumeration of particular doctrines, nor any distinction made between those which are, and those which are not fundamental. So far then from being prepared to judge us in respect to fundamental doctrines, your church, it seems, has not taken care to determine, for its own members, what particular doctrines are to be received as fundamental, all-important as this inquiry must be to them.

It may be said, indeed, that in the articles and covenant referred to, you declare your firm belief in the Christian religion as revealed in the Scriptures, and that such a belief, embracing all the doctrines of Christianity, whether fundamental or not, makes it unnecessary to discriminate between them, or to ascertain precisely what are, and what are not fundamental. Be it so; we also have this firm belief, and hold all the doctrines embraced by it. On this ground, therefore, no difficulty could arise between us about fundamental doctrines. We should rejoice to find you resting upon this safe and solid ground; the ground which was taken by the First Church at its foundation, and which has been maintained with constancy to the present moment. Here we should meet as sister churches, and Christian brethren, receiving the doctrines of Christianity from the same divine source, and seeking alike for truth under the guidance of conscience and by the light of our own minds, as God should enable us to understand the Scriptures.

From this ground you must have departed, before you could find occasion for any such charge as you have brought against this church. How has this happened? The same articles and covenant will show. In "declaring your firm belief of the Christian religion, as revealed in the Scriptures," you add, "and of such a view of it, substantially, as the Westminster Catechism exhibits." Here, indeed, we cannot follow you. This, we think, is to view the Scriptures through a dark and distorting medium. We had rather behold them in their own original and heavenly light.

But let us see whether the Westminster Catechism, this additional guide of your faith, will lead us to a view of the fundamental doctrines, which you charge this church with rejecting. Among the many profound and intricate propositions and articles of faith contained in the Westminster Catechism, we cannot learn, which you receive as fundamental, or whether you receive any of them as fundamental, or otherwise, in the sense or in the terms in which they are expressed. For the framers of your church covenant thought it fit that you should be bound only to adopt them "substantially;" forgetting, probably, that President Clap, the arbiter of orthodoxy in former days, ranked among the signs of heresy a disposition, "to consent to the substance of our catechism and confession, without rigorously insisting upon every article and doctrine in it." Be this as it may, if by this latitude of construction you are at liberty to regard nothing as of substance in them, but truth, this church could not refuse thus far to adopt them, however it might insist upon regarding the Scriptures alone as authority for deciding what is Christian truth, whether contained in those articles, or any other human writings.

Thus we receive, equally with you, the holy Scriptures and all the doctrines which they contain, and, as we humbly hope, endeavor to ascertain their true meaning, in the best manner we can. For this purpose, we would avail ourselves of all the light to be obtained from the works as well as the word of God, from the instructions of human teachers, and the writings of learned and pious men ; rejecting nothing, not even the Westminster Catechism, so far as it contains what is true and useful.

As a church we reject no system of doctrines, every member being at liberty to inquire and judge for himself; so that even those who would go further than you do, and with President Clap adopt all the articles and doctrines of that catechism, might become members with us, without being called upon to receive or reject any thing in repugnance to their principles. They might, in any manner they should choose, make known their belief in those articles, but a profession of belief in them, or any humanly devised articles of faith, could not be required by us, consistently with that supreme regard which we feel bound to pay to the revealed will of God.

Herein appears to consist the main difference, upon this point, between your church and the First Church; you require, as a necessary term of communion, a declaration of belief in "such a view of the Christian religion substantially, as the Westminster Catechism exhibits," while this church requires, in such a case, no act whatever, in relation to that catechism or any similar system of doctrines; and this omission, we presume, is the evidence upon which you charge this church with having rejected those doctrines, which you feel bound to receive as the fundamental doctrines of Christianity.

When we shall have more fully stated to you the reasons why we cannot, in any form, either yield or require assent to the articles of the Westminster Catechism, or any human articles of faith, you will be satisfied, we trust, that the omission to do this furnishes no evidence that we reject any of the Christian doctrines. Had this church, indeed, no express form of a confession of faith and covenant, you would not be justified in drawing such an inference from the fact. It is explicitly laid down in the Platform, as you know, as well as by Dr. Owen and others, that a church may express these, " by their constant practice in coming together for the public worship of God, and by their religious subjection to the ordinances of God there."* Of course nothing can be inferred, as to the doctrines of any church, from its not requiring subscription, or assent, to articles like those of the Westminster Catechism.

Here we think it proper to remark, that we would not be understood as intimating that there are not now, probably, as important differences of opinion on religious subjects between the members of your church and the members of this, as there usually have been between their respective predecessors. We know, indeed, that among members of the same church different views will be entertained upon important points; still more must this be expected of those belonging to different churches, whose religious opinions have been formed under very different influences and associations. But is it not probable, that these differences of opinion appear to be much greater than they really are? We are all apt to confound actual belief with the manner of expressing or manifesting it, the internal assent of the mind with the external assent of words or forms; and, what is still more deceptive, we too often look at the opinions of those who differ from us, through the distorting medium of party names. Could we

---

* Platform of Church Discipline, ch. 4.

see, as with the eye of omniscience, each other's faith, as it really exists in the mind, and the various circumstances under which it has grown up, we should doubtless find, not only that the differences in our faith are less important than we had imagined, but that these, whatever they may be, call for the exercise of mutual charity and tenderness, rather than repulsive coldness, or bitter anathemas.

We would also remark that we are not so sanguine as to indulge the hope that your church, with its strong prepossessions respecting us, can think it agreeable or conducive to edification, to have an interchange of religious services, or to hold any confidential intercourse with this church; but our hope and prayer is, that both churches may yet cultivate the genuine spirit of Christian charity, study the things which make for peace, and endeavor not to think of ourselves more highly than we ought to think, but to think soberly, according as God has dealt to each the measure of faith. With such a spirit, we should be in no danger of unchristian alienations, nor be led to apprehend that there is an insurmountable barrier between us, or a great gulf fixed, so that none who would, can pass from one to the other.

In proceeding to address you further on the subject of human tests in religion, our difficulty is not in finding able and eloquent advocates of Christian liberty among the authors whom you revere, and would therefore listen to with interest, but in selecting the most instructive from the great number of those who present themselves to our choice. The general view which we take of the subject may be presented in the words of the late eminent Adam Clarke. "In every question," he says, "which involves the eternal interests of man, the holy Scriptures must be appealed to in union with reason, their great commentator. He who forms his creed or confession of faith without these, may believe anything or nothing, as the cunning of others, or his own caprices may dictate. Human creeds and confessions of faith have been often put in the place of the Bible, to the disgrace of revelation and reason. Let those go away; let these be retained, whatever be the consequence."*

In justifying this church, even to your satisfaction, for taking this ground, and wholly discarding human creeds as tests of Christian faith or character, it will not be necessary to prove that the Bible alone is the proper rule of faith to all Christians. This, you know,

---

* Commentary on the New Testament, last page.

has been done a thousand times, and will not now be questioned, however it may be disregarded. The Bible, and the Bible only, has all the requisites of a complete rule of Christian faith and practice. It has the authority of such a rule, even that of God himself; it is consequently worthy of our entire confidence ; it is unchangeable, no power on earth can alter it; it is universal, and accessible to all ; it is plain, and intelligible to all ; and it contains all things necessary to be known or believed in order to salvation, for it contains the whole of Christianity. All, too, have the power to use this rule, who are endowed with reason, which, with the aid and direction of conscience, is to all a sufficient power.

Dr. Gale, eminent among the English dissenters for his learning and piety, and who, as his biographer informs us, "embraced with sincerity and faithfulness the doctrine of the Trinity," has a series of discourses on this subject,* all of which deserve your attention. We can only glance at some of the views presented by him. Speaking of all impositions upon conscience as being of the true spirit of popery, he says : " How happy had it been for the Christian world, if this spirit had been confined to the papists. Would to God that the worst of all their doctrines and practices had been truly as much abhorred by all protestants, as the name of popery has been ; then the Reformation would not have been almost only nominal, and rested in transferring this unjust authority from one set of men to another. Let us consider the great evil and wickedness of assuming or submitting to any other authority in religious matters but Christ alone ; for this is not at all less wicked than absurd.—For any to assume a power of directing the consciences of other men, not leaving them to the Scriptures alone, is declaring the Scriptures to be defective and insufficient for that purpose ; and consequently that our Lord, who has left us only the Scriptures, did not know what was sufficient and necessary for us, and has given us a law, the wants and defects of which were to be supplied by some of his own wiser disciples and followers."

"I might, in several other particulars, show the great wickedness they are guilty of, who take upon them to domineer over and prescribe to the consciences of men. They rob God of his just dominion, he alone having the rights they claim. They impeach his justice, in not acquainting us with the doctrines we ought to believe.

* From Matth. xxiii, 8, 9, 10.

and the laws we ought to observe. They set themselves up as more capable to exercise that dominion than God or Christ, and usurp that authority over others, which is expressly forbidden to be exercised by any Christians, who have a strict charge not to lord it over God's heritage. Therefore, all imposers on men's consciences are guilty of rebellion against God and Christ."

"Away, then, with all human forms and compositions; with all decrees and determinations of councils and synods; with all confessions and subscriptions; with all interpretations and pretended scripture consequences; away with all the inventions, agreements, and declarations of men; and let every pious Christian embrace and subscribe only that most valuable form of sound words contained in the Scriptures, which are the word of God, and able to make men wise unto salvation."*

We next invite your attention to some passages from the works of two other eminent trinitarian divines, very dissimilar, however, in some respects; we allude to Bishop Warburton, and the noble-minded Baxter, who might have been a bishop if he would. They both give us striking views of the absurdity and evil consequences of departing from the Scripture rule of faith. "To claim rule or mastery in matters of religion," says Warburton, "on mere human authority, shows so much impudence; and to acknowledge the claim, so egregious folly; that one could hardly conceive any man, who had been 'delivered from the bondage of corruption, into the glorious liberty of the children of God,' should be in danger either of assuming it himself, or of submitting to it when assumed by others."

"But the government of God's church under the gospel, not being administered, as under the law, in person, but by a written rule; the ministers of the word, under pretence of interpreting it, took occasion to introduce their own authority; and on that, by insensible degrees, a very wicked usurpation. The business of interpreting was at first modestly assumed, as a mere act of charity, to assist the brethren in the study of God's word. The pretence for the exercise of this office was the obscurities in sacred Scripture. Unhappily it was not understood, that the very obscurities themselves were a sufficient evidence that the subject of them could never be matter of faith necessary to salvation. What perhaps contributed to obstruct so obvious a truth was the great privileges ascribed to Christian

* Sermons, v. 1, p. 100.

faith. So that men became more solicitous to have it large and full, than to have it pure and perfect."

" Call no man Father upon the earth, for one is your Father who is in Heaven ; neither be ye called masters, for one is your master even Christ. These words plainly imply, that whoever requires religious obedience, or a right over conscience, by his own authority, is a usurper in another's jurisdiction ; and whoever pays obedience to such a claim, is a rebel to his lawful master."*

Baxter, speaking of "the sin and danger of making too much necessary to church union and communion," says : " Addition to Christ's terms is very perilous as well as diminution ; when men will deny either church entrance or communion to any that Christ would have received, because they come not up to certain terms which they, or such as they, devise. And though they think that Christ giveth them power to do thus, or that reason or necessity justifieth them, their error will not make them guiltless. Imputing their error to Christ untruly is no small aggravation of the sin. Nor is it a small fault to usurp a power proper to Christ ; to make themselves lawgivers to his church without any authority given them by him; their ministry is another work. And it is dangerous pride to think themselves great enough, wise enough, and good enough to come after Christ and to amend his work, and to do it better than he hath done."†

" The rule that all must agree in must be made by one that is above all, and whose authority is acknowledged by all. Never will the church have full unity till the Scripture sufficiency be more generally acknowledged. You complain of many opinions and ways, and many you will still have, till the one rule, the Scripture, be the standard of our religion."‡

In pursuing the subject, this fearless advocate of the authority and sufficiency of Scripture, imputes the introduction and multiplication of human creeds among Christians to the artifices of their great spiritual enemy ; who, as he proceeds to observe in the style of his day, " will needs be a spirit of zeal in the church ; and he will so overdo against heretics, that he persuades them they must enlarge their creed, and add this clause against one, and that against another, and all was but for the perfecting and preserving of the Christian faith. And so he brings it to be a matter of so much wit to be a Christian,

---

* Works, vol. v., p. 144.   † Works, vol. 4, 653.   ‡ Ib. 673.

as Erasmus complains, that ordinary heads were not able to reach it. He had got them with a religious zealous cruelty to their own and others' souls, to lay all their salvation, and the peace of the church, upon some unsearchable mysteries about the Trinity, which God either never revealed, or never clearly revealed, or never laid so great a stress upon; yet he persuades them that there was Scripture proof enough of these; only the Scripture spoke it but in the premises, or in darker terms, and they must but gather into their creed the consequences, and put it into plainer expressions, which heretics might not so easily corrupt, pervert, or evade. But what got he at this one game?"

"He got a standing verdict against the perfection and sufficiency of Scripture, and consequently against Christ, his spirit, his apostles, and the Christian faith: that it will not afford so much as a creed or system of fundamentals, or points absolutely necessary to salvation and brotherly communion, in fit or tolerable phrases, but we must mend the language at least. He opened a gap for human additions, at which he might afterwards bring in more at his pleasure. He framed an engine for an infallible division, and to tear in pieces the church, casting out all as heretics that could not subscribe to his additions, and necessitating separation by all dissenters, to the world's end, till the devil's engine be overthrown. And hereby he lays a ground upon the divisions of Christians, to bring men into doubt of all religion, as not knowing which is the right. And he lays the ground of certain heart-burnings, and mutual hatred, contentions, revilings and enmity."*

It will be refreshing to turn from this picture to that of the early Christians, before any such impositions were laid upon them.

The beautiful and divine simplicity of the Christian religion, says Dr. Mosheim, appears from the two great and fundamental principles upon which it is built, Faith and Charity; and the only two rites of Baptism and the holy Supper, instituted by Christ himself. Of the early ages of the church he observes, that whoever acknowledged Christ as the Saviour of mankind, and made a profession of confidence in him, was immediately baptized and received into the church. The Christian system, as it was then taught, preserved its native simplicity, and was comprehended in a small number of articles. The great study of those who embraced the Gospel was rather to express

* Works, vol. 2, 896.

its divine influence in their dispositions and conduct, than to examine its doctrines with an excessive curiosity, or to explain them by the rules of human wisdom. As long as the sacred writings were the only rule of faith, religion preserved its native purity; and in proportion as their decisions were neglected, or postponed to the inventions of men, it degenerated from its primitive and divine simplicity.

This representation, from the highest historical authority, accords with that of other distinguished writers. Robinson, in his 'Ecclesiastical Researches,' says, that in the churches of the earliest times, "the doctrines taught were few, plain, and simple, taken immediately from the Gospel." Dr. Cave, in his 'Primitive Christianity,' observes of the Christian Fathers, that "their creed in the first ages was short and simple, their faith lying not so much in nice and numerous articles, as in a good and an holy life."

The writings of the Fathers themselves show their estimation of Christian liberty. As quoted by Limborch, in his History of the Inquisition, Tertullian says: "Every one has a natural right and power to worship God according to his persuasion; nor can it be a part of religion to compel men to religion, which ought to be voluntarily embraced, and not through constraint." Cyprian says: "Although there may be tares in the church, this ought to be no obstruction to our faith and charity; nor is their being in the church any reason for our departure out of it; it should be our care, that we be found the true wheat. The servant cannot be greater than his Lord; nor should any one arrogate to himself what the Father hath committed to the Son only, to winnow and purge the flour, and separate by any human judgment the chaff from the wheat. When the disciples left the Lord himself, he did not reproach or grievously threaten them, but gently said, 'what, and will you forsake me also?' observing that sacred law, of every one's being left to his own liberty and will, and making for himself his own choice." Lactantius says: "There is nothing which should be more free than the choice of our religion, in which, if the consent of the worshipper be wanting, it becomes entirely void and ineffectual."

The earliest deviation from the gospel terms of communion, appears to have taken place when what is called the Apostles' Creed was introduced; the articles of which were adopted at different periods of time, and which, compared with what followed it in the

Romish church, and with some creeds still existing in Congregational churches, seems scarcely objectionable, except as a precedent leading to further usurpations. In this view, no additions whatever to the Scriptural rule are to be justified. In point of principle, as Bishop Taylor observes, " it is like arbitrary power, which by the same rule it takes sixpence from the subject, may take a hundred pounds, then a thousand, then all." So in fact it happened with Christian liberty. In the language of Dr. Chandler,—" Human creeds were substituted in the room of Scripture; and according as circumstances differed, or new opinions were broached, so were the creeds corrected, amended and enlarged, till they became full of subtleties, contradictions and nonsense."* Christians were thus by degrees stript of their liberties and rights of conscience, and reduced to the most deplorable state of slavery and spiritual darkness.

To restore the Christian world to freedom, and to the light of the Scriptures, was the great object of the Reformation ; and the avowed principles of the Reformers, had they been effectually pursued, would have accomplished this noble object. But, as observed by Robinson, the eminent Puritan before referred to, they had " come so lately out of such thick antichristian darkness, that they could not see all things." They could not attain to just views of Christian liberty, nor clearly comprehend the principles upon which they assailed the papal tyranny. Hence they were soon found acting in contradiction to their avowed principles.

But in their intolerance, if not in their inconsistency, these reformers erred with the age in which they lived. Individuals, indeed, were found even in those times, who had just views of human creeds and of the nature and extent of the reformation in religion which was needed. One of these, whose merits have been little known, furnishes so remarkable an instance in proof of this, as well as of the persecuting spirit which then prevailed, that he deserves particular notice. We allude to Erasmus Johannes, teacher of a Latin school at Antwerp, whose enlightened views and unmerited fate are mentioned in the History of the Reformation in the Low Countries. He published a work, proving how early Christianity began to be corrupted, and maintaining that in order to a true and lasting reformation, it was necessary to conform to the apostolical churches in doc-

* Introduction to Hist. of the Inquisition, p. 111.

trine and discipline; and to that simplicity in expressing matters of religion, of which Christ and his apostles have left us an example. "What can we require more," said he, "of anybody? And if we do, by what authority is it? Therefore, let every one make use of his Christian liberty in this matter, and let him not hinder others. If any man thinks it necessary to use new terms in order to declare his notions and belief about divine matters, insomuch that the words of the prophets and apostles cannot serve him, it is most certain, that not only the words are new, but also his doctrine and religion too ; otherwise it would not be possible for him to fail of good and apposite expressions in holy writ."*

But these principles of reformation were far in advance of the age, and the author, who deserved a crown, was obliged to flee his country. At the present day, perhaps, there are many who would be slow to embrace them in their full extent ; but they may be safely promulgated. Persecution, in every form, is reprobated and disclaimed by all protestant denominations. What apology, then, could there be for us, if we should copy the errors of the early reformers instead of following out their principles, and make subscription to certain human explications of Scripture an indispensable condition to the enjoyment of privileges, which all disciples and followers of Christ are entitled to without it; and thus, "as far as we have power and opportunity," domineer over the consciences of our brethren? This, in our view, would not only be resisting the progress and principles of the Reformation, but returning to that spirit of Romish tyranny and delusion, from which it was the design of the Reformation to rescue the Christian world.

As we earnestly desire to lead you to the same convictions of duty on this subject which we so strongly feel, as well as to the persuasion and acknowledgment that we are sincere in them ; you will indulge us in pursuing the consideration of human tests in religion a little farther, and submitting to you the thoughts of some other authors of high reputation, who have taken views of the subject somewhat different from those already contemplated. Dr. Hartley, distinguished alike for his deep piety and learning, in his great work on "Man, his Frame, his Duty, and his Expectations," speaks with

---

* Brandt's Hist. of the Reformation, v. 1, p. 399.

much force upon the impropriety and futility of forming " any creeds, articles, or systems of faith, and requiring assent to them in words or writing." The whole of his remarks on this subject deserve your attention; a very few only can be introduced here.

"How," observes he, "can a person be properly qualified to study the word of God, and to search out its meaning, who finds himself previously confined to interpret it in a particular manner? If the subject matter of the article be of great importance to be understood and believed, one may presume that it is plain, and needs no article ; if of small importance, why should it be made a test or insisted upon ; if it be a difficult, abstruse point, no one upon earth has authority to make an article concerning it. We are all brethren ; there is no father, no master, amongst us ; we are helpers of, not lords over, each other's faith."

"As to the metaphysical subtilties which appear in some creeds, they can at best be only human interpretations of Scripture words ; and therefore can have no authority. All the real foundation which we have is in the words of Scripture, and of the most ancient writers, considered as helps, not authorities. It is sufficient, therefore, that a man take the Scriptures for his guide, and apply himself to them with an honest heart, and humble and earnest prayer ; which things have no connexion with forms and subscriptions."*

A learned divine of Germany, who wrote " Notes and Additions," which have been thought worthy to accompany the celebrated work of Hartley, enters more fully into this subject, and presents many interesting views, which we can now do little more than allude to. He shows that it is incumbent on the defenders of human articles of faith to prove that, without them, the Scriptures alone would be insufficient to attain the great purpose for which God gave them to us; that these creeds are more powerful instruments against the doubts, ignorance, or wickedness of those who go astray, than the holy Scriptures : or that the sense of the words of Jesus and his apostles may be more clearly and unequivocally laid down in unscriptural expressions, than in those employed by them ; and that without human articles of faith, such a variety of opinions and difference of religion must arise, as would render the uniformity of teaching necessary to general edification utterly impossible.

---

* Page 514, 4to ed.

Adverting to Dr. Hartley's remark upon the uselessness of articles in preventing differences and disputes, he instances the Church of England, in which "experience clearly shows that though the Thirty-nine Articles were established for the purpose of preventing difference of opinion, this end has not been in the smallest degree promoted by them."

He then proceeds to show how superior to the scholastic and abstract style of these artificial formularies of faith, is the simple and natural manner of the Scriptures, which divine wisdom has seen fit to adopt in communicating truth to the human mind. "The instruction given us in the Scriptures is, for the most part, conveyed to us in an historical manner, and is on that account most clear and intelligible to every capacity. The doctrines of our religion are delivered in the history of our Saviour ; and this history is the Christian's system of instruction. To understand the principal facts it relates, nothing more is necessary, than a knowledge of the language in which it is written ; and with a little attention I can discern the doctrines comprised in those facts, and founded on them, with more certainty and facility, than if they stood alone unconnected with any circumstances. The saying of Jesus, for example, 'I am the resurrection and the life,' might admit of various explanations; but if we connect it with the awakening of one from the dead, on which occasion it was spoken, no one can mistake its true sense. The epistles of the apostles refer to the history of Jesus and other facts, and as they elucidate these, they are reciprocally illustrated by them."

After a full discussion of this topic, the learned commentator concludes, that " the holy Scriptures alone, without any human addition, or authoritative interpretations, are sufficient to maintain the unity of doctrine necessary for general instruction and edification ;" and that "the only necessary unity of opinion is intelligible to the common capacity of mankind, without the aid of learning or philosophy."*

In this view of the subject, the author of Paradise Lost has some remarks, in his 'Treatise on Christian Doctrine,' which are entitled to your consideration. "The Scriptures," he says, " being in themselves so perspicuous, and sufficient of themselves to make men wise unto salvation, through what infatuation is it, that even protestant divines persist in darkening the most momentous truths of religion

---

* Ib. p. 699.

by intricate metaphysical comments, on the plea that such explanation is necessary ; as if Scripture, which possesses in itself the clearest light, and is sufficient for its own explanation, especially in matters of faith and holiness, required to have the simplicity of its divine truths more fully developed, and placed in a more distinct view, by illustrations drawn from the abstrusest of human sciences."*

Testimonials in behalf of the pure Bible, as our standard in religion, might be multiplied to almost any extent from the writings of those who have brought to the defence and exposition of it the deepest piety and learning. We will add one more in this connexion, to which we are naturally brought by all the rest, and which can never be too often repeated.

"The Bible, the Bible only," says the immortal Chillingworth, "is the religion of Protestants. I, for my part, after a long, and, as I verily believe and hope, impartial search of the true way to eternal happiness, do profess plainly that I cannot find any rest for the sole of my foot but upon this rock only. This, therefore, and this only, I have reason to believe ; this I will profess ; according to this I will live, and for this, if there be occasion, I will, not only willingly, but even gladly, lose my life, though I should be sorry that Christians should take it from me. I will take no man's liberty of judgment from him ; neither shall any man take mine from me. I will think no man the worse man, or the worse Christian ; I will love no man the less for differing in opinion from me. And what measure I mete to others, I expect from them again. I am fully assured that God does not, and therefore that man ought not to require any more of any man than this, to believe the Scripture to be God's word, to endeavor to find the true sense of it, and to live according to it."†

How happy would it be for the Christian world, if all who profess to be followers of the meek and lowly Jesus would adopt these noble sentiments, discard all human tests of orthodoxy, and, in the spirit of their blessed master, labor to advance the work of reformation according to the pure word of God, till all their churches are restored to the standard of apostolical purity in doctrine and worship. Let us do our part in this great work. However attached we may be to any human articles of faith ; even should we feel as if upon losing them, we should exclaim with Micah, "ye have taken away my gods,

---

* Vol. 2, p. 165.　　　† Works, 271.

and what have I more ?" yet let us be assured that, when we have understood their true nature, we shall rejoice in being released from them. Let us take encouragement from the reply of the truly evangelical Dr. Chandler to some in his day, who inquired what security they should have left for truth and orthodoxy, when their articles of faith were gone : " We shall have," said he, " the sacred Scriptures, those oracles of the great God, and freedom and liberty to interpret and understand them as we can. The consequence of this would be great integrity and peace of conscience in the enjoyment of our religious principles, union and friendship among Christians, notwithstanding all their differences in judgment, and great respect and honor to those faithful pastors, who carefully feed the flock of God, and lead them into pastures of righteousness and peace. We shall lose only the incumbrances of religion, our bones of contention, the shackles of our consciences, and the snares to virtue and honesty; while all that is substantially good and valuable, all that is truly divine and heavenly, would remain to enrich and bless us."*

A distinguished biographer of Baxter, in describing the result of those labors and struggles against ecclesiastical oppression, in which that great man bore so conspicuous a part, considers the leading principles of the Reformation as now completely settled, never again to be called in question. "The untenable and unrighteous exactions of authority," he says, "were exposed, the supreme authority of the Scriptures maintained, and the rights of conscience at last established. That principle stood forth before the world, as no longer to be disputed, that man is accountable to God only for all that he believes as truth, for all that he offers as worship, and for all that he practises as religion. This is the doctrine of the Bible, the dictate of enlightened reason ; and lies at the foundation of all correct and acceptable obedience to God."†

It is not because these were the principles of the Reformation that we attach so much importance to them, but because we regard them as immutable laws of our being, founded in the very nature and constitution of the human mind, and sanctioned by the Gospel of Christ.

The right of free inquiry and private judgment, in the concerns of religion, is an inalienable right, which we could not surrender if we

---

* Introduction to History of Inquisition, p. 110.
† Orme's Life and Times of Richard Baxter, v. 2, 190.

would; the exercise of it being our indispensable duty, as well as our high privilege. It necessarily follows that we are bound to respect in each other the exercise of this right, so far at least as to refrain from doing anything to prevent the perfect enjoyment of it.

That these principles are sanctioned by the Gospel of Christ, we need but open the sacred volume to be convinced. Nothing is clearer in the Christian Scriptures than those commands, which require us to judge for ourselves in matters of conscience, and to refrain from judging others.

Why even of yourselves judge ye not what is right?—Search the Scriptures.—Prove all things; hold fast that which is good.—I speak as to wise men, judge ye what I say.—Be always ready to give an answer to every man that asketh you a reason of the hope that is in you, with meekness and fear.—Judge not.—Condemn not.—One is your master, even Christ, and all ye are brethren.—Who art thou that judgest another's servant? Before his own master he standeth or falleth.—Why dost thou judge thy brother? Why dost thou set at naught thy brother? For we shall all stand before the judgment seat of Christ. Let us not, therefore, judge one another any more; but judge this, rather, that no man put a stumbling block or an occasion to fall in his brother's way.

These directions of our Saviour and his apostles show the spirit which breathes throughout the Gospel. On what account were the Bereans called more noble than some others? Was it because they implicitly received the doctrines taught even by inspired apostles? No. It was for searching the Scriptures daily, to see for themselves whether those things were so. What was the conduct of St. Paul on the occasion of giving the directions just referred to, when disputes and divisions arose between the Jewish and Gentile Christians at Rome about the obligation of the Mosaic ritual? Did he peremptorily require those whom he knew to be in the wrong to renounce their error, and adopt his opinion, or that of their better informed brethren, in order to be entitled to their communion and fellowship? Far from it. He presses upon all equally the duty of mutual forbearance and charity; and enjoins the same rule upon both parties, grounding it on the perfect right which all possessed, to inquire and judge for themselves." "Let every man," says he, "be fully persuaded in his own mind." That is, in the language of a learned expositor of this rule, "Let every man enjoy the freedom of following the light of his conscience, and let no Christians carry their zeal for agreement so far as to break in upon our title to God's favor, which is, acting sincerely according to the inward conviction of our own minds."*

Such is the united voice, which comes to you from the departed worthies of the Protestant faith, who, in different ages and nations, have been among the ablest expounders and brightest ornaments of Christianity. It is full, clear, distinct and harmonious. Will you not regard it, so far, at least, as to be persuaded to make a faithful and conscientious inquiry into the subject, which they so earnestly commend to your attention? Can you in justice to them or yourselves do less than this? Would not such an inquiry enable you more justly to appreciate their views and principles, if you should not be led to adopt them ; and would it not add to your knowledge and expand your charity, even should it fail to enlighten your faith? Is it possible, that proofs and considerations, which carried the fullest conviction to the minds of men, who devoted the highest gifts of intellect and learning to the cause of truth and piety, should bring no light to your minds engaged in the same holy cause? No, surely. You would be brought to question, at least, the right of a Cnristian church to add to the Bible any articles, as a surer test of revealed truth ; and, whatever might continue to be your own usage as to such additional tests, you would not condemn the established practice of this church in relation to them, nor consider it as affording any evidence, that we reject the fundamental doctrines of Christianity.

You will now permit us to call your attention to the principle, which, on the supposition that we reject those doctrines which you receive as fundamental, you assume in charging this church with "a dereliction of the great doctrines of Christianity." Do you not thus usurp the judgment seat, and make your own opinions the standard for judging the Christian faith of others? And what is the spirit of such a proceeding? Is it not of the very essence of popery?—Would it not be so indeed, if, instead of supposition, you had perfect evidence of the fact ; if you had specified the doctrines which your church receives as fundamental, and proved that this church rejects them? Why should your judgment, any more than ours, be the standard of truth ; unless, like the infallible church, you cannot

* Abernethy.

21

err; and, like that, too, claim to hold the keys, and to have authority to judge others? But this ground you will not take. You glory, equally with us, in the name of Protestants. Are you not bound, then, to allow us the same right which you claim to search the Scriptures and ascertain for ourselves the truth of Christian doctrines, be they fundamental or not? Are you not bound to treat us as being accountable, not to you, but, in common with you, to our final judge, for the manner in which we discharge this duty? Will you say, as some have said, that your conscience requires you to denounce those whose religious opinions you consider as essentially wrong, and consequently proceeding from a perverse interpretation of Scripture? But who made you judges of your brethren in the interpretation of Scripture? Is not this an assumption of infallibility? "All that infallibility," says Robert Hall, "which the church of Rome pretends to, is the right of placing her interpretation of Scripture on a level with the word of God; she professes to promulgate no new revelation, but solely to render her sense of it binding."

Can we then, it may be asked, do nothing to suppress what we deem to be gross errors in the faith of our Christian brethren? Yes, much. We may strive to convince them of their errors, and to lead them into a knowledge of the truth by every argument and persuasion which we are able to urge; and to secure their good will and attention to our arguments, we may, by friendly intercourse and Christian kindness, manifest the spirit of love and charity, which our own purer faith inspires. If they refuse to listen to us from a conviction that their errors are precious truths, and that it would be dangerous to consider any arguments opposed to them, we may enforce the great duty of free inquiry into religious opinions, of examining both sides of a question in order to a right decision, of searching the Scriptures and judging for ourselves of the truths of Christianity, and welcoming the light of evidence from whatever source it may come.

With such efforts to reclaim our erring brethren, may we not be satisfied, without usurping the prerogative of Christ, and sentencing them to banishment from his kingdom, or denying their right and title as subjects of it? But receiving, as we do, in common with yourselves, the Bible and all the doctrines it contains, why should you not suppose that we are competent to judge for ourselves what these doctrines are? Why, indeed, should you not suppose that we receive from the Bible the same fundamental doctrines which you receive purely from that source? You doubtless believe the same great truths of Christianity which we do, as far as they go, and differ from us principally in the additions which you make to them. Why should you not suppose, that, in respect to these additions, you may be unconsciously guided by the Westminster Confession and Catechism, which those who become members of your church must approve, as presenting "an excellent system of the doctrines of our holy religion?" Is it not quite possible, that some of the doctrines, which you consider as fundamental, may have been derived from this secondary source, the Scripture foundation of which we should maintain as firmly as you? Take, for instance, the following statement, in the second chapter of the Westminster Confession: "In the unity of the Godhead there be three persons, of one substance, power and eternity; God the Father, God the Son, and God the Holy Ghost. The Father is of none, neither begotten nor proceeding; the Son is eternally begotten of the Father, the Holy Ghost eternally proceeding from the Father and the Son." This statement we cannot adopt, for we find nothing like it in the Bible; but the Scripture views of the Father, Son, and Holy Spirit, are as precious to us as they can be to you. Here, too, we are in company with the excellent Dr. Watts, who is well known to have rejected this statement, and who expressly says, "of the scholastic account of generation and procession I have no idea."*

So also in respect to the doctrines of election, total depravity, &c., there are various statements in this confession, which in your view may contain what is fundamental, but in ours much that is opposite to the sincere word of God. We beg leave to suggest a few of these for your consideration, which, being doubtless familiar to you, need not be recited more at large.

"By the decree of God, for the manifestation of his glory, some men and angels are predestinated unto everlasting life, and others foreordained to everlasting death." These "are particularly and unchangeably designed, and their number is so certain and definite, that it cannot be either increased or diminished. Those of mankind that are predestinated unto life, God, before the foundation of the world, &c., hath chosen in Christ unto everlasting glory, &c., without

---

* Letter to Rev. Mr. Alexander, 1727.

any foresight of faith, or good works, or perseverance in either of them, or any other thing in the creature, as conditions or causes moving him thereunto ; and all to the praise of his glorious grace."

" Neither are any other redeemed by Christ, effectually called, &c., but the elect only. The rest of mankind God was pleased, &c. to pass by, and to ordain them to dishonor and wrath for their sin, to the praise of his glorious justice."

The sin of our first parents, " God was pleased, &c. to permit, having purposed to order it to his own glory. By this sin they fell from their original righteousness and communion with God, and so became dead in sin, and wholly defiled in all the faculties and parts of soul and body. They being the root of all mankind, the guilt of this sin was imputed, and the same death in sin and corrupted nature conveyed to all their posterity, &c. whereby we are utterly indisposed, disabled, and made opposite to all good, and wholly inclined to all evil."

Whether the doctrines here presented amount to antinomianism, we will not undertake to determine, but they appear to us exceedingly like Robert Hall's description of that system : "A system," he says, " which cancels every moral tie, consigns the whole human race to the extremes of presumption or despair, and erects religion on the ruins of morality."* We have not, however, referred to these doctrines, which, as you know, are a mere specimen of what is contained in the Westminster Confession, with any view of controverting them, but to draw your attention to the simple fact, that, whatever may be our repugnance to them, we receive, equally with you, the texts of inspired Scripture upon which they are professedly founded, though we could not make the same use of these texts. We beg you to examine the texts of Scripture adduced by the authors of this Confession, and printed in the margin, and put it to your consciences, after comparing them with other portions of Scripture, whether you could have inferred such doctrines from them, had you not cherished so deep a reverence for this ancient standard of orthodoxy. Could you, for instance, have ventured with various disconnected texts, selected principally from the book of Genesis, and from the most intricate of the apostolical epistles, without one word from the lips of Jesus, the author and finisher of our faith, or a single text from any of the four evangelists, to construct such a Chris-

---

* Hall's Works, v. 1, p. 142.

tian doctrine as that of the total depravity of human nature in consequence of Adam's transgression, its inability to all good, and entire inclination to all evil, insomuch that, as stated elsewhere in this Confession, "Works done by unregenerate men, although things which God commands, and of good use to themselves and others, are sinful, and cannot please God, or make a man more meet to receive grace from God?" And could you think of styling this, by way of distinction, the *evangelical* faith?

If you truly hold this doctrine, is it not because you found it already constructed for you in the Westminster Confession and Catechism? But we can feel no such reverence for these fallible compilations, nor allow them to have any weight except so far as they accord with divine truth. And if in our view they should appear irreconcilably opposed to this, which ought we to take for our guide? You will not hesitate in your answer. Do not then expect us to follow you into these regions of metaphysical divinity, where we look in vain for the pure doctrines and precepts of the Gospel, for the form of sound words, even the words of our Lord Jesus Christ. Let us seek for these at their original source, the Bible, where we are sure to find them unmixed with the delusive speculations of fallible, presumptuous men. Is it not possible, that, in taking a different course, you have been led to adopt as fundamental doctrines some of those metaphysical deductions, which have no real foundation in the sacred volume? May you not be as liable to such an error as some of the greatest and most devout men have been before you?

Transubstantiation was once held to be a fundamental doctrine of Christianity. Sir Thomas More, that learned and pious Chancellor of England, could bring men to the stake for denying it. Luther, with all his boldness of reform, could but half. renounce it, still holding to consubstantiation, scarcely less irrational; and breaking communion with those of his brethren who would renounce it altogether.

From such instances of human weakness and error, let us learn caution how we depart from the pure word of God, in stating and ascertaining the doctrines which he has revealed. What could appear, at this day, more opposed to Scripture, reason and common sense, than the doctrine of Transubstantiation? And can we be certain that some of those doctrines, which were always cherished along with it in the bosom of the Romish Church, and are stated in terms equally remote from the simplicity of the Gospel, may not hereafter appear as groundless as that now does?

Should not this consideration abate our zeal in contending for such doctrines, and keep alive our charity for those who believe that they have no existence in the Bible? Should not the fact, that so many intelligent inquirers fail to find them there, satisfy us that they cannot be fundamental doctrines?

The fundamental doctrines of Christianity are not the deep results of metaphysical skill, or learned investigation, but those evident truths, which all men of ordinary capacity and diligence may receive from a perusal of the Bible. According to the most enlightened and orthodox judgment, among Christians, " no doctrine is a fundamental, a necessary article of a Christian's faith, but what is so plainly and distinctly revealed, as that an ordinary Christian, sincere in his inquiries, cannot miss of the knowledge of it."*

The Westminster Confession alone must be sufficient to satisfy your minds on this point. In the first chapter of that work, it is declared, "All things in Scripture are not alike plain in themselves, nor alike clear unto all; yet those things which are necessary to be known, believed, and observed for salvation, are so clearly propounded and opened in some place of Scripture or other, that not only the learned, but the unlearned, in a due use of the ordinary means, may attain unto a sufficient understanding of them."

With these views accord those of the profound philosopher, John Locke, who was no less successful in his investigation of the Christian Scriptures, than in his inquiries into the human understanding. These Scriptures he studied through with the single purpose of ascertaining what is the faith required to make a man a Christian. The result of his examination was, as may be seen in his ' Reasonableness of Christianity,' that this faith is, "the believing the only true God, and Jesus Christ to be the Messiah whom he hath sent." In a vindication of this work, he quotes bishop Patrick as of the same opinion, and as saying: "It is the very same thing to believe that Jesus is the Christ, and to believe that Jesus is the son of God."

The writers and wranglers in religion fill it with niceties, and dress it up with notions, which they make necessary and fundamental parts of it.—But," adds this great man, "whoever has used what means he is capable of for the informing of himself, with a readiness to believe and obey what shall be taught and prescribed by Jesus, his Lord

---

* Foster on Fundamentals.

and King, is a true and faithful subject of Christ's kingdom; and cannot be thought to fail in anything necessary to salvation."*

"It is very common," says Dr. Gale, "to call those points we are fond of, fundamentals; and then think it very justifiable, nay commendable, to renounce communion with such as err in those fundamentals. But we seldom inquire whether the Scriptures have declared them fundamentals; if not, I am sure we have no power to make them so; and to attempt to do it is to usurp Christ's authority; which he knew human nature too well to entrust with any man or body of men upon earth."†

"All that," says Baxter, "without which a man cannot be a good and holy Christian, is plain and easy in itself; and Christ did choose therefore to speak to the capacity of the meanest." How could it ever have been thought otherwise! To the poor and ignorant, more especially, was the gospel originally preached. It must therefore have been designed for them, and adapted to their comprehension. Among the poor and ignorant of the present day, protestants of every denomination boast of sending the Bible, "without note or comment." But wherefore should it be so sent, if they may not of themselves learn from its pages all that is fundamental, or essential to make them Christians?

Thus, as you must perceive, it is manifest that this church, with the Bible for the man of our counsel, is competent to understand Christian doctrines; and, that, if your church has adopted certain doctrines which we are unable to learn from the Bible, whatever else they may be, they cannot be "the fundamental doctrines of Christianity."

We see not how you can avoid this conclusion, if you allow us common honesty in the use of the Scriptures. It is possible, however, that you refuse to allow us this, and would be understood to mean by "a dereliction from the great doctrines of Christianity," a wilful apostasy from the faith. It is possible that you may have such an assured feeling of the truth of certain doctrines, as stated in the Westminster Confession and Catechism—the Trinity, for instance— that you cannot think us sincere and honest inquirers after truth, if we adopt not the same views and phraseology respecting it. If this

---

* Locke's Reasonableness of Christianity, with the Vindication.
† Sermons, v. 4, p. 443.

be the case, we beg you to consider seriously whether such an assured feeling, even should you think it grounded upon divine illumination, can, of itself, be evidence of truth; since those of every religious persuasion, not excepting deists, have had it, and as they sometimes thought, to a supernatural degree.* And we beg you also to reflect, with an excellent Scotch divine, how widely " we depart from the meekness and humility of the gospel spirit, when we allow ourselves to think and to speak hardly of others, because they do not see every thing just in the same light with us, or have not freedom to express themselves in our phrases, which are, perhaps, not only unscriptural, but were unknown in the Christian church for many centuries, and can claim no better nor higher original than the dregs of the scholastic philosophy."†

Still, whatever you may think of us, or our religious conduct and phraseology, if you admit that any honest, intelligent inquirers could be led by a study of the Bible to embrace the same views on this subject, our argument respecting your supposed fundamentals remains the same. But if you will not admit this, and judge us to be insincere or dishonest in our inquiries, merely from the result of those inquiries, you have to consider the extent of your judgment, and the nature of the responsibility attending it. Together with us you must condemn, as unfaithful inquirers after divine truth, all those great and good men, and enlightened Christians, who have adopted similar views respecting this leading doctrine of the Westminster Confession.

Are you prepared to pass such a sweeping judgment, and to denounce men as unworthy of the Christian name who have devoted the highest powers of mind to the defence and elucidation of the Christian faith, and adorned their profession of it with the brightest virtues of the Christian life? Would you venture to pass such a judgment against Sir Isaac Newton, the renowned supporter of pure Christianity, and whose sincere faith and piety shed a lustre over his character as a philosopher? Or against John Locke, who so profoundly studied the Christian Scriptures, and was no less remarkable for the purity of his life and manners, than for the apostolical simplicity of his faith? Or against Dr. Lardner, who gave himself wholly to the religion of Christ, devoting a long and laborious life to the collection

---

* See Life of Lord Herbert.   † Dr. Leechman.

and exposition of its evidences, to the illustration of its genuine doctrines, and to the manifestation, by his own example, of its purifying spirit?

And, to come within the circle of your own observation, have you not witnessed in the lives of some, whose faith was similar to Dr. Lardner's, proofs of Christian excellence too powerful to allow you to call in question their claim to the Christian character? Did not he, whose century of years has recently closed,* exhibit abundantly to you and your fathers the fruits of a Christian faith and spirit, "walking in all the commandments and ordinances of the Lord blameless?" What professor of Christianity was ever known to you, who more constantly adorned his profession by active goodness and a holy example? Did you not honor, too, the Christian virtues of that venerated man,† who passed his last years in communion with this church, but who, early in life, made a profession of his faith in your church, or in that from which yours was formed, and throughout a long course of public duties and trials, in war and in peace, undeviatingly maintained the purity, sacredness, and simplicity of the Christian character? Would you have hesitated to say of him, what our Saviour said of Nathaniel, "Behold an Israelite indeed, in whom there is no guile?" If such a man be not a Christian, where on earth is a Christian to be found? Must his name be struck from the roll, because his love of truth was stronger than the prejudice of education, and he could not in conscience retain his trinitarian views?

Both these eminent Christians were nurtured in the bosom of Calvinism, and initiated into all the doctrines of the Westminster Catechism. But their profound love of truth, and reverence for the word of God, led them to examine by this unerring standard the doctrines which they had been taught, and to reject what would not abide the test. To go through with such an examination honestly, and surrender to truth long cherished opinions, requires peculiar energy of mind and conscience; and deserves applause, not obloquy. "It is a hard thing," says Baxter, "to bring men to that self-denial and labor, as at age thoroughly and impartially to revise their juvenile conceptions; and for them that learned words before things, to proceed to learn things now as appearing in their proper evidence. And indeed

---

* Edward Augustus Holyoke.   † Timothy Pickering.

none but men of extraordinary acuteness and love of truth, and self-denial, and patience, are fit to do it."*

The distinguished men of whom we are speaking, faithfully accomplished this task. And can you be certain that if you, in like manner, had brought your early opinions to the test of the Scriptures, you would not have arrived at the same result, and enjoyed those clear views of Christian truth and duty, in which, for so many years, they rejoiced on earth, as we trust they now do in heaven? Are such men to be repelled from your communion as heretics, under pretence, too, of apostolic authority; men who are, in the language of Robert Hall, "illustrious examples of piety; men who would tremble at the thought of deliberately violating the least of the commands of Christ, or of his apostles; men whose character and principles, consequently, form a striking contrast with those of the persons whom it is allowed the apostles would have repelled? Are we to separate ourselves from the best of men, because the apostles would have withdrawn from the worst?"

If any of the eminent Christians whose characters we have now pointed out to you, could have honestly studied the Scriptures in forming their religious opinions, which, we think, you will hardly deny; the conclusion before drawn, that your supposed fundamental doctrines cannot be really such, remains in all its force, and the very ground of your judgment against the Christian character of this Church is taken away. The simple fact appears, not that we reject any fundamental doctrines, but that we differ in opinion from you.

Should you still persist in condemning us for opinions, held in common with such honored professors of Christianity, you must perceive that you involve them in the same condemnation with us; a condemnation by which we cannot be much concerned on our own account, while it includes us among those who we feel assured are true Christians according to the rules of judging adopted by our Saviour, whose prerogative it is to judge his followers. Allow us, for a moment, to call your attention to these rules, which you may not have sufficiently considered.

We have shown you from the Gospel what a man must *believe* in order to become entitled to the Christian name and privileges; it is equally clear what he must *be* and *do* in order to possess the Chris-

---

* Vol. 4, p. 502.

tian character. In the Sermon on the Mount, that body of divinity unmixed with any error, left us by our Lord, this is fully and explicitly laid down. How does this divine discourse open upon us? What are the elements of Christian excellence, which have the promise of peculiar blessings? Are they matters of opinion, and doctrine, and subtle speculation? Far from it. They relate to the heart; to those gentle, benevolent, and pure affections, which all may feel, and cherish, and improve. " Blessed are the poor in spirit—the meek—the merciful—the peace-makers—the pure in heart—those who hunger and thirst after righteousness." Such is the foundation of that obedience to Christ, which he makes the test of Christian character. *Obedience* to his commands, *doing* the will of God, is the ground of his constant approbation. Who is great in the kingdom of heaven? Whosoever shall *do* and teach his commandments. Not every one that saith, Lord, Lord, shall enter into the kingdom of heaven; but he that *doeth* the will of God. And what is the whole conclusion of these plain, practical, sublime precepts of Christian virtue and piety? He that heareth these sayings and *doeth* them, builds his house upon a rock; he that doeth them not, builds upon the sand.

The same principle, of course, pervades the Gospel, and indeed all the Scriptures. " Fear God and keep his commandments, for this is the whole duty of man.—Whoever, says our Saviour, shall *do* the will of my father in heaven, the same is my brother, and sister, and mother. He that hath my commandments and *keepeth* them, he it is that loveth me.

So far as our Lord has seen fit to unveil the scenes of the Judgment day, what must be our hope of mercy, in appearing before him? In that day, deeds of charity and kindness, shown to the humblest of his disciples and followers, will be accepted and regarded as if done to himself. Even a cup of cold water only, given in the name of a disciple, will in no wise lose its reward. What, then, we may tremblingly ask, must be our reward, if, instead of such acts of Christian kindness, it shall appear that we have condemned some of his sincerest followers as unworthy to bear his name!

The reflection must have occurred to you, that there may be among Christians an apostasy more awful than that of an erroneous faith; an apostasy from the spirit and precepts of Christ. Let us give to this a moment's consideration.

The great Dr. Owen gives, in his discourse on this subject, " A few instances of the means and ways whereby a general apostasy from the holy precepts of the Gospel, as the rule of our obedience, hath been begun and carried on." "That religion," he says, "is alien from the Gospel, at least includes a notable defection from it, whose avowed profession does not represent the spirit, graces, and virtues of him who was its author. Yea, conformity unto him in all things is the sum and substance of that obedience which he doth require."

"The Lord Christ hath declared and appointed, that the mutual love of his disciples should be the great testimony of the truth of his doctrine, and the sincerity of their obedience."

"Do not some seem to aim at nothing more than to multiply and increase divisions, and to delight in nothing more than to live and dispute in the flames of them ?"

"It is not unusual to see persons, who are under the power of some singular opinion and practice in religion, to make one thing almost their whole business ; the measure of other things and persons, the rule of communion, and of all sincere love : to value and esteem themselves and others according unto their embracing or not embracing of that opinion. And it were to be wished, that such principles and practices were not visibly accompanied with a decay of love, humility, meekness, self-diffidence, condescension, and zeal in other things ; seeing where it is so, let men's outward profession be what it will, the plague of apostasy is begun."*

This quotation we can hardly forbear extending, so excellent are Dr. Owen's remarks upon the subject, so seasonable, too, and so full of instruction. It is as true now as it was in his day, or in the days of the primitive church, that our religion is a religion of love and peace. The spirit of mutual love and charity among its professors is now as convincing "an argument of the truth, efficacy, and holiness of the doctrine which they profess," as it was then. So also "strifes, contentions, and divisions" among them are as great an obstacle to "the progress of the Gospel," as corrupting to "the conversations and spirit" of Christians, and as strong proofs of apostasy from the spirit and precepts of Christ.

The apostasy which Dr. Owen so clearly points out, the guilt of which we may unwarily incur while we are charging others with

---

* The Nature of Apostasy, by John Owen, D. D., 1676.

apostasy from the faith, should fill us with dread, as the great moral evil to which Christians are ever exposed, and which they should most anxiously avoid. To succeed in avoiding, or subduing it, we must begin at its source, and resist its first motions. The sin which leads to it most easily besets us, and gains strength with every indulgence. Censorious judging in matters of faith and conscience is the source from which it springs. This leads directly to that dividing, exclusive, and bitter spirit among Christians, which is itself "the plague of apostasy."

"To judge other men's consciences," says the excellent Howe, "is of so near akin to governing them, that they who can allow themselves to do the former, want only power, not will or inclination, to offer at the other too." When, therefore, we once allow ourselves to judge the consciences of our brethren, we feel a strong desire to control them, and if this cannot be done directly, we attempt to do it by indirect means. Hence proceed exclusions, divisions, contentions, animosities, revilings, and all those calamitous consequences, which the professed followers of Christ, by thus apostatizing from his spirit and precepts, have brought upon themselves, upon mankind, and upon the Christian cause. Let us then look at the fountain head of these bitter waters, and stay them at their source. Let us refrain from judging one another. "One would think," says the author just quoted, "it is the easiest thing in the world *not to do*, especially not to do a thing of itself ungrateful to a well tempered mind, and a great privilege not to be obliged to judge another man's conscience and practice, when it is so easy to misjudge and do wrong."*

The venerated Matthew Henry has some remarks on this subject which cannot fail to influence your minds. "Christ," he says, "is the sovereign of the heart, the rightful sovereign; for him the throne is to be reserved; conscience is his deputy; by him it is to be commanded, and to him it is accountable."

"It is a good reason why we should not judge one another, or be severe in our censures one of another; we thereby invade Christ's throne, for it is his prerogative to call his disciples to account; and though he designed them to be one another's helpers, he never intended they should be one another's judges."†

Is it not entirely mistaking the province of our own conscience,

* On Union among Protestants.　　　† Henry's Works, p. 663.

174

when we thus take oversight of the hearts and consciences of others?
As declared by the same venerated author, in his Commentary,—
"They are not accountable to us, nor are we accountable for them.
If we can be helpers of their joy, it is well; but we have no dominion over their faith. In judging and censuring our brethren, we
meddle with that which doth not belong to us. We have work
enough to do at home; and if we must needs be judging, let us exercise our faculty upon our own hearts and ways."* Can anything
but evil proceed from thus interfering with the most sacred rights of
others? Does it not work evil to our neighbor, evil to the community in which we live, evil to the cause of Christ, evil to our own
souls, evil now, and evil forever? Can it possibly come in aid of
truth, or love, or peace, or joy, or any of the ends of Christianity?
Is it not essentially and eternally opposed to them all?

These are momentous inquiries, and you may justly think that
they deserve to be pursued with some further illustrations from the
same class of admired authors, to whom we are already so greatly
indebted. But we can add a few only of the passages which have
occurred to us as important in this connexion.

We begin with Dr. Evans, a distinguished preacher among the
English Dissenters, and the "worthy friend" of Watts, who, with
Doddridge, thought his 'Christian Temper' one of the best works of
the kind in our language. In this work, alluding to the apostle's
discourse about judging one another, Dr. Evans says: "In such matters every man is to give account of himself to God, but men have
no right to call one another to account; therefore, to judge another in those things, is to thrust ourselves into God's province.
And will not God, think you, chastise such arrogance? It is also
very injurious to our neighbor. Evil surmises of him weaken our
own affection; and, if we spread them abroad, may lessen his reputation with others, and draw many pernicious consequences after
them; for which we shall be justly accountable, as long as they
spring from a sinful action of ours, and such effects might be fore-
seen likely to ensue."

"The way of peace among Christians seems to be plainly declared
in the Gospel.—Not by pretending to bring all Christians to a perfect
uniformity of sentiments or practice in matters of religion. That

* Exposition, Rom. 14.

was not in the apostolical days themselves; nor can be hoped for till we come to heaven. Nor by arbitrary forms of agreement devised by men and prescribed by some to others. There was more of the unity of the spirit in the bond of peace during the primitive times, before ever such methods were invented, than since the Christian world has abounded with them. One would think that now, when the canon of Scripture is completed, we should be ready to own all them our fellow Christians, who own the same sacred books as we do, for the only and perfect rule of Christian faith and practice. Though they and we should differ in understanding many particulars contained in that rule; yet, if we judge them 'weak in the faith,' we are directed to receive them, but not to doubtful disputations."

The judicious Henry, to whom we have so repeatedly referred, will show you in what spirit of candor and equity we ought to conduct all our religious inquiries and disputes. "In matters of doubtful disputation," he says, "while we are contending for that which we take to be right, let us at the same time think it possible that we may be in the wrong. When we contend for the great principles of religion, in which all good Christians are agreed, we need not fear our being in a mistake, they are of undoubted certainty, we know and are assured that Jesus is the Christ. But there are many things which are not so clearly revealed, because of not so much moment, in which the truth indeed lies but on one side, and yet wise and good men are not agreed on which side it lies. Here, though we both argue and act according to the light that God has given us, yet we must not be over confident of our judgment, as if wisdom must die with us. Others have understanding as well as we, and are not inferior to us; nay, perhaps they every way excel us, and therefore who can tell but they may be in the right ?"*

In recommending the same spirit, another eminent old divine declares: "This I say, and I say it with much integrity; I never yet took up religion by parties in the lump. I have found by trial of things that there is some truth on all sides: I have found holiness where you would little think it, and so likewise truth. And I have learned this principle, which I hope I shall never lay down till I am swallowed up of immortality; and that is, to acknowledge every good thing, and hold communion with it in men, in churches, or

---

* Henry's Works, p. 480.

whatsoever else. I learn this from Paul, I learn this from Jesus Christ himself."*

The tendency of an opposite course is stated by Baxter, in his usual plain and direct manner. "When men are incorporated into a sect or uncharitable party, and have captivated themselves to a human servitude in religion, and given up themselves to the will of men, the stream will bear down the plainest evidence, and carry them to the foulest errors.—The interest of Christianity, catholicism and charity is contrary to the interest of sects, as such. And it is the nature of a sectary, that he preferreth the interest of his opinion, sect, or party, before the interest of Christianity, catholicism and charity, and will sacrifice the latter to the service of the former." †

From the following observations of the learned Grove, an intimate friend of Watts, whom in the opinion of Doddridge he resembled as a writer, you may learn how dangerous it is to rely upon our conscience to justify us in such conduct, or in any uncharitable treatment of others.

" Though conscience is our immediate rule, yet the rule of conscience is truth, as God hath manifested it to us in his word, or by the reason and nature of things, and we are capable of apprehending it ; and by this external rule, or the truth, as discoverable by us, we are to be judged in the last day. This is a matter of such importance, that every one will do well to reflect seriously upon it, that he be not too precipitate in forming his judgment of opinions, and of the persons who hold them. For what if I should err in my judgment, and in my practice as consequent upon that judgment, spending my zeal upon things that are no part of Christianity, perhaps of a very opposite nature, and treating those as unworthy of Christian fellowship, and hardly objects of common charity, who are really an honor to their profession? It will be a poor excuse that I did but what my conscience told me was my duty to do, since I ought to have taken care to inform my conscience better."‡

An eminent divine of the English church has demonstrated the innocency of involuntary errors ; and that in respect to those which are voluntary, we are accountable not to man, but to our final Judge for neglecting the means in our power of learning the truth. How

* Dr. T. Goodwin's Sermons, p. 488.   † Life of Baxter, fol. part 2, p. 144.
‡ Grove's Works, v. 8, 155.

deeply then does it concern us all, before we presume to denounce our brethren for their religious opinions or practices, to examine impartially the evidence and arguments which they offer in support of them!

"The only punishable errors," says Dr. Sykes, in his tract on this subject, "are such as are voluntary, and proceed from negligence; and in this case, too, to speak properly, it is the negligence, and not the error, which is punishable. Punishable, I say, but not by man, unless the errors betray them into such acts as are inconsistent with the civil interests of mankind. For since the fault lies only in negligence, what man alive can tell what industry, pains or labor has been used to attain the truth? God, the searcher of hearts, can easily discover this."

To judge for another in religion is as impossible, according to the great Dr. Clarke, "as that any one man should see or taste, live or breathe for another.—The only rule of faith to every Christian," he says, "is the doctrine of Christ; and that doctrine, as applied to him by his own understanding. In which matter, to preserve his understanding from erring, he is obliged indeed, at his utmost peril, to lay aside all vice and all prejudice, and to make use of the best assistances he can procure. But after he has done all that can be done, he must of necessity at last understand with his own understanding, and believe with his own, not another's faith."[*]

Hence every evil inflicted upon a fellow Christian on account of his faith, is stamped with absurdity, as well as injustice.

"Every one," says Dr. Gale, "naturally and necessarily believes his own opinions and sentiments to be true.—We cannot forbear judging as the evidence appears to us, any more than we can with our eyes wide open, and in the face of the sun at noon, judge it to be midnight."

"To what has a man a greater right, than to the entire free enjoyment and direction of his own conscience; and to a full power to act uprightly, and in sincerity before God and man? And yet men are not by far so much disturbed and wronged in any other possessions and enjoyments, as in these."[*]

"The iniquity of uncharitableness," says Dr. Watts, "has more springs than there are streams or branches belonging to the great

river of Egypt ; and it is as fruitful of serpents and monsters too."
Sometimes this iniquity, he observes, proceeds "from a malicious
constitution of nature, an acrimonious or a choleric temper of blood."
To suppress the angry motions of such a temper, " is a work of toil
and difficulty, perpetual watchfulness and unceasing prayer." Sometimes it springs from " self-love, and pride, and a vain conceit of our
own opinions." Hence a man "who is almost always in the wrong,"
will be prompt " in pronouncing error and heresy upon every notion
and practice that differs from his own. He takes the freedom to
choose a religion for himself, but he allows no man besides the same
liberty. He is sure that he has reason to dissent from others, but no
man has reason to dissent from him."

Thus this ardent advocate of "orthodoxy and charity united" proceeds to examine into other sources of this unchristian spirit; such
as perverting " the principles of those that dissent from us," so as to
" be sure to find some terrible absurdity at the end of them ;" making " every punctilio of our own scheme a fundamental point ;"
seeking " the applause of a party, and the advance of self-interest ;"
and "fixing upon some necessary and special point in Christianity,
and setting it up in opposition to the rest." And finally he mentions
as the most common cause of uncharitableness, " that a great part of
the professors of our holy religion make their heads the chief seat of
it, and scarce ever suffer it to descend and warm their hearts.—While
they boast of their orthodox faith, they forget their Christian love."

But Dr. Watts instructs us by his example still more than by his
precepts. He was as anxious to preserve in his own breast the sacred flame of charity as to kindle it in others. To this end, by his
own account, he studied and labored, watched and prayed. "I confess," says he, "now and then some opinions, or some unhappy oc-
currences are ready to narrow and confine my affections again, if I
am not watchful over myself, but I pray to God to preserve upon my
heart a lasting remembrance of those days and those studies whereby
he laid within me the foundation of so broad a charity." If we will
labor, like him, for this crowning grace of the Christian life, we may
be sure to enjoy, as he did, the delightful persuasion that Christians
of widely different opinions may be equally sincere, and that many of
them may travel abreast in the road to heaven. "Though they do
not trace precisely the same track, yet all look to the same Saviour
Jesus, and all arrive at the same common salvation. And though

their names may be crossed out of the records of a particular church on earth, where charity fails, yet they will be found written in the Lamb's book of life, which is a record of eternal love, and shall forever be joined to the fellowship of the Catholic church in heaven.''*

" There is no one point of our religion," says archbishop Sharp, in his Discourse on Church Communion, "more necessary to be daily preached, to be earnestly pressed and insisted on, than that of peace, and love, and unity.—What the worship of one God was to the Jews, that peace, and love, and unity is to the Christians, even the great distinguishing law and character of their profession. And to the shame of Christians it may be spoken, there is no one commandment in all Christ's religion, that hath been so generally and so scandalously violated among his followers, as this."

" Christianity," says archbishop Wake, "commands us to love our enemies, and sure then we cannot but think it very highly reasonable not to hate our brethren ; but especially on such an account as, if it once be admitted, will, in this divided state of the church, drive the very name of brotherly love and charity out of it ; seeing, by whatsoever arguments we go about to justify our uncharitableness to any others, they will all equally warrant them to withhold in like manner their charity from us. There is no honest, sincere Christian, how erroneous soever he may be, but what at least is persuaded that he is in the right, and looks upon us to be as far from the truth, by differing from him, as we esteem him for not agreeing with us. Now if, upon the sole account of such differences, it be lawful for us to hate another, we must for the very same reason allow it to be as lawful for him also to hate us. Thus shall we at once invert the characteristic of our religion, 'By this shall all men know that ye are my disciples, if ye have love one to another ;' and turn it into the contrary note ; while we make our hatred to our brother the great mark of our zeal for our religion, and conclude him to love Christ the most, who the least loves his fellow Christians."

" The faith once delivered to the saints, is that which the holy apostles had once for all instructed them in ; and which, therefore, both they and all succeeding ages in the church were faithfully to retain and earnestly to contend for. It is not the faith of this or that church or party ; it is not the faith of this or that country or

---

* Collection of Tracts by J. Sparks, vol. 6, Isaac Watts.

century. Let men and time make what alterations they please in it; the faith once delivered to the saints, is what we are to contend for, not for any inventions or additions of men that have since been brought into it."*

Here, you may think, we might properly close our observations on this subject; but we cannot forbear to add a brief passage or two from the works of Dr. Barrow and Dr. Balguy, two eminent divines of the English Church, who have described with great truth and energy the evil nature and effects of uncharitable judging among Christians.

"By taking upon ourselves to judge unduly," says Dr. Barrow, "we do invade God's office, setting up ourselves as judges in his room; we usurp his right, exercising jurisdiction over his subjects, without order and license from him. It is St. Paul's argument, 'Who art thou that judgest another's servant?' That is, how intolerably bold and arrogant, how sacrilegiously injurious and profane art thou, to climb up into God's tribunal, and thence to pronounce doom upon his subjects?"†

"We are offended at our brethren," observes Dr. Balguy, "think and speak ill of them, and practise hostilities against them. Why, what have they done? They have, it seems, presumed to differ from us in opinion, and followed their own judgment instead of ours."

"Do we pretend to set up our sentiments as a common standard? Or would we, in resemblance of a noted tyrant, reduce all men's understandings to the model and measure of our own? If we presume that we are in the right, and others in the wrong, what hinders them from making the same supposition in favor of themselves? And whether it is made by the one or the other, assurance and confidence are by no means certain marks of truth."

"The practice here complained of may be considered as producing evils of the highest malignity. To this have been owing most of the calamities which have often so cruelly infested the Christian world.—The chief blessings of society it has corrupted and poisoned; it has robbed men of their mutual affection, benevolence, and esteem; infused jealousies, kindled contentions, and spread variance and discord far and wide; it has divided friends, families, kindred; crumbled communities into parties and factions; and burst

---

* Sermons and Discourses, p. 192.　　† Barrow's Sermons, 1, 448.

asunder the strongest obligations, both natural, civil and religious. It perverts men's understandings, corrupts their judgments, and alienates their affections; it confounds their ideas of merit and de- merit, and makes them estimate characters by false rules and falla- cious measures; it creates uneasy sentiments, productive of ill-will ; it nourishes presumption, confidence, and self-conceit; and destroys the kind instincts of humanity and compassion."*

What inconsistency! What delusion ! When will Christians learn the spirit of their religion? When will Protestants act upon their avowed principles? What but a practical and consistent adherence to this spirit, and to these principles, can restore to us the blessings of peace and unity, and ensure to the Gospel a complete triumph ?

Here is an object worthy of our constant efforts and prayers. Let us promote it by every means in our power, and especially by our example. Let us resolve to be Protestants in deed, as well as in name. Let us regard integrity of conscience, not sameness of opin- ion, as the true Christian bond of union, and embrace as brethren all who conscientiously follow what they believe to be the doctrine of the Gospel, and repel none from our communion, "that love our Lord Jesus Christ in sincerity." Let no mere differences of opinion em- bitter our affections, or obstruct the flow of our charity. In the words of an eminent and devoted servant of Christ, addressed to one of a very different persuasion from himself, "Let the points wherein we differ, stand aside; there are enough wherein we agree, enough to be the ground of every Christian temper, and of every Christian action.—If we cannot as yet *think alike* in all things, at least we may *love alike.* Herein we cannot possibly do amiss. For of one point none can doubt a moment, God is love ; and he that dwelleth in love, dwelleth in God, and God in him."†

Thus, Christian brethren, for so we must be allowed to address you, we have endeavored to collect and lay before you such state- ments and considerations as might lead you to clearer views of the mutual rights and duties of Christians, and to a deeper abhorrence of that exclusive, uncharitable spirit which is opposed to them all.

The dark, antichristian character of this spirit is manifest from its past history; and is there anything to brighten the prospect of its

---

* Discourse on Diversity of Opinion, &c.
† Wesley, to a Roman Catholic—Works, v. 9, p. 535.

future progress? Suppose its mode of operation changed, will not its nature and its object remain essentially the same? And can it produce better fruits by means of exclusions, denunciations and anathemas, than by fines, imprisonments and tortures? Religion has as little affinity with the one as the other. Truth and piety can no more be promoted by destroying a man's usefulness, reputation, or peace of mind, than by maiming or burning his body. Even the poor reward of uniformity cannot be attained by all these or any other means of coercion. Bishop Taylor is not too strong in his expression, when he says that he who attempts to prevent variety of opinions is "like him who claps his shoulder to the ground to stop an earthquake;" nor Chillingworth when he declares that "taking away diversity of opinions touching matters of religion, is not to be hoped for without a miracle."

Let, then, this evil spirit itself be banished from the hearts of Christians. All who would be true disciples of Jesus, and 'followers of God as dear children,' must be filled with brotherly love, and actuated by the divine principles of charity and freedom which the Gospel inculcates. How easily would they then follow the eminent theologian last named, and "learn to set a higher value upon those great points of faith and obedience wherein they agree, than upon those of less moment wherein they differ ; and understand that agreement in those ought to be more effectual to join them in one communion, than their difference in other things of less moment to divide them." You have seen how earnestly the wisest and most devout Christians of other times pleaded for this, and with what generous sentiments of freedom and benevolence they were animated. Will not their example of Christian charity rise in judgment against this generation? Are not many of us wanting in these noble sentiments? Are not some of us relapsing into that very spirit of antichrist which they so resolutely opposed? Yet these distinguished worthies were far from enjoying our advantages for gaining light and knowledge. Many of them lived in times of comparative darkness, and did but imperfectly understand the rights of conscience. Hence they were not always able to act and speak in perfect consistency with their general principles. This, with the light of our times, they would be the first to see and lament. Could they now speak to us, how full of heavenly peace would be their voice! How affectionately would they warn us to avoid their errors, and never forget the Saviour's law of love!

Baxter[*] has given us some faint idea of this, in the speech which he believed that his friend Owen, who departed before him, would address to the disputers in religion whom he left behind, could he have spoken to them from his heavenly rest. And we know not how we can better take our present leave of you, than with this heaven-breathing address:

"Though all believers must be holy, and avoid all known wilful sin, they must not avoid one another, or their communion in good, because of adherent faults and imperfections; for Christ, who is most holy, receiveth persons and worship that are faulty, else none of us should be received. There is greatest goodness where there is greatest love and unity of spirit, maintained in the bond of peace. O call not to God to deny you mercy, by being unmerciful; nor to cast you all out, by casting off one another. O separate not all from Christ's church on earth, lest you separate from him, or displease him. God hath bid you pray, but not told you whether it shall be oft in the same words, or in other; with a book or without a book. Make not superstitiously a religion by pretending that God hath determined such circumstances. O do not preach and write down love and communion of saints, on pretence that your little modes and ways only are good, and theirs idolatrous or intolerable; and do not slander and excommunicate all, or almost all, Christ's body, and then wrong God by fathering this upon him. You pray, 'Thy will be done on earth as it is in heaven;' why, here is no strife, division, disunion, animosity, sects, or factions, nor separating from, or excommunicating, one another. Learn of Christ, and separate from none further than they separate from him, and receive all that he receiveth. While you blame canonical dividers, and unjust excommunicators, do not you renounce communion with tenfold more than they. I was, in this, of too narrow, mistaken principles; and in the time of temptation I did not foresee to what church confusion and desolation, hatred and ruin, the dividing practices of some did tend; but the glorious unity, in heavenly perfection of love to God and one another, bids me beseech you to avoid all that is against it, and to make use of no mistakes of mine to cherish any such offences, or to oppose the motions of love, unity and peace."

In behalf of the Church,

D. A. WHITE, } *Committee.*
H. DEVEREUX, }

---

[*] See Orme's Life and Times of Richard Baxter, v. 2, p. 184.

NOTE.

In this reprint, to shorten it, many of the quoted passages contained in the original are omitted ; also some of the accompanying remarks, and some others, abridged or condensed. Prefixed to the first publication was the following certificate of proceedings, adopted at a meeting of the Church, Feb. 18, 1832 :

" The Committee appointed to correspond with the Tabernacle Church, on the subject of Mrs. Baker's application to be recommended to the communion of the First Church, and who were subsequently instructed to consider and reply to the charge of that Church respecting the Christian character of this Church, having reported a full answer thereto, in the form of a letter addressed to the Tabernacle Church, it was thereupon voted, that the same be accepted.

And whereas the Tabernacle Church, in their last communication to this Church, appear to have taken leave of the correspondence on this subject, while they manifest a perfect readiness to receive information and satisfaction that their said charge is unfounded ; and whereas the answer now reported is designed to give such information and satisfaction to all the members of that church, and may be useful to others, also, laboring under similar erroneous impressions, which purposes cannot be accomplished without printing the same : therefore voted—

That the Committee who reported the answer, be directed and authorized to cause the same to be printed, together with so much of the correspondence and proceedings connected therewith, as they may judge expedient ; and that a copy of the publication be communicated to the Tabernacle Church.

Copy of Record.

Attest,   JOHN PRINCE,
Senior Pastor of the First Church in Salem."

The occasion of this second discussion, which took place in 1854, will best appear from references to various publications on the subject, after the Correspondence with the Tabernacle Church was closed. At the time of the discussion,—which that correspondence involved respecting the Christian character of the First Church,—no suspicion had ever been heard of that her noble old Covenant was not truly the genuine original "confession of faith and covenant drawn up by Francis Higginson," or that she had ever adopted or used a test creed or confession of faith distinct from the Covenant. The publications alluded to will show how such a suspicion was started, to what confidence of assertion it arose, and on what grounds it has been so resolutely maintained.

In 1835 was published: "A Discourse, delivered on the First Centennial Anniversary of the Tabernacle Church, April 26, 1835. By Samuel M. Worcester, A. M., Pastor of the Church." An Appendix, consisting of notes, marked alphabetically, was added to the discourse. In note U., the author presents the Covenant of the Tabernacle Church,* and thereupon his views of the original Covenant of the First Church as follows:

---

* See ante, pp. 85, 87,—the record of the adoption of the "New Direction," &c., from the first part of which this covenant of Mr. Leavitt's church was taken.

24

Extracts from the Covenant of the First Church, as adopted April 15th, 1680—which was subscribed by Mr. Leavitt and twenty-one brethren of his Church on the day of his ordination, 24th of October, 1745.

"We, who (through the mercy of God) are members of this Church of Salem, being now assembled in the presence of God, and in the name of our Lord Jesus Christ, after humble confession of our manifold breaches of covenant with the Lord our God, and earnest supplication for his pardoning mercy through the blood of Christ, and deep acknowledgement of our own unworthiness to be owned as the Lord's covenant people; also acknowledging our inability to keep covenant with God, or to perform any spiritual duty unless the Lord enable us thereunto by the grace of his spirit, and yet being awfully sensible that in these times by the loud voice of his judgments both felt and feared, the Lord is calling us all to repentance and reformation: we do, therefore, in humble confidence of his gracious assistance through Christ, renew our covenant with God, and one with another in the manner following:—

1. We do give up ourselves to that God whose name alone is Jehovah, Father, Son, and Spirit, as the only true and living God, and unto our Lord Jesus Christ as our only Redeemer and Saviour, as the only Prophet, Priest, and King over our souls, and only Mediator of the Covenant of Grace, engaging our hearts unto this God in Christ by the help of his Spirit of grace, to cleave unto him as our God and chief good, and unto Jesus Christ as our Mediator by faith, in a way of Gospel obedience, as becometh his covenant people forever.

2. We do also give up our offspring unto God in Jesus Christ, avouching the Lord to be our God and the God of our children, and ourselves with our children to be his people, humbly adoring the grace of God in Christ Jesus, that we and our children may be looked upon as the Lord's.

3. We do also give up ourselves one to another in the Lord according to the will of God, to walk together as a Church of Christ in all the ways of his worship and service; according to the rules of the word of God, promising in brotherly love, faithfully to watch over one another's souls, and to submit ourselves to the discipline and government of Christ in his Church, and duly to attend the Seals and Censures, and whatever ordinances Christ hath commanded to

be observed by his people according to the order of the Gospel, so far as the Lord hath or shall reveal unto us."

I would here take occasion to notice an error which has long been entertained, concerning the Covenants of the First Church. In the letter of Messrs. Diman, Barnard & Holt, (Appendix I,) it is stated that the First Church in Salem were accustomed formerly, from time to time, to renew their original Covenant. The language would seem to refer to the *first* Covenant of the Church, that is, the Covenant adopted in 1629. In the Records of the Tabernacle Church, there is a Transcript of a Pamphlet, entitled, "A Copy of the Church Covenants which have been used in the Church of Salem, formerly, and in their late reviewing of the Covenant on the day of the Public Fast, April 15, 1680. * * * Boston : printed at the desire and for the use of many in Salem, for themselves and children, by J. F., 1680." It begins as follows :—"There was a Church Covenant agreed upon and consented to by the Church of Salem, at their first beginning, in the year 1629, Aug. 6th." "The following Covenant was propounded by the Pastor, was agreed upon and consented to by the brethren of the Church, in the year 1636 :"

" We, whose names are here underwritten, members of the present Church of Christ in Salem, having found by sad experience how dangerous it is to sit loose from the covenant we make with our God, and how apt we are to wander into by-paths, even unto the loosing (losing ?) of our first aims in entering into church fellowship ; do therefore solemnly in the presence of the eternal God, both for our own comforts, and those who shall or may be joined unto us, *renew the Church Covenant we find this Church bound unto at their first beginning*, viz: 'That we covenant with the Lord, and one with another, and do bind ourselves, in the presence of God, to walk together in all his ways, according as he is pleased to reveal himself unto us in his blessed word of truth;' *and do more explicitly, in the name and fear of God, profess and protest to walk as followeth*, through the power and grace of our Lord Jesus Christ.

1. We avouch the Lord to be our God, and ourselves to be his people, in the truth and simplicity of our spirits."

So continued to the 9th clause, inclusive, through the original Covenant, as on pp. 13 and 14 of this volume, upon which the author observes as follows :

"I have seen fit to throw into the form of a quotation that part of the Preamble of the foregoing Covenant, which I suspect was, in substance at least, *The Covenant* 'which the Church was bound unto at their first beginning.' And I have italicised the sentences immediately preceding and following, so that the sense of the whole may be more obvious. It was the *first* Covenant which was *renewed*. Not satisfied, I suppose, with this brief formula, and wishing to notice some points suggested by the circumstances of the times, the members of the Church in 1636, 'did more explicitly profess and protest to walk as followeth;' that is, according to the more detailed expression of their obligations and engagements. Any one who is acquainted with the history of the town from 1630 to 1637, will perceive that this 'more explicit profession and protestation' *contains divers local allusions* which would be utterly inexplicable upon the supposition that it was prepared for the Church at its beginning. In fact, almost the whole of it implies that the Church had been for some years in existence, had had 'sad experience of the danger of sitting loose' from their Covenant,—and had suffered grievously from 'jealousies,' etc., from unwillingness 'to take advice,' etc., from 'forwardness to show gifts or parts in speaking,' etc., etc. The dissensions which were occasioned by Roger Williams, shed light upon the 6th and 7th articles. It would not have been so natural, in August, 1629, as in 1636, to speak of the duty of 'not laying a stumbling-block before any, no, not the Indians.' The conclusion is to my mind irresistible from the *internal evidence a'one*, that the Covenant printed in the Magnalia of Mather, and often cited as the Covenant of the First Church at its beginning, could not have been the *first* Covenant of that Church. . It was, as is stated in the Transcript alluded to above, 'the Covenant propounded by the Pastor, agreed upon, and consented to, by the brethren, in 1636.' Hugh Peters was at this time the Pastor."

The italics are all the author's. In regard to articles 6th and 7th, alluded to as more applicable to 1636 than 1629, we should recollect that early in the year 1629, Gov. Cradock enjoined it upon Mr. Endicott and his people here, as "the earnest desire of the whole company," that they would " demean themselves justly and courteous towards the Indians, thereby to draw them to affect our persons, and consequently our religion;"* and that the 7th is the very article which, as Morton states, in his account of the original confession of faith and covenant, was adopted because they *foresaw* that this wilderness might be looked upon as a place of liberty,†" &c.

The letter (referred to) of Messrs. Diman, Barnard & Holt, declining the invitation of the Third Church to be present at Dr. Whitaker's induction as their minister, contains the following declaration :

"Our worthy and pious ancestors of this Province esteemed the Congregational plan of Church polity most agreeable to the Gospel, and most favorable to the religious liberties and rights of individuals and societies. The First Church in Salem, (and in the Province,) from which we all descended, did formerly from time to time solemnly renew their original Covenant, and professed their adherence to Congregational principles, and particularly that they will in no way slight their sister Churches, but use their counsel as need shall be."

Certainly, the language here used by these venerable divines, who so well understood whereof they affirmed, would most clearly "seem to refer to the *first* Covenant of the Church; that is, the Covenant adopted in 1629."

In 1849, was published "The Discourse delivered at Plymouth, December 22, 1848, by Samuel M. Worcester, D. D. ;" which (at p. 12,) contains the following remarkable passage :

"A most egregious and singular error has been committed in representing the founders of the First Church in Salem,—the first, as I need not say, in the Massachusetts Colony,—as having organized themselves, without any Confession of Faith ; and as having had a form of Covenant, designedly so framed as to give liberty to all who might choose to call themselves *Christians*, to enter their communion

---

* 1 Felt's Annals of Salem, 48.   † See ante, p. 3.

and fellowship. What has been generally printed, for a hundred and fifty years, as the First Covenant of that Church, and adopted Aug. 6, 1629, *is not that Covenant.* It was adopted as a Special Covenant in 1636. The Covenant of 1629 was a very brief and comprehensive document, by which the signers pledged themselves to walk together in obedience to the rules of the Gospel ; while the "Confession of Faith" was as explicit and decided,—*Trinitarian and Calvinistic,*—as would of course be expected from men, who would rather have been burnt at the stake, than have given the least occasion for a doubt concerning their interpretation of " the faith once delivered to the saints."

In the Appendix to this Discourse, (p. 54) we find a note, in which the author, after repeating substantially what he had before represented as evidence of error concerning the Covenant, and which we have already referred to, proceeds as follows :

In a printed Tract, without date, but undoubtedly issued in the year 1680, we have the " Confession of Faith," with a form of " Covenant," " for substance," as adopted 6th of August, 1629. The expression "*for substance*" implies, of course, that the original was neither less in quantity, nor different in quality. The Tract may be found in the Boston Athenæum, B. 76, Sermons. It is entitled,

" A Direction for a public profession in the Church Assembly, after private examination by the Elders. Which direction is taken out of the Scripture, and points unto that faith and covenant contained in the Scripture. Being the same for substance which was propounded to and agreed upon by the Church of Salem, at their beginning, the *sixth of the sixth month,* 1629."*

THE CONFESSION OF FAITH.

" I do believe with my heart and confess with my mouth.

" *Concerning God.*—That there is but one only true God in three persons, the Father, the Son, and the Holy Ghost, each of them God, and all of them one and the same Infinite, Eternal God, most Holy, Just, Merciful and Blessed forever.

---

* Here was omitted a quotation, on the title page, indicating that this " Direction," was not to be imposed on any.

" *Concerning the works of God.*—That this God is the Maker, Preserver and Governor of all things according to the counsel of his own will, and that God made man in his own Image, in Knowledge, Holiness and Righteousness.

" *Concerning the fall of man.*—That Adam by transgressing the command of God, fell from God and brought himself and his posterity into a state of sin and death, under the wrath and curse of God, which I do believe to be my own condition by nature as well as any other.

" *Concerning Jesus Christ.*—That God sent his Son into the world, who for our sakes became man, that he might redeem us and save us by his obedience unto death, and that he arose from the dead, ascended into heaven, and sitteth at the right hand of God, from whence he shall come to judge the world.

" *Concerning the Holy Ghost.*—That God the Holy Ghost hath fully revealed the doctrine of Christ and the will of God in the Scriptures of the Old and New Testament, which are the word of God, the perfect, perpetual, and only rule of our Faith and obedience.

" *Concerning the benefits we have by Christ.*—That the same Spirit by working faith in God's Elect, applyeth unto them Christ with all his benefits of justification and sanctification unto salvation, in the use of those ordinances which God hath appointed in his written word, which therefore ought to be observed by us unto the coming of Christ.

" *Concerning the Church of Christ.*—That all true believers being committed unto Christ as the head, make up one Mistical Church, which is the body of Christ, the members whereof, having fellowship' with the Father, Son, and Holy Ghost by faith, and one with another in love, do receive here upon earth forgiveness of sins, with the life of grace, and at the resurrection of the body they shall receive ever- lasting life.

" THE COVENANT.

"I do heartily take and avouch this one God who is made known' to us in the Scripture, by the name of God the Father, and God the Son, even Jesus Christ, and God the Holy Ghost, to be my God, according to the tenour of the Covenant of Grace ; wherein he hath' promised to be a God to the faithful and their seed after them in their generations, and taketh them to be his people, and therefore' unfeignedly repenting of all my sins, I do give up myself wholly to this God, to believe in, to love, serve, and obey him sincerely and faithfully, according to his written word, against all the temptations of the devil, the world, and my own flesh, and this unto the death.

"I do also consent to be a member of this particular Church, promising to continue steadfastly in fellowship with it, in the public worship of God, to submit to the Order, Discipline, and Government of Christ in it, and to the ministerial teaching, guidance and oversight of the Elders of it, and to the brotherly watch of the Fellow-Members; and all this according to God's word, and by the grace of our Lord Jesus Christ, enabling me thereunto. AMEN."*

In 1853, was published the Sermon preached at the Installation of Rev. George W. Briggs, as Pastor of the First Church in Salem, by Rev. John H. Morison, of Milton. Appended to the publication were "Notices" of the First Church and its ministers, 1629 to 1853, by a Member. These were prepared by the present writer, and in speaking of the founders of the Church, and of their Covenant, he briefly repeated his own opinion, adding a reference to New England's Memorial, as follows :

"Mr. Felt justly observes : 'They called no man master. They resorted to the Bible as the ultimate standard of moral distinctions and religious principles.' Such, too, was the truly liberal spirit of the covenant they adopted, drawn up, undoubtedly, by Mr. Higginson. It engaged them to walk together in all the ways of God, "according as he is pleased to reveal himself to us in his blessed word of truth ;"—"to reject all contrary ways, canons, and constitutions of men;" and "to study the advancement of the Gospel in all truth and peace."†

---

* Here were omitted the " Questions to be answered at the baptizing of children, &c," showing the special purpose of this " help " (as its proposer, Rev. John Higginson, termed it,) in practising the doctrine of the Synod of 1662, as to Baptism. Members under the half-way covenant were subject to discipline, &c., though not admitted to full communion.

See ante, p. 62, the origin and explanation of this "Direction." The year 1680 was here mistaken for 1663.

† Morton, in his New England's Memorial, speaking of this covenant, says, it "was acknowledged only as a direction, pointing unto that faith and covenant contained in the holy Scripture, and therefore no man was confined unto that form of words, but only to the substance, end, and scope of the matter contained therein."—Davis's Ed.

The extracts here taken from the two Discourses referred to, present in full the evidence relied on to prove that what had always been considered the original Covenant of the First Church, adopted in 1629, was, (all but the three or four lines excepted,) adopted as a special covenant in 1636; and also the evidence to prove that, together with these three or four lines as a covenant, was originally adopted a test creed, or confession of faith, "explicit and decided—*Trinitarian and Calvinistic*." The evidence in each case consists in the discovery of a new inference from an old statement; in the one case, as if Rev. John Higginson had stated that his "Direction," proposed as a "help," &c., was the same *in form* instead of "*for substance*," &c.; and, in the other case, as if the Covenant set forth as "propounded, &c., in 1636," was an original one instead of a *renewal*, with an original preamble only.

At the time of this second discussion, we had received an impression that the First Church co-operated with Mr. Higginson in his said "Direction," but, as before stated, (p. 66,) they took no action in regard to it. We had also been led to suppose that the "Transcript of a Pamphlet," referred to by Dr. W., was among the "Records of the Tabernacle Church," in the "hand-writing of Deacon Timothy Pickering," but we now understand that it is a little pamphlet, not in his hand, but evidently more ancient, in an unknown hand, and attached to the Tabernacle Records. This is here mentioned to prevent misapprehension from any expressions used in the Discussion under review.

From the Salem Gazette of March 7, 1854.

The last two evening meetings of the Essex Institute have been occupied with an interesting discussion on the subject of the Covenant of the First Church in this city. The subject was commenced, on Thursday evening of the week before last, by Rev. Dr. Worcester.

* * Dr. Worcester's discussion was directed to two points, which are entirely distinct from each other. In the first place, he affirmed that at the beginning of the First Church, 6th of August, 1629, there was "a Confession of Faith," or articles of doctrinal belief, as well as "a Covenant."

In the second place, he affirmed that what has been commonly received as *the first* covenant of the First Church, *is not that covenant;* but is that first covenant *as it was renewed and enlarged in* 1636.

These two points respectively were argued, from the internal evidence of the document purporting to be the covenant of 6th of Aug. 1629; from the witness of early historical records; and from various minutes in the Records of the First Church, together with the explicit witness of a document in the Tabernacle Church Records, while these were called the Records of the First Church.

It is much to be regretted that the old book of Records of the First Church, or that previous to 1660, has been "utterly lost, excepting the Ch. Covenant," which appears on the third page of the Records, as copied by Rev. Mr. Barnard, who was settled in 1755.*

If that old book could be found, the question now raised would easily be put to rest; or rather, such a question, probably, would never have been raised.

It will be observed that the points at issue have no reference to the doctrinal belief of the founders of the First Church. There has never been any dispute that they were known and read of all men, as Trinitarians and Calvinists, or, in other words, as Orthodox.

It should also be noted that the error, alleged in regard to the first Covenant, does not appear to have originated with any now living. It may be considered, therefore, as it has now been, merely as a question of history.

————

The subject was resumed at the meeting of the Institute, on Thursday evening of last week, when the President, D. A. White, explained his views of the subject of the First Covenant of the First Church, and adduced authority of contemporary writers in support of the same.

* Here must be a mistake. Mr. Higginson added the Quaker clause to this covenant in 1660.

Judge W. commenced by observing that he would not be considered as antagonistic to Rev. Dr. Worcester, on this occasion, but rather as a fellow-laborer for the truth of history. Dr. W. had sought to explode what he conceived an historical error ; he himself would prevent, if possible, the introduction of a gross error into our history. He was glad that Dr. W. had brought the subject before the Institute, where the question could be fully discussed and settled. It was one of the important duties of the Institute to guard the truth as well as to preserve the facts of history. In the present case they owed it especially to the venerated Fathers of the First Church in Salem, whose character was implicated in the question. The truth, the whole truth, and nothing but the truth, was due to them, and conduced more to their honor than would a monument of marble that reached above the clouds.

The question was whether the foundation of the First Church in Salem, was laid upon broad Protestant principles, as exhibited by the noble confession and covenant prepared by its first teacher, or upon a sectarian creed, Trinitarian and Calvinistic, of the strongest stamp, as maintained by Dr. W.

Judge W. could not but regard the requiring of subscription or assent to such a creed, from all who would join the Church, as not possible in the nature of things. Orthodox as the founders of the First Church unquestionably were, they did not manifest their orthodoxy in such a way. The occasion for it had not come, even had their principles and views been consistent with it. But their earnest purpose on coming to New England was " Reformation of the church according to the written word of God," rejecting " all contrary ways, canons and constitutions of men," and studying " the advancement of the Gospel in all truth and peace."

Extracts from their writings, and from those of their contemporary friends in England, were read, showing how abhorrent to their principles would have been the imposition of such a sectarian creed, at the foundation of the First Church in Salem. The covenants of other early churches, as of Plymouth, Charlestown, the first, second and third in Boston, and that of Watertown, were referred to, as alike free from all disputed theological dogmas.

Judge W. said he had brought to the meeting the old book containing the records of the First Church from 1629 to 1736, together with Morton's New England's Memorial and Mather's Magnalia, as containing all the original authorities respecting the subject in question. The Book of Records has on its first and second pages the original Covenant of 1629, preceded by the preamble adopted on its renewal in 1636, and the clause to "beware of the leaven of the doctrine of the Quakers," added at the end. This addition is in the handwriting of Rev. John Higginson, made in 1660, which proves conclusively that this was then the recognized covenant of the church. So, indeed, it has ever since been regarded, till Dr. W.'s imagined discovery reduced it to about one half of its first sentence, as given in the Magnalia. But is it possible that such was the covenant that Francis Higginson would draw up for the foundation of his church, in compliance with a formal request to prepare a suitable one in Scriptural language? This could not be. The covenant which he *did* produce was worthy to be transcribed at length, that each of the thirty members might have a copy.

Judge W. showed, from the Records of the church, that nothing had been lost from them but what had been deliberately considered by the Church as better lost than preserved; and that everything important had been retained. If there ever had been such a Trinitarian and Calvinistic confession of faith as Dr. W. supposed, it would, of all things, have been most carefully preserved and transmitted. That such a document cannot be found, is full proof that it never existed.

Morton's New England's Memorial was relied upon as showing clearly the character of the confession of faith and covenant drawn up by Francis Higginson, and that it was *one* document only; and also as showing the freedom of access to the church.

But Mather's Magnalia was considered as settling the question beyond all controversy. The author was on intimate terms of friendship with both the ministers of the First Church, Messrs. Higginson and Noyes, and doubtless received from them the account he gives of that church in his Magnalia; and if not, both of them prefixed to this work their solemn "Attestation" to the truth of it. And here we find the genuine original Covenant of the First Church, without the "Preamble" of 1636, or the "Quaker clause" of 1660, together with Cotton Mather's declaration that "by this instrument was the covenant of grace explained, received, and recognized by the First Church in this colony, and applied unto the evangelical designs of a church estate."

Cotton Mather, also, like Morton, speaks of the various manner of admission into the church, and then adds: "which *diversity* was perhaps more *beautiful* than would have been a more *punctilious uniformity ;*" a clear refutation of the idea that subscription or assent was required to any fixed articles of faith.

The Gazette, of March 14, contained a report of some additional remarks by Dr. W., according to which,—

"He re-affirmed that the testimony of Morton's Memorial, of Mather's Magnalia, and other early histories, when interpreted in their true import, was entirely on his side of the questions in debate. The positions which he had taken had not been moved, in a single particular, by any of the statements or arguments advanced in the lecture of the evening."

The report closed as follows:

"It may be added that the discussion was an example that much may be said, on both sides of a question. To judge impartially and correctly in the present case, perhaps, both lectures should have been heard, with the rejoinders respectively; or the documents and authorities which properly relate to the subject, should be carefully and candidly examined.

FIRST CHURCH.
Salem Gazette of March 21.

The very imperfect reports of the discussion before the Essex Institute in relation to the foundation of the First Church, which have appeared in the Register and the Gazette, and especially the closing portion of them, require that something more explicit should be added, in order to a right understanding of the question. "To judge impartially and correctly in the present case," as suggested in the conclusion of the report in the last Gazette, "the documents and authorities, which properly relate to the subject, should be carefully and candidly examined."

This we now propose to do. It may strike some persons as of little importance how the question is considered or settled. But *truth* is always important, the *truth of history* highly so, and the truth of our own history in relation to the principles and proceedings of our venerated fathers, in framing the confession and covenant of the First Church they established,—the mother and model of so many other churches,—must be of the highest importance. It is due also in gratitude to these venerated fathers, to set their character and principles in a true light. It may by some be thought honorable to them to say, as Dr. W. does, in one of the notes to his Centennial discourse : "From their whole proceedings, it is indisputable that the fathers of the First Church, and of this town, were not less rigorous and uncompromising than any of their descendants or successors have been, in respect to the terms of church-membership, and admission to the Table of the Lord."

But such is not the honor which they deserve. They are entitled to the honor that redounds from their own noble spirit and conduct. Their true glory is, that highly orthodox as they were, they thought infinitely less of fastening their opinions upon others, than of carrying out their lofty principles of Christian reform. They came to New England with the earnest design of advancing the reformation of religion, and modelling their church according to the pattern of the New Testament. The word of God, not of man, the divine, not human Scriptures, was their steadfast rule.

Mr. Higginson, the first Teacher, was therefore commissioned "to draw up a confession of faith and covenant in Scripture language." He accordingly produced a document free from all sectarian terms and dogmas, and as beautiful, for its simplicity and union of faith and practice, as it is comprehensive and truly Christian. In its spirit and character, it is still worthy to be regarded as a model by all Congregational churches. Christian faith and practice are admirably blended in it ; *faith* in God, in Jesus Christ, in the word of his grace, and in reliance on him for spiritual strength, and *practice*, in all the duties of a Christian, associated in church fellowship. Before it can be justly said that it " is in no respect a confession of faith," it must indeed be reduced to its first sentence only ; and then who could possibly mistake it for the honored document that Francis Higginson,—" the father and pattern of the New England clergy,"— with so much deliberation and formality prepared ?

The idea that there was adopted a distinct confession of faith to which those who joined the church were required to give their assent as well as to the Covenant, is altogether imaginary. No such distinct confession of faith appears to have been thought of at the institution of the First Church in Salem, or at the beginning of any of the early churches in New England. No, not even at the formation of the second and third churches, in Boston, though this last was the

Old South itself. Not a trace can be found, in the history or records of the First Church, of the adoption or use of such a document, but everything shows the contrary.

The confession of faith and repentance required for admission into the church, was made in the freedom of each individual conscience, and varied accordingly. "The weakest measure of faith," as afterwards expressed in the Cambridge Platform, adopted in 1648, was accepted, and "such charity and tenderness used, as the weakest Christian, if sincere, might not be excluded nor discouraged." Morton, in his New England's Memorial, says: "The circumstantial manner of joining to the church, was ordered according to the wisdom and faithfulness of the elders, together with the *liberty* and ability of any person." Hubbard, in his history of New England, and Mather, in the Magnalia, bear the same testimony, the latter adding that such "diversity was perhaps more *beautiful* than would have been a more punctilious uniformity."

In another place, he says: "The churches of New England make only vital piety the terms of communion among them." The famous Mr. Cotton, of Boston, in his "Doctrine of a Church and its Government," says:—"Nor do we pinch upon any godly man's conscience in point of covenant in case he be willing to profess his subjection to Christ in his church, according to the order of the Gospel. Nor do we limit him to our own way of the order of the Gospel, but as it shall be cleared and approved to his own conscience." Burton, a distinguished English Independent, contemporary with our first Higginson, in his Rejoinder to Prynne's Reply, says: "It is the greatest possible tyranny over men's souls, to make other men's judgments the rule of my conscience." Similar testimony, to almost any extent, might be added, to show that no such confession of faith, as Dr. W. supposes, could possibly have been adopted with the original covenant of the First Church. Even the little "Tract,"—which has so egregiously misled Dr. W.,—containing forms of a confession of faith and covenant, prepared by Rev. John Higginson in 1665, as a "help," &c., upon the introduction of the half-way covenant, bears on its title-page a quotation showing that this confession of faith was "*not to be made use of as an imposition upon any.*" The quotation was taken from a passage in the preface to the Savoy Confession of Faith, declared by the English Congregational Churches in 1658, and substantially adopted by the Synod here in 1679;—viz.: "The genuine use of a confession of faith is," &c., accordingly, &c., and in no way to be made use of as an imposition upon any : whatever is of force or constraint in matters of this nature, causeth them to degenerate from the *name* and *nature* of confessions, and turns them from being *confessions* of faith into *exactions* and *impositions of faith.*"

The late venerable Judge Davis, having given, in the appendix to his edition of Morton's New England's Memorial, the genuine original covenant of the First Church, remarks as follows : "The people at Salem consulted with those at Plymouth, in the settlement of their church order, and this instrument, which is to be considered as expressing the character and views of those memorable worthies, is venerable for its antiquity, and estimable for its mild and benignant spirit. As the reverend author of the *Description of Salem* justly observes, " It may be esteemed, if not for its theology, for its simplicity. If it speak not the language of a sect, it breathes the spirit of Christian union."

It remains for us to examine more particularly Cotton Mather's account of the First Church, together with its old records, which will enable us to explain the origin and purpose of the two pamphlets which appear to have so misguided Dr. W. Both afford evidence that the world has been right in its judgment as to the original covenant of the First Church.

FIRST CHURCH.
Salem Gazette of March 24.

The question, be it remembered, is not about the orthodoxy of the confessions of faith that were actually made on joining the church, any more than it is about the orthodoxy of the founders of the church, but whether they were free, or exacted according to a prescribed written form.

Dr. Cotton Mather settles this question, as well as that respecting the original covenant, for his authority cannot in reason be doubted. Being on terms of intimate friendship with the ministers of the First Church, Messrs. Higginson and Noyes, at the time he was composing his Magnalia, or Ecclesiastical History of New England, he would naturally apply to them for an account of their church, and they would as naturally comply with his request. Dr. Mather, at the beginning of his notice of Rev. James Noyes, of Newbury, says, that he had sent to his "excellent friend, Mr. Nicholas Noyes, minister of Salem, for some account" of him, and gives it "in his own words," as not needing "any alteration." To whom else would he think of applying for an account of the Salem Church? And would he not publish the account as received? But, however this might be, both Mr. Higginson and Mr. Noyes must have read portions, at least, of the Magnalia, in manuscript, for both attested to the truth of the history before it was printed. In "An attestation to this Church History of New England," prefixed to the London edition of the Magnalia, published in 1702, signed "John Higginson," dated "Salem, 25th,—1st month—1697," he says, I "have known the beginning and progress of these churches unto this day, and having read over much of this History, I cannot but in the love and fear of God, bear witness to the truth of it." Mr. Noyes, as was his wont, speaks in verse, if not poetry, and is equally strong in his testimony, closing it as follows :—

> "The *stuff* is true, the trimming neat and spruce,
> The workman's good, the work of publick use,
> Most piously designed, a publick store,
> And well deserves the publick thanks and more."
> '*Nicholas Noyes, Teacher of the Church at Salem.*

These eminent ministers must have known perfectly well the constitution and history of their church. Mr. Higginson was present at its formation, and a member of it in his minority. Besides, he had with him, as his right hand man, during the greater part of his ministry, Deacon Horne, .(or Orne, as he wrote the name in his will,) one of the first thirty members, who must have been familiar with the original covenant and its various renewals. Mr. Higginson, (Jan. 12, 1679–80,) enters the following record of him : "Our bro : Horne having been Deacon of this church above this 50 years, and being now very antient, the church proceeded and agreed to choose 2 Deacons to be added unto him."

The account given by Dr. Mather may therefore be entirely relied on.

Here was introduced the original Covenant of 1629, with Dr. Mather's remarks preceding and following it— (see ante pp. 5, 6, 7 ;) also the preamble of 1636, and the postscript, or Quaker clause, of 1660, with Mr. Fisk's marginal note, all taken from the old Church book, (as ante, pp. 13, 14,) printed in italics.

We have no room for comment; nor is it needed. Every reader may perceive clearly what the original "confession and covenant" was, that it was but one "instrument," and that no *uniform* confession of faith was exacted on admission to church membership.

A. W.

FIRST CHURCH.
Salem Gazette of March 31.

Mather's Magnalia and Morton's New England's Memorial are both original authorities respecting the institution of the First Church. Hubbard, Neal, Prince, and others, who have copied from these, can afford no additional light on the subject. We give Dr. Mather the first place, because, for the reasons mentioned, we consider him as entitled to it. But Morton deserves entire confidence. He was the nephew of Governor Bradford, and in composing his works had the use of his uncle's manuscripts, and probably derived his information from this high source; more probably, however, from Rev. John Higginson himself, then minister of the First Church, whose name, together with that of Thomas Thatcher, the first Pastor of the Old South Church, in Boston, appears prefixed to the Memorial, on its publication in 1669, in attestation of its merits. We copy from Davis's edition of the Memorial, p. 145, the following unbroken passage, being all that immediately relates to our question, and all, as will be seen, substantially in accordance with the account already given from the Magnalia.

See ante, pp. 3, 4.

Here we see, as in Dr. Mather's account, that the confession of faith and covenant was *one* "instrument," and that the manner of admitting members into the church was various, and not according to any fixed creed or confession of faith. The article alluded to by Morton, respecting the "power of the magistrate in matters of religion," was doubtless the seventh,—promising "all lawful obedience to those who are over us in Church or *Commonwealth*,"—an article peculiar to the Salem Church covenant, and therefore likely to attract particular attention.

Were the meaning of the passages taken from the Magnalia and New England's Memorial doubtful, the Church Book of Records,

"1629 to 1736," would at once determine it. This is a folio volume, paged, apparently, at the same time, from 1 to 290.

For a brief account of the Church Book, and its contents, see ante, pp. 11, 17.

It is manifest from this Book of Records, that no confession of faith, distinct from the covenant, was ever recorded in it. And from the proceedings of the church at its first meeting, Sept. 10, 1660, after the settlement of Mr. Higginson, it appears that nothing valuable could have been lost with the old missing volume. At this meeting, "Major Hawthorn, Mr. Batter, Mr. Price, the two Deacons, together with the Pastor,"—were desired "to review the Church Book, and report such things to the Church as they conceived worthy of consideration."

For their report on this subject, and the vote of the Church—"To renew our covenant, and to add that clause of taking heed of the leaven of the doctrine of the Quakers,"—see ante, pp. 47, 48.

The clause was accordingly added by Mr. Higginson himself, apparently with the same pen and ink with which he made his record of this vote. The Covenant, therefore, must have been recorded where we find it, before 1660, and then well known by the Church as the original Covenant.

In 1736, just one hundred years after its first renewal, it was renewed for the last time in its own pristine excellence, without the Quaker clause, or any allusion to it. This took place after Mr. Fisk's dismission, at a meeting of the brethren adhering to the ancient principles of the First Church in Salem.

See ante, pp. 112, &c.

Now, after such a universal recognition of the original covenant of the First Church, for more than two hundred years, with no appearance of a confession of faith, adopted along with it, what has sprung a doubt upon the subject?

Simply, as we understand it, looking at two ancient pamphlets with eyes that see in them what was never found there before. The first, in order of time, is the little "tract," printed anonymously, and without date, but evidently belonging to the year 1665. In November, 1664, Mr. Higginson, at a meeting of the First Church, in-

formed the brethren that he would "at a time convenient" communicate "a short writing as a help for the practice" of baptism, according to the propositions of the synod of 1662. In October, 1665,
the pastor made known to the church, that "the writing he had formerly mentioned and read unto them as a 'help' to reduce the doctrine of the synod into practice, it being a direction for a public profession, after private examination by the elders, which direction is
taken out of the Scripture, and points to the faith and covenant contained in the Scripture; it being the same, for substance, propounded and agreed on by the Church of Salem, in their first beginning,
1629, 6th of 6th month."* The first Covenant, as identified by Mr.
Higginson in the renewal of it in 1660, and by adding the Quaker
clause, is undoubtedly referred to by him here,—the "direction," which
contained a reduced covenant, with confession of faith, and questions and answers suitable for baptism, being the same for *substance*,
though in a Trinitarian *form*. And here is the page of the Book of
Records, (85) which Rev. Mr. Fisk points out in his "marginal note"
to the ancient record of the covenant, to show that its true date was
August 6, 1629. But the "tract," as before mentioned, indicates on
its title page that the confession of faith is "*not to be imposed on
any.*"

The other ancient pamphlet, or rather *transcript*, of one, (which
we have not seen,) purports to be,—"A copy of the church covenants which have been used in the Church of Salem, formerly, and
in their late reviewing of the covenant on the day of the public Fast,
April 15, 1680."

It is sufficient here simply to copy Mr. Higginson's record of this
Fast, as follows:

"1680, April 15, was a Fast observed according to the order of
the Council, when the first Church Covenant was read, and the new
direction, propounded by the Pastor, and more accommodated unto
our times, was also read, and both of them consented to as helps in
renewing our covenant with God and one with another." This
"*first* Church Covenant" was indisputably the one identified by
Mr. Higginson himself, as above mentioned. "The new direction,"
therefore, could contain nothing inconsistent with the fact, that such
is the genuine original Covenant of the First Church.

---

* See ante, p. 62.

As observed in the outset, what gives importance to the question now considered, is its connexion with the character and principles of our forefathers. The truth, above all things, is due to them; and this cannot be clearly understood without attention to their ecclesiastical history, and especially to the constitution of their early churches.

.es.   A. W.

FIRST CHURCH.

Salem Gazette of April 4.

Three articles have appeared in your paper, on the subject of the "First Church," which evidently were occasioned by a lecture, delivered at the Essex Institute, on the 16th of Feb. last. The question, as presented in two distinct points, was discussed by myself, simply as a matter of historical importance and general interest ; —precisely as I would have discussed the question, recently agitated, whether John Endicott, or John Winthrop, is entitled to be considered the first Governor of Massachusetts Colony. A theological, or denominational question or discussion, would, of course, be foreign to the legitimate objects of the meetings of the Institute.

I wish to have all understand distinctly what the two points are, which were discussed in my own lecture. I copy from my manuscript:

"Permit me, gentlemen, to present before you in order, and in detail, the proof

I. That at the formation of the First Church, 6th of Aug., 1629, there was a *Confession of Faith*, as well as a Covenant,—to which candidates for membership were required to give their approval and consent.

II. That the Covenant called the first Covenant, was not that Covenant; but was the first Covenant, as *renewed and enlarged*, in 1636."

On some accounts, I should be glad to submit to your readers the historical evidence, adduced in my lecture, with other evidence of the same kind, which to my mind is most clear and decisive. But I am admonished of the liability, of which, in 1664, good Mr. John Allin thus wrote : "I see men are too apt to make use of sentences of Authors, that seem to favor their opinion, though indeed contrary to the meaning and judgment of those authors ; and this tends to amuse and puzzle the common sort of readers, and enlarge disputes, but doth not tend to clear up the Truth."

As regards *documents*, however, without any inferential or argumentative note or comment, the same liability cannot be said to exist. I therefore request you, first, to give a place in your columns to the following paper,—issued by Rev. John Higginson and the First Church, in 1665.* It is submitted as an answer to the question,—

Was there a Confession of Faith, as well as a Covenant, 6th of Aug., 1629?

Here comes in the "*document*," as already presented, at page 190, from Dr. W.'s Plymouth Discourse, with the following quotation, (there omitted,) preceding "The Confession of Faith,"—

In the preface to the Declaration of Faith owned and professed by the Congregational Churches in England :—

The genuineness of a confession of faith is, that under the same form of words, they express the substance of the same common salvation, or unity of their faith. Accordingly, it is to be looked upon as a fit means whereby to express *that* their common faith and salvation, and not to be made use of as an imposition upon any.

"1 Thes. 5: 12-13,—We beseech you, brethren, to know them that labor among you. He. 13: 17,——Obey them that have the rule over you. Lu. 12: 42—Who then is that faithful and wise steward. Ep. 4: 5,—One faith, one baptism. Tit. 1: 4,—The common faith. Jude, v. 3,—The common salvation. He. 3: 1,—Christ Jesus, the High Priest of our profession. He. 10: 23,—The profession of our faith. 2 Tim. 1: 13,—Hold fast the form of sound words. Rom. 2: 20,—The form of knowledge and of the truth. Rom. 6: 17,—That form of doctrine delivered unto you."

Subjoined to "The Covenant," come in " Questions," &c., (also there omitted,) viz :

"Questions to be answered at the baptizing of children, or the substance to be expressed by the Parents :

Quest. Do you present and give up this child, or these children, unto God the Father, Son, and Holy Ghost, to be baptized in the Faith, and engaged in the covenant of God professed by this Church ?

Quest. Do you solemnly promise, in the presence of God, that,

---

* Not issued by the Church.

by the grace of Christ, you will discharge your covenant duty towards
your children, so as to bring them up in the nurture and admonition
of the Lord, teaching and commanding them to keep the way of
God, that they may be able (through the grace of Christ) to make a
personal profession of their Faith, and own the Covenant of God
themselves in due time? FINIS."

In your next paper, I should like to answer the other question, and
in this same manner. S. M. W.

FIRST CHURCH.
Salem Gazette of April 6.

We refer to page 187, for an account—taken from Dr.
W.'s Centennial Discourse—of the "Transcript Pamphlet,"
here presented by him in answer to his last mentioned
question. All that he appears to have considered material for this purpose, is there pointed out, and need not be
repeated. But, though impertinent to the question, yet
wishing to present, in connection with the record of its
origin, (see ante, p. 85,) the "new direction," &c., which
forms the latter part of this "transcript pamphlet," we
take from the Gazette all that is necessary to supply it,
in addition to what is contained on pages 186 and 187.

Dr. W. introduces the document as follows:

I submit the whole document, although but a part is necessary, in
answer to the question,—

*Is the covenant called the first, the original covenant of Aug. 6,
1629; or is it that covenant, enlarged, and as it "was expressed and
enforced," when, according to Mather, it was solemnly renewed, about
seven years after?*

The portion omitted on page 187,—as indicated by
three stars,—is the following:

A direction, pointing to that covenant of God's grace in Christ,
made with his Church and people in the Holy Scriptures.

"Gather my people unto me, which have made a covenant with
me by sacrifice.—Psal. 50: 5. Jesus, the mediator of the new covenant.—Heb. 10: 29. The blood of the everlasting covenant.—

Heb. 13 : 20. Who is this that engageth his heart's approach unto me? And ye shall be my people, and I will be your God.—Jer. 30 : 21, 22. They shall go and seek the Lord their God, they shall ask the way to Zion, with their faces thitherward, saying, come let us join ourselves to the Lord, in a perpetual covenant that shall not be forgotten.—Jer. 50 : 4, 5.

At the end of the Covenant, as renewed in 1636, and referred to as on pp. 13 and 14, follows in the Gazette the Quaker clause of 1660, and then is introduced the "new direction," thus :

Also the following Covenant was in several Ch. meetings in the beginning of this year 1680, considered and agreed upon, and consented to by the generality of the Church, to be used as a direction for the renewing of our Church Covenant, as being more accommodated to the present times and state of things amongst us.

Accordingly it was made use of in that way, at the conclusion of the publick Fast, April 15, 1680, viz : "We, who, &c.," (as at p. 186,) completed as follows :

And whereas the elders and messengers of these churches have met together in the late Synod to inquire into the reasons of the Lord's controversy with his people, have taken notice of many provoking evils, as the procuring causes of the judgments of God upon New England, so far as we or any of us have been guilty of those evils, or any of them, according to any light held forth by them from Scripture, we desire from our hearts to bewail it before the Lord, and humbly entreat for pardoning mercy, for the sake of the blood of the everlasting covenant. And as an expedient unto reformation of those evils, or whatever else have provoked the eyes of God's glory amongst us, we do promise and engage ourselves in the presence of God :—

1st. That we will—by the help of Christ—endeavor every one to reform his own heart and life, by seeking to mortify all our sins, and to walk more close with God than ever we have done, and to uphold the power of godliness, and that we will continue to worship God, in public, private and secret, and this—as far as God shall help us—without formality and hypocrisy, and more fully and faithfully than heretofore, to discharge all covenant duties, one towards another, in a way of church communion.

· 2d. We promise by the help of Christ to reform our families, and to walk before God in our houses with a perfect heart, and that we will uphold the worship of God therein continually, as he in his word doth require, both in respect of prayer, and reading of the Scriptures, and that we will do what lies in us to bring up our children for God, and therefore will—so far as there shall be need of it—catechize them, and exhort and charge them to fear and serve the Lord, and endeavor to set an holy example before them, and be much in prayer for their conversion and salvation.

3d. We do farther engage,—the Lord helping of us,—to endeavor to keep ourselves pure from the sins of the times, and what lies in us, to help forward the reformation of the same, in the places where we live, denying all ungodliness and worldly lusts, living soberly, righteously, and godly, in this present world, making conscience to walk so as to give no offence, nor to give occasion to others to sin, or to speak evil of our holy profession. Finally—giving glory to the Lord our God, that he is the faithful God, keeping Covenant and mercy with his people forever, but confessing that we are a weak and sinful people, and subject many ways to break our covenant with him ; therefore that we may observe and keep these and all other covenant duties required of us, in the word of God, we desire to deny ourselves, and depend wholly upon the grace of God in Christ Jesus for the constant presence and assistance of his Holy Spirit to enable us thereunto, and wherein we shall fail, we shall humbly wait upon his grace in Christ for pardon, for acceptance, and for healing, for his name's sake. Amen."

We have now presented the two "documents" in the order in which they were first brought out, and by references have endeavored to afford a complete view of each, so as to exhibit the whole evidence adduced in support of Dr. W.'s theory respecting the constitution of the First Church. For his discursive views and observations, with a mass of extraneous matters, we must refer to the volume of the Salem Gazette, for 1854, which may readily be found in the library of the Essex Institute, at Plummer Hall. The real evidence, as we have seen, depends on the interpretation, not of the "documents" themselves, but

of a single accompanying remark or statement in each
case.   As to the original covenant, the latter of the two remarks, recited on page 187 from the "Transcript pamphlet,"
and with which "it begins," involves the whole question as
in a nutshell.   The "covenant" therein said to have been
"propounded," &c., in 1636, was confessedly a renewal of
the first covenant, whatever that was, with a preamble
to the renewal ; and the simple inquiry is, what is the
"preamble," and what the "covenant renewed."   The
inquiry is interesting chiefly as it affects the more important question, whether a test confession of faith was
adopted, together with the first covenant.   If the preamble can be made to swallow up, almost entirely, the
reputed original covenant, with all its nine articles,
there will be room left for an " explicit" and ample confession of faith, and the only difficulty would be to find it,
but if that is suffered to remain in its full strength, the
existence of such an additional confession of faith can
hardly be imagined.

FIRST CHURCH.
Salem Gazette of April 11.

We are sorry to feel obliged to say a single word more respecting
the foundation of the First Church ; but truth and justice require it.
A mist seems to have been thrown over the subject, that ought to be
cleared away.

The two ancient "documents," or copies thereof, published in
your last two papers, are valuable to illustrate the ecclesiastical history of Salem, and indeed of New England, taken in connexion with
the two great Synods that called them forth.   In this view of them,
we thank Dr. W. for their republication.   But as presented by him
without explanation, or any allusion to the notice we had taken of
their origin and purpose, they could hardly fail to make false impressions on the popular mind, in relation to the question under consideration.

The proceedings of the Church, represented by these "documents," afford evidence directly the reverse of that for which they

are now adduced, as we think sufficiently appears from the brief notice of them at the close of our last communication, following the inquiry—"After such a universal recognition of the original covenant of the First Church, for more than two hundred years, with no appearance of a confession of faith adopted along with it, what has sprung a doubt on the subject?" To that notice we would now refer, instead of repeating the same here.

The most ancient of the reprinted documents resulted from proceedings which were occasioned by the Synod of 1662, and was adapted to the Synod's propositions for baptism of children, upon the parents' owning the covenant, called the "half-way covenant." Mr. Higginson, the pastor, was for some time earnestly engaged in preparing a "Direction," &c., as a help to reduce the doctrine of the Synod into practice;" which he finally accomplished in 1665. Though he gave a trinitarian *form* to the reduced covenant contained in this "Direction," he regarded it as "being the same *for substance* propounded and agreed upon by the Church in Salem in their first beginning, 1629, 6th of 6th month." And Rev. Mr. Fisk refers to it in his "marginal note" to the ancient record of the first covenant as evidence of its true date. Mr. Higginson, indeed, could have alluded to no other than the covenant which he had specially recognized in 1660. A trinitarian phraseology, not found in our earliest church covenants, had now become fashionable, but could not have been regarded as affecting "the substance." A striking illustration of this we find in the history of the Charlestown Church. The historian, after copying "the covenant proposed to particular persons," &c., beginning, "You do avouch the only true God [Father, Son, and Holy Ghost] to be your God, &c.," remarks that "the important words in brackets, which are interlined in the original, are of different colored ink from the rest, and as evidently in the hand-writing of Rev. Charles Morton, who was installed in 1686."

The ancient "document" of 1665, therefore, so far as it has a bearing on the subject, proves that "the covenant called the first covenant," *is* "that covenant,"—while it affords no evidence of "a confession of faith as well as a covenant, to which candidates for membership were required to give their approval and consent."

The same may emphatically be said of the "document" of 1680, resulting from proceedings of the church, consequent upon the great reforming Synod of 1679. It declares that "there was a church covenant agreed upon, &c., at the beginning," and afterwards gives the covenant at length, together with the renewing "preamble" of 1636, so as to make it perfectly clear what was the first covenant, showing it to be the same as recorded in the old church book, and as printed in the Magnalia, without the "preamble." It also agrees with Mr. Higginson's record of the Fast of April 15, 1680, in representing the covenant then agreed on, as "a direction for renewing our church covenant, as being more accommodated to the present times," &c. But the record gives the pre-eminence to the original covenant, as follows,—"The *first* church covenant was read, and the new direction propounded by the pastor, and more accommodated unto our times, was also read, and both of them consented to as helps in renewing our covenant with God and one with another."

While Deacon Pickering copied from the "new direction" of 1680, the covenant for the church which had seceded with Mr. Fisk, —"the brethren adhering to the ancient principles of the First Church," did, in 1736, "confirm, recognize, and renew the first covenant made and entered into by our forefathers at their first settlement into a church state in this place;" recording it at length on the second page of the new Church book,—without the "preamble of 1636," and without the "Quaker clause of 1660," —thus affording another indisputable evidence of what was the genuine original Covenant of 1629.

We have nothing to do in this discussion with theological opinions, and cheerfully yield to Dr. W. whatever he may wish as to the number or orthodox character, of the confessions of faith, alluded to by Cotton Mather,—only insisting that their *free nature* be remembered—as indicated on the title page of the "document of 1665." In the preface to the Savoy Confession of Faith declared in 1658, and adopted substantially by our Synod of 1679 ; we find described "the genuine use of a confession of faith," stating that they are "not to be made use of as an imposition upon any; whatever is of force or constraint in matters of this nature causeth them to degenerate from the *name* and *nature* of confessions, and turns them from being *confessions of faith* into *exactions* and *impositions of faith*."

In our historical argument, we, of course, followed Dr. W., who had quoted from Mather, Morton, Prince, and others who copied from the two first,—excepting that we confined ourselves to these two original authorities, and gave from each in one "continuous unbroken passage" all that immediately respected the question. *We*, therefore, certainly, are not within the scope of the admirable remark, of which Dr. W. was "admonished," and "which in 1664, good Mr. John Allin thus wrote : "I see men are too apt to make use of sentences of authors, that seem to favor their opinions, though contrary to the meaning and judgment of those authors; and this tends to amuse and puzzle the common sort of readers, and enlarge disputes, but doth not tend to clear up the truth."

We have endeavored, equally with Dr. W., to discuss the subject as a matter of historical interest, without regard to any "theological or denominational" questions. But had we not considered it as more important than "whether John Endicott or John Winthrop is entitled to be considered the first Governor of Massachusetts colony," we should have taken no trouble about it. The question is of far higher importance.

The primitive Fathers of Salem are entitled to the glory of having founded their Church upon the broad platform of Christianity, and Francis Higginson, their model Teacher, deserves immortal honor for the confession and covenant which he so felicitously drew up in Scripture language, according to their injunctions ;—a truly noble document, which, while it united them in Christian brotherhood, formed an admirable manual of faith and duty, for their constant advancement in piety and all Christian virtues. It is still worthy of profound attention. Every one of its nine articles contains an important lesson for study and practice. It has accordingly been honored in history, both here and in England, above every similar document, for its intrinsic excellence as well as for its antiquity. Our primitive fathers must not be robbed of the glory to which they are so justly entitled, nor must their posterity be deprived of the benefit of their example. If we are ever to be rid of the plague of sectarianism, our churches must return to the Christian Scriptural foundation of the First Church in Salem—"the First in the Massachusetts Colony." A. W.

"THE PLAGUE OF SECTARIANISM," &c.
Salem Gazette of April 14.

For the whole long communication under this head, signed S. M. W., and evidently occasioned by a misapprehension of A. W.'s meaning in the use of the expression quoted, we must refer to the volume of the Salem Gazette for 1854. It is sufficient to copy here the following sentences only:

But what affinity or connection has the "plague of sectarianism" with those instructive, and, for my argument, perfectly conclusive documents of the First Church, in 1665 and 1680? ✻   ✻   ✻

I was not at all afraid to trust those documents, to speak for themselves ; nor any more should I fear to trust Prince, Mather, Hubbard, and Morton, to speak from their own intelligence, without a word of mine. I wish that the two of them quoted, and commented upon, had been permitted so to speak; and the longer and more abundant the " continuous unbroken passages," without any mystifying comments—" contrary to the meaning and judgment of those authors"—the more should I have been gratified and satisfied.

"THE PLAGUE OF SECTARIANISM."
Salem Gazette of April 19.

This unfortunate expression, of which S. M. W. so bitterly complains, is not original with A. W.,—though incidentally, and very innocently, used by him without a thought of its application to any particular denomination of Christians.—He was indebted for the leading word as well as for the sentiment, to the great and good Richard Baxter, of whom the eminent Dr. Bates, in his funeral sermon upon him, says:—"He would as willingly have been a martyr for love as for any article of the creed."

" Two things," says Mr. Baxter, " have set the Church on fire, and been the *plagues* of it above one thousand years. 1. Enlarging our creed, and making more fundamentals than ever God made. 2. Composing, and so *imposing*, our creeds and confessions in our own words and phrases."

" And," again he says, " it is the nature of a sectary that he preferreth the interest of his opinion, sect, or party, before the interest of Christianity, catholicism and charity, and will sacrifice the latter to the service of the former."

In his " Directions for young Christians," Mr. B. says,—" It is a most dangerous thing to a young convert to be ensnared in a sect ; it will before you are aware, possess you with a feverish, sinful zeal for the opinions and interest of that sect ; it will make you bold in bitter invectives and censures against those who differ from them ; it will corrupt your Church communion, and fill your very prayers with partiality and human passions : it will secretly bring malice, under the name of zeal, into your mind and words; in a word, it is a secret, but deadly enemy to Christian love and peace.''

Nothing but an imperative sense of the duty which A. W., under the circumstances of the case, felt that he owed to the truth of history and to the memory of the primitive fathers of Salem, would have induced him to undertake the responsible task of vindicating their just claims,—claims, unquestioned for more than two centuries,— against a novel and threatening inquisition. It appeared to him that the alleged discovery of an historical error in relation to them was itself an error, and tended not only to deprive these noble fathers of the glory of founding their Church, upon a truly Scriptural platform with a complete Christian Covenant renowned for its intrinsic excellence ; but to subject them to the reproach of adopting a sectarian test creed, together with a covenant so meagre as to contain no recognition even of Christ or Christianity !

Having no private interest or views to serve by the present investigation, A. W. wishes to confine his attention as much as possible to the public purpose which first engaged it ; and being strongly impressed with its importance he will make no apology for pursuing it so long as it appears necessary for clearing up the truth. He certainly has no disposition to indulge in personalities, and he hopes to spare himself and others the trouble of replying to any personal or extraneous matters, however confidently presented in the place of argument, or answers to argument.   A. W.

For the whole of the very extended communication under the following heading, we refer to the original in the volume of the Salem Gazette, for 1854, taking from it the first and last sentences together with several other connected passages, which may suffice to accompany the reply to it. Italics, capitals, &c., are exactly copied.

''THE DOCUMENTS''
Relating to the Confession and Covenant of the First Church,
August 6, 1629.
Salem Gazette of April 21.
A confession of faith differs from a covenant, both in matter and form, as much as the Constitution of Massachusetts differs from the

oath of office, or as an inventory of an estate from a will. And yet it has been assumed and argued, as if indisputable, that all which has been said by our early and most intelligent writers, respecting the first confession of faith and covenant of the First Church, refers to but " one instrument"—and *that,* a mere unmixed form of covenant, without one sentence which, by any authorized usage, would suggest the idea of a *confession,* or, which is the same, a CREED !

*　　*　　*　　*　　*　　*　　*

" This following covenant was propounded by the pastor, [it must have been Hugh Peters,] agreed upon, and consented to by the brethren of the church, in the year 1636."

What then is that " following covenant?" It begins :

" We, whose names are here underwritten, members of the present Church of Christ in Salem, having found, by sad experience, how dangerous it is to sit loose from the covenant we make with our God, and how apt we are to wander into by-paths, even to the loosing of our first aims in entering into church fellowship, do therefore solemnly, in the presence of the eternal God, both for our own comfort and those who shall or may be joined unto us, [☞] renew the church covenant, we find this church bound unto at their first beginning, viz : THAT WE COVENANT WITH THE LORD, AND ONE WITH ANOTHER, AND DO BIND OURSELVES IN THE PRESENCE OF GOD, TO WALK TOGETHER IN ALL HIS WAYS, ACCORDING AS HE IS PLEASED TO REVEAL HIMSELF UNTO US IN HIS BLESSED WORD OF TRUTH ; [☞] and do *more explicitly,* in the name and fear of God, *profess and protest to walk as followeth,* thro' the power and grace of our Lord Jesus Christ.

" We avouch the Lord to be our God, and ourselves to be his people, in the truth and simplicity of our spirits," &c.

The remainder is the same as is in the covenant, claimed for 1629.

I submit to any impartial judge, whether the above record represents the covenant of 1636 to be the same as that of 1629? And I submit, whether that part which I have distinguished by small capitals may not have been intended to express the covenant of 1629, in the very words, so far as cited, and as the substance of the whole? What could be more comprehensive, scriptural, and beautiful in its kind? What more was really needed for its time, when the enterprise of the founders of the church was but an experiment?　　*　　*　　*　　*　　*　　*

That Morton, Hubbard, Mather and Prince did not know a Confession from a Covenant, or that they stultified themselves by incongruous language, are suppositions alike preposterous. In sober earnest, I add, that if each of them had said that, when Francis Higginson read aloud the Confession of Faith and Covenant, he made a most dignified and reverential appearance in his *wig and surplice*, I should just as soon have inferred that there was no manner of ' wig,' except in the silk of the ' surplice,' as that there was no kind of Confession, or Creed, except in the Covenant.

S. M. W.

FIRST CHURCH.

Salem Gazette of April 28.

The elaborate and curious speculations about the so called " documents," in last Friday's Gazette, seem to demand some notice, if they contain no argument to be answered. The various ingenious conjectures, queries and surmises, touching matters which pertain to ages after the institution of the First Church, tend to divert attention from the real points at issue, and the main facts relating to them. To a few of these, therefore, we advert once more, briefly as possible.

Learning and ingenuity are not required to decide the simple, though important, question of historical fact under consideration. Nothing more is necessary than a capacity to read writing as well as print, and to open our eyes upon the appropriate page, with something of that common sense construction which our predecessors invariably used in reading it, to understand its contents perfectly. Let us then glance at the page of record and of history which settles the whole question. First, look at the ancient Church book of records, which we have before described and given a fac simile of its first and second page. Here we see " the members of the Church of Christ in Salem," solemnly renewing the first covenant, and we read their preamble, expressing their penitential sorrow, and introducing that covenant as follows: we—" renew that Church Covenant we find this Church bound unto at their first beginning, viz," then repeating at full length that very covenant,—consisting of an introductory clause and nine articles—without the slightest intimation that a single word of it originates with themselves. At the close we see the Rev. John Higginson's hand recognizing it as the Covenant renewed in 1660, and recording the new clause then added to it. In the margin we see the Rev. Mr. Fisk referring, by a note, to the 85th page of the book for evidence that this Covenant was " signed and declared," on the " sixth of the 6th month, 1629."

Viewing with unbiassed judgment, this plain record, can we possibly doubt as to what is the original Covenant, and what the prefix of the renewers, any more than we can doubt what belongs to Mr. Higginson and what to Mr. Fisk? The several parts could not be more distinctly indicated.

So, accordingly, in Cotton Mather's Magnalia, doubtless received by him from Messrs. Higginson and Noyes, ministers of the First Church, both of whom sanctioned his account, we find the whole of the first Covenant as renewed in 1636 without a word of what was then prefixed, or of what was added in 1660,—nothing but the pure original covenant of 1629. These ministers and this historian, certainly, had no doubt as to what constituted this Covenant; nor does it appear that for more than two centuries any such doubt was conceived by any human imagination.

The "house" illustration used by Dr. W. may, with some amendment, be truly applicable. Supposing this Covenant the spacious mansion, which the renewers of 1636 wish to enter, their preamble is the porch built for the purpose; afterwards this porch is removed, and the noble edifice is exhibited to Cotton Mather just as it came from the great master-builder himself.

But now, it would seem, Francis Higginson, after all, is to have little credit for his admirable work. Part only of the introductory clause is yielded to him,—just what. is printed in small capitals and no more! Why not allow him, at least, all this clause? Is it because if all were allowed it could not be detached from what follows and the whole must go with it? The criticism which thus mangles the great "Instrument," by which, as Dr. Mather declares, " the covenant of grace was explained, received and recognized by the first Church in this Colony," is certainly as original as it is remarkable. Cotton Mather, with this instrument before him and which he thus shows to be " one instrument," calls it a Confession and Covenant, however "preposterous the supposition." If not a sentence of it " by any authorized usage," could be considered a confession the same would doubtless be said of Christ's sermon on the mount. Indeed, had Francis Higginson made this his model—as perhaps he did,—he could not have more beautifully blended faith and practice in his noble instrument. Being restricted to Scripture language he could not, if he would, have introduced the trinitarian phraseology, which in 1665 John Higginson used in the form accompanying his "half-way Covenant."

Sufficient has already been said of the "direction," of 1665, and the "new Direction," of 1680, to show that both afford evidence corresponding to that of Cotton Mather. Mr. Fisk's marginal note is not a "blind guidance." The 85th page, to which he refers, shows us that Mr. Higginson, in 1665, pointed expressly to what was "propounded and agreed upon by the Church of Salem *at their first beginning,* 1629, 6th day of 6th month;" and thus fixed the *date* of what a few years before he had recognized as the Covenant of the Church "*at their first beginning.*"

The Church record book commencing with 1736, as before shown, contains the most indisputable evidence of what had ever been regarded as the first Covenant;—introduced too in a manner as if to preclude forever all possible doubt on the subject. "We do," say the brethren of the Church, "confirm, recognize and renew the first covenant made and entered into by our forefathers at their first settlement into a Church state in this place, which runs in the following words." Then follows at length, *without the preamble of* 1636, *or the addition of* 1660, the genuine original Covenant of 1629.

How could our respondent consider "the witness of Mather" as favoring the theory that this Covenant belongs rather to 1636, than to 1629, when Mather subjoins to his copy of it the explicit declaration just alluded to, so evidently connecting it with the first organization of the Church? And how could he fail to notice this passage, and that which follows it, in which Mather most clearly shows, as Morton does in New England's Memorial, that the manner of admitting members to the Church was such as forbids the idea of a written confession of faith to which assent was required?

Both Mather and Morton thus prove conclusively that no such written Confession was used in the admission of Church members, and the fact that no trace of its existence is found in the records or history of any of the first New England churches, shows that the supposition of such an instrument is altogether imaginary. John Higginson in his "Direction," of 1665, referred for substance to what he had known, to exist, which was the first Covenant, and the "half-way covenant" was the main part of that "direction."

That confessions of faith were made by those who joined the

Church, and that these were sometimes very long as well as very orthodox, nobody doubts. But they were *free*—made according to each person's faith and conscience. And, as says the Cambridge Platform, "such charity and tenderness is to be used that the weakest Christian, if sincere, may not be excluded nor discouraged. In his philological distinction of "confession" and "covenant," Dr. W. seems to forget the *freedom* which our early fathers considered so essential to the very "*name* and *nature* of confessions." A. W.

RESPONSE TO FIRST CHURCH.
Salem Gazette of May 2.

For the article in full under this head, signed S. M. W., we must refer to the volume of the Salem Gazette, for 1854, copying here the following unbroken passage, which is about one fifth part of the whole.

As so many assertions and repetitions of assertions have been made, I may be pardoned, I think, if I make one summary reply to all the particulars which I have not specifically reviewed. It is this: I am not aware of a single historical passage of our early writers, which, in the smallest degree, militates against what I have maintained; and I have yet to see the first argument in opposition to my views, which I have not already met, or am not fully prepared to meet, with a direct, plain, honest, manly, and sufficient answer.

On the other hand, I appeal to every competent and candid reader,—(of course, *I mean such only as know a* CREED *from a covenant*,)—if a single statement of *mine*, in my own words, has been *disproved*, a single item of *testimony* has been *confuted*, or one single argument has been fairly met and logically answered !

It is fully conceded that Morton, Mather, and others, have explicitly spoken of a confession of faith and covenant, as used on the 6th of Aug. 1629. I have shown, that a confession is so fundamentally and totally different from a covenant, both in matter and form, that, according to universal usage, *it is impossible* that they could have meant *a covenant* only, and *that* the covenant claimed for 1629.

By the document of 1665, I have shown to a moral certainty, that *there must have been*, both a confession and a covenant, Aug. 6th, 1629. And not to say anything of Mather,—I have also shown by the document of 1680, that the covenant claimed for 1629, *is not that covenant*, but is the covenant of 1636; and that there was another and a different form of covenant, Aug. 6, 1629. The witness of this document *cannot be denied;* neither has it been, nor can it be, *disproved or invalidated.*

Upon these positions, I plant my feet. I will leave all others, some of which are not unimportant. But until these can be overthrown or undermined, there may be a succession of " First Church" numbers, in an infinite series,—and they will avail nothing, except as examples of how much can be said in opposition to what is true.

RESPONSE TO FIRST CHURCH.

Salem Gazette of May 12.

Such a very extraordinary " Response" as appeared in Tuesday's Gazette, of last week, cannot be passed without some notice. The kindly sentiment expressed in the conclusion, is duly appreciated, and sincerely reciprocated; but the higher sentiment of the great Roman orator and moralist—" Amicus Plato, amicus Socrates, magis tamen amica veritas"—is imperative. TRUTH must not be compromised. Yet a greater than Cicero has taught that one is not therefore to be deemed an enemy because he declares the truth.

What was there in the article responded to, which could have produced such a tissue of excited and sweeping assertions ? A. W., in recalling attention from extraneous and irrelevant matters, to " the real points at issue, and the main facts," referred, briefly as he could, to the original evidence of record and of history, proving that the first Covenant was truly what it had ever been supposed to be, and that no distinct confession of faith, or test creed, was adopted along with it. He pointed to the first pages of the ancient Book of Church records, " 1629 to 1736," and to those of the succeeding Book, commencing with 1736,—both presenting the first covenant in full,—the former explicitly as " *that Church Covenant which the Church was bound unto at their first beginning,*"—and the latter declaring it to be " the first covenant," and that it " runs in the following words"—setting forth the very words at length.

He pointed also to the pages of Mather's Magnalia, which he had before given in " one continuous" extract,—containing the original historical evidence, furnished undoubtedly by Messrs. Higginson and Noyes themselves,—certainly authenticated by them,—which presents *the same first covenant,*—clear of all renewing preambles or postscripts,—together with the following explicit declaration:—" By THIS INSTRUMENT was the covenant of grace explained, received, and recognized by the First Church in this Colony," &c., together with a particular account of the *various* manner of admitting members into the church. "Some were admitted by expressing consent unto their confession and covenant; some after their first answering to questions about religion propounded unto them; some, when they had presented in writing such things as might give satisfaction, &c., and some orally addressed the people," &c.; " which *diversity,* "it is added, " was perhaps more *beautiful* than would have been a more *punctilious uniformity.*"

These two passages immediately subjoined to the " Confession and Covenant," as Mather here calls "this instrument," appear to settle completely the points at issue. The one, declaring that "by *this instrument* was the covenant of grace explained," &c., excludes the idea of any *other* instrument in the case, and connects *this* indissolubly with the first organization of the Church, August 6, 1629. And the latter, showing the *free* and *various* manner of admission to church membership, proves incontestably that there could have been no such thing as a written confession of faith or creed to which subscription or assent was required upon admission to the Church.

These passages having failed to attract any particular attention, A. W. took the liberty to inquire as follows: " How could our respondent consider ' the witness of Mather' as favoring the theory that this Covenant belongs rather to 1636, than to 1629, when Mather subjoins to his copy of it, the explicit declaration just alluded to, so evidently connecting it with the first organization of the Church? And how could he have failed to notice this passage, and that which follows it, in which Mather clearly shows, as Morton does in New England's Memorial, that the manner of admitting members was such as forbids the idea of any written confession of faith to which assent was required?"

Yet these essentially material passages, thus again brought distinctly to the respondent's view, are not noticed in the " Response." This is the more remarkable, as it was to one of these that A. W. referred in his allegation that Cotton Mather called "this instrument" a " Confession and covenant," which the respondent answers by commenting on a different passage in which the expression is not used, and by quoting from " Mather's Sketch of Francis Higginson's life," a passage which without mutilation or addition, would clearly show that by "Confession and Covenant," as there used, is meant one instrument only. However variously denominated, it appears from Mather and Morton, the two original authorities, that but one instrument was drawn up by Francis Higginson, "whereof thirty copies were taken for the thirty persons." And in this "Sketch," it is added, "These thirty persons did solemnly and severally profess their consent unto the confession and covenant *then read unto them.*" By omitting these italicised words, and adding the following,—"i. e. not only 'unto the confession,' but also to the covenant," it is made to *seem*, contrary to the *reality*, that there were *two* instruments. There is a perfect consistency between the particular account given by Cotton Mather of the organization or "the nativity of the First Church," as he terms it, and the brief notice of it in this "Sketch." It should be remembered that Francis Higginson was directed to draw up a confession of faith and covenant in the language of Scripture, the acknowledged standard of faith and practice, and not according to "any authorized usage" of technical theology. He accordingly combined in his one instrument, the substance of both faith and practice, recognizing the great undisputed truths, as well as duties of Christianity ; and thus producing, in the scriptural manner, what might well be called, "a confession and covenant."

The omission to notice the important passages referred to, is a sufficient acknowledgment of the facts they establish. But how could the respondent so confidently assert in this "Response" that he was "not aware of a single historical passage of our early writers, which, in the smallest degree, militates against what" he had "maintained ?" No man can, by mere force of will, or boldness of assertion, change an historical fact, any more than he can by mere violence of criticism tear asunder a "venerable instrument" consolidated by the probation of centuries.

Whence comes such overwhelming assurance ? Entirely from two anonymous pamphlets, one of which is known only through an uncertain copy, and both pertaining to ages after the institution of the First Church. Dignified with the name of "documents," they seem to have acquired a sort of magical influence. The records of the First Church, showing their origin and purpose, afford evidence directly the reverse of that which has been so strangely attributed to them. That this may appear in the fullest light, it is thought proper to extract from the Church records all that relates to them, and present the whole in one view.

For these extracts, already substantially given, see ante, pp. 59, 62, 84, 85.

These records of Mr. Higginson speak for themselves. In the last he refers to the "*first* Church Covenant;"—in the former, to what was "propounded and agreed upon by the Church of Salem *in their first beginning*, 1629." Can there be a doubt that he refers to the same Confession and Covenant which he renewed and identified in 1660, and which he and Mr. Noyes afterwards certified to Cotton Mather with the declaration by "this instrument was the covenant of grace explained, received and recognized," &c., at "the *nativity of the First Church* in the Massachusetts Colony?" Is this explicit testimony of record and history, unquestioned for two hundred years, to be controlled by an uncertain copy of an anonymous pamphlet? What sort of "logic" would this be? But even the quotation from this copy shows that the first Covenant *with* the "preamble" was propounded &c. in 1636, while by giving both together it shows that all but the "preamble" was the covenant "which the Church was bound unto *at their first beginning*."

The pamphlet containing the "short writing," or "Direction" of 1665, bears evidence on its face that the confession of faith therein was "not to be used as an imposition upon any." What "logic" could infer from this alone—against all evidence, too,—that there was at first a written confession of faith, or creed, "used as an imposition upon" all who would join the church? The covenant in this "Direction," it is said, "is no more the same as that of 1629, than Washington's Farewell address is the same as the Declaration of American Independence." No *two* things are the *same*. Mr. Higginson says "same *for substance*;" which implies difference in phraseology, and makes manifest his reference to the first covenant,—the only instrument ever recognized or alluded to by him as such, or as the "first propounded."

A few words must be added in conclusion, occasioned by queries in the "Response," which suggest so strongly the great principle that gives to this discussion all its interest and value,—the protestant principle of the sufficiency of the scriptures and the right of private judgment, on which was founded the First Church in Salem, and indeed all the first churches in New England, for in none of them was there a written confession of faith imposed, or any "human test" of religious opinion, as President Stiles calls it. This learned and truly liberal divine well observes that we should remember "that liberty of thinking and choosing our religion, *liberty of conscience*, was the great errand of our pious forefathers into America." And we, their descendants, should never forget how gloriously the primitive fathers of Salem fulfilled their mission. It cannot but be of the highest importance that the true constitution of our early churches should be clearly understood and constantly held up as a model for the time to come. What could afford better hope or means of healing the painful divisions among Christians, caused by "human tests" in religion, which have been so deeply deplored by the wisest and best of men, from the days of the great Apostle down to the late Dr. Arnold, the brightest recent ornament of the English Church?

Dr. Arnold never ceased to lament the great error of his Church in establishing sectarian articles of faith, and he earnestly sought a reform in this respect. "Differences of opinion," he observes, "will exist, but it is our fault that they should have been regarded as equivalent to differences of principle, and made a reason for separation and hostility." "Since disunion," he again says, "is something so contrary to the spirit of Christianity, and difference of opinion so inevitable to human nature, might it not be possible to escape the former without the folly of attempting to get rid of the latter?"— Again, "I groan over the divisions of the Church, of all our evils I think the greatest,—Christ's Church, I mean,—that men should call themselves all sorts of various appellations, forgetting that only glorious name of CHRISTIAN, which is common to all, and a true bond of union. I begin now to think that things must be worse before they are better, and that nothing but some great pressure from without will make Christians cast away their idols of Sectarianism; the worst and most mischievous by which Christ's Church has ever been plagued."   A. W.

For the entire article under the following date, signed S. M. W., we refer to the Salem Gazette, for 1854, copying here the introductory sentences, together with several connected passages, which appear most nearly to relate to the subject.

Salem Gazette of May 16.

"The violence of some men's tempers makes them raise debates, when they do not justly offer themselves, and like mill stones grind one another, when they want other grist."·

I fully concur in this shrewd and quaint reflection of the same New England historian who said that " a copy" of the confession of faith and the covenant of the First Church, 6th of Aug., 1629, was "retained" at his time of writing, "by some that succeed in the same church ;" and which, I am not without expectation, will yet come forth, as did the document of 1665. However this last may be, I am very sure that there is too much of such "grinding" as he speaks of; and, for myself, I have neither "temper" nor time for such childishness or unprofitableness. Besides, *Sirius* will soon make his appearance, even in "the cool of the day." * * * *

I now very respectfully repeat and reaffirm that there is not one word in all that has been quoted from Cotton Mather, which conflicts in the least with the positive statement of the document of Mr. Higginson and the First Church in 1680, viz : that the covenant as given by Mather, was the covenant propounded and agreed upon in 1636. I also reaffirm every word of my last article, and of all that I have said, from the first sentence of my Lecture, Feb. 16. More particularly, I reaffirm, with "*overwhelming assurance,*" as A. W. calls it, that I am not aware of a single historical passage of our early writers, which, in the smallest degree, militates against what I have maintained.

Moreover, I say explicitly and most positively, that not " a single sentence of *mine*, ☞ *in my own words*, has been *disproved*, nor a single item of testimony *confuted*, nor a single *argument* fairly met and logically answered." And both unmoved and immovable are all those positions upon which, as I said, I plant my feet.

I appeal to those undeniably authentic and genuine documents of 1665 and 1680, as in themselves alone a perfect demonstration of all that I have undertaken to prove. * * * * *

Salem Gazette of May 19.

"'THE VIOLENCE OF SOME MEN'S TEMPERS," &c.

What a renewed exhibition (in last Gazette,) of bold and sweeping assertions! But a repetition of bare assertions, with whatever increased energy of emphasis, creates no necessity for repeating their refutation.

S. M. W. is once more respectfully reminded of those "essentially material passages,"—being conclusive of the whole question,—subjoined by Dr. Mather, with the sanction of Rev. Messrs Higginson and Noyes, to his full and pure copy of the original covenant, viz.:—

1. "By this instrument was the covenant of grace explained," &c. &c., at "the nativity of the First Church," &c.

2. As to the circumstances of admission into this Church," &c., showing the various and free confessions upon which members were admitted;—a "diversity—more beautiful than would have been a more punctilious uniformity," and in perfect accordance with the apostolic doctrine—"With the heart man believeth unto righteousness, and with the mouth confession is made unto salvation."

A. W. has made no "assaults" in this discussion, but has been wholly on the defensive. When an important historical truth was assailed, he undertook its defence, and has pursued it without a thought of its being a personal matter. He will enter into no dispute with his learned respondent as to precedency in point of "temper," "courtesy," or "logic." Let the truth of history stand upright, and he is satisfied.   A. W.

Of the lengthy article under the following date, signed S. M. W., we copy a connected portion, near the beginning, being about one seventh part of it, and for the whole must refer, as before, to the original publication. This is the less to be regretted, as the volume of the Gazette, containing the various articles, can so readily be found at Plummer Hall, accessible to all who may wish to consult it.

Salem Gazette of May 26.

"ESSENTIALLY MATERIAL PASSAGES."

As I have before stated, there is much depending upon the meaning of terms, in the present issues. I will, therefore, repeat that the terms "confession" and "Covenant" are *never synonymous, never equivalent, and never interchangeable*. If not expressly modified, they no more denote one and the same thing, or "instrument," than prayer and sermon, or invocation and benediction, in our public worship. I challenge a disproof, c. g. of the following definitions by Webster.

"*A confession, or confession of faith*," is "a formulary in which the articles of faith are comprised; a creed to be assented to or signed, as a preliminary to admission into a church." A "covenant, —*in church affairs*, is a solemn agreement between the members of a church, that they will walk together according to the precepts of the gospel, in brotherly affection." No exception is indicated. Can any be produced? Are there not many, who detest and denounce *Confessions*, or *creeds*, while they do not at all object to a covenant?

In matter and form, as thus defined, Confessions and Covenants must have been as familiar as the alphabet, to the Higginsons and the primitive members of the First Church; and equally so to the early historians of New England, Morton, Mather, &c. The same must be true of "*substance*," which, as Webster says,—is "the essential part; the main or material part. In this epitome we have the *substance* of the whole book." One of the N. E. fathers said:— "Substance for *matter*, yea, *words*, for the most part." Thus understanding the terms, "Confession," "covenant," and "substance," I have discussed this "First Church" subject. And I claim that they are "*conclusive of the whole question*" in *my favor*. * * *

Salem Gazette of June 2.

"THOSE 'ESSENTIALLY MATERIAL PASSAGES,' *being conclusive of the whole question, subjoined by Dr. Mather, with the sanction of Rev. Messrs. Higginson and Noyes, to his full and pure copy of the original covenant.*"

Had S. M. W., (in last Friday's Gazette,) presented these passages in their just light—so that they might be clearly seen and understood, nothing more would have been called for. But he has seen fit to encumber them with a mass of matters and glosses, tending to obscure their real meaning, as if they could not be trusted alone to speak for themselves. A. W. is therefore constrained to make a few additional remarks in answer to the interrogatory proposed—"What proof appears that there was no confession distinct from the covenant of 1629, to be used as I have said, or that Mather considered the covenant, copied by him, to be the original, *unaltered* covenant of 1629?"

"Let the reader keep in mind," that the definitions given by Webster, of "Confession," &c., were made after *creed making* came into fashion, and do not express the meaning which was "familiar to the Higginsons and the primitive members of the First Church," but that these worthies held that *freedom* was essential to the very *name* and *nature* of confessions,"—and that "whatever is of force or constraint" therein, "turns them from being *confessions of faith* into *exactions and impositions of faith*," and that in the use of the words, "Confession and Covenant," they have clearly signified the meaning which they attached to them. The instrument, drawn up by Mr. Higginson, was required to be in scriptural language, and it blended together faith and practice, in like manner as the Scriptures do,—Christ's Sermon on the Mount, for instance,—uniting the essential Christian faith common to all believers with the practical duties to which all are alike bound. It was therefore well called by them "a confession of faith and covenant,"—though it left each individual member of the Church, or candidate for membership, to make confession of his own particular faith, freely and fully, according to his own conscience.

"Let it also be kept in mind," that the two anonymous pamphlets, called "documents," to which so much importance is attached, are not in themselves evidence, but depend wholly on the records showing their origin and purpose, and that these records afford evidence directly the reverse of that for which the so called "documents" have been adduced. If "John Higginson and Mr. Noyes furnished Mather with these "documents," he does not appear to have found in them what is now thought to be discovered there, nor to have paid any regard to them in his account of "the *nativity* of the First Church."

Now let us look at this account, (which need not again be recited) bearing in mind that John Higginson, who so expressly sanctioned it, having been a member of the Church at the beginning, and long conversant with deacon Horne, who was deacon from 1629 to 1684, must have perfectly well understood what was the first covenant of his Church. The most ancient record of this Covenant being coupled with the preamble to its renewal, seven years after its adoption, Mather, of course, gives it as "then expressed and enforced,"—*not* "enlarged." But it is the *first* covenant *purely* that he gives, without a word of what was prefixed in 1636,—or of what was added upon its renewal in 1660, or of what was adopted when it was renewed in 1680,—nothing but the true original covenant of 1629,—the very same as afterwards confirmed anew, on the re-organization of the Church, in 1736, and set forth in the identical "words" of "the first covenant made and entered into by our forefathers at their settlement into a church state in this place."

This would seem sufficient to settle the fact of its being truly the first covenant—as heretofore universally received. But Mather's explicit declaration, subjoined to it,—"By *this instrument* was the covenant of grace explained, &c. by the First Church in this Colony, and applied unto the evangelical designs of a Church estate," &c., would remove all doubt on the subject, if any could possibly exist. When, but in 1629,—at "the *nativity* of the First Church,"—could "this instrument" have had its operation? And how could Mather have more decidedly manifested that he considered it "to be the original, *unaltered* covenant of 1629? How, too, could he have more strongly implied that *no other* instrument was used in the case?

That no written form of confession, distinct from "this instrument," was adopted, is demonstrable from his account, in the next subjoined passage, of the various manner of admission into the church. Each candidate for church membership made confession of *his own faith* in his *own way*, not of *others' faith* in a *way prescribed* to him : a most essential distinction.

Morton, it should be remembered, in New England's Memorial, the other original historical authority, entirely agrees with Mather in showing that but *one* instrument was used in constituting the Church, and that no test confession of faith could have been adopted. "It was desired of Mr. Higginson," he says, "to draw up a confession of faith and covenant in Scripture language ; which being done was agreed upon." Again,—"The confession of faith and covenant, forementioned, was acknowledged," &c. "And for the circumstantial manner of joining to the Church, it was ordered according to the wisdom and faithfulness of the elders, together with the *liberty* and *ability* of any person. Hence it was that some were admitted by expressing their consent to THAT written confession of faith and covenant ; others did answer to questions about the principles of religion that were propounded to them ; some did present their confession in writing, which was read for them ; and some, that were able and willing, did make their confession in their own words and way."

With such *positive* facts established, is it competent for any man to *imagine* a form of confession inconsistent with them, and then to require proof of the *negative?* These established facts are in accordance with the Cambridge Platform, of 1648, with the constitution of all the first Churches in New England, and resulted necessarily from the avowed principles of our forefathers in the formation of their churches. Mather begins his account of the First Church by stating the general principle, in which all were agreed, to be :— "That the reformation of the Church was to be endeavored according to the written word of God." In John Higginson's Election sermon, 1662, which has been referred to, the great cause is represented to be: 1. Reformation of religion according to God's word. 2. *Progress* in that reformation. The fathers of Massachusetts, orthodox as they were, sought not to perpetuate their peculiar views by embedding them in a test creed, and fastening that upon the constitution of their churches. This, as before observed, is the important fact which gives interest to the present inquiry. It is comparatively immaterial, except so far as historical truth is concerned, whether our primitive fathers had a longer or shorter covenant, or no written covenant at all; and it is of little consequence whether they were more or less strict in the examination and admission of candidates for church membership, provided they had no test forms to shackle conscience, but left their posterity in the church the same liberty to adopt new opinions, that they themselves enjoyed in forming their own. The glorious fact that our first New England Churches were founded upon the broad platform of Christianity, ought to be known and never forgotten, for the example must have its influence, and may serve to bring to an end those bitter sectarian divisions, over which the Baxters and the Arnolds of the Christian Church have so deeply mourned.   A. W.

We give the introductory and closing passages of this last article, by S. M. W., as sufficiently indicating that no reply to it was expected or required.

"CREED MAKING."

Salem Gazette of June 6.

I had my reasons for quoting those "definitions." In my youthful days, I was once sitting in an Athenæum, where two older sons of my Alma Mater were quietly reading. The silence was broken by this inquiry,—" *Can you tell me the difference between sanctification and justification?*" From the answer and the colloquy which ensued, I was not a little amused to find, that neither of the two had any more knowledge of the meaning of the terms, than of *abracadabra;* or of the Indian word of thirty-five or more letters, which, if I do not greatly err, was, at *Nonantum,* the word for one of five letters only in our English Bible. At a little later day, I heard in another place, from a liberally educated man, that, after a recent search in the Magnalia, &c., he thought, that "*a covenant is the constitution and the confession is the legislation of the Church.* * * * * *

Webster's "*definitions*" may not have been "made," until "after creed making came into fashion;" but they somehow happen, retrospectively and marvellously, to agree to an iota with those New England confessions and covenants, as well as with the confession and covenant, which, according to Mr. Higginson, were the same for substance as those of the First Church, 6th of Aug., 1629.

If, however, A. W. really thinks that "covenant" and "confession," as defined by Webster, and as commonly understood among us, have a different "meaning," from that which "was familiar to the Higginsons and the primitive members of the First Church, I shall not further contend with him. And as the rest of his article on Friday last, was answered by me, some weeks since, I will not, at present, say anything more. S. M. W.

The Christian Examiner, for July, 1854, under the head of "Religious Intelligence," contains a notice of the preceding Discussion, and we introduce a portion of it here, as a fitting appendix.

CONFESSION AND COVENANT OF THE FIRST CHURCH IN SALEM.

A discussion has recently been pursued in the columns of the "Salem Gazette," in reference to a very interesting point in the ecclesiastical polity of the Fathers of New England. It was introduced by a lecture before the Essex Institute, in Salem, delivered by the Rev. Dr. Worcester, Pastor of the Tabernacle Church in that city. A brief report of the lecture appeared in the Gazette of March 7. Dr. Worcester impugned the truth of a statement which has passed unquestioned for a long time, concerning the primitive practice of the

First Church in Salem, and of others in this Colony, and affirmed that that Church, from the beginning, required of all whom it received to its communion the acceptance of a written *creed*, embodying the views of Augustine and Calvin ; and that this *creed*, as well as the covenant into which church members entered with each other, was a distinct and unalterable standard of religious fellowship, intended to be of binding force upon the founders of the Church and upon their successors.

....D. A. White,....a member of the First Church, denied the historical truth and the documentary authority of what was affirmed by Dr. Worcester, and asserted that neither the Salem Church nor the other primitive churches of the Colony imposed upon their members a set formula of doctrines embodied in a written creed of human construction. *   *   *   *   *   *   *   *   *

The point in debate is simply this,—whether those suffering witnesses and those bold assertors of the sufficiency of the Bible, and of the right of private judgment, under a responsibility to God alone, undertook to shape and fashion out a Calvinistic formula of their own devising, to be written in their records and accepted word by word, as a positive test of fitness for church membership.   Dr. Worcester asserts, and Judge White denies, this statement.   In our opinion, the weight of argument and evidence is with the latter.   We gather three prominent and distinct facts to sustain this position :—

1. No such creed as is alleged is to be found on the records of the First Church, nor is its use or existence even recognized.

2. Cotton Mather and Secretary Morton, who had the best means of information on the subject, give a very particular account of the formation and some of the subsequent history of the church, and inform us that when a candidate entered into covenant with the church, he was at liberty to make his own statement as to religious convictions and experience,—that he was sometimes questioned, that he sometimes read from a written paper, and sometimes gave an oral account of the matter, according to his pleasure ; both writers speak distinctly of the delight which was derived from this liberty and variety of utterance.

3. What is called the Confession and Covenant of the First Church, is on record ; an admirable composition, partaking of the nature both of a formula of faith and of a bond of brotherly fellowship in the Gospel.   This was drawn up by the pastor, by the re-

quest of the church, under the express condition that it should be in the language of Scripture,—a condition which could not have been complied with in the construction of a Calvinistic formula.

The conclusion, to our minds, is obvious and irresistible. The founders of the Salem Church were thorough Calvinists. * * * Yet while the fathers of our Colony held Calvinistic opinions, it is very evident to the reader of what they have left us from their own pens, that they did not lay the stress of Christian discipleship and of the conditions of church membership on a formula of Calvinistic doctrine. * * * * * *

It plainly appears that in the church at Salem there was no written creed or Calvinistic formula imposed upon the members. The pastor, teacher, or elders satisfied themselves as to the faith of candidates for communion by a private examination, and when they came before the church to accept the confession and the covenant, they made such a statement of their views and experience as they pleased, either orally or by reading. If in the private examination or in the answers to questions put to them before the church it had been made to appear that they were heretical, they would, of course, have been rejected. But no set Calvinistic formula was administered to each and all. They expected more light to break from the word of God, and they left the doors and windows open to receive it. We have had to straighten many of their crooked and narrow streets in these regions, nor should we probably have been withheld from doing so if they had put prohibitions on record against it. In matters which concern our own freedom of soul, and our accountability to God, we are glad to know that we can follow with reverence the *principles* of our fathers, even while we utterly reject some of their *opinions.*

This third discussion, so immediately succeeding that which we have just reviewed, was as unwelcome as it was unexpected; but it appeared to be imperatively demanded.

In 1855, was published at Boston, by the Congregational Board of Publication, "The Ecclesiastical History of New England, &c., by Joseph B. Felt, Vol. 1."

It was with high expectations that we opened this volume and read from its first page the "Report of a committee on the character of this work," containing among other lofty encomiums, the following attestations:

Having been appointed by the Congregational Library Association, to examine this first volume of Mr. Felt's Ecclesiastical History of New England, we take pleasure in certifying that, in our judgment, it everywhere discloses a thoroughness of research and an accuracy of statement, in regard to matters of fact, which the early history of New England has never before had, and will never again need.

The gathering of the first churches in New England, and the settlement of their pastors, are given in minute, but not unnecessary detail. From these circumstantial sketches the attentive reader will better learn the genius of our ecclesiastical polity than from any platform or learned treatise that has been subsequently put forth. This attempt to lay bare the first foot-prints of New England Congregationalism, will win for the author the thanks of many earnest minds long exercised with care, to regain "the old paths," and "walk therein."

Here then we confidently hoped to find that full justice

was done to the founders of Salem and the First Church.
We knew that Mr. Felt appreciated the supreme regard
which they manifested to the Bible in "the establishment of
their Church," as indicated by our quotation (p. 192) from
the first edition of his Annals of Salem ; and we also
knew that he had identified the true original covenant by
specifying the remarkable article contained in it against
"being stumbling-blocks in the way of the Indians."*—
And how could he better teach "the genius of our ecclesiastical polity," or more truly "lay bare the first foot-
prints of New England Congregationalism," than by completely and faithfully setting forth the principles and the
proceedings of the First Church in Salem,—the first constituted in America,—and the most deliberately formed
Congregational church that had ever been gathered. Let
us now see how these high expectations were met.

This volume consists of about 660 pages, extending to
the year 1647. The author, having quoted, under the
date of July 20, 1629, the Letter of Charles Gott, (for
which see ante, p. 1,) proceeds at p. 115, under the date
of August 6, as follows :

The ordination mentioned in Gott's letter takes place. The
church platform of rule, covenant,† and articles of faith, being Calvinistic, and drawn up by Mr. Higginson, are accepted, by thirty
members. These had been individually supplied with a copy of the
covenant, which is read publicly, and receives their consent. With
regard to the doctrines now professed, Chalmers says, they "formed
the seed plot of the independent churches of New England." To
the numbers received, many of good report are speedily added. The
covenant and confession of faith here spoken of were evidently not
contained together in one document, but were separately and individually acknowledged. A pamphlet printed about 1660, which com-
prises both of them "for substance," as distinct articles, proves that
the first independent church of Salem, at their outset, had articles of

* Annals of Salem, 28.

faith. Governor Bradford is a delegate from Plymouth Church, but, detained by adverse winds, he arrives during the services, and proffers the right hand of fellowship. This he does, though, as Hubbard remarks, Higginson's principles ' were a little discrepant from theirs of Plymouth.' Among the attendants on this occasion, was Edward Gibbons, who had resided at Mount Wallaston. The services seriously affect him. He was subsequently a prominent and useful inhabitant of Boston.

By the account of Gott, it seems as though the ministers were ordained the 20th of July, and a similar ordinance performed for ruling elders, of whom was Henry Haughton and the deacons, in August. Still there is an evident propriety in believing that a like service took place with regard to the clergymen on the latter date. The chief objection which arises with this view, is that a two fold consecration appears unnecessary. Morton's Memorial observes on this subject,—' After the sermons and prayers of the two ministers, in the end of the day, the confession of faith and covenant being solemnly read, the forenamed persons (members of the church) did solemnly profess their consent thereunto, and then proceeded to the ordination of Mr. Skelton, pastor, and Mr. Higginson, teacher.' This refers to the last date. Hubbard confirms the same position. Prince offers an explanation : ' As Mr. Skelton and Higginson had been ministers ordained by bishops in the Church of England, this ordination was only to the care of his particular flock, founded on their free election. But as there seems to be a repeated imposition of hands, the former, on July 29, may only signify their previous separation for their solemn charge, and this latter, of August 6, their actual investiture therein.' Thus the question is completely decided, what the leading men in Massachusetts mean to have as the mode of their ecclesiastical polity.

The following is the author's note on the word covenant, referred to on the preceding page :

† This covenant differs from the second, formed 1636, which has long been supposed to be the first, and from the hand of Higginson, when it was probably drawn up by Peters, at the later date.

This note renders it proper that, to complete the author's view of the constitution of the First Church, we should give his account of the renewal of the covenant in

1636, which is introduced under this year, at p. 267, as follows :

December 21, Hugh Peters becomes the pastor of Salem Church. They renew their covenant,* somewhat altered from the first. It evidently had reference to events of the time. One passage of it is,— 'Resolving to reject all contrary ways, canons and constitutions of men in his worship.' This evidently bears on the experience of the dissenters in England, who had refused compliance with Episcopal requisitions. Another,—'We will not in the congregation be forward either to show our own gifts or parts in speaking or scrupling.' It was common in our ancient congregations for persons to rise after the sermon, and express approbation or the contrary to its different parts. A further passage,—'No way slighting our sister churches, but using their counsel as need shall be ; not laying a stumbling-block before any, no, not the Indians, whose good we desire to promote.' There had been several cases wherein much difficulty had arisen, because such advice was not seasonably sought. The great object of evangelizing the original inhabitants, is still cherished. The last extract, here taken from the Covenant, runs as follows : 'We do promise.to carry ourselves in all lawful obedience to those that are over us in church or commonwealth.' This relates to the troubles occasioned by the stand of Roger Williams and his advocates, and to those arising from the controversy about Mrs. Hutchinson's doctrine."†

Simultaneously with this "Ecclesiastical History of of New England," or in quick succession to it, appeared a new edition of Morton's Memorial, viz,—"New England's Memorial. By Nathaniel Morton, Secretary to the Court for the Jurisdiction of New Plymouth. Sixth Edition, &c. With numerous Marginal Notes, and an Appendix, &c. Boston: Congregational Board of Publication. 1855."

At page 99, is found a reference to the Appendix,—

---

* Mather's Magnalia.
This general reference to 'Mather's Magnalia,' is by the author. For both Morton's and Mather's account of the First Church, see ante, pp. 3, 4, 5, &c.

† For a similar dissection of the old Covenant, see ante, p. 188. These fragments are all that we find of it in "Mr. Felt's Ecclesiastical History of New England."

"For a copy of the confession and covenant," described by Morton, in his account of the foundation of the First Church,—by a note on "direction," in the following passage:

"The confession of faith and covenant, forementioned, was acknowledged only as a direction* pointing unto that faith and covenant contained in the Holy Scriptures, and therefore no man was confined unto that form of words, but only to the substance, end and scope of the matter contained therein. And for the circumstantial manner of joining to the church, it was ordered according to the wisdom and faithfulness of the elders, together with the liberty and ability of any person. Hence it was that some were admitted by expressing their consent to that written confession of faith and covenant ; others did answer to questions about the principles of religion that were publicly propounded to them ; some did present their confession in writing, which was read for them ; and some that were able and willing, did make their confession in their own words and way ; a due respect was also had unto the conversations of men, namely, that they were without scandal."

Turning to "A," in the "Appendix," at page 459, we read as follows:

(A. page 99.)

THE ARTICLES OF FAITH AND COVENANT OF 1629.

Judge Davis, in his edition, seems to have overlooked the fact that the "Direction," of which Morton speaks, contained both a Confession of Faith and a Covenant. Hubbard, Mather, and Prince, have also spoken of a Confession of Faith as well as a Covenant. And this should not be omitted in a faithful history of the Fathers.

In 1665, the First Church in Salem issued a new "Direction," which was occasioned by the action of the Synod of 1662, in regard to baptism and the half-way covenant.

From this it appears that there was a Confession of Faith and a Covenant, 6th of August, 1629.

Mr. Higginson and Mr. Skelton, and other good people that arrived at Salem in the year 1629, resolved, like their father Abraham, to begin their plantation by calling on the name of the Lord.

*For a copy of this confession and covenant, see Appendix, A.

On their arrival at Salem, they consulted with their brethren at Plymouth what steps to take for the more exact acquaintance of themselves with, and conforming themselves to, the word of God, in their church organization and polity. And the Plymotheans, to their great satisfaction, laid before them the authority they had in the laws of their Lord Jesus Christ for every particular in their Church order.

Whereupon, having the concurrence and countenance of their Deputy Governor, John Endicott, esq'r, and the approving presence of the messengers from the Church of Plymouth, they set apart the 6th day of August for fasting and prayer, and for their making a confession of their faith, and entering into an holy covenant, whereby that church state was formed. See Magnalia, 66.*

Here follow "A Direction," &c., containing "The Confession of Faith," "The Covenant," and "Questions to be answered at the Baptizing of Children," &c., for which see ante, pp. 190, 206.

After the "Direction," &c., the Appendix proceeds as follows:

Cotton Mather says, "the Covenant whereto these Christians engaged themselves, which was about seven years after solemnly renewed among them, I shall here lay before all the churches of God as it was then expressed and enforced." Mag. 1, 66.†

Mather further says, "By this instrument was the covenant of grace explained, received, and recognized by the first church in this colony. This instrument they afterwards often read over, and renewed the consent of their souls unto every article in it, especially when their days of humiliation invited them to it."

The Covenant published in Magnalia, and by Judge Davis, in his Appendix, was probably enlarged from this original at the time of the renewal, seven years after this first covenant was adopted, in Aug., 1629, which is here given.

The following Covenant was propounded by the pastor, agreed upon and consented to by the brethren of the church, in the year 1636‡:

"Gather my saints unto me that have made a covenant with me by sacrifice." Psal. 1, 5.

"We whose names are here underwritten, members of the present church of Christ in Salem, having found by sad experience how dangerous it is to sit loose from the covenant we make with our God, and how apt we are to wander into bypaths, even to the loosing of our first aims in entering into church fellowship, do therefore solemnly, in the presence of the eternal God, both for our own comforts and those who shall or may be joined unto us, renew the church covenant, we find this church bound unto at their first beginning, namely, that "we covenant with the Lord and one with another, and do bind ourselves in the presence of God, to walk together in all his ways, according as he is pleased to reveal himself unto us in his blessed word of truth;" and do more explicitly, in the name and fear of God, profess and protest to walk as followeth, through the power and grace of our Lord Jesus Christ.

We avouch the Lord to be our God, and ourselves to be his people. in the truth and simplicity of our spirits.

For the other eight articles, see ante, pp. 6, 7.

At the end of the old First Church Covenant, "Appendix A" closes with the following quotation:

COVENANT OF THE FIRST CHURCH IN CHARLESTOWN.

June 30, 1630, the first church in Charlestown was formed, and a covenant entered into; and this was the foundation of the first church in Boston. It is in these words: "We whose names are here underwritten, being by God's most wise and good providence, brought together into this part of America, in the Bay of Massachusetts, and desirous to unite into one congregation or church, under the Lord Jesus Christ our head, in such sort as becometh all those whom he hath redeemed and sanctified to himself :—

Do hereby solemnly and religiously (in his most holy presence) promise and bind ourselves to walk in all our ways according to the rule of the Gospel, and in all sincere conformity to his holy ordinances and in mutual love and respect each to other, so near as God shall give us grace."—*Drake's Hist. Boston*, 93.

In 1855, was also published a pamphlet, entitled "A Memorial of the Old and New Tabernacle, Salem, Mass.,

1854–5. By Samuel M. Worcester, D. D., Pastor of the Tabernacle Church."

This publication must have been subsequent to the new edition of Morton's Memorial, though of the same year,—as the appendix to that edition is referred to repeatedly in "Preliminary Notices," at the beginning of this pamphlet.

In these "Notices," after an allusion to "the Records" of the "Tabernacle Church" as having been "withheld" by the pastor, Rev. Mr. Fisk, and supposed "to be lost," it is stated as follows:

The Book of Records of the First Church, previous to 1660, is also lost, or was destroyed. Some portions were copied, and are still preserved. It is not known when the Records actually began. As in respect to the affairs of the city, it is probable, that the early transactions of the First Church were not properly recorded. In the circumstances, this is not unaccountable, however much to be regretted.

We have, for instance, no accredited and no professed copy of the original "confession of faith," which, with a "covenant in Scripture language," was prepared by Rev. Francis Higginson. (See Morton's "New England's Memorial," Mather's "Magnalia," Hubbard's "History of New England," etc.) According to Hubbard, there were copies "retained by some" as late as 1680 or 1681. A printed copy of the confession of faith and covenant, "*the same for substance*," is in the Boston Athenæum, (B. 76, Sermons.) It is entitled "Direction for a Public Profession in the Church Assembly, after giving examination by the elders, which direction is taken out of the Scripture, and points unto that faith and covenant in the Scripture; being the same for substance which was proposed to and agreed upon by the Church of Salem, at their beginning, the 6th of the 6th month, 1629." This was prepared by Rev. John Higginson, of the First Church, and was ready for the members in Oct., 1665. (See Records First Church. A copy may be seen in Morton's "Memorial," etc., by the Congregational Board of Publication, 1855, pp. 459-464. Also, with the covenants of 1636 and 1680, in the Salem Gazette, March 31, etc., 1854.)

The original form of *the covenant* of 1629, very nearly, if not exactly, is inserted in the preamble of the Covenant of 1636. It is this : "We covenant with the Lord and one with another, and do bind ourselves in the presence of God, to walk together in all his ways, according as he is pleased to reveal himself unto us in his blessed word of truth." With the same brevity and beauty of expression, the First Church in Charlestown, which was the foundation of the First Church in Boston, entered into "covenant with the Lord and one with another." (See Morton's Mem ; Cong. Board Pub. p. 464.)

From the imperfect or incomplete mode of transcription upon a *leaf*, the oldest of the known manuscripts or papers of the First Church, it would seem most likely that the Covenant of 1636 has been mistaken for that of 1629, and thus has been undesignedly but unfortunately misrepresented, in most of the publications respecting the Church. That it is not the covenant of 1629, appears from an explicit statement in a copy of the covenants of 1636 and 1680, as issued by the First Church in 1680, and still preserved in a little book, prefixed to the Records of the Tabernacle Church. There is other proof, also, abundant and unanswerable.

We have thus introduced the three publications, which appeared in the course of the year, immediately following the preceding "Second Discussion," bearing directly on the main subject of it—the original constitution of the First Church—yet without the slightest recognition by either of them of that discussion, or the respectable notice taken of it in the Christian Examiner; while they all show, as if in concert, an extraordinary contrivance and unity of design to subvert the long established truth of history in relation to this subject.

Mr. Felt, in his elaborate and copious Ecclesiastical History of New England, ignoring or directly contradicting the standard authorities on the subject, begins his account of the constitution of the First Church, (as may be seen by comparing it with those authorities,) with several gross and manifest errors. "The church platform of rule, covenant, and articles of faith," he says, "being Calvinistic, and drawn up by Mr. Higginson, are accepted by thirty members." And in his confused note on the word "covenant," he would seem to deny its being "the *first*, and from the hand of Higginson," and to assert that "it was *probably* drawn up by Peters," in 1636. But he gives no authority whatever for his assertion or *supposition;* nor does he intimate what his own views or notions are, either of the "first" covenant, or of that "drawn up by Peters," or of the difference between them, not admitting into his history any portion of either except the "fragments," (ante, p. 238) from the "covenant somewhat altered from the first;" of which "altered" covenant he gives no other account or information.[*]

The curiously contrived Appendix to the new edition of Morton's "New England's Memorial," is a still more glaring outrage upon the sanctity of history. The old standard authorities in relation to the institution of the First Church, are so distorted and perverted as to be made to contradict their own authentic statements, and to present views of the subject altogether fallacious.[†]

The extract taken from the last mentioned of the publications of the year 1855, appears to have a peculiar connection with this remarkable appendix; and as it receives no particular attention from the "Third Discussion," (occasioned by the two more important publications,) it deserves a passing notice here. The confident manner in which the grave errors respecting the constitution of the First Church, which had recently been so amply discussed, and by indubitable original authorities so clearly refuted, are again brought up and re-asserted as unquestionable truths, and those very authorities referred to in proof of them, is truly wonderful. So, too, as it appears to us, is the ingenious way in which is carried out to some extent the practice, mentioned by "gooɑ Mr. John Allin," (ante, p. 205) of making "use of sentences of authors," and parts of sentences, with allusions and references,—"contrary to the meaning and judgment of those authors," so as to produce impressions seemingly true and just, but really the reverse.

It is sufficient here to point attention to a single instance,—that of the patriarch, John Higginson,—whose "Direction," &c., designed by him in 1665 "as a help" in baptism and the "half-way covenant," is referred to in such a manner as, with the aid of the new appendix to Morton's "Memorial," to convey an impression that it represents "articles of faith and covenant of 1629."—But this venerated patriarch, who was present with his father at the formation of the First Church, and a living oracle on the subject for more than seventy years, is himself the incontrovertible authority for the fact that no such "articles of faith" ever existed,—that the "confession of faith and covenant"—drawn up by his father, "in Scripture language,"—was one instrument, and that the only "confession of faith," adopted, was blended in it together with the "covenant." These, consequently, are settled facts of history, and no power of will, or strength of assertion, with whatever sincerity urged, can change them.

"It is a hard task," says a sagacious observer, "to unwrite history, and prove facts fictions." And, we may add, it is quite as hard to prove fictions facts. Yet, as we often see, it is easy for a man, a good man, too, to delude himself into a belief of what he ardently wishes to be true; and when deluded himself, he will of course carnestly and conscientiously seek to delude others into the same belief, and will commonly find it an easy task to succeed among those who sympathize in his wishes and views, and yield to him their confidence. And even good men, when once fixed in a favorite belief, are apt to disregard all reasons presented against it; sometimes, indeed, they seem to be fortified in it by opposing arguments. Thus in the case before us, the singular opinion that the first sentence only of the original covenant, as anciently understood, really formed the whole of it, was broached with modest hesitancy (ante, p. 188) as follows :

——" which I suspect was, in substance, at least, *The covenant* which the church was bound unto at their first beginning."

But with what strength of asseveration has it been asserted against argument and invincible authorities !

The delusion must have become complete under which the following statement could be gravely made :

" The original form of the covenant of 1629, very nearly, if not exactly, is inserted in the preamble of the covenant of 1636. It is this : " We covenant with the Lord and one with another, and do bind ourselves, in the presence of God, to walk together in all his ways, according as he is pleased to reveal himself unto us in his blessed word of truth."

Now we have only to consult for a moment the patriarchal oracle on the subject, Rev. John Higginson, and he will show at once the delusiveness of this singular theory, and give us the exact truth both in relation to the "covenant" and the "preamble." Looking back to pp. 6, 7, we see the lucid statement sanctioned by himself, with a complete copy of the "covenant of 1629," just as it came from the hand of his father, Francis Higginson, without any prefix or addition whatever. Then turning to page 13, we find the "Preamble" (not "of the covenant of

1636," but "of the renewal, in 1636, of the covenant of 1629," expressly recognizing it as the covenant which the church was bound unto at *their first beginning ;* together with the covenant renewed, and the clause against the Quakers' doctrine, added in 1660, by his own hand, all just as they stood in the Church book when he recorded in it the notice given of his "Direction," &c., in 1665, and made a reference to that "propounded to and agreed upon by the Church of Salem in *their first beginning,* 1629, 6th of 6th month."

It is a strange idea that from the "mode of transcription upon a *leaf*," &c., " it would seem most likely that the covenant of 1636 has been mistaken for that of 1629." This mode of transcription, as practised by the founders of the Salem Church, rendered it impossible that any such mistake should take place, had there really been such a thing as a "covenant of 1636." There were thirty such "transcriptions" made of the "confession of faith and covenant," at the "first beginning," one for each of the thirty members, (see ante, p. 41, &c.,) all of which would naturally be preserved with care; but we must suppose them all to be lost sight of, and that within seven years, to imagine such a mistake possible.

The "explicit statement," &c., said to be contained in "a little book, prefixed to the records of the Tabernacle Church," affords not the slightest contrary evidence. This "little book" is the "transcript copy" (in an ancient unknown hand) of "A copy of the Church covenants," &c., printed "by J. F., 1680," and the "explicit statement" referred to, whether made by the editor or the transcriber of the printed copy, amounts to nothing more, (see ante, p. 187,) than what was otherwise obvious, viz. : "There was a church covenant agreed upon, &c., 1629, Aug. 6th," and—"The following covenant [the *first* with the *renewing preamble*] was propounded, &c., in the year 1636." It is said (p. 188) that "it was the *first* covenant which was renewed," and then again, that this first covenant "is inserted in the preamble of the covenant of 1636." It can hardly be imagined that the original members of the church, with their precious copies of the covenant in their hands and hearts, should, on renewing it, "about seven years after," mistake the preamble of 1636, or anything else, for the covenant renewed.

The record of the Fast of April 15, 1680, and the renewal of the covenant with a "new direction," &c., (ante, p. 85) shows the priority given to the "first Church covenant,"—the "confession of faith and covenant" of which so many "transcriptions" were made,—and which was recorded upon its first renewal, in 1636, with the renewing preamble, in more than one church book.* The "new direction," &c., which was occasioned by the reforming synod of 1679, appears never to have been entered upon the records, or used in the Church after the special occasion for it had passed by.

Mr. Higginson's felicitous designation of the original confession of faith and covenant, in his account of it, to Morton for "New England's Memorial," as "only a direction pointing unto that faith and covenant contained in the holy Scripture, and therefore no man was confined unto that form of words;" and his repeated use of similar expressions on other occasions, illustrate his true protestant spirit, and his constant care to hold up the Bible as su-

---

* See ante, pp. 20, 42.

preme in matters of faith, and to avoid the appearance of attaching any authority whatever to mere human formularies.

There is one other matter which deserves a more particular notice. The covenant of the First Church in Charlestown, formed about eleven months after that of Salem, is erroneously represented as of "the same brevity and beauty of expression" as the one imagined to be "the original form of the covenant of 1629." The same "beauty of expression" it may have, but certainly not the same brevity and baldness.

The copy of the Charlestown covenant here referred to, is incorrectly taken from that in Drake's History of Boston, which was copied from Foxcroft's Century Sermon, 1730, and by the word "his," near the beginning, shows the omission of something preceding; the change of which word for "God's," makes a material difference.

A comparison of the first covenant of the Church of Charlestown, (being also the first of that of Boston,) with the first Salem covenant, appears to be of sufficient interest to justify its introduction here in a complete and correct form; together with an illustrative fact connected with its record, and to which we have before alluded.

In the History of Charlestown, by Richard Frothingham, Jr., page 70, we find the covenant of the Charlestown Church, "organized, in 1632," (by members dismissed from the Boston Church,) which, the historian observes, "was copied almost word for word," from the covenant of the Church, formed in Charlestown, "June 30, 1630," and transferred to Boston in November of the same year.

It is as follows, the orthography being modernized:

"THE FORM OF THE COVENANT.

In the name of our Lord God, and in obedience to his holy will and divine ordinances :

We whose names are here written, being by his most wise and good providence brought together, and desirous to unite ourselves into one Congregation or Church under our Lord Jesus Christ, our head, in such sort as becometh all those whom he hath redeemed and sanctified unto himself, do here solemnly and religiously, as in his most holy presence, promise and bind ourselves to walk in all our ways according to the rules of the gospel, and in all sincere conformity to his holy ordinances, and in mutual love and respect each to other, so near as God shall give us grace." (1)

In a foot-note, the author remarks as follows :

(1) On the other side of the leaf on which the covenant quoted in the text was written, there is another in the following words :—

"The Covenant proposed to particular persons for their consent, when they are to be admitted, viz. :

"You do avouch the only true God [father, son and Holy Ghost] to be your God, according to the tenor of the covenant of his grace, wherein he promiseth to the faithful and their seed after them in their generations, and taketh them to be his people : and accordingly therefore you do give up yourself to him, and do solemnly and religiously, as in his most holy presence, covenant through his grace, to walk in all your ways and in communion with this particular church in special, as a member of it, according to the rules of the gospel."

Our exact and very intelligent historian adds the following remark :

This covenant, without date, was written sometime after 1632, as it evidently is in the hand-writing of Rev. Thomas Shepard, who was ordained in 1659. It is worthy also of remark, that the important words in brackets, which are interlined in the original, are of different colored ink from the rest, and are as evidently in the hand-writing of Rev. Charles Morton, who was installed in 1686.

The interlining of the "words in brackets" is the illustrative fact alluded to, as showing that subsequent to the institution of the earliest New England churches, a *trini-*

tarian form of expression was introduced in church covenants, while they continued "the same *for substance.*"

On comparing these ancient covenants, we see at once
how entirely they agree in their Scriptural character and
truly catholic spirit. The Salem "instrument," as we
should expect from the peculiar circumstances under
which it was formed, and the profound deliberation given
to it, is the most comprehensive and finished of the two,
being fitted, as it was doubtless designed, to be a manual
of Christian piety and virtue, as well as a bond of
Christian brotherhood. Both might be accepted and subscribed to by all sincere believers in Christ.

A volume has just fallen under our observation, published
this very year, (1860,) entitled "The Book of Religions,"
&c., by John Hayward. Casting a look at the index, we
were struck with the two following references in close
proximity, as suggesting interesting contrasts : "Ancient
American Covenant," "Andover Orthodox Creed." We
here notice the former only, and that merely for the sake
of a quoted remark, added by the compiler of the volume
to a full and true copy of the ancient confession of faith
and covenant "of the First Church in Salem." It is as
follows :

"The above is a covenant," says a learned divine, "to which all
good Christians, of every denomination, to the end of time, will be
able to subscribe their names, written in a style of touching simplicity, which has seldom been equalled, and containing sentiments which
are felt to be eloquent by every amiable and pious heart, and should
form the bond to unite the whole church on earth, as they will unite
the church of the redeemed in heaven. This Covenant might well
be adopted by all Congregational and Protestant churches ; and it
will forever constitute the glory, perpetuate the fame, and render precious the memory of FRANCIS HIGGINSON, the first minister of
Salem."

In this connection we are tempted to introduce from a more learned and important work,—"Allibone's Dictionary of British and American Authors,"—the following just eulogium upon the son and successor of Francis Higginson :

"John Higginson accompanied his father to America in 1629. He was pastor of the Church in Salem, from 1660 to 1708..... He published a number of sermons, theological treatises, &c., and a most eloquent Attestation to Cotton Mather's Magnalia."

Dr. R. W. Griswold is referred to as saying :

"John Higginson was one of the great men of New England, and incomparably the best writer, native or foreign, who lived in America during the first hundred years of her colonization."

We here dismiss the last of the publications of 1855, referred to, and return to the two former, which were the occasion and the subject of the "Third Discussion," now under review ; namely, "The Ecclesiastical History of New England," and the new edition of Morton's "Memorial." We could think of no adequate corrective of the radical errors contained in these publications—errors subversive of truth at the very foundation of our ecclesiastical history—but a presentation of the real original, indubitable authorities respecting the foundation of the First Church in Salem, together with its early records and the avowed principles of the founders. The attempt to do all this seemed in prospect a formidable octogenarian undertaking, but not without its encouragements. No accounts, in all American history, are better authenticated than those relating to the origin and constitution of the First Church, sanctioned as they are, by John Higginson, the truthful witness from the beginning of the facts recorded. We had therefore only to extract the material portions of the clear and explicit statements communicated (as well as sanctioned) by him to secretary Morton, for "New England's Memorial," and to Dr. Mather for the "Magnalia," and to transcribe from his own Church records all that appeared important and illustrative of the subject, together with a view of the principles of the founders, the genuine principles of Congregationalism, and such explanatory remarks as might be suggested.

Having accomplished the undertaking in the best manner we could, the result was presented to the Essex Institute, (where the discussion originated,) in a lecture before the members, at their meeting, May 12, 1856, with an exposition of the errors in question. At the close of the meeting, "It was voted, that the thanks of the Institute be presented to the President for his interesting remarks, and that he be requested to deposit a copy of his communication and his transcript from the records in the archives of the Institute."

A brief sketch of the lecture, with an appendix, containing a copy of the original covenant of 1629, the preamble of 1636, &c., as ante, pp. 13, 14, and the substance of the historical authorities referred to, ante, pp. 3, 5, 8, was published in the first volume of "Proceedings of the Essex Institute." A few impressions of the Brief Sketch, &c. were struck off separately for distribution, and a copy was sent to the author of "The Ecclesiastical History of New England," and also to the publishers of the new edition of Morton's "New England's Memorial." It was thought sufficient, in this way, to call attention to the erroneous passages in these publications, without the more particular exposition of them given in the lecture, and to be deposited, with other papers, in the Institute.

But instead of a correction or candid acknowledgment of the errors thus pointed out, no notice whatever was taken of them by the publishers of the new edition of the "Memorial," while an evasive and delusive pamphlet appeared, in the name of the author of "The Ecclesiastical History," asserting its entire correctness, and even claiming for it the honor of exemplifying the noble rule of Cicero, referred to in the Sketch.

The evasiveness of the pamphlet as a reply to the Sketch, appears at once from its title and from its first page. "Did the First Church of Salem originally have a confession of faith distinct from the Covenant?" is the "title," omitting the gist of the question,—"TO WHICH SUBSCRIPTION OR ASSENT WAS REQUIRED IN ORDER TO CHURCH MEMBERSHIP." On the first page of the pamphlet, the author undertakes "to state the bill of indictment," &c., (as he calls the charge in the Sketch, for support of which the 115th page of the Ecclesiastical History was referred to) as follows :—

"On the 115th page there is a note, saying, the covenant of 1629 differed from that of 1636."

Now the charge of the Sketch was in these words,— "more especially the very important error that instead of the one truly Scriptural 'confession of faith and covenant' adopted by the First Church at its foundation, there was established together with the covenant, a test creed, or sectarian articles of faith, to which subscription or assent was required in order to church membership." For support of this charge, the 115th page of the History was referred to for the following statement, viz: "The Church platform of rule, covenant, and ARTICLES OF FAITH, being CALVINISTIC, and drawn up by Mr. Higginson, are accepted by thirty members." Yet the pamphlet takes no notice whatever of this specific charge, or of the statement thus referred to in proof of it; but substitutes for it the said marginal note, not alluded to in the Sketch.

The delusiveness of the pamphlet appears throughout. The gist of the question being thus evaded, immaterial, undisputed, or already exploded, matters are delusively pursued, as if involving the real question, so that any appropriate answer to the pamphlet must have consisted in an exposition of its false reasonings, unfounded assertions, and perversive representations. It was therefore thought proper not to answer this fallacious publication otherwise than by publishing and depositing in the Essex Institute a number of the printed copies of the "transcripts," &c., (instead of the one manuscript copy requested,) together with the substance of previous discussions on the subject.

To accomplish this, and to complete our review of the "Third Discussion," we have now only to add to the preceding pages the "Brief Sketch," before mentioned, (omitting the Appendix and Notes,) followed by a more particular exposition of the errors referred to, and a fuller view of the genuine Congregational principles which actuated the founders of the First Church in Salem.*

BRIEF SKETCH,

FROM "PROCEEDINGS OF THE ESSEX INSTITUTE."

Monday, May 12, 1856.

Evening Meeting. The President, D. A. WHITE, in the chair.

After reading records, list of donations and correspondence since the last meeting, the President occupied the hour with a lecture upon certain matters of record and history which he deemed important, pertaining to the Fathers of Salem and the First Church. A brief sketch only will be presented here.

Judge W., referring to a remark of the late Mr. Adams, the "old man eloquent," in his Address on the New England Confederacy, before the Massachusetts Historical Society, that it was one of their pre-eminent duties to preserve the good name of our forefathers, observed that it became our more especial duty to protect that of the

---

* Note C.

fathers of Salem from all injurious representations as we ever might with the broad shield of truth. With such views he had explored some of our ancient church records and other historical documents as faithfully as he could, and now brought the results of his humble labor, octogenarian labor—and to be appreciated accordingly. Yet he could truly say that it had been a labor of love from his grateful veneration of our forefathers—a veneration that had grown upon him as he more nearly approached the world where they are. It was a trite remark, because so obvious and just, that no people on earth owed more to their ancestors than the people of New England; and Salem, perhaps, of all New England, was the most deeply indebted. Here they had exerted, in a signal manner, their wisdom and energy in planting the seeds of freedom, piety and learning, the fruits of which we so richly enjoyed. We were bound to study their principles and institutions, and to preserve them unimpaired.

The main purpose of the lecture was to correct certain errors contained in two recent publications in relation to the institution of the First Church in Salem, the first organized church in New England; and more especially the very important error that instead of the one truly scriptural "confession of faith and covenant," adopted by the First Church at its foundation, there was established together with the covenant a test creed, or sectarian articles of faith, to which subscription or assent was required in order to church membership. These publications are,—"The Ecclesiastical History of New England," by Mr. Felt,* and a new edition of "Morton's New England's Memorial," containing an appendix, so arranged as to misrepresent the real meaning of the author, as well as that of Cotton Mather, the two original and indubitable authorities on the subject.† The correction of these errors is demanded of us in justice to the memory of our forefathers, as well as by the sanctity of history and the importance of the principles involved in the question. The fundamental rule inculcated by Cicero, that "the historian must never dare to utter what is false, or to suppress anything that is true, and must always keep his mind above prejudice or partiality," has been sanctioned and enforced by the highest Christian authorities ; "Truth being the very life and soul of history." The publications referred

---

* The Ecclesiastical History of New England, by Jos. B. Felt, Boston. 1855—pp. 115 and 267. [See Note A.]

† New England's Memorial—6th ed. Boston: 1855—p. 459. [See Note B.]

to, having been issued by the "Congregational Board of Publication," and one of them highly extolled for its "thoroughness of research and accuracy of statement," it becomes the more necessary to
correct their misrepresentations concerning the First Church, as otherwise error might supplant truth at the very foundation of our ecclesiastical history.

There are three sources of evidence, each of which is conclusive,
to prove that the First Church has never adopted any such test creed,
or articles of faith.

1. The avowed principles of the founders of the church.
2. The authentic history of its foundation.
3. The ancient records of the church.

1. The principles of the founders were purely congregational, and
as understood by themselves, required their strict adherence to the
Scriptures in constituting the church.   This, too, was their declared
purpose.   Great wrong is done them in confounding their principles
with their opinions ; things essentially distinct.   Opinions are varia-
ble and transient ; principles, fixed and eternal.   Opinions belong
exclusively to the individual holding them ; principles, to the whole
community in common.   Opinions cannot be a guide to any but the
holder of them, nor always a safe guide to him ; but fixed principles
safely guide all, both in forming their conduct and their opinions also.
This distinction was well understood by the fathers of Salem, and
nobly manifested by them in constituting their church according to
their genuine congregational principles, and not in perpetuation of
their peculiar opinions.*

2. This glorious fact is confirmed by authentic history.   The
foundation of the First Church, being a memorable transaction, has
been recorded with more fulness and accuracy than that of any other
church.   Governors Endicott and Bradford, with the ministers Higginson and Skelton, and other eminent characters, were earnestly engaged in their inquiries to ascertain the true scriptural foundation of
a Christian church.   "And accordingly it was desired of Mr. Higginson to draw up a confession of faith and covenant in Scripture
language ; which being done, was agreed upon."   So states Secretary Morton, in his New England's Memorial, and Cotton Mather, in
the Magnalia, records it at length, omitting the preamble of its re-

[* See Note C.]

33

newal in 1636, and the postscript added in 1660, giving the true original "Confession and Covenant" of 1629. Though variously termed, and most commonly "the Covenant" simply, one and the same instrument is always intended;—"the instrument," as Judge Davis calls it, "venerable for its antiquity, and estimable for its mild and benignant spirit;"* which was published in London in 1644, and included by Hanbury among his select "Memorials of the Independents," and which Dr. Bentley, in his History of Salem, says, had been "recorded in every History of New England." Yet in the recent copious Ecclesiastical History of New England, it finds no place excepting some mutilated sentences introduced apparently to disprove its authenticity. And in the appendix to the new edition of Morton's Memorial, it is treated in a way still less worthy and more perversive of its true character.

Morton and Mather entirely agree as to the manner of admission into the church, particularly described by the latter as follows:—
" Some were admitted by expressing their consent unto their Confession and Covenant ; some were admitted after their first answering to questions propounded unto them ; some were admitted, when they had presented in writing such things as might give satisfaction to the people of God concerning them; and some, that were admitted, orally addressed the people of God in such terms as they thought proper to ask their communion with ; which diversity was perhaps more beautiful than would have been a more punctilious uniformity. But none were admitted without regard unto a blameless and holy conversation."†

The accounts of both Morton and Mather were expressly sanctioned by Rev. John Higginson, an eye witness of the foundation of the church, and perfectly acquainted with its discipline and history.‡ The facts stated by Mather had doubtless been furnished by Mr. Higginson himself; and they demonstrate that no test creed, or prescribed form of confession, could have been used in the admission of members.

3. The records of the church afford the same clear demonstration. These records, as contained in the present old church book, consist of transcript records from 1636 to 1659, and of original records from the settlement of John Higginson in 1660, to the dismission of Sam-

---

* Morton's Mem. Davis's ed. p. 391. † Magnal. 1. 19. fol. ed. [Ante p. 7.]
[‡ Ante, pp. 3, 5.]

uel Fisk in 1735. The transcript records, copied from a former book, comprise the original covenant as given by Dr. Mather, under the sanction of Mr. Higginson, with the preamble of its renewal in 1636, and the postscript, or Quaker clause, added in 1660 by Mr. Higginson, and a marginal note in the hand writing of Mr. Fisk ;* also, the names of the first thirty members of the church, and those afterwards added before the settlement of Mr. Higginson, together with an account of baptisms from 1636 to 1659.

As regards the present question the records may be considered complete. It sufficiently appears from the proceedings of the church, at its first meeting, after Mr. Higginson's settlement, Sept. 10, 1660, that all important matters must have been copied from the former book. A committee, then appointed "to review the church book," &c., consisting of "Major Hawthorn, Mr. Battis, Mr. Price, the two deacons, together with the pastor,"—reported, "That they conceived the book itself and the paper of it being old, not well bound, and in some places having been wet and torn, and not legible, is not like to continue long to be of use for posterity ; therefore they thought it best if it were kept in safety by the elders, *by that means it may be of good use so long as it will last.* Only some few passages in it which do reflect upon particular persons, or upon the whole church without any church vote, and without due proof, they did mark in the book as thinking they should be struck out."†

Mr. Higginson thus had possession of the whole former book as well as the transcripts from it. He was very exact in his church records, especially in what related to the admission of members. But no intimation is to be found in the whole church book of any test creed, or prescribed articles of faith, having ever been adopted, or used, in the First Church.

A single instance from his records of admission is enough to show the spirit of the whole. "1678. At a church meeting, March 9, (after naming eight persons)—these eight having been propounded a month, no exception coming against them, they making their profession of faith and repentance in their own way, some by speech, others by writing, which was read for them, they were admitted to membership in this church, by consent of the brethren, they engaging in the covenant."‡

[* Ante, pp. 13, 14.]   [† Ante, p. 47.]   [‡ Ante, p. 83]

Thus appears the entire agreement of authentic history and church records with the principles of the founders in proving the freedom of candidates for church membership in making confession of their own faith in their own way. The Cambridge Platform, of 1648, shows the spirit in which such confessions were to be met on the part of the church; inculcating "such charity and tenderness to be used as the weakest Christian, if sincere, might not be excluded nor discouraged."

It might be asked, as it sometimes had been, "what possible difference," whether such candidates were required to subscribe to "a written confession," or to make in some other satisfactory mode a profession of their faith? The difference in the two modes is self-evident and manifestly essential. One accords with the right of private judgment and the acknowledged sufficiency of the Scriptures; the other contravenes these fundamental principles of Protestantism. The one is in harmony with the spirit of Congregationalism; the other, adverse to it. The one in its tendency is beneficent; the other, pernicious. The one leads to increasing knowledge and love of Christian truth; the other tends to stifle the spirit of free inquiry. The one, in short, is a delightful privilege, the other, an odious imposition.

Our forefathers, of the first generation, were, indeed, "noble Bereans" in settling their principles of church polity,—searching the Scriptures daily for divine guidance. We all venerate their principles, though in following them out we may now be led to different conclusions and reject some of their opinions. So, too, we all admire the spirit which actuated them, and bless God for its glorious results, while we feel obliged to disapprove some parts of their conduct; for where on earth is to be found human perfection? Charity will gladly throw her mantle over errors, which our fathers committed in common with other great and good men of their day, while gratitude delights to indulge her warmest admiration of the wisdom, energy, and fidelity to principle, which raised them above the spirit of their age, above all sectarian influence, and even above the bias of their own darling opinions, in their steadfast adherence to the Scriptures as their only guide and standard in the constitution of their churches.

NOTE A.—Page 244.

It is due to Mr. Felt's Ecclesiastical History of New England, as well as to Truth, that a more particular exposition of its errors in relation to the First Church in Salem, (omitted in the Brief Sketch) should be given in connection with our review of the "Third Discussion." If the peculiar circumstances and singular influences under which these errors were committed are lost sight of, they might be regarded as characteristic of the whole work. Such an inference would doubtless be unjust,—however manifest may be the "serious defect," as stated by a friendly noticer of the first volume—"namely, the want of a copious, continuous and minute reference to the original sources from which the author has drawn." We would not prejudice, but, on the contrary, essentially improve the work by correcting errors lying at the foundation of its important subject, and therefore, if persisted in, fatal to its character as a truthful history.

A comparison of the author's account of the constitution of the First Church in Salem, at its formation, with that transmitted to us by Rev. John Higginson, through Secretary Morton and Dr Cotton Mather, shows the striking contrast between them ; and just so far as the former varies from the latter, it becomes erroneous, confused and fallacious.

First look at the clear and explicit account of the institution of the church, doubtless given by Mr. Higginson himself to Morton, for "New England's Memorial," in a style worthy of "incomparably the best writer" of the time in America,—describing the scriptural "confession of faith and covenant," by which the First Church was constituted in 1629, and identifying it by specifying one of its peculiar articles. Look also at the clear and exact account, furnished in like manner to Mather, for "Magnalia, &c., or the Ecclesiastical History of New England," presenting a true copy of the original "instrument" itself, declaring its character and the veneration with which it was ever regarded. These two authorities are quite sufficient, though added to them may be seen extracts both from Hubbard and Bentley ; and also Mr. Gott's letter to Gov. Bradford, informing him of the preparatory proceedings, on July 20th, pursuant to Gov. Endicott's order upon consultation with Messrs. Higginson and Skelton and other principal founders of the church.

Next look at the account (ante, p. 236,) taken from Felt's "Ecclesiastical History of New England," where it is preceded by Gott's letter. You here find the briefest statement of the institution of the First Church, and that strikingly erroneous. Instead of the "confession of faith and covenant in scripture language," described and set forth so exactly by the patriarch John Higginson, you are met with "The church platform of rule, covenant and articles of faith, being Calvinistic," &c. Morton & Mather, as authorities on this subject, are ignored or disregarded. But Gott's letter receives particular attention, and in commenting upon an apparent repetition of the form of ordination, our author refers to "Morton's Memorial," as he afterwards does to "Mather's Magnalia," in a manner which shows that these standard authorities were before him. Why were they so signally disregarded at his very entrance upon the most important part of his whole subject—the Congregationalism of New England? The inquiry may be best answered by a recurrence to certain facts.

In the year 1854, (see ante, p. 205,) Rev. Dr. Worcester delivered a lecture at the Essex Institute, in which he maintained the two following points:

"I. That at the formation of the First Church, 6th of Aug., 1629, there was a Confession of Faith, as well as a Covenant,—to which candidates for membership were required to give their approval and consent.

II. That the Covenant called the first Covenant, was not that Covenant; but was the first Covenant, *as renewed and enlarged* in 1636."

In proof of the first point, was adduced the "Direction," &c., prepared by Rev. John Higginson, in 1665; a pamphlet which, as stated by Dr. W., was found by Rev. J. B. Felt, soon after his attention was called to the subject by a Discourse delivered at the centennial anniversary of the Tabernacle Church in 1835."

In proof of the second point, Dr. W., as we have seen, (ante, p. 188) curiously analyzed "the Covenant called the first Covenant"—and from a particular examination of some of its parts, alleged the following result:

"The conclusion is to my mind irresistible from the *internal evidence alone*, that the Covenant printed in the Magnalia of Mather, and often cited as the Covenant of the First Church at its beginning, could not have been the first Covenant of that Church. It was, as stated in the Transcript alluded to above, the 'Covenant propounded by the Pastor, agreed upon and consented to, by the brethren, in 1636.' Hugh Peters was at this time their Pastor."

Now let us see what is the new source of evidence substituted by Mr. Felt, in his Ecclesiastical History, for that of Morton and Mather, in relation to the two points thus maintained by Dr. Worcester.

First,—"A pamphlet, printed about 1660, &c., proves that the first independent church of Salem at their outset had articles of faith." But why have we no explanation of the origin or purpose of this ancient pamphlet? Why are we not informed how it came to be imagined that a pamphlet, without name or date, and supposed to be printed about 1660, could supersede the old established historical authorities on the subject of the formation of the Salem Church in 1629? This must have been the very pamphlet "found by Rev J. B. Felt," in the Boston Athenæum, and first noticed by Dr. W. in the Appendix to his Plymouth Discourse, 1848," and then considered by him as "undoubtedly issued in 1680,"—though afterwards the true year was ascertained to be 1665. Why did not our author assign the true year of the pamphlet's issue, and refer to the discoverer of its paramount authority? Why made he no allusion to the public discussion which had just before taken place respecting the constitution of the First Church, (or to the learned and impartial notice of that discussion in the Christian Examiner,) in which the character of the pamphlet was clearly unfolded, and its origin traced to Rev. John Higginson, who had himself so identified what it was likened to "for substance," that nothing else could be mistaken for it? Why indeed was not a document to which so much importance was attached, presented entire in this copious Ecclesiastical History of New England? A single page or two would have sufficed for the whole of it—confession of faith, half-way Covenant, and "questions to be answered at the baptizing of children." Would it not bear the light, and was its mystical character therefore preferred? So it would seem.

Next, as to the "second point,"—the Covenant,—a like mystical obscurity attends it. A foot-note introduces us to Hugh Peters as its chief author, in the following manner: "This Covenant differs from the second, formed 1636, which has long been supposed to be the first, and from the hand of Higginson, when it was probably drawn up by Peters at the later date." Why are we not informed what was the "first," and what was the "second" covenant, and how they differed? Why is no attempt made to explain the contradiction between the note and the text, or to account for the strange conceit that the covenant, "which has long been supposed to be the first, and from the hand of Higginson, was probably drawn up by Peters"—a conceit never before heard of? Why did not our author refer to the originator of it, or assign some reason for it? If not at liberty to do the former, and unable to do the latter, why should he introduce a conjectural *note*, to confound his own positive assertion in the *text?* The Covenant, which, as he there states, was "drawn up by Mr. Higginson," and of which "thirty" copies were made, could have been no other than that very Covenant "which has long been supposed to be the first, and from the hand of Higginson." The *note* and the *text* cannot stand together.

Our author's account of the renewal of the covenant in 1636, makes confusion worse confounded, besides departing entirely (excepting the mere *fact* of renewal) from the authority cited in the margin—the only authority referred to—"Mather's Magnalia." He flies off at once from the clear light of this authority into the mists of error and delusion,—evidently captivated by a new authority, not historical but controversial, yet seeming to blind his judgment and his conscience too as a faithful historian. As this account, confused as it is, contains all that we find in addition to the note to support the surmise of a "second" covenant "in 1636"—or that the one "long supposed to be the first and from the hand of Higginson—was probably drawn up by Peters,"—it may deserve a more particular consideration.

From the manner in which Mather's Magnalia is referred to, in connection with this account, there was reason to expect here what is related in Magnalia on the subject. And had the author faithfully followed his guide we should have been presented with the luminous and true statement, (ante, p. 6,) beginning as follows: "Now the Covenant whereto these Christians engaged themselves," &c., giving the genuine original covenant at length, and adding at the end, "By this Instrument," &c., closing with "So you have seen the nativity of the First Church in the Massachusetts Colony."

But instead of such a worthy and truthful exhibition of the noble old Covenant, what do we find? A pitiful medley of fragments, with not a single entire article of the "venerable instrument," or a clear idea of anything pertaining to it, as if it were the purpose of history to conceal facts, as it is sometimes said of language in regard to thoughts. These fragmentary extracts or broken articles, as before observed, are all that we find in the whole volume of any covenant of the Firt Church, whether of 1629 or 1636,—whether the first "drawn up by Mr. Higginson," and "accepted by Thirty Members," or the "second—probably drawn up by Peters,"—or that "somewhat altered from the first." Why did not our author, on coming to the year 1636, give us the "second" covenant, mentioned in this note, if any such existed, or, if not, correct his mistake and give us the first which he had failed to do before? Why not, at least, give us the renewed "covenant somewhat altered from the first," or tell us *what* it was, *how* and *when* altered? We are indeed told,—"It had reference to events of the time." But what is the time referred to? From certain allusions to Roger Williams, &c., connected with "the last extract," it would seem to be the time when the covenant was renewed, 1636, but from the "extract" itself, and from that immediately preceding it, we should infer that it was when the covenant was made, viz.: 1629. This "last" extract promising "lawful obedience," &c., is taken from the 7th article—which is the one specially referred to in Morton's account of the original "confession of faith and covenant." The extract preceding it, relating to "the Indians," forms a part of the 6th article, which was adopted pursuant to repeated instructions from the "Governor and Company in England." It happens, too, to be the very article, as already intimated, (p. 236,) which, according to our author's own statement was contained in the original covenant of 1629. In the first edition of "The Annals of Salem," published by him in 1827, he adds, at the close of a copy of Gott's Letter to Gov. Bradford, (p. 28,) as follows: "When the 6th of August came, &c.: A platform of church government, a confession of doctrines in general and a covenant were adopted . . . . One particular contained in their covenant was, that they would endeavor to be clear from being stumbling blocks in the way of the Indians." It is thus demonstrated, and by Mr. Felt himself, that the covenant from which these fragmentary extracts are taken was the true original covenant of 1629. The author must have forgotten his own authority when, following a powerful example, (ante, p. 188) he was led into such a contradiction of it.

It is easy to see how the author was misled and deluded in this part of his History, however hard it may be to account for it. His distinguished friend, the pastor of the Tabernacle Church, having conceived from the discovery of an old "Transcript of a pamphlet" that the Covenant of the First Church, at its foundation in 1629, consisted of a single sentence only of what had long been supposed the first covenant, and that a second covenant was formed upon the renewal of the first in 1636.—being comprised in the renewing preamble,—he expressed his strong conviction that with this brief covenant there was originally adopted a distinct confession of faith, to be assented to by all who joined the church—which confession of faith however "had not been discovered." Mr. Felt's interest in the matter was thus excited, and he was so fortunate as soon after to find in the Boston Athenæum an old pamphlet which his friend could interpret as evidence of just such a confession of faith as he had imagined. Both would of course be delighted with the discovery, and disposed to make the most of it. Cordially sympathizing in their sentiments and views on the subject, they would naturally strengthen each other's confidence in this new evidence till it seemed to them conclusive. Mr. Felt too would naturally adopt his honored friend's interpretation of the old "transcript of a pamphlet," and the inferences he had drawn from it in regard to the first covenant, without troubling himself to inquire much into the reasonableness of them. And such appears to be the fact from his various representations connected with the constitution of the First Church, in the text of his History, in the note, and in his account of the renewal in 1636. Excepting the statement in the text (which is not true) as to the "covenant and articles of faith being Calvinistic," he scarcely ventures upon a positive assertion, while he takes for granted the two main points before mentioned, as argued by Dr. Worcester in his lecture at the Essex Institute. Thus, in his note on the first covenant he assumed that there was a "second, formed 1636— probably drawn up by Peters"—and on arriving at the year 1636,—when "Hugh Peters becomes the pastor,"—he adds, "They renew their covenant, somewhat altered from the first. It evidently had reference to events of the time." He then proceeds to comment on fragmentary extracts from divers articles of the covenant, but does not positively say for what purpose, leaving us to conjecture that it might be to show that the covenant is a "second," or one "somewhat altered from the first." But, as we have seen, two of the articles thus commented on by him, viz.: that engaging "lawful obedience," &c., and that relating to "laying stumbling blocks before the Indians," are specially proved to belong to the genuine first Covenant of 1629, the latter upon his own authority, and the former upon that of Morton's New England's Memorial. The other extracts referred to in like manner must appear to any unprejudiced mind equally applicable to the time when the covenant was "first made" as to that when it was "renewed." And had the author presented entire the whole nine articles of the covenant renewed, it would have been seen at once that they are just what Francis Higginson would naturally have conceived in drawing up the original " confession of faith and covenant," and what no self-humbling Christians would have thought of adding in a penitential preamble to renewing their church covenant. Yet these fragmentary comments are the only evidence presented by our author for the statement in his note on the first covenant that it "differs from the second, formed 1636, which has long been supposed to be the first, and from the hand of Higginson, when it was probably drawn up by Peters, at the later date." No authority is assigned for the statement. Neither Dr. Worcester, nor any of his publications on the subject, is referred to at all. And, what is most remarkable, no allusion whatever is made to the " transcript of a pamphlet" to which such importance is attached by Dr. W. as proof,—" That the Covenant called the first Covenant, was not that Covenant; but was the first Covenant *as renewed and enlarged* in 1636."

Our author is quite as far from explicitness as to his authorities on the other point,—viz: " that at the formation of the First Church, 6th of Aug., 1629, there was a confession of faith as well as a covenant, to which candidates for membership were required to give their approval and consent." While ignoring the long established authorities, he makes no reference to any that are substituted in their place. except the mere assertion that " A pamphlet printed about 1660," &c., proves that the first independent church of Salem, at their outset, had articles of faith." The reference to Chalmers amounts to nothing—besides being incorrect—for he speaks not of " doctrines," but of " a characteristic covenant and peculiar profession of faith, which formed," &c. On the point touching the Covenant the author might have found an apposite proof in the specification by Chalmers, (in his Political Annals) not only of the 6th article, but of the 8th, (" nor will we deal oppressingly," &c.,) as parts of the original Covenant of the Salem Church. This would have well accorded with his own specification of the 6th article, (about "laying stumbling-blocks in the way of the Indians," &c.,) in the first edition of his Annals of Salem, where he so justly denominates the original "instrument,"—"a confession of doctrines in general, and a covenant."

The little care or thought exercised by the author upon what he calls "A pamphlet printed about 1660,"—found by himself and used as before seen, by Dr. Worcester, is remarkably manifested by the manner in which he quotes and remarks upon the church record respecting it in the second edition of the Annals of Salem, (2 vol. p. 586,) where it is stated as follows: "1665, Oct. 5. The pastor informs the church that their covenant, 'being ye same for substance agreed upon in 1629,' is now printed and ready for their use. As Mather's Magnalia says that this covenant was renewed about seven years after its adoption, and does not accompany the statement with the qualifying phrase ' for substance,' many have incorrectly concluded that this covenant was literally and verbally the same as it was in its beginning." By recurring to the true record (ante, p. 62,) it will n what a mistaken view our author here took of it. This edition of his Annals of Salem was published in 1845, after he had become possessed with the notion of a "second," or an "altered covenant," and he thus heedlessly represents the pastor, (who was John Higginson,) as applying to the church covenant what he says of his "short-writing," proposed as a "help," &c., and then remarks upon the Covenant in Mather's Magnalia, (sanctioned by Mr. Higginson himself) as incorrectly given because the same egregious mistake is not made there.

Such is the erroneous, confused and fallacious account given by the author of this new Ecclesiastical History of New England, of the foundation and constitution of the First Church in Salem, compared with the clear, explicit and authentic relation of the same memorable transaction, presented by Rev. John Higginson, through Secretary Morton and Dr. Cotton Mather, the incontrovertible authority and only standard of truth on the subject. May we not rely on the fidelity of the author to correct the manifest errors of his account according to this authentic relation and standard of the truth? No historian can be under higher obligations to be faithful, than the writer of an Ecclesiastical History of New England; and no chapter in such a history can be more important than that demanded by the institution of the First Church in Salem, involving as it does the origin, principles, and true character of New England Congregationalism.

NOTE B.—PAGE 244.

History being a "record of truth for the instruction of mankind," the historian's first duty is fidelity to the truth; and just so far as he fails in this, his work tends to the deception of mankind, and, of course, deserves their condemnation. This rule is applicable to every writer of history, more especially to the compiler, who purposely contradicts authentic history, and most strictly to the contriver of alterations in authentic history, to produce impressions contrary to the author's meaning, as well as to the truth.

Of this most aggravated degree of the offence a remarkable instance is presented in the Appendix to the new edition of Morton's New England's Memorial. Judge Davis, the late eminent jurist and antiquarian, after giving his attention for many years to the early history of New England, published an improved edition of the Memorial in 1826, with an Appendix, containing the rich fruits of his learning and research. From the passage in the Memorial describing the original "confession of faith and covenant" of the First Church in Salem, which states that the "aforesaid confession of faith and covenant was acknowledged only as a direction, pointing unto that faith and covenant in the holy Scriptures," &c., Judge Davis refers by a marginal note "for a copy of this covenant" to his "Appendix &c.," where we accordingly find it as taken from Mather's Magnalia, (ante, pp. 5, 6, 7,) to which the learned editor adds the following remarks: "The people at Salem consulte l with those of Plymouth in the settlement of their church order, and this instrument, which is to be considered as expressing the character and views of those memorable worthies, is venerable for its antiquity, and estimable for its mild and benignant spirit. As the reverend author of the *Description of Salem* justly observes : It may be esteemed, if not for its theology, for its simplicity. If it speak not the language of a sect, it breathes the spirit of Christian union." Such was the natural, simple and truthful course pursued by Judge Davis.

Let us now look at the course taken by the editors of this new edition of the Memorial. Like their distinguished predecessor they refer from the passage describing the Covenant of 1629, "for a copy of t iis confession and covenant," to their "Appendix A." But upon turning to this Appendix, instead of finding what we were sent there to see, we are surprised by the following delusive heading :—"The Articles of Faith and Covenant of 1629." This at once introduces us to a most remarkable process of mystification, seemingly designed to substitute for the true " confession and covenant " of 1629, a very different one, together with articles of faith, and to transfer the genuine " instrument " from 1629 to 1636. Judge Davis's authority is first disposed of with a gentle rebuke for his ignorance or oversight of what was material to a " faithful history of the principles and proceedings of the Fathers." It is intimated that he " overlooked the fact that the " direction " of which Morton speaks, contained both a confession of faith and a covenant, while they ignore the *real* fact that the word " direction " was here used as a mere descriptive term, (a favorite one with Rev. John Higginson,) indicating that the " confession of faith and covenant " referred to, was *one* instrument,—a blended " confession of faith and covenant," and purely scriptural. In like manner they ignore the fact that it was to this blended " confession of faith and covenant " that Hubbard, Mather and Prince alluded when speaking, as alleged, of a " confession of faith as well as a covenant."

It is next erroneously said :—" In 1665 the First Church in Salem issued a new direction," &c. The " new direction " was adopted by the Church in 1680, (ante, p. 85,) consequent upon the Reforming Synod of 1679. The " Direction " of 1665 was not " issued by the Church," nor was it called a " new direction." It was simply a proposal from the pastor, Mr. Higginson, consequent upon the Synod of 1662, " as a help," &c. The first notice of it may be seen (ante p. 59,) when upon reading the Propositions of the Synod touching Baptism, &c., " the pastor promised that in time convenient he would communicate unto the brethren a short writing as a help for the practice of the Synod's propositions." And (p. 62) it may be seen that on presenting the " short writing," he called it a " direction for a profession," and which " is taken out of the Scriptures, it being the same for substance propounded to and agreed upon by the church in their first beginning, 1629, 6th of 6th month ; it being now printed, any that desired it should have one of them for their use."

These are all the notices that we find in the church records of this " short-writing," or the print of it. It seems to have been little used, and soon forgotten. Having upon its recent discovery been perverted into evidence that the First Church, at its formation, adopted test articles of faith, and also been made the ground of a perversion of the authentic history in relation to this matter, it is proper here to give to it a more particular attention.

Mr. Higginson's views in relation to "children of the covenant," or the church, and the baptism of *their* children, &c., may be seen from his records, ante, pp. 49, 60, 70, and together with his colleague, Mr. Noyes, pp. 91, 2, 3. The result of the Synod of 1662, on this subject, agitated the people throughout New England, and many of the ablest divines of that day engaged in earnest controversy for and against it.

The late Dr. John Eliot, in his biographical sketch of Richard Mather, says :—" It was the fifth proposition discussed by the Synod," ' Whether those who make a profession of religion, whereby they give themselves up to God in a solemn covenant, and subject themselves to the discipline of the church, shall have the privilege of baptism for their children.' There were several who opposed the voice of the Synod,—among them President Chauncey, Mr. Davenport of New Haven, and Mr. Increase Mather, minister of the second church in Boston. Three very eminent divines were elected to manage the controversy with them,—Mr. Allen of Dedham, to answer President Chauncey, Mr. Richard Mather, to write against Mr. Davenport, and Mr. Mitchel of Cambridge, a younger divine, but *Vir, claro nomine*, to discuss the subject with Mather the younger. The books were well written, but the manner of writing which Mr. R. Mather adopted, pleased old Mr. Higginson of Salem so much that he said, ' he was a pattern to all the answerers in the world.' "

Mr. Higginson was among the most zealous for carrying out the doctrine of the Synod in its fullest extent, but the brethren of his church were divided in their opinions respecting it. He desired, of course, to afford every facility for the practice of baptism, and at the same time to reconcile the brethren to his own views. " Because," as both he and Mr. Noyes were persuaded, " baptizing belonged to their office." Hence the " short writing " furnished by him " as a help," and hence his recommendation of it as " the same for substance propounded," &c. What was " propounded, &c. in their first beginning, 1629," was as well known as it was dear to the brethren of the church, and it has been clearly ascertained to us by Mr. Higginson himself. (See ante, pp. 63, 4, &c.) The first page of this little print, which was without date, contained the title, (as ante, p.190,) with the following quotation added, (ante, p. 206):—"In the preface," and closing with,—"not to be made use of as an imposition upon any." On the second page were the references to texts of Scripture, as given ante, p. 206. The third, fourth and fifth pages contained "The Confession of faith" and "The Covenant," as ante, pp. 190–1, &c., and on the sixth page were the "Questions to be answered at the baptizing of Children," &c., as ante, pp. 206–7. The covenant was, (like the "solemn covenant" alluded to by Dr. Eliot,) adapted to members of the church, not admitted to full communion, though subject to discipline, &c., that is, what has been called the Half-way Covenant. Such was Mr. Higginson's "short writing," which he gave notice of to the church as a "Direction," &c., the same for substance propounded, &c., 1629, 6th of the 6th month.

Recovered from its long oblivion, the old pamphlet has been clothed with a new character, the reverse of that given to it by Mr. Higginson, and instead of being judged for its *substance* by what was "propounded, &c., in their first beginning," &c., it is made use of to determine what that was both as to *form* and *substance*. Indeed, the contrivers of "Appendix A." seem to have done what they could to substitute the confession of faith and half-way covenant of 1665, for the true confession of faith and covenant of 1629. Their inimitable manner of proceeding in attempting this, can hardly be described, but it may easily be perceived on comparing the 6th and 7th sections of chapter 4th, and book 1st (ante pp. 5, 6, 7,) of Mather's Magnalia, with "Appendix A." The 6th section alone is sufficient for the comparison, comprising, as it does, under the sanction of John Higginson, the "confession of faith and covenant in scripture language," as drawn up by his father, Francis Higginson, 1629, with pertinent remarks preceding and following it, in clear, explicit language, not to be mistaken. Now, how is this important and most authentic passage of history treated in "Appendix A?"

After introducing a portion of the remarks, which, in the Magnalia, precede the true covenant of 1629, this true covenant is set aside, and the "Direction," &c., of 1665 is foisted in, at the end of which other remarks, applied in like manner, in Magnalia, to the true original "instrument," are quoted as follows: Cotton Mather says, "The covenant whereto these Christians engaged themselves, which was about seven years after solemnly renewed among them," &c.

Mather further says, " By this instrument was the covenant of grace explained, and recognized by the first church in this colony," &c. Hereupon the framers of " Appendix A." make the following remarks : " The covenant published in Magnalia, and by Judge D i- vis, in his Appendix, was *probably enlarged* from *this original*, at the time of the renewal, seven years after *this first covenant* was adopted, in August, 1629, *which is here given*." We have italicized several expressions in this sentence, which appear to us inexplicable. " The covenant published in Magnalia, and by Judge Davis," &c., was the very one set aside as before mentioned, to make way for " Direc- tion," &c., and that certainly was itself the " original," the " first " covenant. 'What, then, can be meant by the expressions—" *proba- bly enlarged* from *this original*, at the time of the renewal sev^n years after *this first* covenant was adopted, &c., *which is here given ?*" What *first* covenant was here intended ? It could not possibly be the half-way covenant contained in the " Direction," &c., of 1665—the only covenant previously given, and therefore seemingly referred to by the expression, " which is here given." It might well be the " holy covenant whereby that church state was formed,"—as represented by the quotation in " Appendix A." from Magnalia, (ante, p. 240,) in- troducing the " Direction," &c., but this was the very covenant set aside or displaced from its rightful position by the framers of this Appendix, to be afterwards presented as a covenant of 1636 ; of course, this, though really the *first covenant*, could not have been what was here intended. From a statement referred to, ante, p. 246, it would seem that the brief sentence, marked as if a quotation, in the covenant so displaced, and transferred to 1636, must be ' the one intended by the expressions, " this original," " this first covenant," and " which is here given." Yet, if so, why is it not given now with as much explicitness, at least, as before ? And why do we find no intimation, except by marks of quotation, that this brief sentence is the covenant intended ? Had the framers of " Appendix A." too strong misgivings to be explicit on the subject ? They must, indeed, have perceived that this sentence, so marked by them, formed the beginning, only, of the true first covenant,—the covenant clearly and explicitly expressed in Magnalia by Higginson and Mather, for they both sanction it, and consequently that the preamble, introducing the covenant when renewed, was all that belonged to the year 1636. Nor could they have failed to observe also that it was to this complete original covenant, given in Magnalia, that the clear and emphatic declaration, (ante, p. 7,) was subjoined, viz.: "By this Instrument was the covenant of grace explained," &c. Yet this most explicit declaration is disjoined from the covenant to which it relates; and the "Instrument,"—the very covenant of 1629,—with the preamble to its renewal in 1636, is gravely set forth as "the covenant propounded by the pastor, agreed upon and consented to by the brethren of the church, in the year 1636."

In immediate connection with this proceeding, and in conclusion of "Appendix A.," is introduced the "COVENANT OF THE FIRST CHURCH IN CHARLESTOWN, June 30, 1630," &c., but without any intimation for what purpose, or a single word of comment. The natural and just inference from a comparison of the confession of faith and covenant of the Salem Church, drawn up by Francis Higginson in 1629, with the covenant of the Charlestown Church, formed in 1630, would be, That as no distinct confession of faith was adopted with the latter, so *a fortiori*, none with the former, containing as it does, in itself, a more full "confession of faith and covenant in scripture language." But from the manner in which this copy of the Charlestown covenant has been referred to, (ante, p. 243,) it would seem considered as countenancing the supposition that "the original form of the covenant of 1629," was as brief as is there represented, comprised in a single sentence.

For a more particular notice of the "Covenant of the First Church in Charlestown," see ante, p. 249, where the incompleteness of the copy of it in "Appendix A." is shown, and a full and correct copy presented from Frothingham's History of Charlestown.

We trust that this remarkable portion of the Appendix to the new edition of Morton's Memorial will not fail to attract the particular notice of the Reverend Board, under whose auspices it has gone forth to the public, and that it will receive from them the attention which the importance of the subject deserves, and the correction which the truth of history demands.

NOTE C.—PAGE 255.

There are three sources of evidence, as before stated, to prove the purely Scriptural constitution of the First Church in Salem, viz. : The authentic history of its foundation; the ancient records of the church; the avowed principles of the founders. The two former have already been exhibited in sufficient fulness. Our purpose here is to adduce some passages and historical authorities (not included in the Brief Sketch) illustrative of the principles of the founders, which were the true principles of Congregationalism.

The late John Quincy Adams, in his Address on the New England Confederacy, before referred to, quotes Edmund Burke as calling " the Puritan spirit the Protestantism of the Protestant religion." This the Congregational spirit may still more justly be called. The primitive Congregationalists, or Independents, were actuated by the cardinal principles of protestantism in the purest degree, and re-asserted them with explicitness and constancy. Sir James Mackintosh says of Locke : " By the Independent divines, who were his instructors, our philosopher was taught those principles of religious liberty which they were the first to disclose to the world."*

Dr. Belknap, in his biography of John Robinson, one of the fathers of Congregationalism, after showing that the members of his Church were called Robinsonians, and Independents, but the name by which they distinguished themselves was a " Congregational Church,"—begins his account of their church as follows :—

" Their grand principle was the same which was afterwards held and defended by Chillingworth and Hoadley, that the Scriptures given by inspiration contain the true religion ; that every man has a right to judge for himself of their meaning, to try all doctrines by them, and to worship God according to the dictates of his own enlightened conscience." And he closes the account with the following sentence : " And finally they renounced all right of human invention, or imposition in religious matters."†

---

* "No man can, if he would," says Locke, " conform his faith to the dictates of an other." "True and saving religion consists in the inward persuasion of the mind without which nothing can be acceptable to God." 2 Works, fol. 234.

† Dr. Sprague, in "Historical Introduction" to the first volume of his great work "Annals of the American Pulpit," says of John Robinson, "that he, especially in

Prince, in his " New England Chronology," refers to governor Winslow as saying,—" As the Churches of Christ are all saints by calling, so we desire to see the grace of God shining forth, at least seemingly, (leaving secret things to God) in all we admit into church fellowship, and to keep off such as openly wallow in the mire of their sins ; that neither the holy things of God, nor the communion of the saints may be thereby leavened, or polluted. And if any, joining to us when we lived at Leyden, or since we came to New England, have with the manifestation of their faith and profession of holiness, held forth therewith separation from the Church of England, I have divers times in the one place heard Mr. Robinson our pastor, and in the other Mr. Brewster our elder, stop them forthwith, showing them that we required no such thing at their hands, but only to hold forth faith in Jesus Christ, holiness in the fear of God, and submission to every divine appointment ; leaving the Church of England to themselves and to the Lord, to whom we ought to pray to reform what was amiss among them."

Prince proceeds as follows : " Perhaps Hornius was the only person who gave this people the title of Robinsonians. But, had he been duly acquainted with the generous principles both of the people and their famous pastor, he would have known that nothing was more disagreeable to them than to be called by the name of any mere man whatever ; since they renounced all attachment to any mere human systems or expositions of the Scripture, and reserved an entire and perpetual liberty of searching the inspired records, and of forming both their principles and practice from those discoveries they should make therein, without imposing them on others. This appears in their original covenant in 1602. And agreeably to this, governor Winslow tells us, that when the Plymouth people parted from their renowned pastor, with whom they had always lived in the most entire affection, he charged us before God and his blessed angels to follow him no further than he followed Christ ; and if God should reveal anything to us by any other instrument of his, to be as ready to receive it as ever we were to receive any truth by his ministry ; for he was very confident the Lord had more truth and light yet to

view of the relation he sustained to the Plymouth Church, may be considered as the father of at least New England Congregationalism." Among " The points which gave to them their distinctive character," Dr. S. states the following: "That all human inventions or impositions in religion are to be discarded."

break forth out of his holy word. He took occasion, also, miserably to bewail the state of the reformed churches who were come to a period in religion, and would go no farther than the instruments of their reformation.....Here, also, he put us in mind of our Church Covenant, whereby we engaged with God and one another, to receive whatever light or truth should be made known to us from his written word; but withal exhorted us to take heed what we receive for truth, and well to examine, compare, and weigh it with other Scriptures before we receive it. For, said he, it is not possible the Christian world should come so lately out of such antichristian darkness, and that full perfection of knowledge should break forth at once," &c.

In the same spirit Dr. Thomas Goodwin, a member of the Westminster Assembly of Divines, and regarded as the master-spirit among the Congregationalists in that body,—in giving an account of a Congregational church, describes their covenant as " leaving their spirits free to the entertainment of the light that shines, or shall shine out of the word."*

In the famous " Apologetical Narration," which this Dr. Goodwin together with four other eminent Congregational members of the Westminster Assembly, addressed to Parliament in 1643,† we find among the great principles avowed by them, the following : "First, the supreme rule without us was the primitive pattern and example of the churches erected by the Apostles. A second principle we carried along with us in all our resolutions, was, not to make our present judgment and practice a binding law unto ourselves for the future, which we in like manner made continual profession of upon all occasions ; which principle we wish were (next to that most supreme, namely, to be in all things guided by the perfect will of God) enacted as the most sacred law of all other, in the midst of all other laws and canons ecclesiastical in Christian States and Churches throughout the world."‡

The eminent John Cotton, one of the early ministers of the Boston Church, in his " Doctrine of the Church," &c., says,—"When a

---

* Cong. Dict., 129.

† " An Apologetical Narration, humbly submitted to the Honorable House of Parliament, by Thomas Goodwin, Philip Nye, Sidrach Simpson, Jeremiah Burroughs, William Bridge."

‡ Hetherington's Hist. Westm. Assembly, p. 160.

church is suspected and slandered with corrupt and unsound doctrine, they have a call from God to set forth a public confession of their faith, but to prescribe the same, as the confession of the faith of that church, to their posterity ; or to prescribe the confession of one church to be a form and pattern unto others ; sad experience hath shown what a snare it hath been to both."

Again he says,—"Seeing our faith resteth only on the word of the Lord and his spirit breathing therein ; and the word hath promised [that] more and more light shall break forth in these, till Antichrist be utterly confounded and abolished ; we shall sin against the grace and word of truth, if we confine our truth either to the divines of the present or former ages."*

Mr. Cotton's Answer to the Letter of Sir Richard Saltonstall, expressing his grief for the sad things he heard reported of New England, sufficiently shows that imposing human creeds formed no part of the " tyranny and persecution " complained of. " You know not," Mr. C. says, " if you think we came into this wilderness to practise those courses here which we fled from in England. We believe there is a vast difference between men's inventions and God's institutions ; we fled from men's inventions, to which we else should have been compelled ; we compel none to men's inventions.".... " We are far from arrogating infallibility of judgment to ourselves, or affecting uniformity ; uniformity God never required, infallibility he never granted us. We content ourselves with unity in the foundation of religion and of church order."†

The fathers of New England professed their regard for the rights of conscience, while they felt bound to punish offences, though committed under pleas of conscience, which appeared to them subversive of all religion as well as order. The law against such offences, passed in 1646, bears on its face evidence of respect for sincere consciences—premising as follows : " Though no human power be lord over the faith and consciences of men, and therefore may not constrain to believe or confess against their conscience," &c. This was in the very spirit which led to the scriptural constitution of the first New England churches, and forbade the adoption of human tests of faith. The idea of dictating confessions of faith, or submitting to such dictation, would doubtless have been as abhorrent to their feel-

---

* Hanbury's Hist. Mem., ii, 162.   † Hutch. Coll., 401.

ings as to their principles. In justice to their memory, we must never forget the essential distinction they made between rights of the conscience and wrongs of the will,—nor the obstinate type of the latter which they had to contend with, and which so severely tried their own consciences, as well as their patience.

Of all the American divines, since the patriarch John Higginson, the late Dr. Styles, President of Yale College, appears the best informed on the subject of the Congregational churches of New England. While he laments that some in his day were " fond of substituting human interpretations given by authority of councils and learned men, exacting that the sacred Scriptures be understood according to senses fitted and defined in human tests;" and, on the contrary, declares that " There ought to be no restrictions on the conscience of an honest and sober believer of revelation;" he explicitly testifies to the true scriptural foundation of our early churches. " I have observed," he says, " that our churches, in a distinguished sense from almost all the protestant world, are founded on the Bible. Our worthy and venerable ancestors (be their memories dear to posterity) did not like other protestant patrons, form a system of what they thought and judged to be the true sense of revelation, and establish this for the truth :—no, it was enough for them that the Bible was the inspired rule, and this they made the only rule."*

We have already repeatedly alluded to the spirit of Christian freedom manifested by the Congregational Churches of England, met in a Synod at the Savoy, in London, 1658. It may be seen, from the following extract, how faithfully the English Congregationalists have adhered to their first principles. The Declaration of the Congregational Churches of England and Wales " adopted at a general meeting of the Congregational Union, held in London, May, 1833," contains the following : " Disallowing the utility of creeds and articles of religion as a bond of union, and protesting against subscription to any human formularies as a term of communion, Congregationalists are yet willing to declare, for general information, what is commonly believed ; reserving to every one the most perfect liberty of conscience."†

We add a few passages from more recent writings in relation to

---

* Christian Union, 119.   † See Appendix to Hanbury's Hist. Mem., III, 598.

the corruption of primitive Congregationalism in our country, and the hopeful prospect of its restoration to its true principles: and first, from a valuable and thorough work, entitled, "ORGANIC CHRISTIANITY, &c. By Leicester A. Sawyer":—

"The Westminster confession of faith and discipline are the platform of Anglo-American and Scotch Presbyterianism, and the supreme organic law of the churches adopting them. Congregationalism is built less on human constitutions and confessions, and more on the Bible, than any other systems. Its earliest confession of faith is that which was drawn up by John Robinson, and published at Leyden, 1619. Next follows the Savoy confession, adopted by the ministers and delegates of the Congregational churches of England, more than one hundred in number, at their meeting at the Savoy, London, Oct. 12, 1658.....With some slight alterations, it was adopted by the New England Synod, at Boston, in 1680, and has ever been regarded as one of the standards of New England theology. It is not, however, imposed by authority, and cannot be, without an entire abandonment of the principles of Congregationalism.....The Bible is the Congregationalist confession of faith and constitution. It is the highest and sole supreme organic church law of Congregationalism; and has no other enforcement than what arises from the counsel and advice of sister churches and the providence of God."[*]

"Congregationalism, as a system of church democracy, is corrupted when any foreign element is introduced into it. Its principal liabilities to corruption are from Presbyterianism. Many imagine that the two systems are essentially the same, with only slight unimportant differences between them. But this is a great mistake. The two systems are fundamentally different. Presbyterianism is a modified Episcopacy," &c.[†]

"Consociationalism is a corruption of Congregationalism. It constitutes permanent courts above and over the churches. Consociated churches resign their independency just to that extent to which they commit jurisdiction to the consociations."[‡]

Dr. Bacon, in "Historical Discourses," represents the Saybrook Platform as "a compromise between the Presbyterian interest and the Congregational." But he says that in the County of New Ha-

---

* Page 403.   † Ib. 414.   ‡ Ib. 416.

ven, " the influence of Davenport in favor of the simplest and purest Congregationalism was still felt."*

" Consociations have learned that if they are to do any good, nay, if they are to have any being, it must be as Congregational Councils, and not as Presbyteries. The spirit of Congregationalism, such as Congregationalism was when Thomas Hooker and John Davenport, and the Synod at Cambridge were its expounders, prevails throughout the churches of Connecticut, and with perhaps a few exceptions, throughout the ministry."†

That able periodical, THE NEW ENGLANDER, published in New Haven, and largely indebted, doubtless, to the genius of Dr. Bacon, has exhibited, from time to time, the true old spirit of Congregationalism. In the second number of the XIVth volume, 1856, there is an interesting article, touching the subject, which contains the following evidence :—

" We may as well own it before the world, that our system hinders all interference with the free and honest differences of Christian minds in their examinations of truth ; that it is impracticable to make all our churches sign precisely the same articles of faith, that men in our order can and will think for themselves ; and that it is impossible so to constrain Congregationalism that it will banish from its communion, or exclude from its fellowship, any who give good evidence of their oneness with Christ."‡

A still more remarkable article may be seen in the number of the New Englander for August, 1860, on " The adaptation of the Congregational Polity to develop a true Biblical Theology," &c. A single sentence or two from this article will be sufficient to show its true scriptural character. This adaptation appears first, " In the fact that it leaves the minister untrammeled by human systems and authorities," &c. And in reference to the Congregational fathers, Robinson, Cotton and Hooker, the writer adds : " These fathers were never afraid of liberty for new light."...." New light, progress in theology, improved methods of stating, arranging, harmonizing, applying the old familiar truths, were looked for then as the result of studying the word of God, with minds unshackled by confessions and catechisms."‖

We must introduce a single passage from a recently published

---

* pp. 191-2.   † Ib. 272.   ‡ p. 314.   ‖ p. 637.

work—there can be no higher authority on the subject,—we allude to Dr. Palfrey's History of New England. At page 36 of the 2d volume, we read as follows :—

" The religious objects of the colonists claimed attention immediately after their arrival. The planters at Plymouth had no new scheme of church order to devise. Theirs was the scheme of the English Independents, already put in practice and amended by themselves at Scrooby and at Leyden. It was imitated in Massachusetts by Skelton and Higginson, was adopted by the immigrants of the following year, and was carried to Connecticut and New Haven by the founders of those colonies. A church was a company of believers associated together by a mutual covenant to maintain and share Christian worship and ordinances, and to watch over each other's spiritual condition. The *covenants*—remarkably free, in the earliest times, from statements of doctrine—were what their name imports : they were mutual engagements, in the presence of God, to walk together in all his ways, according as he was pleased to reveal himself in his blessed word of truth."

In a note on this passage, the author observes that,—The covenant of the First Church of Salem contains no statement of doctrine, nor that of the First Church of Boston, nor that of the Second Church of Boston. " I do not remember," he adds, " a material deviation from this catholic character in any of a considerable number of early covenants which have come under my eye."

We close with an important historical statement respecting the covenant of the first Church in Salem, (unnoticed by us before,) contained in the Appendix to the new edition of Morton's New England's Memorial, (preceding in the volume the " Appendix A.") parts of which we give in italics, for their decisive evidence as to the origin of the " articles " mentioned.

At page 423 of the volume, after a quotation, stating that the members of the Church of which Robinson was pastor, "joined themselves by a covenant of the Lord, into a church state, in the fellowship of the gospel, ' to walk in his ways made known and to be made known to them,' according to their best endeavors," it is added as follows :—

" The covenant of the First Church in Salem, *which was formed in* 1629, under the advice of the Plymouth church, was of the same import, *with the addition of some articles of discipline.*"

As a fitting SUPPLEMENT to the early Records of the First Church, already presented, we conclude this volume with some account of the several Pastors and Teachers, abridged from " Notices of the First Church in Salem and its Ministers, 1629 to 1853. By a Member." These notices were compiled by the present writer, and published together with " A Sermon, preached at the Installation of Rev. George W. Briggs, as Pastor of the First Church in Salem. January 6, 1853. By John Hopkins Morison, Pastor of the First Church in Milton."

I.
REV. FRANCIS HIGGINSON.
1629 TO 1630.

Of the early ministers of the First Church, it may truly be said, in the language of a recent biographer of one of them, that they were "divines who had won the highest respect in their native land, and who were among the holiest and most gifted men of the age."[*]

" The venerable Higginson, the father and pattern of the New England clergy," as Mr. Savage so happily calls him,[†] deserves the first place among them. He received his education at Jesus College, Cambridge, and took his first degree in 1609. He was minister of one of the parish churches in Leicester, where, it is said, " He was so popular a preacher, that the people flocked to hear him from all the neighboring towns." Neal, the historian of the Puritans, says : " He was a good scholar, of a sweet and affable behaviour, and having a charming voice, was one of the most acceptable and popular preachers of the country." Becoming a non-conformist, by his conscientious study of the Scriptures, he was ejected from his living, and forbidden to preach in England. His remarkable gifts and graces qualified him to be a chief agent in the great enterprise for which he was so earnestly sought. Nor did he disappoint the high hopes entertained of him. Few as were his days after arriving here, he accomplished his great work. " He lived," says Dr. Bentley, " to secure the foundation of his church, to deserve the esteem of the colo-

---

* Elton's Life of Roger Williams.   † Savage's Winthrop i. 2.

ny, and to provide himself a name among the worthies of New England."

He died on the 6th of August, 1630, just one year from his installation. "He was grave in his deportment," adds Dr. Bentley, "and pure in his morals. In his person he was slender, not tall; not easily changed from his purposes, but not rash in declaring them. He held the hearts of his people, and his memory was dear to their posterity." He left a widow, Ann, and eight children. The children's names and ages at the time of his arrival, as given by Dr. Young, (Chron. Mass.) were as follows:—John, 13. Francis, 12. Timothy, 10. Theophilus, 9. Samuel, 8. Ann, 6. Mary, 4, (who died on the passage.) Charles, 1. Neophytus, born in Salem.

With the cares of such a family, added to his arduous public duties and labors, in a feeble state of health too, Mr. Higginson must have possessed uncommon energy and power, to undertake the task of writing the "Journal of his Voyage," and the "New England's Plantation," and to finish the task in the manner he did.

II.
REV. SAMUEL SKELTON.
1629 TO 1634.

The high character of Mr. Skelton is sufficiently proved by the confidence reposed in him, not only by Gov. Endicott, who looked up to him as his spiritual father, but by the company in England, who selected him as one of the two who were to take the governor's place, in case of Mr. Endicott's death.

Mr. Skelton was educated at Clare Hall, Cambridge, taking his first degree in 1611. It has been inferred, as Dr. Young observes, from his being appointed Pastor, that he was older than Mr. Higginson. But as he took his first degree at college two years later,* it would seem that he could not have been much older. And if he were, it does not appear that on that account he was chosen Pastor, and Mr. Higginson Teacher.† He survived Mr. Higginson about

---

* See Mr. Savage's Gleanings, &c., 3 Hist. Coll., viii., 248.

† The terms pastor and teacher, as applied to our early ministers, seem to have had no reference to age. Some difference of office was doubtless intended, according to the import of the terms, but it soon came to be more a distinction than a difference.

Of all the ministers of the First Church, but four sustained the title of teacher, viz:

four years, during which he was sole pastor, excepting the two brief periods that Roger Williams was his assistant. He died August 2, 1634. Though a strict disciplinarian, he was a friend to the utmost equality of privileges in church and state. " No particular records," says Dr. Bentley, " were kept of his services. As he never acted alone, he yielded to others all the praise of his best actions." Edward Johnson, his contemporary, describes him as " a man of a gracious speech, full of faith, and furnished by the Lord with gifts from above, to begin this great work of His."

Dr. Eliot, in his biographical notice of Mr. Skelton, observes: "There was a want of friendship between the ministers of Boston and its neighborhood, and the ministers of Salem. Everything which one party did, was found fault with by the other. It is remarkable," he adds, " that no kind of notices of the character of Mr. Skelton, a man so distinguished among the first planters, should have been given by writers of that or the succeeding generation. Gov. Winthrop just mentions his death ; Dr. Mather mentions very little about him."

Mr. Skelton left a son, Samuel, and three daughters. His wife died in March, 1631. Governor Dudley, in his letter to the countess of Lincoln, says : " She was a godly and helpful woman, and indeed a main pillar of her family, having left behind her a husband, and four children weak and helpless, who can scarce tell how to live without her."

III.
REV. ROGER WILLIAMS.
1633 TO 1636.

Roger Williams was born in Wales, in 1599. Late in life he says : " The truth is, from my childhood, now above three score years, the Father of lights and mercies touched my heart with a love to himself." He emigrated to this country a resolute non-conformist, and arrived at Boston, early in February, 1631,—six months after the death of Francis Higginson. The Salem Church invited him to settle as teacher and colleague with Mr. Skelton. He accepted their

---

Francis Higginson, Roger Williams, Edward Norris, and Nicholas Noyes—the last of whom, in his record of the ordination of Mr. Curwin, his young colleague, as pastor, styles himself " the Teacher."

invitation, and became their minister on the 12th of April following. But the governor and magistrates interfered and made such opposition to his settlement, that he was induced to leave Salem before the close of the summer, and to become assistant to Mr. Ralph Smith in the ministry at Plymouth. The opposition from the civil authorities to his remaining in Salem, sprung from certain opinions divulged by Mr. Williams soon after his arrival. He thought that the ministers and people of Boston had conformed, to a sinful degree, with the English church, and ought to declare their repentance; that the royal patent could give them no title to their lands without a purchase from the natives: that the civil power could not rightly punish breaches of the Sabbath, nor in any way interfere ‚with the rights of conscience,—with other offensive opinions of less importance. Open, bold, and ardently conscientious, as well as eloquent and highly gifted, it cannot be surprising that he should have disturbed the magistrates by divulging such opinions, while he charmed the people by his powerful preaching, and his amiable, generous, and disinterested spirit. After laboring among the people of Plymouth about two years, with great acceptance and usefulness, he asked a dismission, in 1633, upon being invited by the church at Salem to return to them as assistant to Mr. Skelton. He returned accordingly, and during Mr. Skelton's life labored with him in great harmony and affection, and after his death, was sole minister of the church till November, 1635. At this time, the renewed opposition of the magistrates, strengthened as it was by a treatise he had written against the patent, had come to a crisis, and Roger Williams was driven from Salem, and became an exile in the wilderness. But what was then his reproach, is now his honor; and his banishment led directly to his chief glory,—the glory of founding a state upon the basis of civil and religious freedom. He died in his Colony of Rhode Island, in 1683, in the 84th year of his age.

Dr. Elton, the latest biographer of Roger Williams, says, " The conduct of Williams on the occasion to the magistrates and clergy was mild and conciliating; and although he did not retract his opinions, he offered to burn the offensive book, and furnished satisfactory evidence of his " loyalty."* Dr. Elton consequently regards the sentence passed upon him as " cruel and unjustifiable." The

* Life of Roger Williams, 25.

truth appears to be that there were faults on both sides, and that they were faults of the age rather than of the heart. It is the peculiar glory of Roger Williams, that in his great doctrine that *the civil power has no jurisdiction over the conscience*, he rose above the age, and that he was stout enough to sustain himself nobly against opposition and difficulties which would have crushed any common man.

" His excellent wife survived him, and, as far as can be ascertained, the whole of his family, consisting of six children. His lineal descendants are numerous, and may justly rejoice in the diffusion alike of the fame and of the principles of their ancestor."*

IV.
REV. HUGH PETERS.
1636 TO 1641.

Hugh Peters, (or Peter, as he himself spelt his name,) was born at Fowey, in Cornwall, in 1599, and was educated at Trinity College, Cambridge, where he took the degree of A. M. in 1622. Upon leaving the University, he came to London, and was appointed lecturer at St. Sepulchre's. Towards the close of 1629, when Laud began his persecution of the Puritans, he went to Holland, and became pastor of an independent church at Rotterdam, having for a colleague, the celebrated Dr. William Ames. After remaining six years in that country, he came to New England, Oct. 6, 1635. For some time after his arrival, he divided his Sabbath labors between Boston and Salem. The church at Salem invited him to settle with them, and he became their pastor Dec. 21, 1636. According to Dr. Bentley's account of him, he entitled himself to the lasting gratitude of Salem, both as a minister and citizen. The town never saw greater peace, prosperity, or increase, in so short a period.

He interested himself in reforming the police of the town. The best regulations obtained. He stimulated industry, and the spirit of improvement. The arts were introduced. A water-mill was erected; a glass-house; salt works; the planting of hemp was encouraged, and a regular market was established. Commerce received most earnest attention. He formed the plan of the fishery, of the coast-

---

* Ib. 149.

ing voyages, of the foreign voyages ; and, among many other vessels, one of three hundred tons was undertaken under his influence.

Ever active and engaged in business, at home and abroad, he did not forget his church. He was the first to object to the unreasonable avocations from business by the numerous weekly and occasional lectures, which he suppressed. Being frequently absent, Mr. John Fiske, a worthy man, from King's College, Cambridge, then residing in Salem, assisted him in his pulpit.

As Mr. Peters was much engaged in trade, and had often done the business of the colony, he was thought a proper person to return to England, and to represent the sense of the colony upon the laws of excise and trade. Such was the affection of his people, that every remonstrance was made against the proposition. The court pressed, then solicited, and at length entreated that he might be in the commission with Mr. Weld and Mr. Hibbins. No man ever possessed more sincerely the affections of his people. Mr. Endicott, too, opposed it with great warmth. But it was finally agreed to, and Mr. Peters, with his two colleagues, left the colony on the 3d of August, 1641. We need not follow him into England. It was a melancholy separation to the people, and it was awful in its consequences to him. He rose into high favor with Cromwell and his Parliament, who granted to him Archbishop Laud's library, with various rich donations from noblemen's estates. No wonder, then, that he suffered with the regicides after the restoration. He fell a martyr to the cause he had so zealously espoused, on the 16th of October, 1660.*

V.

REV. EDWARD NORRIS.

1640 TO 1659.

Mr. Norris, who had been a clergyman in England, came to Salem in 1639, and joined the church here in December of that year. As he was a man of distinguished learning and influence, he was doubtless educated at one of the English Universities. Not long after his arrival he was duly elected a colleague with Mr. Peters, and ordained March 18, 1640. Under this date, Gov. Winthrop, in his History of New England, says: " Mr. Norris was ordained Teacher of the

---

* 1 Hist. Coll., VI., 250.

church of Salem, there being present near all the Elders of the other churches, and much people besides."* Dr. Bentley says : "This is the first ordination which was performed with great public ceremonies in Salem." Mr. Savage, the learned editor of Winthrop's History, says of Mr. Norris: " Much influence in the State was exerted by him, of which evidence will appear in this history."

After the departure of Mr. Peters, Mr. Norris was sole minister of the church about eighteen years, and during his whole ministry, he was highly esteemed for his ability and faithfulness. Nor was his attention confined to his parochial duties. He took an active interest in the public affairs of the colony.

In 1642, he replied to a book, written by Mr. Saltonstall, one of the assistants, on the subject of a permanent council. Gov. Winthrop was pleased with the reply, and said, that this grave and judicious Elder treated the book with that just severity it deserved.

In 1646 he preached the Election sermon. " He represented his church," says Mr. Felt, " in the synod, at its session, Oct., 1647 ; and was on a committee of seven, to draw up the system of Ecclesiastical Discipline, substantially contained in the Cambridge Platform."

In 1653 he wrote an able letter to the General Court, signed by himself, and his ruling elder, Samuel Sharpe, in the name, and by the vote of the church, remonstrating against an order, just passed, forbidding any person to preach without the approbation of elders belonging to the four next churches, or the County Court.

The first of the three reasons urged by him against the order, being in the true spirit of the founders of the First Church, is copied here :—" First, because it incroacheth upon the liberties of the several churches, who have power to choose and set up over them, whom they please for their edification and comfort, without depending on any other power, and if a break be once made into these liberties, we know not how far it may proceed in time, there being such a leading example as this." The order was repealed the same year.

Dr. Eliot says that Mr. Norris interfered so little in the affairs of other churches, that when the Platform of church discipline was adopted, in 1648, he persevered in a platform of his own church, and preserved not only the love of his people, but the respect of his neighbors to his death. He was more liberal in his ideas of tolera-

---

* Ib. 329.

tion than most ministers in New England, and was never active in proceedings against the baptists or other sectaries.

Mr. Norris died Dec. 23, 1659, aged about 70. He left one son, Edward, teacher of the school, to whom he bequeathed his house, land, books, and all his property. "With Mr. Norris," says Dr. Bentley, " we close the history of the ministers of the first generation. The consistent politics, the religious moderation, and the ardent patriotism of Mr. Norris, entitle him to the grateful memory of Salem. He finished in peace the longest life in the ministry which had been enjoyed in Salem, and died in his charge."

VI.
REV. JOHN HIGGINSON.
1660 TO 1708.

For the settlement and ministry of Mr. Higginson in Salem, see "Original Records," ante, p. 45, whence the account of him in "Notices," &c. was chiefly taken. For that account, therefore, we substitute here the first and last portions of Dr. Sprague's condensed sketch of Mr. H., in the first volume of his admirable Annals of the American Pulpit:

John Higginson (1636–1708) was the son of the Rev. Francis Higginson and Ann his wife, and was born at Claybrook, England, on the 6th of August, 1616. He came with his parents to New England in 1629, and joined the church in Salem, of which his father was "teacher," when he was but thirteen years of age. After his father's death, he was assisted in his education by the ministers and magistrates of the Colony,—a favor for which, in after life, he often expressed the warmest gratitude. He was chaplain of the Fort at Saybrook in 1636, and continued there about four years; in 1639, we find his name as witness to the articles of agreement between the settlers at Guilford, Connecticut, and the Indians, concerning the lands which were then purchased. In 1641, he was engaged as the teacher of a school at Hartford, and at the same time continued his theological studies under the direction of the Rev. Thomas Hooker. Having been thus occupied for about two years, he removed to Guilford in 1643, where he was employed as assistant to the Rev. Henry Whitfield, whose daughter he married. In 1647, he transcribed nearly two hundred of the sermons of his friend and benefactor, Mr. Hooker, who had then recently died; and about half of them were afterwards published in England.

After Mr. Whitfield returned to England in 1651, Mr. Higginson remained in sole charge of the church at Guilford until 1659, when he took leave of them, with the intention of returning to his native country. The vessel in which he had taken passage for England, put into Salem harbour, in stress of weather; and, as the church there was in want of a minister, they made proposals to him which issued in an engagement, on his part, to remain and preach for them a year. Before this time had expired, he received an invitation to become their pastor. He accepted it, and was ordained in August, 1660. At his ordination, the hands of the deacons and one of the brethren were imposed, in the presence of the neighboring churches and elders. Mr. Norton of Boston gave the Right hand of Fellowship. Mr. Higginson continued in the pastoral relation to this church until his death, which occurred on the 9th of December, 1708, at the age of ninety-two. He had been in the ministry seventy-two years.

. . . . Mr. Higginson was regarded as a person of excellent judgment, and his opinions generally had great weight. An agent from England, supposed to be Edward Randolph, wrote home, about 1677, that Mr. H. was one of the three most popular divines in New England. John Dunton* visited him in 1696, and writes thus concerning him :—

"All men look to him as a common father, and old age for his sake is a reverend thing; he is eminent for all the graces that adorn a minister; his very presence puts vice out of countenance; his conversation is a glimpse of Heaven."

Cotton Mather says of Mr. H. (1696) ,—

"This good old man is yet alive; and he that from a child knew the Holy Scriptures, does, at those years wherein men are to be twice children, continue preaching them with such a manly, pertinent, judicious vigour, and with so little decay of his intellectual abilities, as is indeed a matter of just admiration."

---

* JOHN DUNTON was an extensive bookseller in London, but came to this country in March, 1686, for the double purpose of selling books and collecting debts. He remained here eight months, and formed an extensive acquaintance, particularly with the prominent clergymen of the country. In 1705, he published in London, "The Life and Errors of John Dunton;" in which he gives an amusing account of his visit to New England, and describes many of the people whom he saw there.

Mr. Higginson's first wife died before 1678; for in that year he was married to Mary ——, a widow of Boston, who died March 9, 1709, leaving two daughters, one of whom was married to Jeremy Dummer.* By his first marriage, Mr. Higginson had seven children. Of these, *John* was of the Governor's Council, and lived in Salem. *Nathaniel* was born at Guilford, October 11, 1652 ; was graduated at Harvard College in 1670 ; went to England in 1674 ; and was with Lord Wharton about seven years, as steward and tutor to his children. He was employed in the mint of the Tower in 1681 ; and in 1683 went in the East India Company's service to Fort St. George, East Indies ; was member and Secretary of the Council, and afterwards Governor of the Factory at said Fort. He married Elizabeth Richards in 1692 ; returned to England with his wife and four children in 1700 ; and established himself as a merchant in London, where he died in 1708. *Thomas* went to England, learned the goldsmith's trade, came home, embarked for Arabia, and was never afterwards heard of. *Francis* went to his uncle, at Kirby Stevens in England, was educated at the University of Cambridge, and died of small pox in London, aged twenty-four. *Henry* was brought up a merchant, went to Barbadoes as Factor, and there died of small pox, 1685.

Mr. Higginson published the following works :—An Election Sermon, 1663. Our dying Saviour's legacy of peace to his disciples in a troublesome world, with a Discourse on the duty of Christians to be witnesses unto Christ, unto which is added some help to self-examination, 1686. An Attestation to Dr. Mather's Magnalia, prefixed to that work, 1697. A Sermon, entitled, " New England's duty and interest to be an habitation of justice and holiness," 1698. A Testimony to the order of the Gospel in the churches of New England, with Mr. Hubbard, 1701. An Epistle to the reader prefixed to Hale's Inquiry into the nature of Witchcraft, 1702. A Preface to Thomas Allen's Invitation to Thirsty Sinners, 1708. The deplorable state of New England, 1708.

---

* JEREMY DUMMER was a native of Boston; was graduated with the most brilliant reputation at Harvard College, in 1699; afterwards went to Europe and spent several years at the University of Utrecht, where he studied theology, and received the degree of Doctor of Philosophy; returned to this country, and finding no prospect of any congenial employment here, went to England, where he devoted himself to politics, and wrote an admirable pamphlet in defence of the New England Charters.

VII.
REV. NICHOLAS NOYES.
1683 TO 1717.

Mr. Noyes was the nephew of Rev. James Noyes, first minister of Newbury together with Rev. Thomas Parker, and was born in that town, Dec. 22, 1647.

In his letter to Cotton Mather, giving an account of his uncle's life, he says : " In the same ship came Mr. Thomas Parker, Mr. James Noyes, and a younger brother of his, Mr. Nicholas Noyes, who then was a single man : Between which three was a more than ordinary endearment of affection." Of this Mr. Nicholas Noyes he was the son, and by this Mr. Thomas Parker he was supported in his education at Harvard College, where he took his first degree, in 1667.

Before preaching in Salem, Mr. Noyes had been thirteen years in the ministry at Haddam. For account of his ordination in Salem, see ante, p. 89.

Mr. Noyes sustained a high reputation for learning in theology and general literature. But with other great and good men, he was carried away by the witchcraft delusion. It should be remembered, however, that he had the magnanimity afterwards to confess his error, and make all the reparation in his power.

Mr. Noyes was never married. He died Dec. 13, 1717, a few weeks after his lamented colleague, at the age of 70.

His character as given at the time, together with that of Mr. Curwin, is recorded in the church book.* He is there represented as having been extraordinarily accomplished for the work of the ministry. He is extolled for his superior genius, his pregnant wit, strong memory, solid judgment, and his great acquisition in human learning ; for his conversation among men, especially with his friends, so very pleasant, entertaining and profitable ; for his uncommon attainments in the study of divinity, his eminent sanctity, gravity and virtue, his services and learned performances in the pulpit ; and for his wisdom in human affairs, and his constant solicitude for the public good. John Dunton, an intelligent English traveller, who visited Mr. Noyes in 1686, says of him : " He is all that is delightful in conversation ;

---

* See ante, p. 102.

it is no lessening to his brother Higginson to say that he is no ways inferior to him for good preaching or primitive living." Mr. Noyes preached the Election sermon, 1698, which was published, and, besides his excellent Letter to Cotton Mather, as Mr. Savage calls it, he was the author of a poem on the death of his venerable colleague, and also of one on the death of Rev. J. Green; but it was not as a poet that he became so famous in his day.

VIII.
REV. GEORGE CURWIN.
1714 TO 1717.

Mr. George Curwin was the son of Hon. Jonathan Curwin. He was born in Salem, May 21, 1683, and graduated at Harvard College in 1701.

Having been for a number of years an assistant in the ministry with Mr. Noyes, he was ordained as pastor and colleague, on the 19th of May, 1714. The record (by Mr. Noyes) says: "May 19, the Rev. Mr. George Curwin was ordained Pastor of this church." For the record, see ante, p. 100.

Mr. Curwin died Nov. 23, 1717. His ministry was short, but in the highest degree meritorious. The church record says that he was "very eminent for his early improvements in learning and piety, his singular abilities, and great labors, his remarkable zeal and faithfulness in the service of his master."[*]

The Rev. John Barnard, of Marblehead, his early friend, preached in Salem on the public Thanksgiving, a few days after Mr. Curwin's death. The sermon was published, and dedicated to Hon. Samuel Brown, a relative of the lamented minister. Mr. Barnard, in his discourse, says of his "reverend and beloved brother, Mr. George Curwin," that "he seemed to have been peculiarly formed from his youth for that great and noble design in which he afterwards spent a short and laborious life. The spirit of early devotion, accompanied with a natural freedom of thought, and easy elocution, a quick invention, a solid judgment, and a tenacious memory, laid the foundation of a good preacher; to which his acquired literature, his great reading, hard studies, deep meditation, and close walk with God, rendered him an able and faithful minister of the New Testament."

Rev. Mr. Curwin married in 1711, Mehitable, daughter of Deliver-

---

[*] See ante, p. 102.

ance Parkman, a distinguished merchant of Salem. Two of his sons, Samuel and George, were graduates of Harvard College, in the class of 1635: the former of whom was the author of "Journal and Letters of the late Samuel Curwin, Judge of Admiralty, etc.," edited by his kinsman, George Atkinson Ward, A. M.

IX.
REV. SAMUEL FISK.
1718 to 1735.

Mr. Samuel Fisk was the grandson of John Fiske, already mentioned as assistant to Hugh Peters, and afterwards minister of Wenham, and was graduated at Harvard College in 1708. For account of his call and settlement over the First Church, &c., see records, ante, p. 103, &c.

Simultaneous with the settlement of Mr. Fisk was the formation of the second church by members dismissed from the First Church to settle Rev. Robert Stanton in the east part of the town.

Dr. Bentley says of Mr. Fisk : " He was a man of real abilities : but his high thoughts of church authority prevented his usefulness, and he was dismissed from the First Church in 1735, and accepted a new house provided by his friends, in the same street, westward, on the north side of the street. He was succeeded in the old church by Mr. John Sparhawk." Mr. Fisk's " high thoughts,"—so repugnant to the spirit of the First Church and its founders,—led to a fierce controversy, which continued many years after he was excluded from the pulpit, but was finally settled in a Christian spirit and manner. He was dismissed from the Third Church in 1745, and succeeded by Rev. Dudley Leavitt. He died in Salem, April 7th, 1770, aged 81. He preached the First Century Lecture, of the First Church, August 6, 1729. The Election Sermon, delivered by him in 1731, was published, and may be ranked among the best. His wife was Anna Gerrish. The late Gen. John Fisk, a gentleman of much distinction in Salem, was his son.

X.
REV. JOHN SPARHAWK.
1736 to 1755.

On the 5th day of August, 1736,—" at a meeting of the brethren adhering to the ancient principles of the First Church in Salem,"

Mr. John Sparhawk was chosen as a "meet person to discharge the office of a Gospel minister among them."

By a letter dated Cambridge, October 23, 1736, Mr. Sparhawk accepted the call, and his ordination took place on the 8th of December following."*

Mr. Sparhawk was the son of the Rev. John Sparhawk, of Bristol. He was born in September, 1713, and graduated at Harvard College, in 1731. He married Jane, daughter of Rev. Aaron Porter, of Medford, Oct. 4, 1737. He died April 30, 1755, in the 42d year of his age. He left three sons, Nathaniel, John, and Samuel, and four daughters, Priscilla, married to Hon. Nathaniel Ropes; Catharine, married to her cousin, Nathaniel Sparhawk; Jane, married to John Appleton; Susanna, married to Hon. George King, of Portsmouth.

Of Mr. Sparhawk it has been said, that he was much esteemed and beloved in his life, and in his death sincerely and universally lamented.

The late venerable Dr. Holyoke, whose minister he was, described him as "large in person, a man of dignity, and an excellent preacher."

XI.
REV. THOMAS BARNARD.
1755 to 1776.

Mr. Thomas Barnard was the son of the Rev. John Barnard of Andover, born Aug. 16, 1716, and graduated at Harvard College in 1732. He was installed Pastor of the First Church in Salem, Sept. 17, 1755; "the Rev. Mr. Lowell of Newbury began with prayer; Rev. Mr. Clark of Danvers preached from Malachi 2:6; Rev. Mr. Barnard of Marblehead gave the charge."

Mr. Felt, in Annals of Salem, says of Mr. Barnard: "He was ordained at Newbury, Jan. 31, 1738,—left his people there because of difficulties about Mr. Whitfield's preaching,—studied and practised law, represented Newbury in General Court, re-entered the ministry, and was installed over First Church of Salem. He left children, Thomas, John, Benjamin,—and Sarah, who married Jonathan Jackson of Newburyport. He published sermons at the ordination of his brother Edward, in Haverhill, 1743,—of Josiah Bayley, at Hampton Falls, 1757,—before Society of Industry, 1757,—at Artillery Election, 1758,—at ordination of William Whitwell, in Marblehead, 1762,—and at Election, 1763. He possessed a strong and cultivated

mind. He was much beloved by his society here, and highly esteemed by the public." To this list of his publications should be
added his able discourse at the Dudleian Lecture, 1768, in defence
of Christianity, from 1 Cor. 2:5, " That your faith should not be in
the wisdom of men, but in the power of God."

He died August 5, 1776, aged 60.

" Mr. Barnard having been taken off from his labors by the palsy,"
adds Mr. Felt, " and his son Thomas having supplied his place,—the
church had a fast, Oct. 31, 1770, preparatory to the choice of a minister." Mr. Thomas Barnard, Jr., and Mr. Asa Dunbar, preached as
candidates, and upon the choice of the latter, the minority, friends
of the former, separated peaceably, and established the North Society, settling Thomas Barnard, Jr. as their minister. The First Church,
" for the continuing of peace and brotherly love," made an equitable
division with them of the " temporalities of the church," though it
could see no reasons for a separation, Mr. Dunbar being " admirably
qualified for a Gospel preacher."

One or two matters of permanent interest in the proceedings of
the church may be noticed here.

At a meeting of the church, Dec. 3d, 1760, Deacons Joshua Ward
and John Beckford were chosen to receive and improve the legacy of
eighty dollars, bequeathed to the church by the late Judge Lindall,
" to be improved (by such persons as the church shall choose.) by
good bonds on interest,—the interest or improvement being for the
Deacons of the church for the time being,—the principal not to be
diminished." The deacons of the church successively received and
improved the same, using the interest, till April 21, 1819, when the
principal was deposited in the Savings Bank, pursuant to a vote of
the church, " in such manner that the Deacons of the said First
Church, for the time being, may receive the interest thereof."

At a meeting of the church, August 2, 1762, it was unanimously
voted, for the sake of peace and Christian communion, to give up to
the church, formed by those who went off with Rev. Mr. Fisk, in
1735, one half of the plate belonging to the First Church, at the
time of the separation, or its value in money ; and also to pay them
an equivalent for one part of the Deacons' Marsh.*

---

* The original grant of the Deacons' Marsh, as recorded in the Town's Book, is as
follows:

"Item, There is granted to John Horne, two acres of Marsh ground, until the town
do further dispose of the same."

" Item, To Charles Gott two acres of Marsh ground, upon the same conditions;

XII.
REV. ASA DUNBAR.
1772 to 1779.

Mr. Dunbar was born in Bridgewater, May 26. 1745, graduated at Harvard College, in 1767, and ordained as colleague with Rev. Thomas Barnard, July 22. 1772. Rev. Mr. Adams of Roxbury, prayed; Rev. Mr. Appleton of Cambridge, preached; Rev. Mr. Swain of Wenham, gave the charge: Rev. Mr. Whitwell of Marblehead, concluded with prayer; Rev. Mr. Payson of Chelsea, gave the right hand of fellowship.

Mr. Dunbar's services were interrupted by the bad state of his health, and in a few years he was induced to ask a dismission. The following letter, being characteristic of the man and the times, may be interesting to members of the society.

" To the First Church and Propriety in Salem.

" My dear Christian brethren and friends,

" Such is the general state of my health, that I judge it expedient for me to ask a dismission from your service in the Gospel ministry. This request I doubt not you will think to be reasonable, and I hope your compliance with it will be greatly to your own interest.

" It would be disagreeable to me to say anything to you concerning past salary or support, did not the representation I must now make of the matter, bear a very honorable testimony to your constant generosity. I would not, however, abuse your generosity by asking any favor, nor do I mean to make any demands. Not that I scruple your readiness to do me any reasonable favor, should I request it; but with respect to my expenses, I would have you regard equity alone, and act as your own integrity shall determine you. Perhaps you will think them extravagant, or if not, yet that you ought not to defray them wholly. Judge ye what is right, and settle the affair accordingly. Betwixt you and me there shall be no contention.

and that the said Charles Gott shall have one acre more, if there be any in the town's hands, when other men are provided for."

Both were deacons, and their *successors*, not their *heirs*, took the Marsh. John Horne, or rather *Orne*, (for so he signed his will, proved in 1684,) was deacon from 1629 to 1684. From him descended all the Salem Ornes. He left four sons, John, Symon, Joseph, Benjamin. Joseph was great-grandfather to the late Dr. Joseph Orne, of H. C., class of 1765.

" Such necessary family expenses as I am able to recollect and account for, since my return to preach with you in September, 1777, amount to   -   -   -   -   -   £1524. 0. 0.
" I have received of your treasurers, Mr. Rand and Mr. Woodbridge, by taxation and subscription,   -   £441. 4. 2.
" By privatedonations, of which I have kept a scrupulous account, estimating them as justly as I could, I received,   -   -   -   432. 16. 0.
—————874. 0. 2.
    " Your most affectionate, humble servant,
        " ASA DUNBAR.
" April 23, 1779."

The society more than complied with Mr. Dunbar's request, by voting him seven hundred pounds.

As little seems to be known among us of this estimable man and minister, we have taken some pains to ascertain his history after he left Salem. From the church records it appears that he was recommended, in 1786, to the church in Keene, under the care of Rev. Aaron Hall.

After his dismission from the ministry, Mr. Dunbar studied law, and settled in the profession at Keene, N. H., where he was known as the honest lawyer, and greatly respected. He died in Keene, as appears by the records of that town, on the 22d of June, 1787, (not 1788, as Dr. Bentley states,) and was buried from the meeting house, Rev. Mr. Hall preaching his funeral sermon, and giving him a high character.

Mr. Felt observes of Mr. Dunbar, that when settled here he belonged to Weston, and married Mary Jones, of the same place, 1772. By the church records it appears that at his ordination he came recommended from the church of the late Rev. Dr. Gay, of Hingham. His places of residence, as well as the members of his family, may be conceived from the following extract from the Town records of Keene:

" Dunbar Asa :
" Polly, daughter of Asa Dunbar and Mary his wife, born in Salem, Nov. 24, 1773. William, their son, born at Weston, Sept. 28, 1776. Charles Jones, their son, born at Harvard, Feb. 28, 1780. Sophia, their daughter, born at Harvard, July 19, 1781. Louisa, their daughter, borne at Keene, May 11, 1785. Cynthia, their

daughter, born at Keene, May 22, 1787. William Dunbar, son of Asa and Mary his wife, died at Harvard, July, 1779,—buried at Lancaster." Mrs. Dunbar survived her husband, and was married to Mr. Minot of Concord, Mass., father of Judge Minot of Haverhill.

Dr. Bentley, who must have known Mr. Dunbar well, says: "He was a man of genius."

XIII.
REV. JOHN PRINCE, LL.D.
1779 to 1836.

Dr. Prince was born in Boston, July 22, 1751, and graduated at Harvard College in 1776.

"Mr. John Prince was ordained to the pastoral care of the First Church in Salem, Nov. 10th, 1779. The Rev. Mr. Payson made the first prayer, the Rev. Mr. Williams preached from Luke 2:14; the Rev. Mr. Howard prayed before the charge; the Rev. Mr. Diman gave the charge; the Rev. Mr. Willard prayed, and the Rev. Mr. Barnard gave the right hand of fellowship."

The sermon, by Mr. Williams, of Bradford, (afterwards professor at Cambridge,) was published. To the people he says: "No church can be under stronger obligations than you are to preserve the religion of Jesus pure and undefiled. Here those good men who came into this part of America for the sake of religion, formed *the first Church.* We reverence their memories."

In 1817, a legacy of $3000 was received from the late Charles Henry Orne, merchant, a worthy member of the church, which, when accumulated to $5000, was to form a permanent fund for the support of the settled minister of the First Church. From accumulation and subscriptions, the fund has increased to nearly $8000. Upon receiving this legacy, the Proprietors of the First Church became incorporated by the name of the "First Congregational Society in Salem."

Here may be gratefully noticed another benefactor and most worthy member of the First Church. The late Mehitable Higginson, the sixth in descent from the first minister, and the last in Salem to bear that venerated name, was an honor to her ancestry and her sex. As the teacher of successive generations of children she was a blessing to the church and the town, exhibiting through life an example of exalted female excellence. She left at her death a lasting memorial of her interest in the Society of the First Church by a generous bequest; also providing that a legacy of five hundred dollars given to the Salem Athenæum on certain conditions, should, "in case of the non-fulfilment of said conditions, go to the use of the Ministerial Fund of the First Congregational Society in Salem."

In February, 1824, at a meeting of the First Congregational Society, in Salem, called for the purpose, it was voted that it was expedient to settle a colleague; and that the salary of Dr. Prince should be continued to him if a colleague was settled. Rev. Henry Coleman, having preached as a candidate, was earnestly desired by a considerable portion of the Society. A majority, however, not being in favor of his settlement, his adherents seceded from the first Church in 1824, and built for him the house in Barton Square; and he was installed as their minister, Feb. 25, 1825,—Mr. Upham having been recently ordained the colleague of Dr. Prince. This secession made the fourth religious society in Salem, formed from the First, in a little more than one hundred years.

Dr. Prince lived in Christian union and brotherly love, for more than thirty years of his ministry, with Dr. Barnard of the North Church, and preached his funeral sermon, which is a beautiful memorial of their mutual friendship. He was also happy in his young colleague, who by his devoted attentions cheered and brightened his latter days, and paid a just and eloquent tribute to his memory, in a discourse preached at his funeral, which was published, and may be referred to for a full and clear view of Dr. Prince's merits as a philosopher, and his character as a Christian divine. We cannot forbear to take from it a sentence or two, showing the beautiful relation which the venerable minister and his faithful people bore to each other.

After speaking of the steadfast kindness of his people, and observing that for twelve years they had "released him from labors," and yet "continued to him an unabated support;" the author adds: "Your late venerable pastor has himself attested to your goodness and faithfulness to him. On his death bed he bore a testimony in your favor which will not and cannot ever be forgotten by you or your successors. He has bequeathed a munificent donation of nearly 150 invaluable books, selected with the greatest care, and constituting a theological library such as few clergymen possess, for the perpetual use of your ministers." It is then stated that the will providing for the donation had been executed some years, and that just before his death Dr. Prince called for the catalogue containing the titles of the books, and dictated, in Mr. Upham's presence, the following words to be written on the catalogue over his signature: " Sensible of the kindness of my people through my long ministry and life, I bequeath these books as a lasting memorial of my affectionate gratitude."

Dr. Prince died on the 7th of June, 1836, aged very nearly 85 years. He was twice married. Mary Bailey, of Boston, was his first wife, and the mother of his children. His second wife was Mrs. Millie Waldo, who survived him. His eldest son, John, a graduate of Harvard College, class of 1800, was a lawyer, and the late Clerk of the Judicial Courts in the County of Essex.

The eminent character of Dr. Prince is well known. He possessed the spirit of a true philosopher and a true Christian, and was alike distinguished for his mechanical ingenuity, his attainments in natural science, in theological and general learning,—for his various genius and taste, his ardent love of nature and of art,—his single-heartedness and truly Christian temper, and for his amiable and generous disposition, especially as manifested in the gratuitous diffusion of his scientific discoveries and improvements, and in imparting his rare knowledge, at all times, for the gratification and entertainment of others. His character will long be remembered with sincere admiration.

XIV.
REV. CHARLES WENTWORTH UPHAM.
1824 to 1844.

Mr. Charles W. Upham, son of the Hon. Joshua Upham, formerly of Massachusetts, and a graduate of Harvard College in the class of 1763, was born at St. John, New Brunswick, May 4, 1802. He received his education at Harvard College, and took his first degree in 1821. He was a graduate of the Theological School in Cambridge, in the class of 1824.

Having accepted an invitation to settle as colleague pastor with the Rev. Dr. Prince, Mr. Upham was ordained Dec. 8, 1824. The record (made by the senior pastor) gives a full account of his ordination. The ecclesiastical council was organized by choosing Rev. Dr. Thayer, of Lancaster, moderator, and Rev. Mr. Walker, of Charlestown, scribe.

The candidate read before the council a statement of his views of religion and the sacred office.

Rev. Dr. Channing made the introductory prayer; Rev. President Kirkland preached the sermon; Rev. Dr. Lowell made the ordaining prayer; Rev. Dr. Thayer gave the charge; Rev. Mr. Brazer offered the right hand of fellowship; Rev. Mr. Flint addressed the Society.

During his ministry Mr. Upham published his Dedication sermon and the 2d Century Lecture. He also published, at an early period of his ministry, "Letters on the Logos," the "Life of Sir Henry Vane," and "Lectures on Witchcraft,"—with various other interesting publications.

Mr. Upham resigned his pastoral office in December, 1844, from regard to his health, as did his predecessor, Mr. Dunbar;—the only instances of resignation among the ministers of the First Church. Upon accepting this resignation, the Society presented Mr. Upham with the sum of fifteen hundred dollars. In his excellent farewell address, in writing, which was entered upon the records of the Society, he warmly expresses "the gratification with which he contemplated their unanimity, kindness and generosity," concluding "with the most fervent wishes and prayers for the welfare of the Society collectively and individually, and with the liveliest sensibility in the remembrance of all their kindness, fidelity and sympathy."

Mr. Upham was soon called into public life. He has been a Representative of Salem in the General Court; a member of the State Senate from the County of Essex, and President of that body; also a member of the Congress of the United States, and Mayor of the city of Salem.

XV.
REV. THOMAS TREADWELL STONE.
1846 to 1852.

Mr. Stone was born at Waterford, Me., Feb. 9, 1801, and was educated at Bowdoin College, taking his first degree in 1820. He was ordained in the ministry at Andover, Me., Sept. 8, 1824, and remained there till Sept. 1830, when he became preceptor of Bridgton Academy, where he continued two years. He resumed the ministry, and was installed at East Machias on the 15th of May, 1833. In June, 1846, he was chosen Pastor of the First Congregational Society in Salem, and installed on the 12th of July following.

The mode of Mr. Stone's induction into the pastoral office, on this occasion, was somewhat peculiar. No invitations were given to the pastors of sister churches to be present. The ceremony of installation took place on Sunday morning, at the usual hour of meeting for worship, in the manner prescribed by the Committee of the Society, and in designed imitation of ancient practice. Dr. George Choate, in behalf of the Committee, standing together with Mr. Stone, in front of the pulpit, made an address, first to the congregation, then to the Pastor elect, combining in the latter both a right hand of fellowship and a charge. The pastor responded in suitable terms. He was then " taken by the hand, and conducted into the pulpit. Then followed an anthem ; next an appropriate prayer by Mr. Stone, and a discourse adapted to the occasion."

The vote of invitation to Mr. Stone contained a peculiar provision, viz :—" That either party may terminate the contract by giving to the other party six months notice of an intention or wish so to do." The Society, on the 23d of August, 1851, by a major vote, gave such notice to Mr. Stone, and his ministry terminated accordingly in February, 1852.

Mr. Stone had greatly endeared himself to many persons in the society ; and all, it is believed, entertained for him a high respect, and the sincerest good wishes. One thousand dollars was contributed at once by members of the Society, and cordially presented to him upon the close of his ministerial connection with them.

Mr. Stone is again settled in the ministry at Bolton.

XVI.
REV. GEORGE WARE BRIGGS
1853.

Mr. Briggs was born at Little Compton, R. I., April 8th, 1810, and was educated at Brown University, taking his first degree in 1825. He graduated at the Theological School in Cambridge, with the class of 1834; and was settled in the ministry at Fall River,

Sept. 24, 1834. He was installed at Plymouth, Jan. 3, 1838, as colleague Pastor with the Rev. Dr. Kendall.

The installation of Mr. Briggs as Pastor of the First Church in Salem, took place on the 6th of January, 1853. Invitations were extended to various clergymen in the vicinity to be present on the occasion, but no ecclesiastical council was organized. The services in the church were as follows:

Introductory Prayer, by Rev. William O. White, of Keene, N. H.; Reading of the Scriptures, by Rev. O. B. Frothingham, of Salem; Sermon, by Rev. John H. Morison, of Milton; Ordaining Prayer, by Rev. Dr. Thompson, of Salem; Right Hand of Fellowship, by Rev. Dr. Flint, of Salem; Concluding Prayer, by Rev. Dexter Clapp, of Salem; Benediction by the Pastor.

Rev. Mr. Briggs is the sixteenth minister of the First Church,—the tenth of those who had been approved ministers elsewhere before their settlement here, and the second that came from the ancient church of Plymouth,—from the church first assembled for Christian worship, to the church first gathered and organized, in New England.

We have thus endeavored to give an account of every ordination or installation in the First Church, as found in its records, or elsewhere. It does not appear that any sermon was preached at the induction of any of the first five ministers. At the three next, it was preached by the ministers themselves,—Higginson, Noyes, Curwin,—and at all since, except the fifteenth, by a pastor of some other church. The right hand of fellowship appears to have formed a part of the services from the beginning, but no charge is noted till the ordination of Mr. Curwin, when it was given by "the teacher," Mr. Noyes. There is no instance to be found of any examination of the candidate as to his doctrinal views, and but one in which they were spontaneously given. In this case (the fourteenth) there was the most complete observance of ecclesiastical form and etiquette; yet in the next, (the fifteenth,) they were wholly disregarded. The various manner of introducing the ministers of the First Church, may be taken as an illustration of the spirit of Christian liberty, which actuated the founders. Through every variety of form, and all diversities of sentiment, the church has been steadfast to its first principles. The only contentious controversy with a minister that occurs in its history, sprung from a disposition on his part, believed to be inconsistent with these principles and the rights of the church.

With a single exception, all the ministers were settled for life. No one of them ever resigned his office here to preach elsewhere. All were liberally educated ; the first five at one of the English Universities ; the sixth without any university; the next eight at Harvard ; the fifteenth at Bowdoin, and the present pastor at Brown University.

Of the fifteen, whose ministry has closed, one was banished by the civil authorities, and one sent on a foreign mission,—both against the wishes of their people ; one was excluded from the pulpit, two resigned, and the ministry of one was terminated by its own special constitution. The other nine died in their pastoral charge. In no case has the salary of a minister been diminished upon settling a colleague with him.

The facts we have given, though brief, sufficiently show how learned, able and faithful were the ministers, and how just and generous the people have been to them ;—and also, we may add, to their seceding brethren, who, at different periods, went from them to form other churches.

We find no mention of any council before the ordination of Mr. Fisk, in 1718. The free election of a minister being conclusive, it would hardly seem consistent to submit it to any ecclesiastical authority. The Society accordingly "voted that the installation of the Rev. Mr. Briggs should be consecrated by public religious services in the First Church, consisting of a sermon, right hand of fellowship, reading of the Scriptures, prayers, and appropriate music." But no ecclesiastical council was organized.

With the auspicious settlement of the present pastor, our desultory notices are brought to a close. We rejoice most devoutly in the auspices under which his ministry has commenced. May the blessing of God rest upon it, and make it more abundant in " the fruit of the spirit,—love, joy, peace,"—than any that has gone before it.

It is hoped that these notices, imperfect as they are, will be acceptable, and serve to inspire a more lively interest in the prosperity and perpetuity of the First Church, and a deeper attachment to the principles upon which it is founded.

ADDITIONAL NOTE.

The following certificate, subjoined to Rev. John Fiske's Original Record, and unintentionally omitted in its proper place, (ante, p. 36), is added here, together with some other matters:

BOSTON, MAY, 1857.

The foregoing twenty-seven pages, comprising the Original Covenant of the First Church in Salem, (and its renewal), with names of members, and certain Church records in 1637, were copied by me, at the request of Hon. Daniel Appleton White, of Salem, from an ancient book of Church records (now in my possession) in the well known handwriting of the Rev. John Fiske, for several years the assistant preacher of Hugh Peter, while pastor of the said First Church, being the first portion of said ancient book, and all of it which pertains to the Salem Church, next to which appear records of the Wenham Church, from the year 1644 to Nov. 1655, followed by records of the Church of Chelmsford, from Nov. 1655, to July 25th, 1675, of which Churches Mr. Fiske was the minister.

The record of " The Children of John and Anna Fiske," also in his handwriting, was copied by me from the beginning of his said book of Church records.

DAVID PULSIFER.

Among the fifty members of the First Church, in Salem, residing at Marblehead, and dismissed " to be a Church by themselves," (ante, p. 90,) with Rev. Samuel Cheever their minister, it may be seen that twelve have no given name except the single letter G., doubtless standing for " *Goodie*," as "Goodie Guppa," for instance, on p. 71. For the sake of genealogical inquirers we here supply their christian names from a list of the fifty-four original members of the new Church, as found on the 12th page of a " Discourse on the History of the First Christian Church and Society of Marblehead, &c., 1816. By Samuel Dana, A. M., Fifth Pastor of said Church." They are as follows: G. (Mary) Dixy, G. (Mary) Bartoll, G. (Elizabeth)

Watts, G. (Abigail) Ellis, G. (Miriam) Pedrick, G. (Mary) Meritt,
G. (Mary) Merritt, G. (Sarah) Henly, G. (Alice) Darby, G. (Charity) Sandin, G. (Joanna) Hanley [or Hawley] G. (Abigail) Clarke.
Tab. Pedrick is *Dorcas* Pedrick, in Mr. Dana's list. His four additional names appear to be Ruth Cheever, (the minister's wife), William Beal, Sarah Ward, and Sarah Buckley.

Charles, before Pitman, in the Salem list, should be *Charity*—the
i in this word not being dotted, nor the *t* crossed, an omission very
common in Mr. Higginson's records, occasioned the mistake. *Hanley*
in his list is undoubtedly the same as *Hawley* in the other.

———

The ancient record of Mr. Fiske, to which Mr. Pulsifer's certificate
relates, is curious and interesting, taken in connection with Thomas
Letchford's "Plain Dealing, or Newes from New England," as well as
in the important respects before mentioned. They strikingly illustrate each other, particularly in respect to the Salem Church. The
three or four years that Letchford, who was a London lawyer, resided
in Boston, were the very years that Mr. Fiske passed in Salem. The
Plain Dealing, which was published in London, in 1641,* gives a
minute account of the early New England Churches, their formation, admission of members, mode of worship, &c., but, like Mr.
Fiske's record, contains no intimation of any test creed or prescribed
formula of faith, and, of course, proves that no such test could have
been adopted or used among them. The Newbury Church, then under the famous Parker and Noyes, must have been very far from
thinking of such a test, if we may judge from the following remark:
"Of late," says Letcher, "some churches are of opinion that any
may be admitted to church fellowship that are not extremely ignorant or scandalous: but this they are not very forward to practise, except at Newberry."† How this ancient Church could have been
brought, in the middle of the 19th century, to interpolate, in its admirable old Scriptural, Christian Covenant,—the Covenant of Tucker
and Popkin, worthy successors of Parker and Noyes,—a glaring
sectarian test creed, longer than the covenant itself, is a hard prob-
lem to solve.

* Re-published in 3 Hist. Coll., III., 55.   † Ib. 50.

ALPHABETICAL INDEX.

A.

Abernethy, on freedom of conscience, 160.
Adams, J. Q., on the N. England Confederacy, referred to, 255, 275.
Additional Note, 307.
Allibone's Dictionary, etc., quoted, 252.
Allin, John, on quoting from other authors, quoted, 205, 213, 245.
Apostles' Creed, earliest deviation from gospel terms of communion, 153.
Arnold, Dr., on sectarian differences of faith, quoted, 225.
"Articles of Faith and Covenant of 1629," 239, 270.
Athenæum, Boston, referred to, 190, 242, 263, 266.

B.

Bacon, Dr., on Congregationalism, quoted, 280.
Baker, Mrs. Martha, denied recommendation to First Church, 121, 124 to 127.
Balguy, Dr., on judging others, quoted, 180.
Baptism of children, 52, 53, 59, 72, 91 to 93, 271.
    "   " Pasea Foote's eight children, 70.
    "   Questions at, 206.
    "   " Joseph Orne, Jr., 111.
Barnard, Rev. John, on Rev. Geo. Curwin, quoted, 294.
    " Rev. Thomas, Notice of Life of, 296.
Barrow, Dr., on judging others, quoted, 180.
Barton Square Church, 301.
Bass River Church, 72, 73, 74.
    "   "   " Members of, 73.
    "   "   " Its covenant and ordination of Mr. Hale, 74.
Baxter, Richard, on peremptory opinions, quoted, 125.
    "   " on terms of Christian communion, quoted, 133.
    "   " on schism, quoted, 144.
    "   " on addition to Christ's terms, quoted, 151.
    "   " on the adversary's artifices, quoted, 151.
    "   " on fundamental doctrines, quoted, 167.
    "   " on change of belief, quoted, 169.
    "   " on sectarianism, quoted, 176, 214.
Belknap, Dr., his biography of Robinson, quoted, 275.
Bentley, Dr, his "Description of Salem," quoted, 9, 10, 80, 200, 258, 269.
    "   "   "   " on F. Higginson, quoted, 283, 284.
    "   "   "   " on Skelton, quoted, 285.
    "   "   "   " on Norris, quoted, 289, 290.
    "   "   "   " on Sam'l Fisk, quoted, 295.
    "   "   "   " on Asa Dunbar, quoted, 300.
    verly, Ordination at, 109.

Bible given to John Massey, 97.
Bible, the standard of Christian Faith, 127.
Boston Church, Trouble in, 76, 77.
Boston Churches, Covenants of, referred to, 195.
Bradford Church, gathered, 91.
"Brief Sketch" of Judge White's Lecture in 1856, 255.
Briggs, Rev. George W., Notice of Life of, 304.
Burke, Edmund, on the Puritan spirit, quoted, 275.
Burton's Rejoinder, on liberty of conscience, quoted, 199.

C.

Cambridge Platform, quoted, 199, 260.
Campbell, Dr., on schism and heresy, quoted, 140, 141.
Catalogue of baptized children, 16.
      "   persons joined in full communion, 15.
Cave on the Christian Fathers, quoted, 153.
Centennial Celebration, Aug. 6, 1729, 109.
Chalmers' Political Annals, referred to, 267.
Chandler, Dr., on making the Scriptures the rule of faith, quoted, 138.
      "   "   on human creeds, quoted, 154.
      "   "   on giving up articles of faith, quoted, 159.
Charlestown Covenant, quoted, 241, 250.
      "   "   referred to, 195, 211, 243, 249, 274.
      "   History of, quoted, 250.
      "   "   referred to, 249.
Chebacko Church, gathered, 91.
Chillingworth, on diversity of opinions in religion, quoted, 182.
      "   on believing the Scripture alone, quoted, 138.
      "   on heresy, quoted, 142.
      "   on "the Bible the religion of Protestants," quoted, 138.
Choate, Dr. George, assists in installing Mr. Stone, 304.
Christian Examiner, Article from, 232.
Church, a new, built, 105.
Church-book, 47, 48.
      "   recovered from Rev. Sam'l Fisk's heirs, 118.
Church in Chelmsford, Moses Fiske joins, 38 to 40.
Church, Excommunication from, 53, 54.
Church-membership of all children of the faithful, 8, 49, 50, 60, 61, 69, 71, 88, 97.
Church-membership, 50, 51, 52, 54, 55, 56, 57, 58, 68, 69, 71, 74, 75, 77, 79, 83, 88, 90, 94, 96, 97, 98, 259.
Church-members, List of, at reorganization of Church, 115.
Church, Withdrawal from, 31 to 36.
Churches, Duty of, 127 to 132.
Cicero, quoted, 221.
      "   his fundamental rule, 256.
Clap, President, regards "consenting to *substance* of Westminster Catechism" as heresy, quoted, 146.
Clarke, Adam, on creeds versus Scripture, quoted, 148.
Clarke, Dr., on judging for another in religion, quoted, 177.
Colman, Rev. Henry, minister of Barton Square, 301.

Communion, Terms of Christian, 132 to 144.
Confession of Faith, Fiske's *negative* evidence on, 23, 24.
    "   " and Covenant, as given in tract in Boston Athenæum, 190, 191.
    "   "   " Preface to, quoted, 206.
    "   " not distinct from covenant, 198.
    "   " Webster's definition of, 228.
Confessions, various, 280.
Congregationalism, True principles of, Note C., 275 to 282.
    "   "   "   " Quotation on, 280.
Consociationalism, Quotation on, 280, 281.
Contribution for captives of Indians, 95.
Correspondence between First Church and Tabernacle, (in 1832), 121.
Cotton, John, on the dependence of the churches on Christ, quoted, 133.
    "   " his testimony to Christian freedom of early churches, 137, 199, 277.
Cotty, Case of Rob., 27, 28.
Councils of Churches, 76, 77, 78, 80, 95.
Covenant, The First, as given by Mather, 6, 7.
    "   " Comprehensiveness of, 251.
    "   " Dr. Bentley's opinion of, 10.
    " identified with Confession of Faith by Neander and Uhden, Morton, and Mather, 22.
Covenant, The first, John Higginson's record regarding, 62.
    "   "   "   "   " discussed, 62 to 66.
    "   " Dr. Worcester's version of, 187, 190, 216, 243, 246.
    "   "   " reasons for his version, 188, 216.
    "   "   "   "   " answered, 217 to 220.
    "   " testified to by Messrs. Diman, etc., 189.
    "   " Discussion regarding, at Essex Institute, 193 to 197.
    "   " Inadvertent admission regarding, in new ed. of Morton, 282.
    "   " The question stated, 210.
    "   " Mr. Felt's earlier view of, 236, 265.
    "   "   " later view of, 237, 238, 240, 254, 261 to 268.
Covenant and confession, Morton's account of, 3, 4, 192.
    "   " propounded to candidates, etc., 68, 69.
    " Mr. Fiske's duplicate record of, discussed, 40 to 44.
    " renewed, 48, 84, 85, 113, 114, 203.
    " Evidence of renewal of, in Rob. Cotty's case, 28.
    " as contained in "New Direction," discussed, 85 to 88.
    " as renewed in 1660, with preamble and P. S., 13, 14.
    " as subscribed by Mr. Leavitt, Dr. Worcester's extract from, 186.
    " Webster's definition of, 228.
Covenants of various early churches, quoted, 137.
    "   "   "   " referred to, 195.
    "   "   "   " Dr. Palfrey on freedom of, 282.
Cradock, Gov., Injunctions of, 188.
"Creed-making," (newspaper article), 231.
Creeds of New Testament, 134.
Curwin, Mr. Geo., ordained, 100.
    "   " Obituary of, 102.
    "   " Notice of Life of, 294.

Cyprian, as quoted by Limborch, on Christian liberty, 153.

D.

Davis's edition of Morton, quoted, 200, 258, 269.
Deacons, 84, 94, 116.
Deacons' Marsh, 42.
" Declaration of Cong. Churches in England and Wales in 1833," quoted, 279.
Devereux, H., 121, 183.
Diman, Barnard and Holt, Letter of, quoted, 189.
    "   "   "   "   referred to, 187.
Direction, The, 211, 242, 245, 247, 262, 263, 268, 270 to 272.
" Direction, The New," Pamphlet containing, discussed, 85 to 88, 203, 204, 212, 224, 248.
" Direction, The New," quoted, 207, 208, 209.
Discussion, First, 121. Second, 185. Third, 235.
" Documents, The," (newspaper article), 215.
Doddridge, Dr., on freedom of thought, quoted, 129.
Drake's History of Boston, quoted, 241.
Dudley, Gov., on Mrs. Skelton, quoted, 285.
Dummer, Jeremy, Notice of Life of, 292.
Dunbar, Rev. Asa, Notice of Life of, 298.
Dunton, John, on Rev. John Higginson, quoted, 291.
    "   "   on Rev. Nicholas Noyes, 293, 294.
Duty of Churches, 127.

E.

Early Records of First Church, Account of, 11, 12, 17 to 24, 117, 118, 258, 259.
Early Christians, Simple faith of, 152.
Earthquake, Fast on account of, 107, 108.
East Parish, gathered, 106.
    "   Ordination in, 107, 108.
    "   Members of, 105, 106.
Elder, Ruling, 46, 48, 58, 116.
Eliot, Dr., on Skelton, quoted, 285.
Elton, on Roger Williams, quoted, 286, 287.
Erasmus Johannes, on Christian liberty, quoted, 155.
" Essentially material passages," (newspaper article), 227.
Essex Institute, Discussion before, 193 to 197.
    "   "   Lecture before, in 1856, 253, 255 to 260.
    "   "   Vote of, 253.
Evans, Dr., on accountability to God alone, quoted, 174.

F.

Feltham's Resolves, on bondage to creeds, quoted, 121.
Felt, J. B., " Ecclesiastical History, etc." of, 235 to 238, 243, 244, 252, 256, 258, 261 to 268.
Felt, J. B, on the Bible the standard of founders of First Church, quoted, 192.
    "   on Rev. Edward Norris, quoted, 289.
    "   on Rev. Thomas Barnard, quoted, 296, 297.
    "   on Rev. Asa Dunbar, 299.

First Church, Foundation of. 1.
  "   " Morton on. 3.
  "   " Mather on, 5 to 8.
  "   " Hubbard on, 8, 9.
  " Reorganization of, 112.
  " Manner of joining, according to Morton, 4.
  "   "   "   " Mather, 7, 8.
  "   "   "   " Hubbard, 9.
  " Intercourse of with other churches, 124.
  " Proceedings of, Feb 18, 1832, 184.
  " How far it accepts the fundamental doctrines of Christianity, 144 to 149, 161 to 171.
First Church, unsectarian at beginning, 195.
  " Newspaper articles on. 197, 200, 202, 205, 207, 217.
  " List of members of, at its reorganization, 115.
Fisk, Samuel, Note of, on book of records, 17.
  " Retention of records by. 87.
  " Method of recording of, 110.
  " Expulsion of from First Church, 111.
  " Notice of Life of, 295.
Fiske, John, Account of, 19, 37.
  " Account of record of the covenants by, 20 to 24.
  " Record of. discussed, 40 to 44.
  " Children of, 36, 37.
Fiske, Moses, recommended by Chelmsford Church, 38 to 40.
Foster, Dr., on mutual forbearance, quoted, 130.
Freedom of judgment, New Testament injunctions to, 160.
French Protestants, Contribution for, 93.
Funds of First Church, 297, 300.
Fundamental doctrines of Christianity, 126, 127, 144 to 183.

G.

Gale, Dr., on judging the members of Christ's body, quoted, 133.
  " on impositions on conscience, 149.
  " on fundamentals, 167.
  " on freedom of conscience, 177
Gloster Church gathered, 56.
Goodwin, Dr. T , on acknowledging good, wherever found, quoted, 175.
  " " on freedom of Congregational covenant, quoted, 277.
Gospel doctrine of *being* and *doing*, 170, 171.
Gott, Charles, orig. witness, Letter of, 1, 2.
  " " " " " referred to, 261.
  " " Felt's explanation of his letter, 236.
Griswold, R. W., quoted, 252.
Grove, on uncharitableness, quoted, 176.

H.

Hales, on heresy and schism, quoted, 143.
Hall, Robert, on free inquiry, quoted, 126.
  " " on the duty of churches, 127.
  " " on party distinctions in churches, 128, 129.

Hall, Robert, on infallibility of church of Rome, quoted, 162.
    "   "   on antinomianism, quoted, 164.
    "   "   on heretics, quoted, 170.
Hanbury's Historical Memorials of the Independents, referred to, 21, 253.
Hartley, Dr., on futility of creeds, quoted, 156.
Haughton, Henry, first ruling elder, 43.
Hayward's Book of Religions, quoted, 251.
Henry, Matthew, on separation from churches, quoted, 139.
    "   "   on schism, quoted, 141.
    "   "   on accountability to Christ alone, 173, 174, 175.
Heresy and schism, Meaning of these terms, 140 to 144.
Higginson, Francis, chosen teacher, 2.
    "   "   ordained teacher, 4.
    "   "   his confession of faith and covenant, 198, 218, 242, 246, 251.
    "   "   Notice of life of, 283.
Higginson, John, original witness, 1, 246, 258.
    "   "   his attestation of Mather's Magnalia, quoted, 5, 201.
    "   "   "   Morton, 202.
    "   "   called to the church, 45, 46.
    "   "   Records of, quoted, 45 to 96, 224.
    "   "   His Election Sermon, 231.
    "   "   His " Direction," 242, 245, 247, 270 to 272.
    "   "   New inference from his old statement, 193, 245.
    "   "   eulogized, 252.
    "   "   Notice of life of, 290.
Higginson, Mehitable, 300.
Holyoke, E. A., a blameless Christian, 169.
Hooker, Thomas, on Christ the church's only lawgiver, quoted, 133.
Howe, John, on narrowing Christian communion, quoted, 130, 131.
    "   "   on judging other men, quoted, 173.
Hubbard's History, &c., quoted, (on the First Church foundation,) 8, 9.
Humiliation, Days of, 51, 54, 57, 58, 59, 67, 68, 70, 71, 74, 75, 81, 82, 93, 96, 97, 108.

I.

Indian war, 82.
Induction of Rev. T. T. Stone, 304.
Installation of Rev. Thomas Barnard, 296.
Ipswich, Ordination at, 107.

L.

Lactantius, on Christian liberty, as quoted by Limborch, 153.
Lardner, Dr., a pure Christian, 168, 169.
Law of 1646, quoted, 278.
Leaf, Transcription on a, 243 247.
Leavitt, Mr., Covenant adopted by church of, 87.
Lecture set up, 116.
Leechman, Dr., on illiberality among Christians, quoted, 168.
Letchford's " Plain Dealing," quoted, 308.
Lin, The church in, hinders the seals, 30, 31.
Locke, John, on the requisite Christian faith, quoted, 166.

Locke, John, on true religion, quoted, 275.
"   "   a simple Christian, 168.
Lord's Supper, Absence from, 50, 51, 52.
"   "   Admission to, 30, 52, 67, 117.
"   "   Suspension of Wm. Walker from, 25, 29.
"   "   Time and charge of it, 47.
Lowth, Bp., on freedom of inquiry, quoted, 126
Lynn, Ordination at, 108.

M.

Mackintosh, Sir James, on Locke, quoted, 275.
Manchester church gathered, 101.
Marblehead church, Members of, 90, 91.
"   "   "   their names, 307.
"   "   Gathering of, 91.
"   "   Ordination in, 101.
Mather's Magnalia, quoted, 5, 6, 7, 8, 199, 239, 240, 248, 258, 272, 273.
"   "   referred to, 196, 257, 261, 264.
Mather's evidence, 200, 201, 218, 219, 221 to 223, 227, 229, 230.
Mather, on Rev. John Higginson, quoted, 291.
Mather, Richard, Dr. Eliot's biography of, quoted, 271.
Middle district church, 99, 100.
Milton, John, on heresy, quoted, 142.
"   "   on darkening Scripture with metaphysics, 157.
Morison, Rev. J. H., Sermon of, 192, 283.
Morton, Rev. Charles, interpolates trinity in Charlestown covenant, 250.
Morton's Memorial, quoted, 3, 197, 199, 239, 257.
"   "   on First Church covenant, quoted, 137, 192.
"   "   Evidence of, on the covenant, 202, 219, 230.
"   "   referred to, 196, 212, 261.
"   New edition of, 238 to 241, 244, 252, 256, 258.
"   "   Note upon, 269.
"   "   Inadvertent admission in, 282.
Mosheim's Commentary of terms of Christian communion, quoted, 135.
"   on the early Christians, 152, 153.

N.

Neal, on Francis Higginson, quoted, 283.
Neander and Uhden, quoted, 22.
Newbury Church, trouble in, 78.
"New Englander," on Congregationalism, quoted, 281.
Newton, John, on heresy, quoted, 142.
"   Sir Isaac, a sincere Christian, 168.
Nicholet, Mr. Charles, Bentley's account of, 80.
"   "   Meeting-house built for, 80.
"   "   Proceedings of Committee, &c. regarding, 81, 82.
Norris, Rev. Edward, Notice of life of, 288.
Note A., 261; B., 269; C., 275.
Notices of First Church and its ministers, 283.
Noyes, Rev. Nicholas, Notice of life of, 293.

Noyes, Rev N., Obituary of, 102.
  "   "   His attestation to Mather, quoted, 201.
Noys, Mr. N., called and ordained, 89.

O.

Obituaries of Curwin and Noyes, 102.
Old South, in Boston, 199.
Ordination of Mr. N. Noys, ⊧9.
  "   Skelton and Higginson, 4, 237.
  "   Rev. John Higginson, 291.
  "   Mr. Geo. Curwin, 100.
  "   Mr. Samuel Fisk, 103, 104.
  "   Rev. Asa Dunbar, 298.
  "   Rev. John Prince, 300.
  "   Rev. C. W. Upham, 303.
Ordination of deacons, 94.
  "   Various forms of, in First Church, 305.
Ordinations in other churches, 56, 57, 91, 95, 98, 100, 101.
Orme's Life of Baxter, on accountability to God alone, quoted, 159.
Orne, Deacon, (also spelt "Horne"), 84, 201.
Orne, Joseph, His house worshipped in by Fiske's adherents, 111.
Owen, Dr., on terms of Christian communion, quoted, 133.
  "   on removing from one church to another, quoted, 139.
  "   on heresy, quoted 143, 144.
  "   on apostasy from the gospel precepts, quoted, 172.
  "   Speech put by Baxter in lips of, quoted, 183.

P.

Palfrey's History, &c., on freedom of early covenants, quoted, 282.
Pamphlet in Mr. Felt's name, 254.
Patrick, Bp., on the requisite Christian faith, quoted, 166.
Peters, Hugh, Dr. Bentley on, 24.
  "   "   Record of, discussed, 40, 41.
  "   "   supposed by Mr. Felt to be author of covenant, 238, 244, 263, 264, 266.
  "   "   Notice of life of, 287.
Pickering, Timothy, "an Israelite indeed," 169.
  "   Deacon, not copier of Tabernacle MS., 193.
Pistorius, on human articles of faith, 156; quoted, 157.
Platform of church discipline, quoted, 147.
Plymouth church covenant, referred to, 195.
Prince's New Eng. Chronology, on liberty of conscience, quoted, 276.
Prince, Rev. John, Notice of life of, 300.
Psalm books, 72.
Pulsifer, Mr. David, 20; certificate of, 307.

Q.

Questions at baptism of children, quoted, 206.

R.

Records, Original, Mr. Fiske's, quoted, 25 to 40.
  "   "   Mr. John Higginson's, quoted, 45 to 96.

Records, Original, Mr. Noyes's, quoted, 96 to 100.
"   "   Mr. Curwin's, quoted, 101.
"   "   Mr. Samuel Fisk's, quoted, 103 to 111.
"   "   Mr. Sparhawk's, quoted, 116, 117.
Records, The first, lost, according to Dr. Worcester, 194, 242.
Records of First Church, referred to, 196, 203, 221.
"   "   "   quoted, 204, 217, 219
" Response to First Church," (newspaper articles,) 220, 221.
Robinson's charge to his congregation, quoted, 136, 154.
"   confession of faith, 280.
"   Ecclesiastical Researches, on early church, quoted, 153.
Robinsonians, Principles of, 276.
Royall Side church gathered, 101.

S.

Salem Gazette, Articles from, 193, 197, 200, 202, 205, 207, 210, 213, 214, 215, 217,
    220, 221, 226, 227, 228, 231.
Salem Gazette, Articles from, referred to, 209, 214, 215, 220, 225, 227, 242.
Salem Village church gathered, 95.
"   "   "   members, 94, 95.
Salvian, on heresy, quoted, 144.
Savage, on Francis Higginson, quoted, 283.
"   on Edward Norris, quoted, 289.
Savoy Confession of Faith, quoted, 199, 200, 212.
"   "   "   referred to, 279, 280.
Sawyer, Leicester A., Work of, on " Organic Christianity," 280.
Saybrook Platform, referred to, 280.
Schism, True meaning of the term, 140 to 144.
Scriptures read as part of public worship, 116.
"Sectarianism, The Plague of," (newspaper article), 213, 214.
Seed, Views of, on uncharitable thinking, quoted, 123.
Sharp, Abp., on Christian charity, quoted, 179.
"   "   on heresy, quoted, 143.
Sheppard, Rev. Thomas, author of Charlestown covenant, 250.
Skelton, chosen Pastor, 2; ordained, 4.
"   Notice of life of, 284
Sparhawk, Mr. John, chosen minister, 115; ordained, 116.
"   Rev John, Notice of life of, 295.
Sprague's Annals, etc , on John Robinson, quoted, 275, 276.
"   "   "   on Rev John Higginson, quoted, 290 to 292.
Stiles, Pres., on liberty of conscience, quoted, 226.
"   on Scriptural foundation of early churches, 279.
Stillingfleet, Bp., on narrowing Christian communion, 131.
Stone, Rev. T. T., Notice of life of, 303.
Stoneham, Ordination at, 108
Supplement, 283.
Sykes, Dr., on punishable errors, quoted, 177.
Synod of 1662, 270, 271.
"   1679, on Platform of Discipline, etc , 83, 84.
"   1680, Confession, etc. of, 280.

T.

Tabernacle Church, Centennial Discourse, 185.
   "   "   Letter to, from First Church, 122 to 184.
   "   "   Memorial of Old and New, 241.
   "   "   Records of, referred to, 187, 247.
   "   "   Resolutions of, refusing to recognize First Church, etc., 122.
Taylor, Jeremy, on narrowing Christian communion, 131, 132.
   "   "   on articles of necessary belief, quoted, 135.
   "   "   on heresy, quoted, 142, 143.
   "   "   on adding to the Scripture rule, quoted, 154.
   "   "   on preventing variety of opinion, quoted, 182.
Tertullian, as quoted by Limborch, on Christian liberty, 153.
Test articles of faith, wrongly imputed to founders of First Church, 85 to 88, 256, 257, 260, 308.
Thanksgiving, Days of, 54, 67, 70, 75, 78, 84, 94, 96.
Thatcher, Thomas, attests Morton's Memorial, 202.
Tillotson, Abp., on heresy, 143.
Topsfield Church gathered, 56.
Transcript of pamphlet printed by J. F., 187, 193, 199, 204, 247, 266.
True Doctrine of New Testament, on Christian unity, quoted, 130.

U.

Upham, Rev. C. W., Notice of life of, 302.

V.

"Violence of some men's tempers," etc., (newspaper article), 226.

W.

Wake, Abp., on Christian charity, quoted, 179.
Walker, Wm., suspended from Lord's Supper, 25 to 27.
Warburton, Bp., on terms of salvation, etc., quoted, 134.
   "   "   on authority in matters of religion, quoted, 150, 151.
Watertown covenant referred to, 195.
Watts, Dr., on differences in religion, quoted, 124.
   "   on uncharitableness, quoted, 177, 178.
Webster's Dictionary, quoted, 228; answered, 229.
Wenham Church gathered, 57.
   "   "   Ordination at, 109.
Wesley, John, on heresy and schism, 141, 142.
Westminster Catechism, "substantial" conformity to, by Tabernacle Church, 144 to 147.
   "   "   Doctrines in, which are not accepted by First Church, 163 to 165.
Westminster Catechism, Declaration of, on clearness of Scripture, quoted, 166.
White, D. A., 121, 183, 233.
   "   "   Discussion by, before Essex Institute, 194 to 197.
Williams, Mr., of Bradford, quoted, 300.
   "   Roger, Notice of life of, 285.
Winslow, Gov., quoted by Prince, 276.
Winthrop, Gov., on Rev. Edward Norris, quoted, 288, 289.
Worcester, Rev. S. M., Articles by, from Salem Gaz., 205, 213, 215, 220, 226, 227, 231.
   "   "   Centennial Discourse, etc., of, 185; quoted, 198.

Worcester, S. M., Discourse of, at Plymouth, quoted, 189, 190.
"   "   Discussion by, before Essex Institute, 194, 197.
"   "   "   "   "   "   quoted, 205, 262.
"   "   Interpretation of, followed by Mr. Felt, 266 to 268.
"   "   Memorial Discourse, etc. of, 241, 244.

ERRATUM.

Page 315, line 31, —for "inadvertent," read "important."

PRINTED AT THE SALEM GAZETTE OFFICE.

www.ingramcontent.com/pod-product-compliance
Lightning Source LLC
Chambersburg PA
CBHW060517030726
47498CB00004B/972